A FORTUNE IN

"Know w
Lieutenant M

"A Kiowa

"It's silve
pace.

"I wonde

"Exactly.
cryptic sym
twelve trade
in silver spe
way to Saint Louis. They came the southernmost route, not far
from where we're now camped. If you look closely at the medallion, you'll see some Spanish markings remain."

"There could be any number of explanations. The Kiowa
could have traded for that coin. Trading was their way of life."

"They didn't even know what they had," Sheets sneered. "My
guess is they made some trinkets and then probably abandoned
or hid the remainder because it was too heavy to transport far.
All we have to do is find out where, and I'll bet my commission
that squaw knows exactly where. It wasn't right, killing those
traders. It's a crime of murder and thievery, and it's our duty as
representatives of the United States government to rectify it."

"What are you suggesting?" McReynolds asked.

"Only that as soldiers we are obliged by our oath to protect
the citizenry of this country. And that's exactly what I intend to
do. The death of those traders needs to be avenged and their
possessions recovered."

BOOK YOUR PLACE ON OUR WEBSITE AND MAKE THE READING CONNECTION!

We've created a customized website just for our very special readers, where you can get the inside scoop on everything that's going on with Zebra, Pinnacle and Kensington books.

When you come online, you'll have the exciting opportunity to:

- View covers of upcoming books
- Read sample chapters
- Learn about our future publishing schedule (listed by publication month *and author*)
- Find out when your favorite authors will be visiting a city near you
- Search for and order backlist books from our online catalog
- Check out author bios and background information
- Send e-mail to your favorite authors
- Meet the Kensington staff online
- Join us in weekly chats with authors, readers and other guests
- Get writing guidelines
- AND MUCH MORE!

Visit our website at
http://www.pinnaclebooks.com

The Savage Trail

Sheldon Russell

Pinnacle Books
Kensington Publishing Corp.
http://www.pinnaclebooks.com

PINNACLE BOOKS are published by

Kensington Publishing Corp.
850 Third Avenue
New York, NY 10022

Pinnacle and the P logo Reg. U.S. Pat. & TM Off.

First Printing: August, 1998
10 9 8 7 6 5 4 3 2 1

Printed in the United States of America

To my father, Ralph James Russell,
a man of the land, a man of his word.

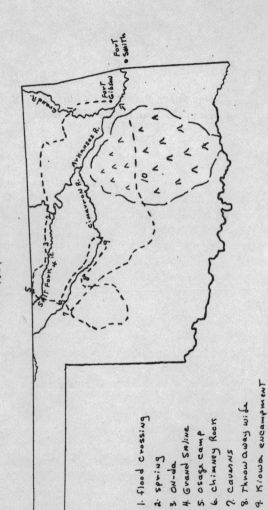

Expedition, Indian Territory
1834

Fort Smith

Fort Gibson

Grand R.

Arkansas R.

Cimarron R.

Salt Fork

1. Flood Crossing
2. Spring
3. Oui-da
4. Grand Saline
5. Osage Camp
6. Chimney Rock
7. Caverns
8. Throw Away wife
9. Kiowa encampment
10. CrossTimbers

One

When he stepped into the Fort Gibson infirmary and saw Nurse Cromley's face, Assistant Surgeon McReynolds knew something was wrong.

"What's going on here?"

"Thornhill's dying," she said, "and two more on their way. There's five more patients just checked in with the same symptoms. What are we going to do?" She clenched her hands. "Dreadful, Doctor, high fevers, convulsions, fast, very fast, and it's spreading."

"I've checked the food," he said. "Aside from being unpalatable, it is fine."

"They're so young, and healthy. It doesn't make sense."

"Are they taking water?"

"Yes, but Surgeon Bloomly ordered a purgative."

A frown crossed his face.

"Anything else?" he asked.

"He's bled the last five, sir."

"And?"

"It didn't seem to help, Doctor. They're very weak. We'd better find out what's happening soon or the whole command's going to be down."

"Let's take a look," he said.

They climbed the stairs to the second floor, stopping in front of each bed. The story was the same. The men looked back with haunted eyes, faces drawn, lips pulled tight over their teeth.

The soldier on the far bunk lay with his head back, eyes flickering beneath closed lids. Saliva drooled from his lips onto his pillow. Dabbing at his cheek with a napkin, Nurse Cromley looked up at McReynolds.

"He's the weakest of them all," she said.

Examining the soldier, McReynolds felt the glands in his throat and neck. There were lesions beginning behind his ears.

"This is Thornhill?" he asked.

She nodded her head, pushing the hair from Thornhill's anguished face.

"What duty are you pulling, soldier?"

"Tending the stock, sir, down by the bog. It's coming spring grass down there and we graze them out, taking four-hour shifts so they don't run off or get stole by Indians." A flush wrapped about his neck like red fingers. "It gets mighty sticky sometimes and them mosquitoes eat man and horse alike, sir."

"Well, you get some rest, soldier. I'll see you're relieved of duty for a day or two."

Turning, McReynolds directed his attention to Nurse Cromley.

"Increase his water," he said, "the others too. Take them off the purgative. They're dehydrated from fever and diarrhea. Liquids are what they need."

"But Dr. Bloomly?" she said, with a startled look on her face.

"I'll talk to Dr. Bloomly."

Opening her pad, she began writing, then hesitated.

"What is it?" he asked.

"It's not my business, Dr. McReynolds, but Dr. Bloomly is quite adamant about his orders."

"I've seen this before, or something like it. But there's a difference. It just doesn't make sense to me."

Silence fell as he thought.

"When was that, Dr. McReynolds?" she finally asked.

"On the syphilis ward, during my residency."

"Syphilis ward?"

"I know. It's crazy. This is not syphilis, but there's something . . ." Turning, he examined the soldier again. "Where is Dr. Bloomly?"

"His quarters, I think. I'm not certain, though."

"Hold off on the orders until I've had an opportunity to talk to him. It's going to be all right," he said, winking at her. "We'll get this thing figured out and under control."

It took three tries before Bloomly answered the door, eyes bleary, smelling of whiskey, store-bought rye delivered discreetly in the packages of pharmaceutical powders brought in once a month from Fort Smith to Fort Gibson, a secret known by nearly everyone in the medical unit.

An intimidating presence, Bloomly filled the doorway, a huge man with a powerful neck and a white beard, so stiff and coarse it wore away the material on his collar, fingers thick as broom handles, back square, legs slightly bent. Pulling at his beard, he turned his head when spoken to as if compensating for a hearing loss.

"What is it you want?" he boomed.

"We've got a problem at the infirmary," McReynolds said.

"We've always got a problem at the infirmary, Doctor, or hadn't you noticed?"

"One nearly dead, seven more down. We'd better get it right soon or we'll have a full-scale epidemic on our hands."

"Bad food or bad shine," he shrugged. "This is the Oklahoma frontier, Doctor. Life can be hard."

"I'm concerned about the purgative. These patients are dehydrated and can't keep anything down as it is."

"Purgatives are standard procedure for this sort of thing," he said, pulling back his shoulders, "and I'll not have my orders questioned."

"Those men need every bit of liquid they can get. It's coming out both ends faster then they can pour it in."

"I'm still head surgeon around here, Doctor," he said, face red against his white beard. "Army procedure for this sort of thing is well established. Procedure was working fine when you was a puking newborn and it'll still be working fine when you're an old man shitting your pants."

Clenching his teeth, McReynolds held his temper. The man's ignorance of modern medicine was as appalling as his language. When he turned to leave, Bloomly called after him.

"And one other thing, McReynolds. Lieutenant Sheets tells me you been coddling the prisoners again. What the hell you think this is, a convent? This is the goddamn army, Doctor, and prisoners get the punishment that's been ordered."

"And let me tell you," McReynolds whirled about, out of control, "that sterile procedures are army policy and I follow them to the letter. Just because Lieutenant Sheets is second in command of this carnage house doesn't mean he makes sound judgments. There's not a soldier in this godforsaken fort, high nor low, who would take him home for soup in a blizzard." McReynolds took a deep breath. "Look, I'm not the one who has broken policy here."

"Well," Bloomly backed off, "in the future check with me before striking out on your own. I've got two years left in this outfit, McReynolds, and I ain't letting no one screw it up."

Both men fell silent as they assessed their positions. Finally McReynolds spoke.

"You ever been on a syphilis ward, Doctor?"

"Surely you are not suggesting that these men are suffering from syphilis?"

"No," he said, looking into the trees surrounding the cabin, "but I am suggesting that this is more serious than bad food or bad shine. It's the smell I think, something about the smell."

When McReynolds returned to the infirmary, Nurse Cromley was in the pharmacy on her knees, her hands clasped together in prayer. What luxury, religious abdication, what convenience to relegate responsibility to God. Life lived as a mission was a clear and simple path.

"It's just a matter of time," she said, weariness in her eyes.

"God's will?" he asked.

"Yes," she nodded, unaware of his cynicism, "God's will. If He wants them to die, there's little to be done."

"Are you all right?" he asked, lifting her chin.

"Just tired, I think. It's been a long day."

"You go back to your quarters," he said, lifting her. "I'll get some of the men to stand in tonight. There's very little you can do here anyway."

"Perhaps I will."

"Before you go, show me again the purgative that Dr. Bloomly prescribed."

Standing tiptoe, she reached for the vial from the cabinet, handing it to him.

"Calomel," he mumbled to himself, turning the vial, studying the amber contents, setting it on the table next to a beaker. "And what is this liquid here in the beaker? Is all of that calomel? I don't remember seeing this before."

"Urine," she said, her face turning scarlet. "I couldn't get free from the patients today, not even for a moment."

"Oh," he grinned, "well, we all do what we must. Better get on out of here for a little rest."

Mortified, Nurse Cromley ducked her head and hurried from the pharmacy.

As soon as she was gone McReynolds began his search through the small collection of medical journals and records kept in the pharmacy. After several hours of reading, he was confident the soldiers' symptoms were consistent with prairie fever, probably from the swamp bordering the fort on the north.

Some of the fort records reported similar episodes in the past, mostly during the spring months. One such report specifically recommended that subsequent quarters be built higher up on the hill and away from the swamp area.

Just before midnight, Bloomly arrived at the infirmary in a bluster. Trying to dissuade him from prescribing the purgatives was futile. Not only did he increase the doses of calomel, but ordered the patients bled once more.

On his way out of the infirmary, Bloomly stopped at the desk where McReynolds was finishing an article from one of the journals.

"Where's Nurse Cromley?"

"Her quarters, exhausted."

"What the hell good is a nurse if she ain't on duty?" he said, puffing his cheeks in disapproval.

"It's too much for one person. There's plenty of men around here who can help."

"Humph," Bloomly snorted, picking up the beaker and studying it curiously. "What is this? My God, there's enough calomel here for the whole Army."

"It's nothing."

"What do you mean, nothing?" He held the beaker against the lantern light. "By God, McReynolds, what are you keeping from me now?"

"It's nurse urine, all right? You've got her so busy she can't even get out of here long enough to relieve herself."

"Nurse urine?" Bloomly's chin dropped.

"That's right," he said, laying aside his journal.

"Well, by God, McReynolds, will you please tell Nurse Cromley to urinate somewhere besides in my beakers?"

"Did you see the lesions on the jaws of some of those men, Doctor?"

"Of course I did. They seemed to have gotten into something, poison oak, nettles, vermin. Hell," he scratched at his beard, "could've been nurse urine for all we know."

"In my opinion, those are lesions of the saliva glands, and they are weeping. That's the smell, the same smell as on the salivation wards, beds reserved for syphilis patients in the final stages of their disease. Lesions of the neck and jaw were common; even their bed clothing would be wet from saliva. The stench was unbearable, and I've never forgotten it."

"By God, that's the craziest thing I've ever heard," said Bloomly, clenching his hands. "Anyone in their right mind could see that those men don't have syphilis."

Picking up the journal, McReynolds shook it at Bloomly.

"I didn't say they had syphilis, Doctor. I said they had lesions, and I think they are gangrenous or soon will be."

"What the hell are you saying?"

"Guess what medication they used on those wards? It says right here in this reference—Calomel, Doctor, Calomel with a mercurial base."

"Will you make your point?" Bloomly cocked his head, pointing his ear at McReynolds.

"Maybe it's the medicine, maybe they're dying from the medicine."

"By God, I'll have no more of this," he said, rising up on his toes. "That medication is as sound and safe as anything there is. Another word about this and I'll have you busted to private for insubordination. And another thing," he shouted from behind as McReynolds made his way up the stairs, "I'll not have nurse urine in my beakers, you understand? I'll not have it!"

Two

Nurse Cromley sat at her secretary, pen in hand, too tired to write, too tired to sleep. Being away from the infirmary was always difficult. No one knew the patients like her, nor understood the myriad details that kept the infirmary running. To leave it in the hands of others, just for a moment, filled her with anxiety. The doctors could have their disagreements, but in the final analysis it would be she and her exacting care that would make the difference.

The lamp flickered in the breeze that bled through the crack under the door. A page of her writing pad lifted upward from the draft, the daily letter, writing as promised no matter the circumstances nor the weariness of body, the inviolate message delivered like clockwork to her father's front door.

The pain of her loss was keen still in her memory, his coming to her room, eyes brimming with tears, pulling her into his arms. The words struck into her soul as he rushed to speak.

"She's gone," he said, "to God, and it is only through God that we will ever see her again."

On their knees they prayed beneath the crucifix that hung above her bed and he clung to her, weeping bitterly into her arms. Stroking his hair again and again, she consoled him, asking God to take away his pain, promising God her life if only He would take away the pain and bring them peace.

In the night, the neighbors came, speaking softly, sitting silently in the room where her mother lay, candles flickering, the murmuring of voices downstairs in the kitchen, voices from her mother's kitchen, and her father alone, alone except for her, and it was that night she vowed to God and to her mother who lay dead in the other room that it would be she who would make the difference, that it would be she to bear the cross farther down the path, that it would be she who would make the family whole again.

In the years to follow, the neighbors marveled at her devotion, at her piety and spirituality, especially for such a young girl. Those hours not caring for her father were spent at the small church, the same church where her mother was buried, yellow flowers, fleeting and guileless, over the ponderous iron casket.

Each morning she walked the foggy New Orleans streets to this same church, moving effortlessly into the sublime music of the mass, the consoling chant of the priest and the promise of paradise. It was her place, her life, and in it she found her truth and center. The church met her needs, the contentment she sought, and all the while brought her closer to her mother, to her God.

Over time, the anguish of confession turned to grace, soul-freeing and cleansing, the purge of vile and base thought. In sacrifice and hard work she found emancipation from vanity, pride, the blackness of her own feelings as they rose in the night, the dark moments of the night when desire clutched at her breasts and fell hot against her neck and raged through her body like the fire of the damned.

"Mary." He looked up from his paper. "I heard you up again last night. Are you not feeling well?"

"I couldn't sleep."

"I hear you often," he said, laying aside his paper, "and I'm concerned, so many hours at the church. Even your studies are neglected."

"I'm just fine. It's God's charge that the most be made of life."

"Father Mark tells me you're at the church nearly as much

as he and that he's concerned about you too. It's not normal for a girl to be so involved, not at your age."

"Perhaps," her eyes narrowed, "Father Mark should take counsel of his own slackness to God's bidding."

"Mary," he scolded, "that's no way to talk of a priest."

"I'm sorry, but I see no reason why I should be chastised simply because I have the conviction of my beliefs. I've been thinking that perhaps I should go to the convent, a place where I can have the kind of relationship with God that I need."

Sunlight from the window fell across them as they spoke.

"Father Mark and I have talked about this," he said. "We could see that it was headed this way. I must be frank with you. We both agree that you are not cut out for life in a convent."

"There is no one more hardworking or dedicated than I," she said, tears welling in her eyes as if she'd been slapped.

"That's just it, Mary." He rose from his chair, putting his arm around her shoulder. "Hard work and dedication are only a small part of monastic life. It's a spiritual world, a cerebral world, a world of prayer, reading, and self-sacrifice. It's in your nature to work your way to God. The convent would only hinder and frustrate you."

"Then there is no place for me."

"The church has established a school of nursing here in New Orleans. It is my opinion that you would make a wonderful nurse, and I think it's time you got out on your own."

"But what about you?"

"It might surprise you," he smiled, "to know that I managed fairly well even before you came along."

Within days of enrolling in Saint Anthony's School for Nursing, Mary Cromley knew that she had at last found her place, a proclivity for the work that was obvious to all, an unflappable bearing in the face of the most startling surgical procedures.

Nursing fulfilled her and she relished even the exhausting physical demands placed on her. It was to Surgeon Bloomly's credit that he picked her from all the others to accompany him as the first female nurse to serve at the furthermost western outpost of Fort Gibson in Oklahoma Territory.

Lifting her hair to cool her neck, she rubbed at her throbbing temples, then signed the letter with bold and precise strokes, creasing the flap with her fingernail. Duty here at Fort Gibson had been rewarding, and she had been content even in her isolation, that is until today.

There was a sadness in Dr. McReynolds, an inconsolable sadness like she'd seen in her father's eyes. In that moment she knew how much he was in pain. As she stood next to him over Thornhill's bed, her arm against his, her knees buckled unpredictably, bearing her against him to regain her composure.

To her surprise, it was not Thornhill's suffering that caused her to swoon, but Dr. McReynolds's touch.

Three

The infirmary reminded Assistant Surgeon McReynolds of the schoolhouse he'd attended as a boy, prominent against the other buildings, constructed of lapboard barged upriver, whitewashed, straight and squared.

Sunlight poured through the large windows on both the east and west sides of the building, and a porch of quarry slate greeted visitors with an unusual expanse. The floors were wooden and fireplaces at each end warmed the rooms. Immense chimneys accommodated the fireplaces and were constructed of the same iron-colored slate as the porch.

A search of the infirmary failed to turn up Nurse Cromley, leaving McReynolds with little option but to conduct rounds alone.

One of Thornhill's feet hung through the iron slat of the bed. Moving cautiously so as not to awaken him, McReynolds lifted back the blanket. Thornhill's head was contorted in a rigid arch, tongue swollen, purple, eyes open, vacant, nothing so certain as a dead man's gaze.

Deportment vanished under the ironic spectacle of youth and death, and McReynolds struggled against the desolation that swept him, before turning his attention to the other soldiers.

All were seriously ill, gowns wet with perspiration, fevers raging, tremulous and unsteady hands. There in their eyes, as in the eyes of Thornhill, was the indisputable mark of death.

The day passed slowly, and by noon six more soldiers signed

in on sick call, fevers, tremors, unrelenting vomiting. Two of the soldiers who had come with Thornhill the day before were dead by the time McReynolds made second rounds.

When the bugler's sad taps rose from the tiny fort at sunset, four soldiers lay on the infirmary porch awaiting burial detail. A line of new victims stretched from the sick call window and down the steps of the infirmary.

Thriving on the bedlam, Bloomly stormed about in a flurry of random activity, ordering purgatives, conducting bleedings, forcing endless vials of calomel down retching soldiers. In between trips to the rye he cursed the cooks, the command, and the scourge of army rations.

When Nurse Cromley failed to report for the second shift, McReynolds sent a man to roust her. Within moments, the soldier was back, Nurse Cromley over his shoulder.

"Damn," McReynolds said, his heart sinking at what he saw.

"Where do you want her?" the soldier asked, as if she were a sack of flour.

"Prepare a bed in the pharmacy. Get some fresh well water down her. See that she takes a glass an hour," he said, fixing on the soldier. "She's to have no calomel, son, do you understand, or I'll turn you over to Lieutenant Sheets."

The soldier's face ashened.

"Yes sir," he said.

By dark, another was dead and carried to the porch of the infirmary. All about McReynolds, lesions drained, jaws pulled at grotesque angles, men heaved bile and blood and moaned from the dark and foreboding rooms of the infirmary.

With some relief, McReynolds worked the upstairs ward, relinquishing the care of Nurse Cromley to Bloomly. He was, after all, a superior, a full surgeon, the man responsible for bringing her to this forlorn and dangerous place. This much was certain—her death must not be on his own hands.

The pharmacy became a fearful place, what lay inside—the need of this woman and his own inadequacy to help her.

Just before daylight, Bloomly found him sitting on the end

of a bed, exhausted from the work, from the suffering and misery of the last hours.

"How is she?" McReynolds asked, trying to calm his voice.

"Sick," Bloomly said, "sick as these other poor bastards and more likely to die. Big mistake to bring a woman out here, I suppose. Still, I thought it was time. Female nurses been getting good reports here and there. They've a better touch, you know, and not so likely to complain about the cleaning up."

"The soldier I assigned is still with her?" McReynolds asked.

"Sent him away. Smelled of horses. Panicked every time I opened Cromley's gown."

"What medication have you prescribed for Nurse Cromley?" he asked, his pulse quickening.

"Calomel," Bloomly said, "and just finished bleeding her."

"Calomel? That doesn't make sense. Didn't you hear a thing I said?"

"Course I did, McReynolds, but that's why I'm head surgeon and you're an assistant. Sometimes things don't make sense, but there's never a doubt as to why you do them. It's called *procedure,* and you'd better learn how to follow it or you won't last long, I tell you."

"You might kill her with your procedure," McReynolds said.

"Look," Bloomly's face reddened, "don't tell me about procedure. I've read your record, see, and offhand I'd say your procedure isn't so all-fired superior."

"What do you mean by that?"

"I know about your wife, how you killed her on the table. If I was you, I'd be a little more cautious about criticizing someone else's procedure."

Turning on his heel, McReynolds rushed up the stairs and as far away from Bloomly as he could get. Hearing it spoken aloud like that, by a man like that, confirmed the deed, caused it to loom real, black, evil.

As the night deepened, a quiet fell, punctuated by an occasional groan and the distant yip of coyotes. With trepidation,

McReynolds made his way to the pharmacy and knelt at her bed.

The heat from her body rose against his face, her breathing shallow, labored. Even in the darkness, he knew that she was near death.

The lamp flame grew under his match, dark shadows rising up the wall, bending where the ceiling joined the wall. Next to her bed was Bloomly's vial of calomel. Pouring it into another container, he refilled the vial with water, too clear for calomel, detectable. Looking around, he spotted the beaker of urine, adding minute amounts to the vial until the desired color was attained.

With calomel in hand, McReynolds slipped from the infirmary and made his way down the path, flinging it into the heavy bramble beneath the blackjack trees. A short way farther and he was back at his quarters, climbing exhausted into his bed. Right or wrong, the deed was done, and for the first time in many hours sleep came.

His timepiece read twelve hours since he'd fallen into his bed. Why hadn't they awakened him? Surely Bloomly wouldn't have allowed him to sleep so long. Taking the stone steps two at a time, he rushed into the pharmacy.

There on her bed, legs over the edge, Nurse Cromley bobbed her feet.

"How are you feeling today?" he asked, out of breath.

"Oh, Dr. McReynolds," she smiled weakly, "my fever is nearly gone and my strength is returning by the hour. In fact, I'm rather hungry." Tears came to her eyes. "It's a miracle, I suppose."

"Yes," he said, "I suppose."

"And there are no new patients, Doctor. The disease seems to have run its course." She hesitated. "Except one."

"Bloomly?" McReynolds guessed.

"I'm afraid so," she said, hair falling across her eyes like a little girl's.

On the upper ward in the far bunk, Bloomly rolled over, his beard like a snowdrift on his massive chest.

"Nothing stays down," he groaned. "I'm going to die. You must do something."

Motioning for the private to assist, McReynolds examined Bloomly.

"It appears that Surgeon Bloomly is suffering from bad food or shine," he said. "Please see that he gets a full measure of calomel every four hours."

"Yes sir," the private said.

When out of earshot, McReynolds stopped.

"Give the others fresh water and leave them alone. The first rule of medicine is to do no harm. Better have Dr. Bloomly bled daily for the remainder of the week," he pulled at his chin, "and see to it that his calomel is taken from Nurse Cromley's vial in the pharmacy."

The private looked at him curiously. "Sir?"

"It has a special ingredient, see," McReynolds smiled, "one conjured up by Nurse Cromley herself."

Four

The little cabin huddled within sight of the fort. Twobirds stood in its doorway, her body trembling against the night air.

"What do you want?" she asked, sleep still in her voice.

Leaning into the shadows, Corporal Adam Renfro savored the delicacy of her face, the rush of her black hair, the way she stood, hip-shot, the glisten of her eyes in the night.

"You are Twobirds?"

"That's what they call me," she said, stepping from the doorway and into the shadows. "You were in the guard that brought me here from Fort Smith. No soldiers are permitted off post, not here, not this place." She lifted her hair between her fingers, pushing it back from her face.

Five hundred feet from where they stood slept those who controlled Renfro's life with unquestionable power, and he shot an uneasy glance toward the gate.

"Saw the coals from your campfire winking in the breeze. Most folks cook inside."

"A pack rat lives in the fireplace," she said, scanning the darkness behind him. Where there was one soldier there were often more. "Why are you here, Corporal?"

Propping his foot on a blackjack stump, Renfro gathered up his story.

"Over there," he pointed north to where the blackjacks thickened, flooding the gully in a tangle, "got my molly mule penned, living alone and lonesome like yourself. She's got to be tended and cussed from time to time or she'll shrivel up and die."

The moon edged over his shoulder, falling on Twobirds's face, spilling her beauty like fragrance into the prairie winds. A year now at Fort Gibson, the hardest year of his life, and hardest of all, the chaste world in which he lived, the starkness of men, the bitter taste of monotony, the unrelenting tyranny of Lieutenant Reginald Sheets. How he longed for the company of women, longed for their quiet spirit and their soft strength.

Twobirds searched for the truth in his eyes.

"Why is your mule hidden in a thicket?"

The black wall of the fort loomed in the darkness.

"The lieutenant says the fort ain't no place for mules," he dropped his eyes, "or Indians or rattlers or busthead liquor for that matter. Says if he sees my molly again, he'll gut her out and run her up the flagpole on a singletree."

Allowing herself to relax, Twobirds leaned against the door.

"Your lieutenant is a warrior without a tribe," she said.

"He's a friend of no man, for certain, and no man's friend that I know."

"You are foolish to risk his anger for a mule."

"Old Molly would lay down her life at sunrise if called," he said. "Can't let her starve, or pine away, or get run up a flagpole."

"But she's a mule, and you are a man," she said, lifting her eyes.

"I never claimed to be smart, just headstrong, I guess." Beyond the fort, a coyote's howl rose into the night, singular, pure. "Had a dog named Bawler back in Tennessee," he continued, "a good dog but never knew when to quit, would hunt all night, come in all tired and wet long after everyone else was asleep. Guess I'm like old Bawler, just don't know when the hunt's over. Wasn't all that good a dog, I suppose," he said, shrugging his shoulders like a little boy. "Weren't no difference between a skunk and a coon far as he could tell."

In the distance the guard changed, the hard voices, the metallic snap of rifles as the command passed. Renfro crouched, his stomach knotting.

"Come inside," Twobirds said.

Flames from the candle danced in her coal-black eyes, shadows frolicking about the room like silent children.

The cabin was a single room, poorly chinked, moonlight peeking through like stars in the sky, but it was her world and he was happy to be there.

The dampness of the river lingered at the door, frogs croaking, old voices rising from the bog that lay to the north of the fort. Fetid gas bubbled and seeped from the bog in a daily reminder of its decay. A log stool occupied one corner of the room. Beyond that there were few amenities, an army blanket folded in half against the wall, a canvas bag at the foot, next to that a small deerskin satchel with brightly colored beadwork, a single reminder of her Kiowa heritage.

There had been rare opportunity to see her during the march from Fort Smith, and she was now even more beautiful than he remembered, riding next to the lieutenant at the front of the column, spending her nights in a tent on the edge of the camp. Even though Renfro was at the rear, bringing up supplies procured for the expedition west, he could see her now and again, mounted on her horse like a queen on a throne, her back straight, her head high, her hair the blue-black of a crow.

As the heat mounted, he watched, a stifling heat silencing the column of men, rounding their shoulders, drawing them down, but not her—not this Kiowa girl. With purpose she rode, with strength and defiance. Here was a woman worth knowing.

"Sit," she said, pointing to the blanket, "and speak softly. Voices carry in the night air."

The tension flowed from between his shoulders as he leaned against the wall, Twobirds taking her place on the blanket across from him, leaning back on her hands, her breasts thrusting forward, their fullness, their lilt, their sensuality concealed beneath the simple cotton dress.

A bullfrog croaked, a resonance belying both its size and

place in the Grand River bog. Is this what she thought of him, all air and noise and bluster in a bog much bigger than himself?

"Why are you here, in my land, Corporal, so far from your Tennessee?"

"I ain't much, not in the way some men are, what with their reading and their educations, but I got a hunger to see and to touch and to know the things of this world and sometimes it just takes me by the scruff and leads me anywhere it wants to go. It's like an itch," he said, stroking his chin, "that can't be reached, like river rock rattling in your belly and then smelling fresh-baked yeast bread, like a back rub in a feather bed on a cold winter night. Some things are too good to deny, and there's nothing to do but go along."

As Twobirds listened, she knew that this was of a distant place, of a world which she would never know.

"It's just the way I am," he said. "Back there as a kid I decided that I would not live as my pa, if you could call it living—litter of five, forty acres of rocks and a gimp-legged mule, a hard life and nothing for it except crying babies and ten acres of shriveled-up corn.

"A man ought not to live like that," he said, picking at the nettles that clung to his woolen pants, "not when there's things to be seen in this world and places to go. No sir, I ain't settling for blisters on my hands and a dirt floor cabin. No sir." He leaned toward her. "I walked out the day I could, left them standing there and never looked back. I want to see this world for all it's got, good or bad, makes no difference to me, but I plan to see it all and when they dig my grave, they'll know that here was a man that sucked the juice out of life and left nothing behind but an empty carcass.

"I don't mean to go on so." He poured the nettles into a pile next to his leg, "but 'times I feel like I might bust inside if one more wall's throwed up between me and the world out there."

Uncrossing her legs, Twobirds pulled them to her side, the delicate bend of her knees, her amber skin, her youthful, firm thighs.

"Only white men reveal their spirits before their names," she said.

"I ain't normally so forthcoming," he lowered his eyes, "but then this ain't exactly a normal situation, a mountain boy like myself here with the prettiest Kiowa girl whatever."

Twobirds spiked her hand on her waist, the same way he'd seen schoolgirls do a hundred times back in Tennessee.

The guards laughed in the distance and Renfro moved into the shadows next to the single-square-foot opening which passed for a window. Even in the pale moonlight, he could see the gaping holes in the crude fort wall. Hardly a single straight tree was to be found west of Fort Smith, mostly the stunted and twisted blackjack that grew from the earth like arthritic black hands.

"My name is Adam Renfro," he said, "Adam, like the first man in paradise. And who are you, Twobirds, and why are you here?"

The flame danced in celebration as she moved close to the candle.

"I am a Kiowa," she said, "kidnapped at thirteen by the Osage, traded for three kegs of molasses and a broken pistol to a trapper and his toothless wife. When I fell sick, from lack of fresh food, and from loneliness, they left me at the fork of a river. They said I was a Kiowa and that I would find my way. The old trapper left me a skinned rabbit, a fruit jar of water, and a saddle blanket. Follow the river, he said, to Fort Smith, keep west from there, follow the sun west to the Cross Timbers and beyond somewhere were my people." Rubbing her hand in the heat of the flame, she grew quiet. "The Cross Timbers are taboo, a dark and evil place, a place where no Kiowa would go."

How sad her story and how sorry he was, how pitiful a thing to leave a young girl alone in such a fearful and untamed place.

"What happened?" he asked.

"I followed the river, walking the bank when I could, keeping sight of the river. When I couldn't, I kept the tree line in sight.

I knew that the river was the only chance I had. During the day I'd catch crawfish, frogs, anything that couldn't escape. At night I'd dig into the soft bank and cover myself with the saddle blanket. There was no fire."

Lowering her head, her hair fell about her face, black, thick, handsome. What of her father, Adam wondered, a chief adorned in regal dress, a proud and fierce warrior, a shaman with godlike powers?

"The coyotes," she said, "packs running the river in search of prey, sometimes so close I could hear them crossing the river, back and forth and back and forth through the water, searching for the scent, never silent, quarreling, yelping, fighting." She looked into the flame. "But then as if by a sign they would gather, circling like a storm on the bank of the river." A shiver passed through her body. "From among them a face would lift to the night, a mournful cry, sorrow of a mother for her dead child," she paused, "more, I think, sorrow of the dead past, tears for all that's happened, will happen.

"He is God's dog," she said, pulling her knees to her chest, "and sometimes sees more than he can bear.

"One night I heard one sniffing, stopping, sniffing again until he was above me. I lay as dead, not even to breathe. For the longest time he waited and with a snort was gone. God's dog saw what is, what will be for me, I think."

The moon edged past the tiny window, blue now, farther away, colder. A tree limb scrubbed against the cabin roof as the breeze picked up from the west. The guards murmured among themselves, the tedium of their duty pressing in on them.

Waiting too long to return to the fort could be risky. Bed checks were random and frequent as the warm spring days lured increasing numbers to desert. These soldiers were a fickle lot, kids mostly, like himself, country boys enticed by the promise of adventure on the frontier. Few were prepared for what they found at Fort Gibson.

The great courage of the Kiowa was well known to Adam,

their uncanny ability to survive in the wilderness, but abandoning anyone alone in this harsh land was unforgivable.

"I know grown men," he said, "wouldn't last the night alone in this country. What did you do? How did you get to Fort Smith?"

"I walked," she said, drawing a deep breath, "always with the river. Who knows the wasted miles I walked following every bend of that river? In this land only rivers have an end, and I knew that sooner or later it would lead me somewhere.

"Ten days and ten nights passed, from the day the wagon drove off until I saw Fort Smith up on the hill. I wanted to turn back to join those coyotes when I first saw that fort."

The second week after Adam's arrival at Fort Gibson, a deserter was captured, a hapless fellow from his own state of Tennessee who'd broken his leg in a gopher hole not ten miles from the fort. When the detachment discovered him, he was out of his head with pain and thirst, and the bog mosquitoes had found him an easy victim. Upon returning to the fort, a general assembly was sounded and Lieutenant Sheets had the deserter clamped in stocks, his broken leg swinging like a tree limb in a storm, head shaved, and a "D" the size of a man's hand branded on his hip, an iron so hot it was held at arm's length to keep the brows of his tormentor from scorching. The deserter's cries of affliction were nothing compared to the humiliation of his new crest.

"I've got some notion," he said, "how mighty frightening all those soldiers can be."

"They took me in," she said, "and put me with an Arapaho girl they'd found while on patrol the week before. Poor girl had been clubbed on the back of the head during a raid and left for dead, couldn't talk nor eat, least not the salt pork and corn mush the Army served up. Maybe with fresh meat, fruit, maybe then she would have lived. I don't suppose, though. The light was gone from her eyes. I never knew her name."

The moon cast its glow through the window and onto Twobirds. What a lovely and wild thing she was, a rare and won-drous thing, like a cougar in the moonlight.

"The soldiers were going to take her back to her people," she said, "a token of the Army's good will. That's why I'm here too, to be returned to my tribe as a gift and token of good will. I heard the lieutenant talking. Tribes are being moved into the Oklahoma Territory from far away. They want my people to share their hunting grounds with strangers. There's to be an expedition soon, beyond the Cross Timbers."

"But why are they returning you?"

"Your chief thinks my people will be grateful." Her voice dropped. "Your chief is wrong. I am but a woman, a woman gone too long from her people, and I'm of no importance. You must go now," she stood, folding her arms across her chest, "and not come again."

"I'll come again."

"No, you must not," she said, picking up the beaded satchel. "These are of my tribe, ways you could never understand. I know what it is to be among people who are not your own. The distance is too great."

Holding up the candle, he took a final look, to store the memory until next time. Changing directions did not come eas-ily to him.

"You stop in and speak to my molly," he said, handing Two-birds the candle. "Tell her you saw me. Scratch between her ears and her heart will be yours."

The distance was considerable from the opening in the wall to the barracks where he and three other soldiers lived in a small cabin. Little happened in that cabin that the others didn't know of, it being barely large enough for two double bunks and four trunks.

Reveille was at sunup and his bunkmates were no doubt aware of his absence by now. Still, silence was a code by which they all lived. It was their only power, a limited power to be sure, but the only power they had against the absolute rule of the first sergeant and the officers of Fort Gibson.

Pushing himself against the stockade wall, he waited. Dawn was breaking, the morning light erasing the few remaining shadows within the compound. The row of cabins on the north provided little cover, their similarity broken only by the brig and the stocks used for the punishment of enlisted men.

Directly in front of him but on the opposite side of the compound was a hand-dug well. Soldiers had carried rock from a quarry three miles upstream to encase the well. Water from the well tasted of fish and smelled of the river that lay to the west, but it gave the fort the capacity to hold off an attack. If he could reach the well, there would be good cover from there to the cabin.

There was less exposure by way of the stocks and then to the well, but the distance would be doubled. Throwing caution aside, Adam struck out directly across the compound, scalp tightening as he reached the halfway point. Lunging forward in a full gallop for the well, his heart roared in his ears as he leaped behind it.

He was not more than a dozen yards from the cabin door, safe now, listening for sounds beyond the surge of his own heart, one last check before racing the final distance.

Somewhere between the decision to move and the first step, the cabin door swung open, the stripes on the first sergeant's sleeve a blaze of color in the new morning sun.

Adam bolted instinctively, then slumped in resignation to the circle of carbines about him.

Five

An order went up for attention; heels snapped; carbines clicked against the metal buttons of woolen uniforms and silence fell as still and torpid as the morning fog over the Grand River. In the distance, Assistant Surgeon McReynolds could hear the bray of horses beyond the compound and could smell the raw slumgullion stew as it wafted from the kitchen.

Gripping the rope above his head, Corporal Adam Renfro smiled at the young doctor who watched on with knitted brow. There was little to fear in this life or any other, as far as Renfro knew. A man didn't grow up in the backwoods of Tennessee without knowing the cost of living, and the cost of living was dying any way it was cut. If the dying was now, then so be it, and those who witnessed it would know before this day was out the man he was.

Raising his head between his arms, he let the light of the territory sun shine red through his lids. Sweat trickled from between his shoulder blades and gathered in the folds of the shirt that hung in shreds about his waist, jaw tightened against the first sergeant's orders to commence the punishment. Many a man died under the lash, but it was a choice, a rare choice given by Lieutenant Sheets to save him from life as a deserter. Forty lashes and thirty days if he survived, and the matter forgotten. It was more than he'd expected and it was his to live, if he could live, the moments to come.

The test of the whip, a cracking sound, like the cracking of a limb on a stormy night and the smell of lightning on the wind and the rumble of thunder in his soul, and he waited for the lash. If he could manage the first without a cry, then maybe.

It came to him not as thunder but as a whine, and embraced his naked back and wrapped its fiery tongue about him. Rib skin opened with a pop, and he turned his scream inward, turned it inward against the core, against the strength that bore deep within him and turned it out as a shudder of final and exquisite light. Gasping for breath, he braced against the pain, to hold back the nausea that rose in his throat, the vileness and wretchedness of life and death and the inevitability of the next lash.

Again it came, and he cried for mercy, begged for death, for God to stop his desolate life, for God to still his crushing anguish. But he begged without words, his tongue clenched between his teeth, a bloody and convulsing gristle.

He opened his eyes to the sun, to burn away the nerves, to burn away the unyielding fear of the next lash, but it came again, his nipple peeling from its place, and the smell of death and dust and urine, and the men about him, their blue coats, their ridiculous hats and blazoned chevrons and their black boots that wore the skin from their heels. These were the men who loved him and they who thanked God that it was he before the lash.

The breath was not there, that single breath between him and the whip and its savage tail. The flesh bore it all, hornets in his blood, wings pulled back and stingers erect, burrowing a thousand strong into his very core, assaulting that which no other should see or touch or know.

Even as he reached for the scream, a scream for mercy, a scream so piteous, so abject, so wretched as to touch even the dark souls of these men, it failed him. It was his time to die and he knew now the purpose of death, to stop the torment that only living can allot. In death was that which all men sought, the end of pain, and he, Adam Renfro, sought that end now.

The foul air of Fort Gibson filled his lungs for a final time, his head falling forward in defeat, and in that moment her face before him, there beyond the men, her eyes filling the emptiness left by the whip, and he clung to them as a man drowning, and settled into them even as the lash bore against his defenseless flesh. Even as the men picked up the count, their voices rising and falling, each count compounding their fervor and their disbelief that the bloodied lump before them remained silent, he clung to them. And even as his flesh bled into the earth between his legs, he clung to those eyes.

The final blow was held in deference to Corporal Renfro's courage, and McReynolds shook his head in disbelief that the man still lived, and, not a sound had he uttered.

The soldier with the slick sleeve and odd hip broke rank at his own peril and saluted Renfro in respect. The first sergeant let it pass and dismissed the formation. But for McReynolds it was amazement more than admiration that he felt for Renfro, a simple man no doubt, one who bore pain well, like a beast of burden.

Men's boundaries for pain were in a far narrower range than most would think, this McReynolds knew, but the simpler the man, the more impervious to pain. Now it fell to him to attend the wound, to scrub the cuts clean of the salt thrown there as a final insult and healing agent, a medical irony lost on all but himself.

It was a job McReynolds had little taste for, the senselessness of inflicting and mending the same wounds on the same day, but more—the despairing practice of nursing men who were largely renegades and illiterates driven by animal needs and a profound disrespect for honest work. Their hygiene was universally appalling and had not the first sergeant driven them to the Grand like a herd of buffalo, bathing would have been a rare event indeed.

Two years earlier, the War Department ordered a military road cleared between Fort Smith and Fort Gibson. As the assigned medical officer, McReynolds learned the hard way that to open a wound in this country was an invitation to the havoc of gangrene, and it was gangrene that accounted for the speed and deftness of his own amputation skills.

Axe wounds were common among the men, but it was gangrene that brought them to the infirmary and gangrene that rotted away their hands and legs and mortified even the bone mass.

So apathetic were they to sanitation that he'd abandoned even the modern techniques of letting blood, because infection and gangrene were inevitable consequences.

Disturbed at the stench brought in on the wind and the fray set up by coyotes fighting over the carnage, Lieutenant Sheets ordered all body parts buried in the fort cemetery. During that time, McReynolds perfected the art of separating limbs from bodies, soldiers staring at their stumps in astonishment, forgetting even to cry out in pain.

Bag over his shoulder, McReynolds crossed the compound. The guard at the brig snapped a salute, his eyes avoiding contact. Enlisted men in the 7th Infantry learned to avert their eyes with officers, like a dog pinned in a fight.

"Assistant Surgeon McReynolds," he said, "to tend the prisoner. Open the door, Corporal."

"Yes sir," the guard said, "if he's still kicking. Not much left to fix I'd say."

Pushing past the guard, he went into the tiny cell, where the prisoner lay against the wall, his knees pulled into his chest. Allowing himself the first groan of pain, Adam Renfro turned his head to see who stood over him.

"Christ," McReynolds said to the guard, "where do they get that salt, off the bottom of the river? Get a bucket of that well water, guard, and a clean towel from the laundry. There's more dirt on his back than on the floor."

"Leave my post, sir?"

"You think this man is going somewhere?"

"No sir, I reckon not, sir."

The guard lumbered across the compound, the powdered dust exploding under his feet, returning with a cedar bucket filled with water and a clean towel tucked under his arm.

Soaking the towel with the cool water, he leaned over Renfro.

"This may hurt some," he said, squeezing the towel, washing the caked blood and salt away. Shuddering, Renfro gasped for breath. "I'm saying this just once, Corporal, you've got to keep these wounds clean or you won't last the week."

From behind the sweat and dust and pain, Renfro smiled.

"I knew they was tendering me up," he said, "but I didn't know I was for supper till they salted me down."

Bewildered by Renfro's remark, McReynolds shook his head. With forceps and deliberate skill, he extracted the loose skin from the wounds. Rock salt and dirt were embedded, an affront promising infection and death. There was small chance Corporal Renfro would survive the week.

"I don't know what you soldiers find out there that's worth this kind of risk, nothing but shine whiskey that won't stay down. There's not a soldier at this fort man enough to get back to civilization without getting lost or starving or stopping an Osage arrow," he said, stepping back and examining his work. "Even those army horses out there have enough sense not to graze more than a mile from the fort for fear of the same end."

"It's the whiskey, sir, the promise of whiskey and freedom that a man can't turn down." Renfro tried to laugh, his wounds tightening like a band of iron around his chest.

By rolling Renfro gently on his side, McReynolds could get a good view of the damage the whip had inflicted, cutting lengths of gauze to close the gaping lash wounds.

"We'll see if that will grow back," he said.

"Never was much of a milker," Renfro said, managing a grin.

Filling his pipe, McReynolds looked out the window and across the compound.

"You have smoke makings?" he asked.

"Don't use it, sir. Guess that's about the only vice I passed up, though."

Touching the match to his pipe, he drew until the tobacco glowed red. Unlike the others, this Renfro fellow had a certain intelligence, crude to be sure, and uneducated like the others, but there was an alertness about him that belied his background and appearance.

"Tell me, Renfro," McReynolds allowed the smoke to rise into his nostrils like small white clouds, "why you took such a risk? It wasn't whiskey, was it? That rotgut coming down the river is not worth losing the skin off your back, not for a clever man like yourself."

"Never been accused of being clever, sir, but to tell the truth the walls just close in some times, all these men, the never-ending lies. An old mountain boy like myself just has to get away once in awhile." Renfro adjusted his position, leaning on one elbow and stretching his legs out. Pain sucked his breath away. "Guess I was holed up with no room to breathe one day more than I could stand. Course, if I'd knowed just how un-comfortable that whip could be, I might have stretched it a day or two longer."

Smoke from McReynolds's pipe drifted through the bars and into the freedom beyond. Whatever Renfro's reason for running, it was not because he couldn't handle the pressure. At this mo-ment he bore more pain than most men would ever know, and without so much as a protest. This was not someone who broke ranks without good cause.

As an army doctor, McReynolds knew better than most what drove men like Renfro, fleeing to the frontier for reasons more fearful than the frontier itself, men like Lieutenant Sheets, driven by self-doubt, self-hatred, secured in the power that his rank afforded.

How many times he'd watched medical students falter at the last moment, a repressed fear buried deep within them, the half-rotted cadaver delivered by the grave robber, the smell of a dead child putrefying in its mother's womb, surgery with nothing but whiskey between flesh and the cold reality of the scalpel.

Perhaps he knew these fears most because of his own luckless past, the old pain returning like an unwelcome guest as he thought of her, of the life he'd left behind.

"Look," he said, "I don't know why you did what you did,

I'm not even certain that I care, but you must think me a fool to believe you risked the lash because you wanted to go for a walk."

"I think you are no fool, sir," Renfro said, rubbing at the pain that burned up his neck and into his head.

The draft shifted, pulling the smoke from McReynolds's pipe and moving it across the room. The nights could be cold here, the clear, thin sky, the wind sweeping from across the river.

Beyond this wall there was little to cause a man to risk the lash, the fort garden he'd requested to provide fresh vegetables, a much-needed supplement to the unhealthy diet of salted meat and corn, other than that, only the cabin built as a temporary cook shack while the fort was under construction. It now housed the Kiowa girl he'd seen watching from the gate during the punishment.

"I'll have the brig scrubbed with vinegar and new wrappings delivered, and even then I risk the lieutenant's wrath for coddling prisoners. The commander is no help here either, Corporal, nor Surgeon Bloomly for that matter. They do not concern themselves with enlisted men's discomfort. Tend your own wounds, conserve your energy. You've days with precious little to eat. If infection sets in, you're done for, and there is sweet little I can do. Stay as clean and warm as you can."

Even as he spoke, he knew that neither of these things was likely, but what else could be done, his position as assistant surgeon being little more than perfunctory.

"Yes sir," Renfro said, "shouldn't be too bad if those bog mosquitoes don't get a smell of this blood and pull out those bars there."

Knocking the coal from his pipe, McReynolds smiled in spite of himself.

"The afternoon sun comes through that door there. Get as much sun on that back as you can. It'll help keep the infection down. Drink all the water they will provide and sleep the rest of the time. Those are nature's cures and they're all you have."

"Yes sir," Renfro said, his skin drawing tight against his skull, his body rigid against the throbbing pain, his eyes closing in fitful sleep.

Saluting, the guard stepped aside as McReynolds left, to walk the path up the hill to the officers' quarters, small squat rooms built of iron-colored slate carried down from the quarry. The rooms were small but, unlike the log cabins of the enlisted, relatively free of vermin and quite capable of stopping the frigid winds of February.

Perhaps most important was the privacy single occupancy afforded him as Assistant Surgeon. To live among men, consumed by their triviality, living void of reflection and deliberation, was more painful than the harshest elements. Privacy was his and he guarded it, shunning the friendships of fellow officers for fear of infringement on time spent reading, thinking, thinking of her.

Men like Corporal Renfro probably bore no such needs, nor concerned themselves with much beyond the demands of the day. These enlisted men were an uncivilized lot, separated from the wild by little more than a log cabin, a fire, and simple tradition; beyond that there was but primal instinct that turned them this way or that or caused them a moment's hesitation.

In his own mind the savage Indians for whom they were responsible were no less wanting of culture and grace than the insolent soldiers of Fort Gibson. But then this was a graceless place, a place fit for the likes of them and for the likes of himself too.

McReynolds released the latch and stepped into the dark room where his own thoughts and his own demons awaited.

Six

Sitting on his bunk, McReynolds looked through the books he'd selected from the commander's library, a small collection of no more than a hundred books, but tastefully chosen, eclectic and informative, donated by an unknown benefactor.

The leather-bound volume of Shakespeare caught his attention. Three years had passed since Alison asked him to read her beloved sonnets.

Pointing her finger at him, she said, "Joseph McReynolds, a man of medicine must guard against his own science or he will lose his humanity. There is more to be read in life than science journals."

Laying down his journal, he looked up at her, green eyes like China jade, full red mouth, skin as white and opulent as marble. When he'd asked Alison Simons to marry him, he'd chosen well—beautiful, intelligent, devoted, a flawless education, a family influential in the small Maryland town where he had started his practice. Unlike other men he knew, there was never a moment that he was tempted by another, for he was fulfilled by her, sustained intellectually, emotionally, sexually.

Taking her hand, he explained.

"It's important for a doctor to keep up with medical advances, Alison. The only way I can do that is to read these journals."

Brushing her lips, soft as goose down, against his, she moved into his lap.

"You must advance your soul equally, Joseph. Medicine without art will harden you."

The only softness he needed in his life was in Alison, her elegance, her warmth and femininity.

"I think it's happening," he whispered in the folds of her hair.

"What's happening?" she drew back, alarmed.

"I'm quite certain of it. I've begun to harden already."

"Oh, Joseph," she leaped up, "you're impossible."

Retrieving her copy of Shakespeare's sonnets from the shelf, she handed it to him.

"Here, I want you to read these. They are very important in my life, and I want to be able to share them with you."

Leafing through the pages unconsciously, he watched her.

"For you, anything," he said. "I'll begin tomorrow."

But tomorrow never came, his medicine absorbing him, intoxicating him once again with its infallibility, feverish study, a flawless practice fueled with a zealot's ardor.

Those times when his own mind and body, emptied and weary, sought something beyond science, Alison awaited, her restorative powers his for the asking.

Success, a happy marriage, Alison's devotion, were but natural extensions of the ideal world in which he was reared, a kind and nurturing mother, a doting sister who supported his success, a prosperous father with royal manners and a hearty laugh that filled the house with joy. Even still sometimes his laughter came, oddly in moments of despair, joy, or the quiet of the night. Dropping the long ash from his cigar in the palm of his hand, his father would look directly into his eyes. "You're a fine lad, Joseph," he'd say, "and nothing in the world can stop you, nothing. You've McReynolds blood in your veins and fire in your belly, and the world is yours to have."

This Joseph came to know and to believe, and there was little in which he failed or feared. Medical school, a successful practice, the most beautiful girl in town were his by decree. For it to be otherwise simply never occurred to him.

As a doctor, Joseph was decisive, confident, even arrogant.

No case gave him pause, no surgery too complex, no procedure too risky, and his reputation soon spread. "The finest doctor in town," they said. "None better."

There were times his reputation exceeded his skills, tested his limits, but he met the challenge, bore the responsibility of life and death. Who better after all, who more qualified, more competent? "A miracle man," they'd said, "brilliant, genius." Accolades, praise, all generously given and accepted, with modesty certainly, but accepted nonetheless. It was, after all, true. Heady with success, confident in his ability, he was the happiest man alive.

The illness was sudden, a raging fever, distress in the lower left quadrant of Alison's back, eyes wide in pain, lips cracked with fever.

Pulling the cover about her, he looked away to compose himself.

"What is it, Joseph?" she asked, her hand hot and thin in his own.

"Appendicitis I think, infection, the pain in your side, the high fever."

Frowning, he traced the veins in her hands, their connecting points, their course, their function in the body system. These veins were familiar territory, untold hours stripping away the flesh of cadavers, inflating arteries with hot wax to trace their origin, their design, their inception.

As a doctor, McReynolds knew the body better, was more comfortable with it, than with the complexities of this woman he loved, this woman who took him into her heart and mind and bed and was now threatened by the very system he venerated.

"It's not good, Alison. If your appendix is not taken out, it might rupture." Her hand tightened on his fingers. "Your fever is much too high. To wait is risky, too risky," he said, averting his eyes, afraid of the fear she might see in them.

Laudanum was powerless against surgery of this magnitude. If Alison didn't die from a ruptured appendix, she might well die from the pain inflicted by the scalpel. Time under the knife was measured in seconds, because it was seconds that separated success from shock and death on the table.

"I know someone," he said, "very good, very fast, some say the fastest there is. I know you," he said, his hand on her forehead, her fever raging under his touch, "and you are strong. This will be all right."

"I know the best doctor of all, Joseph," she smiled, a faint and weaker smile than before.

The decision made, she adjusted her cover and settled against her pillow.

"This must be done very quickly, Alison. I'm not the one for this. I'm a good doctor but too careful, too concerned about the details."

"Go now, Joseph," she waved her hand to dismiss him, "I'm very tired and I want to sleep while I can. You wake me when it's time."

Holding out her arms, she embraced him. It was to be his last embrace of Alison, a memory diminished by the press of his obligation as surgeon, a memory imagined again and again as more than it was, a memory crying of the emptiness that was to become his legacy.

Rising from the table to meet his scalpel, she arched against the leather straps, her white skin opening under his trembling and uncertain hand, and he knew that she was lost, that he was lost, that life would never again be the same.

This fort was his place now, a place of brutality, of ignorance, of futility. No one deserved it more than he, true penance and atonement, so high, so far to fall.

For Alison to have died was devastating, for him to have killed her, inconceivable.

Seven

Grinding out the stub of his cigar, Lieutenant Reginald Sheets pulled the map of the Indian Territory from a drawer. Landmarks were sparse, an outcropping, a bend in the river, a well-worn buffalo trail.

With deliberate care, his finger traced the rivers, the Cross Timbers hatched in black ink, the thin line far to the northwest representing the highly traveled Santa Fe Trail. Somewhere there, his finger stopped in the vast emptiness of the Gloss Mountains, lay a fortune in Spanish silver.

The story had formed from pieces, shards of information scattered and broken by time, a Kiowa pictorial calendar, newspaper accounts of the disappearance of twelve traders from Santa Fe transporting ten thousand dollars in silver specie along the trail, the surreptitious reading of reports, confidential reports transmitted to the commander of Fort Gibson concerning the party's last known whereabouts. Neither the traders nor the silver were ever found.

Turning the map into the light, Sheets held it close to his eyes, as if, were he to look hard enough, the treasure would appear there in the parchment. What coincidence and good luck to get the expedition west, what coincidence and good luck to have the army provide the authority and manpower that he needed for his plan.

The blank space in the map loomed large, his finger lingering in its vastness. This was where his fortune lay, his fame and destiny, and he would have it.

From the window of his office, Sheets watched as McReynolds crossed the compound, indignity in his gate. Men like McReynolds resented a summons, particularly from a junior officer like himself, but as commander of this expedition his power was absolute, that of life and death. All men bent in that breeze.

Leaving McReynolds to stand in front of his desk, Sheets spoke without looking up.

"I've been meaning to discuss a matter with you for some time, Doctor," he said, drumming his fingers on the top of his desk. "As you know, I've only recently arrived from Jefferson Barracks and have assumed second in command for the duration of my stay."

"Yes, Lieutenant, I am aware that you are second in command."

"Then you also know I've been assigned commander of the expedition to contact the plains Indians west of the Cross Timbers," he said, raising his chin.

"Yes, I believe I have heard that."

"And to persuade them to accept the migration into their lands of the civilized tribes from the southeast. There's also a matter of the Grand Saline reported by caravans out of Santa Fe," he said, pushing back his chair. "Salt could be an important commodity in the future, Doctor. As you know, many of the tribes use it as a currency. Whoever controls those salt fields controls the Indians."

"That's true," McReynolds said, "if one is interested in their control."

Hooking his thumbs under his belt, Sheets paced back and forth behind his desk with the swagger and bravado of a peacock.

"It's getting late in the season. We should have been supplied and ready to go. And now I hear from a courier that the army in its wisdom is supplanting one-third of our horses with mules," he snorted, face darkening, "mules, for chrisake, the 7th Infantry in all its glory riding jackasses into Indian Territory." The vein in his neck bulged, like a child on the verge of tantrum. "And even then I can't be certain when they'll arrive. All I've managed to do so far at this miserable post is fight epidemics and flog deserters."

"Your contribution to the epidemic was noted by us all, Lieutenant," McReynolds said, lifting his brows.

The sunlight edged forward into the window, falling across Sheets's face.

"Well," he said, holding his hand over his eyes, "strong leadership always makes a difference, doesn't it, McReynolds?"

"Speaking of flogging, Lieutenant, do you think it advisable to restrict food and blankets to men who have just been flogged? Open wounds are an invitation to infection."

"The guard tells me you had the brig cleaned, Doctor. You should know that I don't hold to coddling deserters."

"That's within my authority as a medical officer, Lieutenant Sheets, and I intend to see that sanitary conditions are maintained."

"Yes, well, Corporal Renfro still lives, doesn't he? Perhaps he will be useful as mule tender for my expedition. The corporal rode in here on a hammerhead molly mule like some Mexican peasant on his way to market. But not for long, I tell you."

"Prisoners would stand a better chance of surviving with decent food, Lieutenant."

Adjusting the fit of his coat, Sheets walked to the window and looked out onto the compound.

"That's out of the question, Doctor. Bread and water are as much a part of the punishment as the flogging. If Corporal Renfro lives, we'll have ourselves a man fit for the mules, if not, the mules will just have to adjust." He turned. "I find the use of these mules an affront and embarrassment, McReynolds. It's good horses that can cover ground fast, always has been, always will be."

"Was that all you wanted of me, Lieutenant?"

Pulling a match from his pocket, Sheets snapped it into a flame on the heel of his boot.

"No," he said, "it isn't all. Reports are reaching us of smallpox among the Indians. The commander and I agree that it would be judicious for you and Nurse Cromley to accompany the expedition."

"To go along?" McReynolds froze. "Me and Nurse Cromley? We're not exactly experienced soldiers, you know. There's not a damn thing to be done for smallpox without vaccine in any case."

The match flame dipped as Sheets touched it to the end of his cigar.

"Well, your function is primarily political. I dare say Nurse Cromley will make the journey less taxing for you."

"Perhaps Surgeon Bloomly will have a different view," McReynolds said, his face flushing.

"Perhaps, but I doubt it. The commander agrees, you see, and we all know how Dr. Bloomly hates conflict with the commander."

"Anything else, Lieutenant?"

"As a matter of fact there is, Doctor. Check the mess for spoilage. The men are complaining of the food and at any given time half of them are behind trees and the other half are waiting in line at the latrine. There's enough shit in those woods to ward off the whole Indian nation, and I can't get a day's work out of any of them."

"It's not spoilage, Lieutenant, but the lack of fresh vegetables and fruit."

"Then I'd suggest you tend your garden."

"I'll have the mess checked again, Lieutenant," McReynolds said, exasperated. Dealing with Sheets was like dealing with a disagreeable schoolboy, pushing, bragging, indifferent to everyone's needs but his own.

"And another thing, McReynolds, I'm having a private tent taken along on the expedition. Protocol prohibits officers from quartering with enlisted."

"On the trail?"

"Anywhere, anytime," he said. "Officers do not do manual labor. Officers do not quarter with the enlisted. As a doctor, you are also an officer and you will quarter in the tent with me. Is that understood?"

"You're the commander," he said, shrugging.

The sun shone red through Sheets's extruded ears, his hands clutched behind his back.

"Yes, Doctor, that is correct. I am the commander."

Eight

Unrolling the map again, Sheets studied the smudge left by his thumb. There somewhere was his fortune, enough to secure him for life. With a command and money no man would dare cross his path nor question his word ever again. Two things he was certain of, that someone out there knew where the silver was, and that he was just the man to find out who.

As a child, he'd been smaller than the others, victim to the larger boys roaming the playground in search of prey. But it was an early discovery and a lesson well learned, that intimidation paled against the certainty of retaliation.

At the first sign of doubt in his adversary, that momentary glint or quiver in the cheek, Sheets would strike with audacity. But it was the sure knowledge that revenge would come, if not now then soon, that mattered most. Unbridled and certain reprisal taught those who dared challenge him that the price was often too high.

Once a classmate sat on his chest in the school yard, tweaking his nose until blood ran salty into the corner of his mouth. Following him home, Sheets watched from behind the field-stone fence as the boy rubbed the white stomach of his tabby, giggling as it curled into a tight yellow ball, holding its cool nose against his face.

That evening, the stone wall casting a shadow across the front porch, Sheets wrapped the squirming tabby in his mother's hair net, lay it in the cedar water bucket that hung over the cistern, and lowered it hand over hand into the dark recess. Hanging the soggy package on the front doorknob, he walked home in the cool evening air, hands tucked in his hip pockets. It was for him a telling moment of power, of strength, of detachment.

From school, Sheets went directly to the military academy. Within its caste system lay the control he craved, and he pursued it with an intensity that drew him ever further into isolation.

The uncompromising enforcement of the rules earned him the nickname of "Regiment Reginald" among his superiors. More derisive terms were applied by his subordinates, who were frequent recipients of his ambition, but Sheets worried little about what the minions thought. Within the walls of the citadel were the agents of power, within the military, the rights of kings. It was wealth he needed now, wealth to complete the circle.

Upon graduation, new commission in hand, the now Lieutenant Sheets was assigned to Jefferson Barracks in Missouri as one of eighteen select dragoon officers. They were joined there by a hundred cavalrymen.

All were to undergo specialized training in Indian control. Come spring they would steam to Memphis on the stern-wheeler *Fred Hartwig*. She'd been designed with a flat hull to accommodate the Mississippi shallows and leased by the U.S. Army for transport of troops to the frontier.

From there they would march west to Fort Smith, Arkansas. It was but a short trip up the Arkansas River on flatboat to Fort Gibson, the departure point of nearly all major expeditions into Indian Territory. This was an opportunity Lieutenant Sheets did not intend to let slip through his hands.

Upon arrival at Jefferson Barracks, his disappointment was matched only by the bitter wind and soaking rain that set him to shaking as he awaited the officer in charge.

The dragoons were to be a crack outfit, the best mounts, the best uniforms, even the best and latest weapons, but neither supplies nor mounts had reached them from upriver and already a thin sheet of ice ran twenty feet out from the shore.

If the river clogged before the flatboats arrived, it would be a long winter indeed. Some of the men had abandoned garments in their optimism and now found themselves chilled and miserable. Many huddled together for warmth, their backs against the cold like buffalo in a blizzard, and waited.

The camp itself was pathetic, two barracks constructed of oak shingles, clinging with tenacity to the banks of the Mississippi River, trees crowding about like stalking enemies, the heavy smell of decaying forest in the air.

A small log cabin on the edge of the camp belonged to Colonel Henry Dodge, regiment commander, warrior, and God almighty.

An hour passed before Lieutenant Swinkoe came out of the far barracks and called them to attention, a thin, wiry man with onion-like skin. The veins in his neck corded when he talked, cold eyes peering down his bony nose like a shotgun, an O-shaped mouth, pink against his white skin, twisting this way and that as he examined the formation of men, stopping in front of each, shaking his head in disgust at the sorry lot who stood before him.

Inspection finished, Swinkoe strutted to the front of the formation and stood, shoulders back, hips forward, pendulum genitals exposed against his tight uniform, on his left hand a ring of turquoise and silver, like a pope's ring for all to kneel and kiss. Crossing his arms, Swinkoe peered at them with bulbous and watery eyes, a dragonfly hovering over a stagnant pool, and Sheets hated him.

"I'm Lieutenant Swinkoe," he said, clearing his throat, "Officer in charge. Officer in charge," he repeated, pacing the length of the formation, looking at his feet. "I want you to think about what that means, gentlemen.

"It means that I am in charge. Your very life depends on me. I have the authority and the will to make your life miserable if I so choose." Swinkoe stopped, turning his back to them, looking down on the Mississippi River. "Believe me, gentlemen, I so choose. Now," he said, turning back, "you have one hour to set up bunks and reassemble. Colonel Dodge wants another barracks built and you are just the merry fellows to do it. Any questions?"

"Two, Lieutenant," Sheets said, stepping forward.

"Oh?"

"Officers do not do common labor, nor do they quarter with the enlisted men."

The look in Swinkoe's eyes grew cold, bearing down on Sheets.

"What was your name again, Lieutenant?" he asked, his voice tight.

"Lieutenant Sheets, Reginald Sheets."

A droll smile spread across Swinkoe's face, spittle gathering in the corners of his mouth.

"Of course not, Lieutenant. For you there is a tent in the far barracks storage room. Pitch it at the edge of the trees."

"A tent, Lieutenant?"

"That's right, for your privacy, and since you have such an aversion to common labor, we'll just put you second in command of building the barracks. You'll answer directly to me."

"Yes sir," Sheets said.

Dismissing the formation, Swinkoe called Sheets back.

"Oh, Lieutenant Sheets, since you are second in command, see to it that the tools are organized for the men, and it will be necessary, of course, for you to study the drawings I've put together for the barracks before the men are ready to start."

"But my tent?"

"Tonight, Lieutenant," Swinkoe smiled, "after you've finished."

And so it was that Sheets pitched his tent in the dark and crawled exhausted under his single blanket.

In the night the rain came. Huddling alone, knees pulled up to conserve heat, he plotted revenge against Lieutenant Swinkoe.

By the second week, the barracks was well underway, with the frame reaching half again as high as the two existing barracks. The men split oak shingles while Sheets resolved the persistent problem of water in his tent by digging a six-inch trench around it for drainage.

Still, he suffered greatly from the night cold and from Swinkoe's determination to humiliate him in front of the men.

It was Swinkoe alone who communicated with Colonel Dodge and any complaints were channeled only through him. On the one occasion Sheets tried to jump command and speak directly to Colonel Dodge, he was rebuffed.

Dodge glared. "It's the officer in charge who handles such matters."

The men complained of the bitter cold, the lack of decent food, the pitiful state of their clothing, but Swinkoe only smiled. By the fourth week, the shingles were ready to cover the walls of the barracks, and that's when Sheets made his discovery.

Feet kicked up, hands behind his head, Swinkoe dozed against a sack of white flour.

"Well," he said, "what is it now, Sheets? Don't we understand how to read the blueprints?"

"I think there's been a mistake here, Lieutenant."

Rising to his feet, Swinkoe peered down his nose.

"I'm sick of this, Sheets," he said. "Every fifteen minutes you're back here with some criticism of my plans. Just follow the goddamn plans, see," the turquoise ring garish on his skinny finger, "or I'll have you in front of the commander!"

"Yes sir," Sheets said, folding the drawings, tucking them under his arm and retreating without a word.

Two days passed before Colonel Dodge and Lieutenant Swinkoe made their inspection of the project. Walking the circumference of the barracks, Colonel Dodge shook his head and walked it again in disbelief.

"Lieutenant Sheets," he said, a slight quiver in his voice, "are you aware there are no doors on this barracks?"

"Yes sir," he said.

"For Christ's sake, Lieutenant, how do you expect anyone to get in?"

"I don't know, sir. I followed Lieutenant Swinkoe's orders

not to change another single item on his drawings. His orders were quite explicit, sir, to 'follow the goddamn plans,' sir."

"Is that right, Swinkoe," the Colonel whirled about. "It's true you wanted barracks with no goddamn doors?"

"No sir, of course not, sir," Swinkoe said, eyes bulging. "There's been a misunderstanding."

"Fix it, Swinkoe! Fix it, you hear, or you'll shovel horse shit until you die of old age!"

Snapping to attention, Swinkoe thrust his hips forward, his feet cocked at a forty-five-degree angle and saluted as Colonel Dodge stomped down the path.

"Yes sir," he said after him, "right away, sir." Turning to Sheets, his voice pitched, Swinkoe shouted, "I'll have you for this, Sheets! Mark my word, I'll have you for this!"

"Following orders, sir," Sheets smirked.

"Whirling about on his heel, Swinkoe headed down the path after the colonel.

"Oh, Lieutenant?" Sheets called after him.

"What do you want, Sheets?" he stopped, not turning around, his head dropping forward.

"Orders, sir?"

"Fix it, you lame bastard!" he shouted. "Fix it!"

The quality of Sheets's rations diminished first, and then endless details, none too dirty, none too dangerous nor too menial to warrant his personal attention.

Sleep was impossible. In the early morning hours, while the night frost still glistened on the dead grass, Swinkoe would stick his head into the tent and order Sheets to conduct the changing of the guard, or to replenish the supply of camp water, or to check the ice depth on the river. And then there was the supervision of the digging of latrines, the disposal of camp garbage, the cutting of firewood, the burying of corpses beyond in the grove of ash trees. Everywhere he turned was Swinkoe spitting and mewling and whining.

Dreams of Swinkoe's demise came to him in the night, the thin milky skin, the grasshopper eyes, the swinging genitalia nesting whole generations of Swinkoes, and his hatred compounded.

By the end of the third week of Swinkoe's vendetta, Sheets could stand no more. Rising from his bed, he dressed in the cold and damp of his tent. Hours passed, shivering there in the dark, before the scrape of Swinkoe's feet could be heard coming up the path.

Stalking prey came naturally to Sheets. This was familiar territory, the waiting, the moment, the revenge.

The tent flap opened with a swish and Sheets lunged for Swinkoe's throat. Finding it in his grip, he held taut, Swinkoe bucking, squirming, kicking in desperation, clawing with bony fingers at the thing snuffing away his life.

They fell to the ground, thrashing about the tent and out onto the frosty grass. Under his grip, Swinkoe's heart tripped, but Sheets endured, cougar and rabbit, predator and prey, held secure the twisted, contorted body and awaited the final contractions.

Minutes passed before Swinkoe's heartbeat faded and he relaxed in death, but even then Sheets hung tight, his arms trembling with exhaustion, and did not stop until he could do no more.

Sitting back on his heels, he rested, his arms burning with fatigue, waiting to see if he moved. Deep in the forest, the melancholic hoot of a owl confirmed the end of Lieutenant Swinkoe.

Bony hands, cool in his own, bird claws cold in the night air, as he began the difficult pull to the river. With each tug, Swinkoe moved only a few feet. With each tug, his head lifted and fell, bulbous eyes opening and closing like the owl in the trees, boots plowing furrows behind him, marking his final grievance and complaint in the earth.

It took an hour and all the strength Sheets could muster to drag the body to the banks of the Mississippi. Gray clouds rolled aside and the moon cast an ivory light onto the water. Beyond the sheet of ice, the river moved, a churning, muddy rush beneath the shimmering surface.

Pulling off Swinkoe's boots first, he tossed them far out beyond the ice, then his shirt, and finally his pants. Naked now, Swinkoe lay on the bank, a dead fish, belly up.

Undressing himself, Sheets rolled his clothes in a bundle, trembling against the cold that blew from across the river. A wet and frozen uniform would most certainly give him away.

Inch by inch, he began the journey to the ice's edge, where the river's current would take Swinkoe away. Twenty feet from the bank the ice cracked, pinging across the surface in a jagged line. Dropping to his stomach to distribute his weight, the ice hot on his belly, Sheets pushed him to the edge. With bare feet he shoved him at last into the Mississippi, Swinkoe floating momentarily, rolling in a single fluid motion onto his stomach, slipping away, a shadow on the current, disappearing from sight.

With each move back the ice fractured more, zinging and skittering across the surface like electrical charges, freezing, rigid with fear, each move bringing him closer to safety.

Dressing was difficult, shaking from the cold, fumbling at shirt buttons, pulling at damp socks, but finally he was done, erasing all signs of struggle away with a branch.

Dawn broke as Sheets made his way back, hoarfrost glistening on his tent in the morning light. Exhausted, he collapsed into his bunk, falling into a deep sleep.

That day, unlike any other day since his arrival, Swinkoe would not be waking him.

Nine

If there was anything to be learned from Swinkoe's death, it was the insignificance of his life, and hardly a pause was given to his sudden disappearance. The assumption was that he'd deserted, easy pickings no doubt for the myriad demons of the forest. No one was surprised when Lieutenant Reginald Sheets was assigned officer in charge.

A brutal winter followed. Men and officers alike suffered from the lack of decent food and clothing. The few horses they'd acquired were inadequate for successful hunting parties, the animals themselves surviving on a paltry mixture of white flour and dried grass.

February was even more daunting, with snow banked to the eaves of the barracks, sifting through the cracks in the walls and onto the men huddled under their blankets. During the day, the men clustered about the fireplace, their faces hot, their backs freezing against the penetrating cold.

Reveling in his duty as officer in charge, Sheets soon enough alienated even the most seasoned of the soldiers. They hated him, as they'd hated Swinkoe, but found him in some ways a more competent leader.

Finding the solitude of his tent to his liking, he elected not to remove, and spent much of his time reading documents from the administrative files or studying military maps taken from a leather trunk stored in the camp supply room.

Colonel Dodge was quick to recognize Sheets's organizational skills but, like the men, found him cold, remote, unlikable. Even he scorned Sheets's company, keeping communications between them to military matters. Still, when spring and supplies finally arrived, it was Sheets who was put in charge of the expedition into Indian Territory and Sheets who would take the first group of men to Memphis on the *Fred Hartwig* and then overland to Fort Gibson. Later, when the mounts arrived at Jefferson Barracks, they would be conditioned on spring grass and brought downriver on flatboats to the fort.

Finally the dragoons boarded the stern-wheeler, steaming away from Jefferson Barracks in a cloud of black smoke. Night and day they plowed their way southward on the Mississippi, the relentless slap of the wheel urging them ever further into the oppressive southern heat.

The men lay on her deck stripped to their waist to cool themselves against the mounting humidity. Clouds hung low, dark, their bellies heavy with water. At night the sky danced with lightning and torrents of rain gorged the Mississippi, the banks brimming with muddy, fuming water.

Great black turtles perched on dry snags, basking in the afternoon sun. Pools of brackish water bred clouds of mosquitoes and crickets clung at the boat's waterline, awaiting dark for their invasion of the *Hartwig*.

The days were interminable, marked only by the insufferable pace and the foul stink of mud.

On the rare occasion the *Hartwig* pulled to shore to stock wood and water, the men stripped naked and swam into the muddy backwashes and holes for catfish. Some cats weighing over a hundred pounds were caught and heaved on deck, their heads severed and spiked on poles for all to see, entrails tossed irreverently into the river, turtles diving after them in a frenzy.

With great care and consternation, the captain made his way to Memphis, but it was Sheets who took to the bow, his temper dark, black, deepening with each day on the river, rising before the others, sleeping not at all.

The men avoided him altogether and talked among themselves of his behavior. But Sheets ignored them, staring into the depths of the muddy waters.

Each day was like another, and the men grew listless from the monotony of the river and the perpetual bank of trees that blocked the world from view. The floodwaters raced past them and left in their wake sandbars where none stood before.

On such a day the stern-wheeler lurched, groaning like an old woman, and turned sideways against the rushing current. Water rose halfway up her side and she shuddered against the force of the river. Her whistle screamed and men scrambled about her deck in panic.

Within seconds, Private Sacks rushed to Sheets, who clung to the rail, his face white with fear.

"Sir," Sacks said, "the captain says we've snagged a sandbar and wants every able-bodied man over the side to heave her free."

"Over the side?" he asked, staring at the private.

"Yes sir. Captain thinks we can rock her loose."

"Well, to hell with the captain, Sacks, we're soldiers, not goddamn river rats!"

"Captain says we'll be here till another steamer comes along if we don't help, sir, maybe weeks."

"Weeks?" he said, leaning over the rail, looking at the churning water.

"Yes sir, that's what he says."

"Put 'em over the side," he finally said.

"Sir," Sacks said, stopping, "Captain says *every* able-bodied man or we'll be here till the snow flies."

"Goddamn it, Sacks," Sheets stiffened, "you don't need to tell me that!"

"Yes sir," he said, saluting.

The men peeled from their clothes as Sheets looked on, some jumping from the railing into the teeming water, but he waited until the last man went over the side before taking off his own clothes, closing his eyes, and dropping into the river.

The turbid water sucked him down, down into its depths as

he swam against its pull, his heart pounding, his lungs burning, bursting from the water with his mouth agape and his arms flailing. Standing in the shallows, river mud oozing between their toes, the men watched the curious performance.

Both footing and composure regained, Sheets barked out the orders.

"Heave. One, two, three, heave," each man black to his armpits with mud.

And the *Hartwig* groaned, turning into the current, her paddle slapping the water, black smoke boiling from her stacks.

Again they tried, and the *Hartwig* edged forward, stopping again with a moan, the rancid smell of river mud filling the air.

Working his way to the stern, Sheets examined the point where she hung tight, to where the paddle whipped the water into a froth, to where the thud of the engines penetrated his body.

Suddenly she pivoted. Without sound or warning, a great swirl pulled him downward and his lungs filled with the muddy water.

Fighting his way to the top once more, he found the *Hartwig* now beyond reach and the river hauling him out and into the deep current, ever further away from the men, who hollered frantic directions from the sandbar.

The distance between him and the stern-wheeler widened and the men's voices grew faint as the river swept him away. Arms burning with exhaustion, he labored against the current, but to no avail. The river was too powerful, too inevitable. What bad luck to die like this, a stinking catfish in the Mississippi ooze.

Giving himself to the river, Sheets's frenzied pawing ceased, a fatalistic calm, his eyes trained on the men, now small figures on the horizon.

Then he saw it, a limb rising from the river, splitting the surface into a dark shimmering fan. Hope, strength, and determination swelled within him, and he swam toward the limb, his lungs bursting, his arms and legs beyond feeling, his heart pounding like the paddle of the *Hartwig* against the relentless power of the river.

Grabbing the limb, he clung to it, an insignificant spot in the mighty waters. Where only moments before there was death, now there was life, and he waved his arm above his head at the stern-wheeler steaming toward him from upriver.

Minutes passed before he realized how precarious his situation, how fragile his raft, how inescapable his death. Even though several limbs ran into the water, with the least movement, the whole tree rocked and twisted into the current. The river sucked at his body, pulled at his arms, and he realized he must position the snag between himself and the current if he was to survive.

Running his hand down the length of the snag, he reached as far under the water as possible before readjusting his position on the tree. Nearly there, the tree rose from the water, its limbs a muddy claw reaching into the sky. Determined to stay the course no matter where it took him, he hung on, but there above in the limbs was a ghost from the past.

The scream that followed was a scream from within, the kind that is neither planned nor controlled but comes from the dark terrors of one's deeds and the destruction of one's soul. There in the limbs a skeleton grinned back, a turquoise and silver ring on its bony finger, river mud bleeding from its eyes.

Panic-stricken, Sheets lunged for the nearest limb and the log rotated once again. The skeleton hung on its perch before falling onto him in a cold and profane embrace. Screaming at the terror, he flung it blindly into the river, where it rolled in the eddies, a fixed and diabolic grin on its face, before disappearing below the surface.

Moments later, a line was thrown from the stern-wheeler and Lieutenant Reginald Sheets was hauled aboard and taken to his quarters. There he stayed for the duration of the trip. The men said little of his mishap and nothing of the cursed skeleton.

Laying the map aside, Sheets shivered, and walked to the window of his office once again. The day had turned cold.

Across the compound, McReynolds was just leaving the canteen, heading for the brig to check on the prisoner no doubt. Getting his bluff in early on the good doctor had been a good idea. Might save him trouble later.

Closing the window against the chill, Sheets rolled up the map. It was time to go now, to the Gloss Mountains, to the Spanish silver, all far from Swinkoe and the muddy Mississippi.

Ten

Cutting into the dense blackjacks, Twobirds followed the winding gully. The setting sun painted the trees with swatches of light and the Grand River shimmered into the shadows of the untamed territory. Frogs tuned their voices for the evening chorus and mosquitoes twisted in union against the orange horizon.

The molly was well hidden in the canopy of trees, dozing in the last of the sun's warmth, her tail swishing in timed intervals at the heel flies. Calling her name in calm, gentle tones, Twobirds approached Molly, who lifted her head, looking about for Renfro.

"It's all right," Twobirds said. "He's sent me to help." Molly snorted, shaking her head, scraping at the dirt with her hoof, ambling toward Twobirds. "That's my friend," she said, reaching her hand over the corral. Sniffing at Twobirds, Molly moved forward with caution. "There," Twobirds rubbed Molly's nose, under her chin, the hair like bristles against her hand, and then between her ears, where large veins surged with warmth. "Your corporal's going to be all right, Molly. I'll see to it."

Pigweed grew in abundance along the wet banks of the stream, ample food for the hungry mule. Carrying large bundles in her arms, Twobirds dumped them over the side of the corral. Green froth gathered at the corners of Molly's mouth as she munched at the stems with a consuming appetite.

"I'll be back," Twobirds said.

The light faded as she worked her way down the gully, turning west toward the clearing where the soldiers' garden struggled to survive. When she saw men still working there, Twobirds changed course, picking her way through the blackjack stumps left at the boundary of the clearing. For each stump, a thousand runners stuck their green fingers through the soil in a tenacious grip on this primitive and ancient place.

Like a deer she slipped along the tree line, moving, listening, moving again until she reached her trap under the fallen elm. The jackrabbit darted into the corner of the trap, to become invisible, its face hidden from the world. Lifting it by the ears, Twobirds clipped it with a stick at the base of the skull, watching it kick out its life in the brush. Tonight she would be one of a few having fresh meat instead of slumgullion stew.

Sitting on the stoop of her cabin, Twobirds relieved the rabbit of its pelt with a single pull, her knife opening the steaming carcass, tossing the entrails into the hole she'd dug in the sand, brushing the pelt, hanging it on the cabin wall to dry.

The tinder started, growing into a flame no larger than the size of her hand. With patience, Twobirds waited for the bed of coals, learning early that a fire need not be large to be hot. Soldiers' fires were always great, to drive the darkness from their camps and the fear from their hearts.

Soon the rabbit was a golden brown, and in the aroma the memories of her family, the sound of their voices, the gentle nights about their own fire.

Riding proud and grand, her father brought to them the buffalo to be skinned. They ate the meat killed with his hands and sat at his fire, the night touching their hearts and building the memories she now held within her.

From the buffalo's neck he fashioned his shield, tucked between the skins the extra moccasins kept dry there from the rains, the strips of sinew to sew their tepee, clothing, horn, hoof, bone, bladders to carry their water, and the great robes that warmed their bodies when the blizzards covered their tents.

The warhorse he rode was untouched by labor, as her father,

and in Twobirds's mind they were the same, his moccasins unfit for walking, with tassels tied too long, his bow of bois d'arc, arrows of white willow quivered at his shoulder. They were as one, but more together, a predator of intelligence and swiftness that no other creature could match.

They were Kiowa, born from a hollow log, child of the sun and an earthly mother and safe with Tai-Me, the Sun Dance medicine. As guardian of the Tai-Me, her father was honored among her people but he was a man too. This she knew from the sounds of the night, her mother's hunger, her husky laughter, her father peering into the dry cottonwood leaves beyond the tepee.

Even as his blood spilled from the Osage lance, his life pooling into the dirt, he spoke not to her of his love, nor as her mother thrashed in death under the feet of horses, did he touch her or bid good-bye, nor as they took the lock from his own head, the waxen white of his skull, a medallion from his raven hair, did he grant her words of the place in his heart or of her place in the world.

It was only the eyes, the words from the eyes, that Twobirds clung to and held to and knew to be true. Beneath her blouse was the Tai-Me, kept there from the hands of the dreaded Osage. This day like no other since filled her with such pride, and it was once more the eyes not the words that spoke to her of courage and love.

Beyond the stockade gate, beyond the sour smell of the soldiers, she'd watched Adam Renfro bear the punishment of his own kind. In those moments he spoke to her with the eyes, as her father had, and she knew the truth of this man.

Pulling the rabbit from the spit, she covered the coals with the damp earth and went into the cabin. In a cloth she wrapped the rabbit, a handful of black walnuts, a forked hackberry stick peeled of its bark.

The surgeon had gone to Adam, his face troubled, but he was an officer and help would not come from his hand.

Stepping into the night, she was certain of what she must do. Stars shimmered in the clear black sky and a current of cold, damp air wrapped around her legs and ankles. Twobirds shivered, pulled her blanket about her shoulders, and made her way through the blackjack stumps toward the brig.

Entering the fort was a risk, she knew, but one she'd have to take. The soldiers were always hungry, spending the few dollars they made on whiskey barged down the Arkansas in the dark of night. Fresh meat was rare, an occasional kill as they cut their foolish roads through the trees, and they hungered for it even more than they hungered for the whiskey.

Hidden in the shadows of the stockade, Twobirds waited and listened. The guards at the gate crouched low behind the wall to escape the cutting breeze, smoking and laughing among themselves. Walking the length of the compound, the brig guard hunched his shoulders against the cold and the long night ahead.

Watching for the others, Twobirds stepped into his view.

"Soldier," she said, "I am a woman and not here to harm you. I have food, rabbit smoked on the spit."

"Step closer," he said, lifting his carbine into the darkness, fear in his voice, "or I'll shoot, woman or no."

"Fresh killed," she said, holding the rabbit in front of her, "and cooked over the coals."

"Who are you and what do you want?"

"I am Twobirds, the Kiowa brought from Fort Smith."

Taking her by the arm, he pulled her into the doorway of the brig.

"Heard there was a squaw in the old cook shack," he said, his hand lingering on her arm, "a pretty one too, but my pay's long gone, sister. There's but half a plug of tobacco between me and the next pay call." The smell of smoked rabbit rose into his nostrils. "You got no business in the compound like this. The commander would have my hide like Renfro in there."

"It's the corporal I want to see," she said, "ten minutes and half this rabbit's yours. There will be another tomorrow night. None will know from me."

"So that's it, is it?" He chuckled under his breath. "I can see why, maybe. Something right special here."

"You get half, another half tomorrow," she said, lifting the rabbit higher, pulling one of the legs from the carcass, "I see the corporal for ten minutes."

"It's the hind half, see," he said, tearing a leg from the carcass, and no more than ten minutes. I'll shoot you between the eyes if I must, and swear you was stealing in. Do we understand each other?" Snapping the rabbit's back, Twobirds handed him the hind quarters. "If he wasn't such a friend and good soldier, I wouldn't be doing this, not for no hindquarter of a jack, mind you," he said, taking another bite of the rabbit, grease glistening on his lips. "I won't be on duty till night after next. Come near morning, most everyone's sleeping by then."

A cold draft from the door penetrated her wrap. In the far corner of the cell Adam lay so still that at first she thought he was dead.

"Adam," she whispered, "Adam, it's Twobirds."

Lifting his head, he tried to smile, his lips tight against his teeth, misery in his eyes.

"What are you doing here?" he whispered. "It won't do for them to find you."

"Some things can't be denied," she said. "I've brought food, meat and nuts. The wounds will heal with fresh food."

Kneeling beside him, she took his head into her arms, giving him the warmth of her own body for the few short minutes they had. When she looked up, the guard's shadow watched from the doorway.

"The ten minutes are to be ours," she said, "alone."

When she looked again, the guard was gone, the door ajar.

"He's not to be trusted," Adam whispered, slumping into her breasts.

"It's all right. He likes the taste of rabbit and he fears you."

"I had cause to thrash him once," Adam said, "for rifling my locker. Guess he figures if I live, it might happen twice." The wound seized like dried rawhide, bending him forward. "Might have to spend the rest of my days just staring at these big feet," he moaned.

Sometimes white men's words fell on her like rocks from the sky.

"You must eat all of this," she said, pulling the strips of meat from the rabbit, laying the walnuts out before him, "and hide the bones when you're finished."

"It's a fine meal, Twobirds. I'd guess the commander wishes he was here right now eating rabbit and keeping company with such a pretty girl." Pausing, he let his arm rest across his chest for a moment. "About my molly . . ."

"Your molly's appetite is as large as yours and her breath could welt the trees."

"Thanks for taking care of her, Twobirds," he said. "She pines something awful without company."

"The fever will come," she said. "That will be the dangerous time, and the time you must eat and drink the most. There are hackberries by the river and ground beans in the nest of the meadow mice beyond the canebrake, but there are no mesquite beans here, which is a shame, for they have much energy and are good to make bread."

"You must go now," the guard said from the doorway.

Handing the hackberry stick to Adam, Twobirds whispered, "This has power. I give it to you."

"I ain't got much faith in stick power."

"You must not joke of these things," she said, thrusting the stick into the dirt floor. "The dead hackberry grew again, life from death, and it is not for you to refuse."

Once more the guard was at the door.

"Now," he said. "You must leave now. There will be a changing of the guard soon. You come back with more meat, but in the morning next time."

"Yes," she said, moving past him.

The smell of rabbit was on the guard's hands as he took her chin. Twobirds fell silent. Only the white soldier lived without his woman, an unwise custom making him both wanton and dangerous. Since her arrival, she'd seen only two white women, the commander's wife and the pale nurse trailing at Surgeon Bloomly's heels like a favored dog.

"Maybe you'd give a little more than rabbit if we made it a whole hour?" he said, grabbing her breast harshly.

Avoiding his eyes, she distanced herself from his passion, his coarse hand mauling her breast, his breath wet against her face. Shoving his hand away, she moved quickly into the darkness. A few days of fatback and his interest would more likely be smoked rabbit than her.

Whatever happened, this much was certain, she would do what she must to see that Corporal Adam Renfro lived.

Eleven

Trips to the brig depended on the luck of Twobirds's trap and the duty schedule of the guard, but with each visit the guard's courage and appetite grew, his manner more brazen. Dealing with him was a dangerous game, a narrow and perilous line.

The moon was full, bright, increasing the risk of discovery, so Twobirds waited, waited as the moon arched high and cool into the sky, waited as it fell below the tangled tree line, before slipping into the fort.

In her hand was the hind quarter of a rabbit, smoked golden brown and smelling like glory itself.

"Open the door," she whispered, stepping into the light.

"What's your hurry?" he asked, snatching the rabbit from her, filling his mouth with meat. "Your man in there would be toes up without me, you know. Maybe you should treat me with a little respect."

"Open it up," she commanded, moving to the brig door.

Turning the lock, the guard forced her to squeeze past. Renfro reached for her hand, pulling her in, his strength returned.

"You've come again," he said.

"For you," she said, opening up the folds of her skirt, "onions from the soldiers' garden. They think there is a very big rabbit about. Here is the smoked meat. It is only the front quarters. The guard insists on the hind parts. He is a greedy man."

"Make a mistake one day," Renfro said, his jaw clenched.

"He thinks only of his stomach," she lied.

Sitting cross-legged on the floor, she watched him devour the rabbit, then rub his hands on his trousers to remove the grease.

"How's my molly?"

"There is no pigweed left in the territory," she said, turning up her palms.

"I'm out soon, Twobirds. I'll come when I can."

"You will not come to me, Adam," she frowned. "I'll feed your molly, but you will not come. I'm tired of crawling through the weeds in the moonlight to feed rabbit to you and that guard out there."

"The expedition leaves soon," he said, reaching for her hand, "then there will be time."

"Now, I must go. We must not tempt the spirits, Adam. Many have died in this place from the illness, but we have been spared. The leaves have grown," she said, pointing to the stick. "It has come to life."

"And what happens when we find your people?"

Stepping to the door, Twobirds spoke to the guard.

"I am ready," she said.

"I'll see you soon?" Adam asked.

"You must let go sometimes, Adam," she said, laying her hand on his arm, "to gain what you most need."

Pushing past the guard, she hurried toward the wall opening.

"Wait there," he called. "When are you coming back?"

"You must hunt your own rabbits now," she said.

Suddenly he was upon her, grabbing her arms, pinning her against the wall, his mouth hot against her neck. Struggling, she tried to free herself, but he held tight, slipping his leg between her thighs, pushing apart her knees, maneuvering his coarse hand up her cotton dress.

Staring at the moon above, she froze, purging her emotions, bracing against the repulsion that rose within her as he pawed, thrusting against her leg. This was a price she knew she might pay, a chance taken, and she choked back the fury that raged within her.

The impact of Adam's blow stunned even her through the

guard's body. There was a rush of air from his lungs as he slumped against her. Gasping, he struggled in vain for breath, raising up his hands in defense, but Adam struck again under his uplifted arm, the guard's rib cage splintering under the staggering blow. Silently, he slid unconscious into the dirt at Twobirds's feet.

"Made a mistake," Adam said, "and didn't lock the door."

"They'll never let you out now."

"Course they will. If Lieutenant Sheets found out you was bringing me food, our friend here would be my cellmate for a mighty long time. A few broken ribs ain't much compared to that."

There was no answer from Twobirds, who had already moved into the shadows, into the night, into the world of the coyote.

Twelve

Holding his ribs with one hand and saluting with the other, the brig guard stepped aside for Dr. McReynolds.

"You all right, soldier?"

"Yes sir," he said, "fell off my horse is all."

When McReynolds entered the cell, the dank smell assaulted his senses as he searched in the pale light for Corporal Renfro.

"Morning, Lieutenant," Renfro said from the corner of the brig. "It's a fine spring day, isn't it?"

"Renfro, is that you?" he said, covering his eyes with his hand, peering into the corner.

"Yes sir. I like it fine here, so thought I'd stay a spell."

"What you been eating in here, Corporal?" McReynolds asked, squatting on his haunches to examine him, finding him in surprising condition for a man on bread and water. "I never knew a man to gain weight on prison rations, and these lash wounds are little more than scars already."

"It's them mosquitoes, sir," Renfro grinned, "once I get one wrestled down and kilt, he'll last damn near a week."

"It's not much to me," McReynolds laughed, "except curiosity, but how you been getting food into this brig? That guard out there your friend or something?"

"No sir, not a close one."

"Well, I suppose it doesn't matter, but I know enough about the human body to say you been getting some fair meals." He leaned over and examined the scars. "You've healed remarkably well."

"It's in the blood, I reckon," Renfro shrugged. "My pa grew back a little finger what was cut off with a corn knife, just like a snake grows a new tail when it's lopped off with a hoe."

"Well, I suppose that could be it." McReynolds smiled to himself. "By the way, Corporal, Lieutenant Sheets tells me one-third of the mounts the army is sending is going to be mules. Says if you live, you'll probably wind up mule skinner. Says the word is you're the best mule driver about."

"Know the lieutenant must be tickled about that," Renfro said, twisting his mouth to the side. "Me and mules think some alike, I guess."

"What brings a man to study mules, Corporal?"

"Well, sir, I guess it comes from relying on them entirely for near everything. Without our mules," he looked out the window at the stockade wall, "I guess my family wouldn't have lasted a week in them mountains."

"Lieutenant Sheets doesn't see riding mules as dignified, Renfro. Thinks soldiers on jackasses is inappropriate."

"That a fact?" Renfro rubbed at his chin. "That's unsettling to hear, sir, especially from a man like the lieutenant, what with his experience and learning and winning ways.

"Had a dog once named Fuzz Face," he said, tugging at his nose in thought, "used to lick my chin every chance he got. Couldn't sleep without him slurping me one right across the mouth. The more ole' Fuzz Face wanted my company, the more I hated him, hated him his whole life, hate him still, come to think on it."

"Is there a moral to this story?' McReynolds asked.

"No sir, not so's you can tell, but the lieutenant does bring back memories of ole' Fuzz Face somehow."

"Don't forget that you're talking to an officer," McReynolds said, stiffening. Renfro fell silent. "Sorry," McReynolds said, "I didn't mean to be short. We lost quite a few men with the prairie fever. I guess I'm still a little jumpy. Anyway," he turned and smiled, "looks like you're in good health."

"Yes sir," Renfro said, but the friendliness had gone from his voice.

"It's just that officers and enlisted men can't get too chummy, you understand?"

"Like mixing mules and horses, I reckon," he smiled.

"I don't know much about mules, I'm afraid."

"No sir, most don't, but there's a heap to know. Someday when I ain't enlisted and you ain't an officer, I'll tell you all about them."

"Tell me about mules, Renfro. It seems I am going on the expedition as well."

"Well, howdy do. You're apt to learn more about mules than you set out to. Course, a man could do worse than teaming up in the wilderness with a mule. They got the size of a horse and the wear of a donkey," he said, scratching his head as if reaching back into time. "Hitched our saddle horse up with our molly mule once to plow the corn patch. Left them in the field while eating my dinner. By the time I got back, that mule had dragged our horse around the field so many times, there was a path worn six inches deep."

Renfro waited for a reaction.

"I guess there are some tall tales in those mountains too?" McReynolds said.

"Some," he grinned, "some. Still, it's a fact there ain't nothing can work longer without food and water than a good mule— except a camel maybe, I wouldn't know about that—and they're smart too. Heap a wagon load of oats in front of a mule and it will eat no more than what's good for it, no matter the temptation. Course it won't take one thing less than what it's got coming.

"Now, a horse will eat it all, or until it blows up, whichever comes first. It's got no temperance and no judgment. Catch it up in the wire, and it will saw off its leg. Jump up a rabbit, it's apt to bolt right over the top of you and break your back. Gives up when the going gets tough, too." Sticking his hands in his pockets, he kicked at the dirt floor with his foot. "A mule, on the other hand, won't never quit and won't never give up.

"Once, my pa found a mule's skeleton standing at the feed trough waiting for oats. Dead as a rock it was, with corn all around but oats's what it wanted and oats's what it figured to have."

"Is that so?" McReynolds said.

"Yes sir, it is. And another thing, treat a mule right, and it will take care of you when the going gets tough. Treat it wrong and it will wait a lifetime for justice."

McReynolds knocked on the door for the guard.

"Thanks for all the information, Renfro." Leaning over, he looked at something protruding from the floor. "What's that there, looks like a stick with leaves growing on it, right out of the floor?"

"That a fact?" Renfro said, turning away.

"You know, I've heard that the Kiowa believe hackberry sticks have sacred powers. But how would a Kiowa stick get here in the brig?"

"No accounting for the Kiowa, I reckon."

"They also say that some Indians won't go into the Cross Timbers, Corporal, because they believe there's dark spirits there."

"That's what they say," Renfro said, tucking his hands into his pockets, "but then dark spirits almost always live where you don't want to go, don't they, sir?"

Thirteen

The book of sonnets lay in McReynolds's lap as he looked out the small window of his cabin. All of nature dozed under the afternoon sun. Picking up the book, he read again.

No longer mourn for me when I am dead
Than you shall hear the surly sullen bell
Give warning to the world that I am fled
From this vile world, with vilest worms to
    dwell:
Nay, if you read this line, remember not
The hand that writ it; for I love you so
That I in your sweet thoughts would be forgot
If thinking on me then should make you woe.
O, if, I say, you look upon this verse
When I perhaps compounded am with clay,
Do not so much as my poor name rehearse,
But let your love even with my life decay,
    Lest the wise world should look into your
        moan
    And mock you with me after I am gone.

His eyes dampened with emotion. Perhaps there were spirits after all, hackberry sticks springing from death to life. Perhaps this was Alison's message from the grave and the world could mock him no more.

Opening the door of the cabin, he leaned against the jamb. Across the way, Nurse Cromley would be on duty now, filling her vials, copying her notes, making certain that each detail was meticulously recorded. What a strange girl, so dedicated, fierce commitment sometimes driving away the very thing she sought. Soldiers flocked about, to be sure, but to no avail. The word soon spread that Nurse Cromley was an iron box, clasped and securely locked.

Uncertain as to her reaction, he had not told her yet of the expedition west. He would have to face it soon.

Lying down on his bunk, the book across his chest, he closed his eyes, the sun falling through the window, warming his back, urging him into a slumber. When he awoke, the sun set low in the sky, an orange ball igniting the storm clouds that darkened on the horizon.

Within the hour, rain drummed on the roof, a sweet and warm rain. Thunder rumbled in the distance and the rain grew heavier. Through the deluge, the lantern light glowed in the pharmacy window.

Throwing his slicker over his head, he searched his way through the downpour to the infirmary, wiping his feet at the door, Nurse Cromley allowing no one in with mud on his boots, no matter the rank or occasion.

The infirmary was warm, cozy, a small fire burning in the fireplace to take away the dampness. He found her as he knew he would, working at her records, bent over the small table in deep concentration, her hair falling loose over her shoulders.

"Hello," he said.

"Oh," she jumped, touching her hair, "Dr. McReynolds, I didn't expect anyone in this rain."

"I came by the path that goes down to the fort. It's a veritable river."

"Is there something I could help you with, Doctor?"

"Ah, no, not really," he said, "just thought I'd check on the patients."

"That would be fine, Doctor, if we had any patients."

"Oh," he said, looking at the chart, "not even Dr. Bloomly?"

"No sir, not even Dr. Bloomly. Said he wasn't going to take another drop of calomel if he died tomorrow for it."

"In that case," he smiled, "why don't we have a cup of coffee and a talk? There's something I've been meaning to speak to you about."

Drawing the water, she wiped the drops from the bottom of the pot with her skirt tail.

"And what could that be, Dr. McReynolds?"

"Your first name. I don't know your first name."

"Mary," she said, lighting the large candle to heat the water. "Is that what you've been meaning to talk to me about?"

Retrieving two cups from the shelf, McReynolds chuckled to himself.

"What's the matter with, Mary?" she asked.

"My name is Joseph," he said. "Haven't we met before somewhere?"

Nurse Cromley beamed and poured the water over the grounds. Soon the aroma filled the little room and they fell silent as the brew percolated. When the coffee was done, she took her place across from him.

"I've checked on the prisoner," he said, sipping at the coffee. "He's doing fine, in fact, rather better than almost anyone at the fort."

"Oh, I'm glad." She shook her head. "Punishment like that is barbaric. I don't understand Lieutenant Sheets, you know. Sometimes he's such a lonely soul, and then to order those horrible floggings."

"But by his own hand," McReynolds shrugged. "I mean, with Sheets everything is extreme, too much, at the wrong time, in the wrong way. Pretty soon he has you against the wall and there's nothing left to do but fight."

"Perhaps you are right," she said. "Some never seem to fit in."

"There's this dead stick in Renfro's cell," he said suddenly, "a forked stick, you know?"

"A stick?"

"Yes, like a forked stick, and it has leaves, like someone just stuck it in the dirt and it started growing." Sitting down his coffee, he looked at her. "Don't you find that odd?"

"I suppose I do, but what is the point, Doctor?"

"No point, really, except I've heard that the Kiowa have a belief about a forked hackberry stick having spiritual powers, like bringing life from death."

"I don't believe in such foolishness. I would hardly think a man of science would either."

The sound of the rain increased as the winds picked up. Thunder rumbled down the valley, tripping off smaller volleys in its path. McReynolds waited until it had passed before speaking.

"I've never known anyone who believed more in spirits than you, Nurse Cromley."

"You mean my religion?"

"Spirits are spirits I should think."

The curvature of her back accentuated the roundness of her hips as she placed her cup back on the shelf.

"My faith could hardly be compared to a hackberry stick, Doctor. Ever since my mother died, I've dedicated my life to God. There was even a time I thought of going to the convent."

"We're all tied to the dead in some way, I suppose."

"And what about you, do you believe in hackberry sticks?"

"Until today, I would've said no."

"And how is today different?"

"Because my wife spoke to me today," he said, dropping his hands in his lap, staring at them. "The words were hers, there on the page, words of forgiveness, words from the grave."

"Like a miracle?" she said.

"In a way."

"Like my surviving the fever? That was a miracle. And Surgeon Bloomly, too. We both survived the fever. It was God's will, Dr. McReynolds, don't you see? Hackberry sticks have nothing to do with God's will." Sitting down, she took his hand.

"What is it? Is there something I could do for you? Do you need my help?"

"We are not always what we seem," he said, pulling away his hand, looking into her eyes. "I've hurt people in my life."

"I could never believe you would hurt anyone, Dr. McReynolds. You care too much."

"You're very kind, but there's a lot of young men out there in that cemetery. I didn't help them much, I'm afraid." The fire crackled in the other room and the rain swept against the pharmacy window.

"Maybe there is no difference between hackberry sticks and anybody's faith," he said. "Maybe Truth is in none of it or all of it. Maybe it doesn't matter, though, because it's the believing that matters, that gives the comfort. Maybe 'Truth' is not the right goal. Maybe we've been asking the wrong question the whole time."

"I'm sorry for your pain," she said, squaring her shoulders. "If it were in my power to take it away, I would, but I have no questions. My faith has no room for questions."

Standing, he rinsed his cup. This was obviously not a subject she was willing to pursue.

"I've something else, Mary, the reason I'm here, actually. You don't mind if I call you Mary like this?"

"Of course not, Doctor."

"The expedition west is in need of medical support, and Lieutenant Sheets has ordered both of us along. He has the commander's ear, you know, and we probably have very little choice."

"On the expedition?" she said, her eyes widening, "what on earth for?

"There are reports of smallpox among the Indians."

"But without vaccine?"

"Yes, I know, but Lieutenant Sheets is a very determined man."

"As long as it is with you," she said, pushing back the hair from her face, "then it will be all right."

Impetuously, he reached for her, putting his arm about her waist, pulling her into him. Startled, Nurse Cromley squirmed to free herself from his hold. Passion doubling and redoubling, he searched for her mouth with his own, his tongue probing for the desire he knew must be there, craving her, desiring her, wanting her beyond reason. Nurse Cromley clenched her fists, tiny and ineffectual, and pounded at his chest.

"Doctor, no, please, no."

"Mary, I'm sorry," he said, pushing her back in astonishment. "I'm sorry. I don't know what came over me. Please forgive me."

Without a word she fled from the infirmary.

Dejected, he walked back to his cabin, the rain stinging his face, soaking his clothes, and fell into his bunk. Never had he acted so cowardly, so contemptuously toward a woman, and toward a woman for whom he had such great respect. How could a day starting so well end like this?

Tomorrow he'd apologize, that's all, when she was feeling better. For now he damned the military for bringing him to this point and the sonnet for freeing such wanton and inexcusable behavior.

The night closed in about him, but he didn't bother shutting the door or lighting the lantern. Lying on his bunk, his hands behind his head, he watched the lightning arch across the sky. Each flash lit the trees beyond the clearing, their tops bowing to the ground.

At first he thought it was an apparition, a shadow, or a Kiowa spirit come to avenge his skepticism. Rising on an elbow, he peered into the darkness. Lightning lit the sky again and this time he saw her, hair down, dress clinging, body trembling.

"Yes?" he said.

"It's Mary," she answered.

"I'm sorry, Mary, for what I did. I was not thinking of you, what you wanted. It was a selfish thing."

"I came to help you, Joseph, to erase the sadness if I can."

She stood at the foot of his bunk, smelling of the rain, of the lightning, of the pungent earth, breath rising with the storm, lifting and falling with the surge of the storm.

Lightning flashed, a fixed and permanent image, her hands cupping her breasts, freed now as she herself was freed, coming to him as only Mary could, with unconditional commitment and sacrifice.

Sometime in the morning hours, the storm a distant murmur on the horizon, he touched her shoulder. Awakening, she turned to him, arms about his neck, hair like down against his cheek.

"Do you know what the Cross Timbers are, Mary?" he asked.

"Yes," she said, sleep in her voice, "a band of trees that cut through the southern part of the territory. They are very thick and difficult to penetrate."

"Yes, very difficult. The expedition won't enter them until it drops south on the return trip. It's not a good time, when supplies are low, horses jaded, energy and will spent. The expedition is too ambitious, too long. It seems poor planning to me."

"Surely the commander knows about such things," she said.

"Yes, but I wonder if Lieutenant Sheets does. There is a mad look in his eyes, Mary. It concerns me to follow such a man into the territory."

"Well," she sighed, "we must not worry. Others have made it through the Cross Timbers, haven't they?"

"Yes, but a few men on horseback, not wagons, not an expedition of this size nor of this duration, nor with this commander.

"The Indians won't go there, you know. They say it's an evil place, a place where spirits dwell, a place that separates their people from the evil beyond. Sometimes I think it's not right that we go there, even if we can. Maybe we don't know all we think we do. Sometimes we should just leave things alone."

"They are a superstitious people, Joseph, a godless people. The Cross Timbers are just trees."

Wrapping his arms about her, he snuggled against her

warmth. She was right, of course. He worried too much, like an old woman.

In the distance the storm died away and from the bog, frogs began a lament, a dirge, a requiem for his wife, for dead soldiers on the hill, for spirits dishonored.

Fourteen

The *Facility,* a seventy-five-ton steamer with two keelboats in tow, loaded with uniforms, horses, mules, and ammunition for the soldiers, arrived at Fort Gibson from downriver.

Ordering all uniforms unpacked to dry, Sheets walked back and forth on the bank of the Grand, hands on his hips, stooping to examine the clothing like a crane searching for minnows. The men murmured among themselves at the array of articles before them.

"Up front, Corporal Renfro," Sheets commanded. "Here's a uniform just your size." Looking around at the other men, he smiled. "We want our mule skinner to be well dressed, don't we?"

There was anxious laughter among the soldiers as Renfro made his way through the ranks, snapping a salute as he approached Sheets.

"Put it on, Corporal," Sheets said, holding up a dark blue double-breasted coat.

"Here, sir?"

"That's right, here."

"We won't be wearing these on the expedition, will we, sir?" Renfro asked, lifting the heavy wool coat.

"A great deal of planning went into these uniforms, Corporal. Military apparel is an important element in warfare. Everyone knows that ornamentation is highly valued by Indians. We must look the part to play the role. One can accomplish much with appearances, if properly executed. We can't go into the territory looking like mountain boys on mules, can we?"

"You mean we're going to scare them to death, sir?"

"Haven't you had enough of the guardhouse, Corporal?" Sheets said, his eyes narrowing.

"Sorry, sir."

"And the pants too."

"Yes sir," he said.

Slipping on the coat, Renfro fumbled at the two rows of gilt buttons. Both collar and cuffs were yellow, gold fringe dangling from the epaulets. Turning his back to the men, he pulled off his worn trousers and slipped on the blues. Yellow stripes three-quarters of an inch wide ran the length of both legs, and then the cap, a heavy tube-like affair adorned with silver eagle, gilt star, and white horsehair plume.

Nearly fifteen minutes passed as Renfro struggled to attach the epaulets, the cape, the silk sash that tied the whole thing together like a brightly colored Christmas ribbon.

Staring straight ahead, he pulled at his collar, sweat beading on his forehead and dripping onto the front of the new uniform. The final touches included black patent leather belt, boots, and sabre with steel scabbard.

"Turn," Sheets ordered, "so they can see."

Looking for the world like an enormous blue jay, he turned about. Laughter rippled among the men.

"Sir?" Renfro asked.

"What is it, Corporal?"

"Sir, it's hotter than Satan's kitchen in this getup. We won't make the bend of the river before we'll be toes up from the heat."

Arms rigid as tent poles, Sheets walked around Renfro.

"Let's have an understanding, Corporal. I am in charge of this outfit. You are in charge of the mules. That should tell you something, shouldn't it?"

"Yes sir, suppose it does, sir, but even a mule's got sense enough to shed its coat come summer."

"These are the uniforms we've been issued," Sheets said, rising up on his toes, "and these are the uniforms we'll wear. Is that understood?"

"Yes sir," Renfro said. "Just trying to be helpful, sir."

"Your job is to do as you're told, Corporal. Now show these men how this all goes on."

Turning an about-face, Renfro mingled among the men as they began the task of fitting their uniforms.

Motioning for McReynolds to follow him, Sheets moved out of hearing, lighting a thin black cigar, letting it dangle from the corner of his mouth.

"You wanted to talk to me, Lieutenant?" McReynolds asked.

"We are leaving in the morning," Sheets said, rolling the cigar to the opposite side of his mouth, "three wagons in all, two for food, one for ammunition, medical supplies, and gifts for the Indians. I assume you've spoken to Nurse Cromley."

"I have."

"Yes," he said, examining the end of the cigar, "well, space is limited in the wagons as you might suspect. Will you require much room for your medical supplies?"

"The only thing worth taking from the pharmacy is Bloomly's rye whiskey. I do have bullet forceps, scalpel, dressings, things of that nature, but they won't take up much room."

"Good, then I'll expect you and Nurse Cromley at the main gate and ready to go at sunup."

"As you say, Lieutenant," McReynolds said. "Oh, by the way, do you have any notion as to the length of this expedition?"

"Hard to say," Sheets said, grinding out the cigar on the heel of his boot. "There's the Grand Saline first, of course, and then the Kiowa girl. Depends on what we run into I suppose."

"And may I ask why the commander is not going? It seems that an expedition this far into Indian territory, of this magnitude . . ."

Sheets stiffened. "The commander is organizing a commission to handle the assignment of the southeastern tribes. I assure you that he has every confidence in me, Doctor."

"Yes, of course. I didn't mean to imply otherwise."

"Well then, if you have no other concerns." He started to leave, turning. "McReynolds, you do understand that we are the only officers going on this expedition?"

"I understand."

"I expect your support, you see. Officers must stick together. Discipline must be maintained."

"Look, Lieutenant Sheets, it's not my intent to undermine your authority as commander. I'm going on this expedition because it was ordered, but it should be understood that I am a doctor, not a soldier. My interest is in providing the best medical care I can under the circumstances."

"Good, good," he said, resting his hand on the side arm he'd started wearing the last few days. "Just one final thing, McReynolds."

"What's that, Lieutenant Sheets?"

"There's a uniform for you as well. Wear it."

The troops stood at the ready as the sun broke over the eastern horizon, their uniforms buttoned, their boots shined, their hats like plumed peacocks in the wind.

At the head of the column, Sheets rode a spirited black mount that danced about, its tail lifted like an ebony fan. Next to him, Twobirds rode a large bay, her hair braided and tied at the end with a scrap of red cloth, deerskin boots accentuating the symmetry of her brown legs.

The column of men behind was divided into two groups, at the lead about thirty men on horseback resembling gallant Roman warriors, at the rear twelve more looking less valiant atop their mules.

Riding near the wagons in the center of the column were McReynolds and Nurse Cromley, while Renfro brought up the drag atop the biggest mule McReynolds had ever seen, a white mule, and from a distance at least, a rather impressive one. Up close, however, was another story, great floppy ears that couldn't decide which way to lay, a nose that twisted and turned, smelling, touching, toiling with a life of its own, the mule's forehead protruding outward like a hammer. With a grating bray, it complained at every opportunity, pulling its lips back and exposing enormous yellow teeth.

His horse prancing against the reins, Lieutenant Sheets circled Renfro's mule.

"Wasn't that a white molly I ordered you to get rid of when you come riding in here, Corporal?"

"No sir," he said. "That was a no good jack, just like you said, sir, and I was glad enough to see him go."

"A hammerhead, just like this one here, wasn't it?"

"Yes sir, a hammerhead, but with a black splotch on his rear and a brain so small I don't know how he breathed regular. Glad he's gone, sir, coyote food, just like you ordered."

The heavy side arm and prancing horse had worked Sheets's britches into an uncomfortable wad, causing him to tug at his crotch unconsciously.

"Well, see to it these mules keep to the back of the column, Corporal, lest the Indians think we're dirt farmers or moonshiners."

"Yes sir," Renfro said.

With a chest like a barrel and a voice like a bugle, First Sergeant Lansdown commanded instant obedience as he ordered the column forward through the gates of Fort Gibson. An anxious look passed between Nurse Cromley and McReynolds as they rode past the bend of the river and turned north up the east bank.

They had agreed that discretion was in order, that it wouldn't do for the troops, or especially Sheets, to know there was anything between them. After a quick, reassuring smile, McReynolds turned his attention to hauling on the reins, which his horse insisted on pulling slack with its head.

With some consternation of his own McReynolds watched Fort Gibson fade from sight. To leave all civilization behind, to march into the unknown, to realize that only wit, luck, and

Lieutenant Sheets would keep him alive in the coming weeks, was at best disconcerting. Yet, as the column moved up the valley, he too sensed the excitement and sat straight in his saddle, his shoulders back.

The plan, he was told by the wagon driver, was to cross the Grand some twenty miles upstream, where the river widened into shallows before turning west toward territorial lands.

"Can horses swim well?" McReynolds asked.

"Oh, no sir," the driver grinned, "they just hold their breaths mostly and walk acrost on the bottom."

By noon McReynolds's legs were raw from the saddle and sweat dripped from his brow. The sun was high and hot and the humidity from the recent rains was oppressive.

Without the burden of a heavy uniform, Nurse Cromley was better off than the soldiers.

"The men are suffering from the heat, Doctor," she said, riding up beside him as they moved into an open stretch. "We're going to have trouble if something isn't done."

"It's these jackets for Christ's sake," he said, pulling on his collar. "They aren't made for this kind of weather. Surely Sheets will soon figure it out."

"Couldn't you ask him to relieve the men of their jackets at least? It's brutal."

"I know it's difficult, but it would be better if I didn't interfere, to wait," he said, jerking the reins up as his horse dropped its head to pull at grass. "Sooner or later he'll discover it for himself."

By late that afternoon, the valley had narrowed into a steep canyon that twisted alongside the river, its walls towering above the column, shutting away any breeze. Mosquitoes swarmed about them in droning black clouds. Humidity hung in the canyon, a suffocating curtain, an invisible ceiling holding the heat of the sun about them.

Within the hour, a soldier not twenty feet from McReynolds teetered and spilled from his horse, his sabre clattering among the rocks.

Dismounting, McReynolds opened the soldier's coat, pouring water from a canteen over his neck in an effort to cool him.

"What's going on here?" Sheets asked, his horse prancing about the downed man.

"Heat," McReynolds said, in spite of his determination to remain silent. "The uniforms are too hot, Lieutenant."

"This is the army, Doctor. Soldiers wear uniforms in the army."

"These jackets are wool, Lieutenant, and this is the Oklahoma Territory."

"Put him on the wagon and keep moving," Sheets said, spurring his horse to bring him about. "We need to make that crossing before dark."

After tying the soldier in the wagon bed to keep him from bouncing off and into the river, McReynolds fell in behind, his pants wet from ankle to crotch with sweat. Within a few miles, another man dropped from his horse, his foot snagging in the stirrup, horse catering askant, eyes white and frightened at the strange thing flopping on its side.

Once again Sheets galloped the length of the column, pulling up just short of McReynolds.

"Now what?" he asked.

"What do you think, Lieutenant?" McReynolds snapped. "These men could die out here with these coats on." He wiped the sweat from his face. "Look, Lieutenant, it's the commander's prerogative to set the uniform of the day. You're the commander, aren't you? So why in God's name don't you relieve the men of their jackets?"

"It's against my better judgment, Doctor," Sheets said, sitting back in his saddle, circles of sweat under his arms, "but if that's your medical opinion, then all right, but only to make time. Coats off," he ordered. A murmur rippled through the column as the men shed the woolen coats. "I want them rolled and tied on the back of the saddles, you understand? I want those coats where they can be put on at a moment's notice." He spun his horse about. "Now can we get to that crossing?"

Relieved of their jackets, the men joked among themselves as they worked their way up the narrowing canyon.

At times there was scarcely room for the wagons to pass between the river and the canyon wall. Voices echoed, eerie rejoinders bouncing and careening against the rocks.

The lead horse on the supply wagon lifted its tail and farted, reverberating through the canyon with a great whooshing sound, and the men laughed. Sheets stood erect in his stirrups, looking over his shoulder.

By mid afternoon, thunderheads boiled overhead, white pillars stretching into the sky. The heat mounted, a sweltering haze deepening about them, and the men fell silent. The sky darkened, black and ominous, lightning dancing within the churning, fomenting clouds. Raindrops splattered about them on the rocks and then a torrent, curtains of rain driving through the canyon, buffeting and stinging their faces like blowing sand.

At times the rain was so heavy McReynolds could not see the wagon in front of him. Water poured from his hat and into his lap as his horse picked its way along the precarious path. Even in the driving rain, McReynolds could hear Renfro's mule protesting as it selected footholds along the trail.

Within half an hour the river began to rise. Where the passage narrowed, the water deepened, at times threatening to spill into the wagon beds themselves.

Convinced now that they were all to drown on the first day out, McReynolds pulled up his horse and examined the terrain. To his left a jagged wall rose into the dark clouds, an impenetrable bank of granite; to his right and across the river, the canyon opened onto an alluvial plain. Water rushed from the surrounding hills in all directions and dumped into the turbulent river.

Ahead, a sandbar stretched a third of the way into the river from the east bank. Once across, they would be safe, but to stay on the canyon side would be disaster. There was no high ground to be had between the water and the canyon wall.

Signaling the column onto the bar, Sheets climbed on top of

a boulder that rose from the water's edge, clothes wet, the white of his underwear showing above his side arm, hair sticking to his forehead in rivulets. Standing atop the supply wagon, McReynolds stretched the cramps from his legs.

"All right, men," Sheets began, "this is the crossing. The river is rising and as you can see there's no place on this side of the river for camp. There's probably an hour of daylight left and plenty of time to make the crossing. I want Renfro and half a dozen men to take the wagons across first and start setting up camp. The rest will follow single file once they're over." Turning, he looked at the men below him. "Are there any questions?"

"Yes sir," Renfro said, "not exactly a question, though, I reckon."

"What is it, Renfro?" Sheets said, frowning.

"Seems to me these wagons aren't going anywhere, not sunk to their hubs in quicksand at least."

"What?" Sheets jumped from the rock and circled the wagon McReynolds was sitting on. "For Christ's sake," he shouted, "the wagons are sinking into the riverbed. Get off the goddamn wagon, McReynolds. Get those jugheaded mules hitched up to these wagons, Renfro. Christ!" he shook his head in disbelief. "Get those men up here to help."

Even as he spoke, the river rose higher and the clouds darkened above them, heavy with rain. The men worked feverishly against the rising water and the setting sun. Each time the wagons were pulled from the muck and forward movement ceased, they sank straightaway like a floundering ship.

At last Renfro and his mules pulled the last wagon onto solid footing at the river's edge just as the sun dropped below the horizon.

"Sir," Renfro said, approaching Sheets, who was pacing the bank, "what we could do, and there's just light to make it I think, is head on across. We'll unpack the supplies from the wagons and float 'em over empty. If the supplies was split up amongst the men, they could pack 'em over on horseback. Once we're across, we'll hang a lantern in one of them trees on the far bank. The others could cross then, keeping the lantern light in sight so that ways they wouldn't drift on downriver somewheres."

"Cross the river in the dark, Corporal?"

"Reckon that's about it, sir," he said, climbing on his mule, pulling at her ears. "There's only about twenty feet of dry bank left. By morning that will be under water and everything what's setting on it, I figure."

"It's a good eighth of a mile across this river, Renfro," Sheets said, staring at the distant bank. "What makes you think we could see a lantern light on a night like this?"

"If it ain't hung, no man will see it for certain."

"And we've got women. You can't ask women to swim a flooding river in the dark."

"Oh, don't know about that, sir," he said, patting his mule on the neck. "Old Molly here is a woman, and she's got more balls than most jacks I know. Besides, we could float the women over on the wagons if that's disturbin' you, sir."

Looking at the canyon wall and then at the rising water, Sheets shrugged in resignation.

"I guess there's no other way, is there. Hang that lantern high, Renfro."

First Renfro directed the men to unload the supplies, and then tied two mules to each side of all three wagons for stabilization, putting Nurse Cromley in one wagon, Twobirds in another. With a wave of his hand, they pulled straightaway into the current. Within moments, all had disappeared from sight.

The remaining men huddled in small groups against the canyon wall to wait for the lantern light, to protect themselves from the downpour as best they could.

Soon enough it was dark and only the rush of the river and an occasional crash of thunder could be heard. They all stared into the blackness until their eyes ached for a sign of the lantern.

An hour passed, maybe more, as Sheets stood at the river's edge, his arms crossed, jaw set, and the night grew blacker. The water inched closer to where the men waited, the inevitable water soaking their shoes and then the cuffs of their new uniforms. At some point there would be no choice but to swim blindly into the river.

And then McReynolds saw it, at least he thought he did, cupping his eyes, peering into the night. Yes, there it was, a yellow dot, downstream maybe 500 feet from where they stood.

"There," he shouted, excitement in his voice, "just there to the left."

Gathering about, the men tried to fix the point of light.

"Yes," Sheets said, staring into the darkness, "there, I see it now. All right," he said, "First Sergeant goes, and then the others, single file, and hang on to those supplies."

They fell silent, the sound of the rushing water intensifying about them.

"Maybe we should follow you, Lieutenant," McReynolds said. "We could all go across together so if anyone gets into trouble . . ."

"No," Sheets said, his breath short, labored, "not together. That wouldn't do, you see. If I should become disoriented, we'd all wind up drowned. Better for each man on his own, keeping the light as a beacon. Now move out."

The men and horses moved into the water as McReynolds looked on, swallowed by the darkness as if they'd been swept over the edge of the earth.

The barrel of Sheets's pistol dangled in the water as he waited against the canyon wall.

"Are you ready, sir?" McReynolds shouted above the din of the river.

"You go," Sheets yelled, "I'll follow."

Leading his horse to the water's edge, McReynolds slipped his arm through the stirrup, and took one last sighting of the lantern light before slapping his horse hard on the rump.

The horse plunged in, pulling McReynolds under for a single terrifying moment. Emerging, he searched for the light over his shoulder, spotting it, a friend and champion there on the horizon.

With power and grace, his horse swam for the distant shore, the current hauling and pushing them away from the speck of light. McReynolds yanked hard on the reins, turning his horse's head into the current, his heroic companion swimming on, powerful muscles churning against the force of the river.

And then they were there, the river bottom firm and alien under his feet. Shouting with relief, McReynolds stood and hugged his horse's neck.

When McReynolds looked up, there was Renfro, Twobirds, Nurse Cromley, and all the others standing on the bank cheering him home.

"You made it," Nurse Cromley laughed with relief, stopping just short of his arms.

"This horse did," he smiled.

"Quite a ride," Renfro said, reaching for McReynolds's hand and pulling him onto the bank. "Where's the lieutenant?"

"I left him, with water to his waist. He couldn't have been more than a few yards behind me."

"Could've been swept downstream," Renfro shrugged, walking toward the grove of locust trees. "Be passing through Texas about now if he was. Come on to camp, sir. Sarge's got the men setting lean-tos. We'll leave the lantern up till morning just in case."

The smell of coffee and bacon awakened McReynolds the next morning. When he pulled the flap of the tent back, he saw the sun just breaking over the east bank, Nurse Cromley and Twobirds standing over the fire chatting like a couple of housewives, Renfro saddling his mule, humming, looking up when McReynolds approached.

"Fine day, Doctor," he smiled and hauled on the cinch. Molly grunted a complaint, turning her head as if to bite. "Here," Renfro scolded, "you wouldn't blow up like a toad, there'd be no need to haul this cinch so tight, now would there? There now," he said, half hitching the cinch, "that shouldn't come off."

"Did Lieutenant Sheets make it across?" McReynolds asked.

"Well, that's the deal, isn't it? Seems Molly and me have to go back over and swim him across."

"What do you mean?"

"Look yonder across the river, sir. See that bump there on that rock?"

"Yes."

"Well, sir, that's Lieutenant Sheets. Been there all night he has, like a frog on a rock you might say. Sarge says me and Molly's got to go get him."

"Where's his horse?"

"Having his breakfast right here in camp just like I'm fixing to do."

After breakfast, they all went down to the bank and watched as Renfro and Molly swam their way back across the river. Within the hour, the three of them climbed the bank, where the column awaited in silence.

Blue streaks running down his face where his hat had bled dye during the night, Sheets stomped past, his face white and drawn from his ordeal on the rock.

"Are you all right, Lieutenant?" McReynolds asked.

"Break camp and get ready to move out," he said, stalking toward the tent, "and I want those goddamn jackets at the ready. Do I make myself clear?"

Fifteen

The next few days were distinct only in their monotony, as the column made its way west and north towards the Salt Fork branch of the Arkansas. On a good day they could make twelve miles with the wagons, but there were more often irritating and time-consuming stops, to forge a creek, to haul the wagons up a steep slope, or to circumvent an impassable gorge.

The all but worthless map led them endlessly wrong or gave them just enough information to confound logic or to set them arguing among themselves.

Afternoons were fierce, as the sun rose high overhead and the locusts mounted their choral chant. Even the mules slowed under their hypnotic troll and the crushing heat.

Liking Renfro's easy manner and uncomplaining ways, McReynolds took to riding with him. They had little in common to be sure, McReynolds educated and well-read, Renfro illiterate and backward. Still, he was pleasant company and a marvelous source of information about the wildlife around them.

Reading the earth like a book, Renfro would point. "Here," he'd say, "sand rose, and just there skunk brush with the red berry, and over there coon track, maybe two days old." Attention to detail was second only to his abiding curiosity and his desire to move ever forward. No man McReynolds ever knew faced the unknown with such zeal and confidence as Renfro atop his beloved molly. There was a wisdom there beneath his rough exterior, sought by most of the men at one time or another, no small comfort under the vexing command of Lieutenant Sheets.

The days passed and the terrain changed with imperceptible subtlety. Large and healthy trees shrank to scrub. Grass grew shorter, browner. Paddle cactus sprang from the rocks like green hands and the sky, wrung of moisture, cleared into infinity.

At times the rough landscape opened into vast grasslands, broken only by the ripple of heat rising from the red earth below, no landmarks, no direction, no distinction except unending distance. The apprehension of sailors bobbing in the sea's immensity was no stranger to McReynolds.

To make matters worse, there were increasing signs of Indians and everyone, including himself, knew the anxiety, sensed the danger, and struggled with the inconceivability of another human wanting them dead. It was foolhardy, as he had always thought, to send men so ruefully lacking in experience on such an expedition.

Bubbling creeks turned brackish, diminishing finally to little more than dry gulches. Food too dwindled, first in variety and then in portions, until they were down to a single meal a day of corn mush and syrup.

The men grumbled about their food and spent much of their time looking for game. But there was precious little to be found, only an occasional rabbit or turkey or a hapless rodent snatched from the watchful eyes of circling hawks.

But it was the want of water that consumed them, gnawed at them even in their sleep, pools and liquid dreams, falling, bubbling, gurgling dreams that sat them upright in the dead of night and kissed their dry, cracked lips.

But they rode on, plodding under the territorial sun, the smell of leather and sweat, leeching hot winds cooking them, blistering their skin, gnats drinking at the corners of their mouths and eyes, whining in their ears to the point of madness.

McReynolds no longer thought of Nurse Cromley or of his dead wife or of Shakespearean sonnets, no longer thought of medicine or of books or of his fellow man, no longer thought of Sheets's injustice or of Renfro's company or of the expedition's success. He thought only of water, the restoring and healing powers of a single drink of water. The thought consumed him, drove him on, as it did the others, ever westward and farther from civilization.

Within a few days, the horses began to suffer. Suddenly and unpredictably they would stumble, spilling their burdens onto the ground.

Looking on, Renfro's mules moved in their tireless and steadfast gait, no faster nor slower than the day they ambled out of the Fort Gibson compound.

Just as the sun edged into evening, they rode upon thick green rushes nestled at the base of a rock ledge. Sliding from his saddle, Renfro examined the pool of water, lifting a handful to his nose, tossing it back into the pool.

"Bad," he said, "thick enough for frogs to walk on. Wouldn't do for man nor animal."

"Looks fine to me, Corporal," Sheets said, walking around the pool. "Water is water and these animals won't last without it."

"Thick as soup and smells of skeeters, sir."

"But for the horses," he said, pushing back his hat, lifting a handful of the water to his nose, "wouldn't they drink it?"

"Yes sir, they'd drink it sure enough. There ain't a horse born that won't eat or drink hisself to death. But a mule won't," he said, leading Molly to the edge of the puddle, letting go of her reins. "A mule won't drink bad water or eat more than she can, neither one." Sniffing the water, Molly pulled her lips back in disgust. "Molly says it's tainted, sir, and she ain't wrong all that often."

"Taking orders from a mule," Sheets snorted, dropping his horse's reins. Burying its muzzle into the brackish water, his horse sucked noisily, water drizzling from its lower lip when it lifted its head. The other horses pulled at their reins and pranced about in anticipation. "It's a puzzle who grouses the most, you or that mule."

"It's a match, sir," Renfro said, ducking his head, but McReynolds could see the ripple in his jaw.

"Make camp," Sheets ordered, stomping off in the direction of a chinaberry grove farther down the hill, "and see if you can't stir up some game."

"Best wait to water them horses, boys," Renfro said, turning to the other men. "Morning's soon enough."

Within the hour, First Sergeant Lansdown, Renfro, and two privates set off for a hunt, returning before dark, three turkeys slung over their saddles. Handing the game to Twobirds, the first sergeant slid from his horse.

"Downed two in the air and winged the third squattin' under a tumbleweed not a quarter mile from here. Wouldn't have took that long if Renfro here had been a little faster on his feet. Took him nearly an hour to chase those turkeys down."

"Weren't nothing," he said, grinning. "Just warming them up some so they'd bleed properly when butchered out."

The turkeys were decidedly skinny, but soon crackled on the spit over a blazing fire. The men gathered about the camp as the night closed in, sucking grease from their fingers, sipping at what little water remained in their canteens.

Coyotes howled, doleful cries from the blackness, and loneliness struck at the hearts of the men as they settled in for the night.

Returning to the tent, McReynolds found Sheets studying the map.

"Evening, Lieutenant," he said, loading his pipe. "Skinniest turkeys I ever saw. Hadn't been for the rocks in their craws, they wouldn't have weighed more than an ounce altogether." Sheets didn't look up from his map. "Better get out there before it's gone, Lieutenant."

"I take my meals alone whenever possible, Doctor, and would advise you to do the same. First thing, these men start thinking you're their closest friend," he said, laying aside the map, looking up. "That's when it begins."

"When what begins, Lieutenant?"

"The smothering needs of the rabble, McReynolds. They'll suck your blood and complain with red lips that it's too tepid for their taste."

"Friends can be a comfort if you let them, even if they do come with a price."

"If it's comfort you seek," said Sheets, his face darkening, "I suggest you look to your own mettle. Now, if you'll excuse me, I've work here to do."

Determined to leave Sheets to his own company, McReynolds joined the others at the fire. Befriending the lieutenant was like petting a rattler, a brooding and venomous anger just there at striking distance.

The men rested after their meal, smoking, talking among themselves, or pondering their own thoughts. They were more subdued than usual, had been since the fresh tracks of horses were discovered a few days back.

Even inexperience was no sanctuary from the fearful reality of Indian pony tracks. The laughing and lightheartedness that had characterized the beginning of the journey ceased as they entered the forbidding world of the hunter and the hunted.

The nights were the worst, wind sounds, crackling fires, the sorrowful lament of the coyote. "God's dogs," Twobirds called them, seers of the future, their mournful wails penetrating their sleep like arrows through the darkness, singular, swift, irrevocable.

Kicking sand around the edges of the fire to narrow its flame, Twobirds retrieved two intricately designed feathers from the bloodied remains of the turkeys and tucked them into her satchel. What a strange and primal creature she was, snatching from death a moment of beauty.

Nurse Cromley followed behind Twobirds as they made their way to their beds. They had become friends, or at least in their isolation, took from each other comfort among common and crude men, but alike in many ways, courageous, feminine, competent, but so different, from such diverse worlds. Their heads together, talking, they faded from the light of the fire.

The night he and Nurse Cromley had together seemed remote to him now, distant, as if it had happened many years ago, his feelings fading at times, without confirmation, without holding her again. It had been exciting, of course, Nurse Cromley being an attractive woman, but he realized now that something was missing, too.

"Jacobs," Sheets snapped, stepping from the darkness and next to the fire, his arms crossed against the smoke that sought him out, "you take the first duty, till midnight. Bledso, you take the second, till daybreak, and keep your eyes open."

"I took daylight last night, sir," Bledso said, tossing the stick he'd been sharpening into the fire. Sparks lifted into the blackness. "I ain't slept a wink in two days. Besides, standing out there alone makes my skin crawl. What's to keep some Kiowa from cutting my throat or running me through?"

Looking about, he searched for help from the other men, McReynolds recognizing him as the guard who was standing duty the day he'd treated Renfro's wounds.

"As commander of this expedition," Sheets whirled, pointing his finger at Bledso, "I got the power of the lash, and I'll not hesitate to use it on slackers. There are those here can testify that there's things worse than being run through."

"Yes sir," Bledso said, insolence in his voice, "midnight till daylight."

Squatting at the edge of the fire, Sheets poked at the coals as if stalling for time. Suddenly he turned to Renfro.

"Corporal, you know anything about critters other than mules?"

"Guess I don't quite get your meaning, sir," Renfro said, pushing back his hat. "I know a little bit about a lot of things and a lot about a few things, mostly mules."

"Well, do you know anything about bloatin' horses?" Sheets asked, squirming.

"Yes sir, I know about bloatin' horses." He paused. "They just pump up sort of and get bigger and bigger and they can't get rid of their air no matter what. Pretty soon they can't breathe or swallow or even stand up, and then they just split wide open like a watermelon in August." He fell silent, letting Sheets stew. "Some say," he finally said, "those that knows horses better than me, that bloatin' comes from too much grain or bad water, say. Why is it you ask, sir? You studying bloatin' horses?"

"No, I'm not studying bloatin' horses, Renfro. That black gelding of mine's pumped up like a toad there by the tent and isn't going to make it till daybreak without some help. That's the best horse in the territory, and by God I don't want him dead."

Taking off his hat, Renfro watched the fire.

"Well?" Sheets said, his face red.

"What's that, sir?"

"Well, don't you agree?"

"Oh, yes sir, he's a fine horse, sir."

"No, goddamn it, Renfro, don't you agree that he's probably a goner before daylight?"

"Oh, yes sir, if he's a bloatin' horse, sure enough. Course, I don't know what he'd be bloatin' for. We ain't had grain to feed since we left Fort Gibson."

"From the water!" Sheets yelled.

"You mean that tainted water my molly mule wouldn't drink, sir?" Renfro said, smiling ever so slightly.

"Goddamn it, Renfro, is there anything you can do for him or not?"

Light danced in Renfro's eyes as he stood at the fire's edge, tipping the toe of his boot into the flames, pushing the wood onto the fire. It was for him, McReynolds knew, a triumphant moment.

"Well sir," he began, "that's hard to say. I ain't much except a deserter and mule skinner as you pointed out earlier and I been riding drag the whole expedition, sir, so I'm a bit dragged out you might say."

Turning, he pointed to Bledso. "Maybe Bledso here could help you out, sir. He's guarded deserters like myself and been riding point up there where the breeze is clean and fresh." Eyes shining, he looked at McReynolds across the fire. "Or even Lieutenant McReynolds here, what with his medical degree. Surely bloatin' horses been a prime topic for an Army doctor."

"All right, Renfro," Sheets snapped, looking first at McReynolds, than at Bledso, "tomorrow you ride point."

"You mean with my molly mule, sir, leading the expedition?"

"Yes, damn it, Renfro, don't push me too far."

"Bloatin' horses got to be stuck, sir," he said, wiping the ash from the toe of his boot onto his pant leg, "else they die ever' time. I've stuck a few in my life. Sometimes they lived. Sometimes they died. It's a matter of luck mostly, sir, and knowing where to set the blade.

"Maybe Lieutenant McReynolds would loan me one of his knives and we'll see what we can do. Take a small blade, sir. Got to go in without disturbing the vitals."

The others prepared torches while McReynolds retrieved his bag, and within minutes they gathered around Sheets's horse.

It lay on its side, eyes wide, legs protruding at stark angles from its strutted stomach. Throwing its head back with each gasp for air, it grunted against the mounting internal pressure.

The horse calmed under Renfro's hand, down its side, along its flank, identifying the point of entry.

"Right there, Lieutenant," he said to McReynolds, "between the muscle and the rib cage. Goes straight into the stomach, and with a little luck, not too much damage."

Even before McReynolds could answer, Renfro plunged the scalpel into the horse. A rush of fetid air whistled from the hole as he extracted the blade. Neither the horse nor the onlookers realized the deed was already done. Within moments, the horse's distended stomach returned to normal and it struggled to its feet.

"By God," Sheets said. "Hobble him so he won't go back to the water."

"He won't do that, sir," Renfro said, handing the scalpel back to McReynolds. "Unlike some men, it's an uncommon horse makes the same mistake twice."

"Hobble him," Sheets commanded, and ducked into his tent.

* * *

Moonless nights were rare on the prairie, but as McReynolds undressed for bed, the blackness was total, and he searched for his bunk with his hands. Only the dying campfire could be seen through the cracks of the tent. Sheets's breathing was steady and deep.

But McReynolds's sleep was fitful and he was awakened by Sheets's horse sometime in the night as it grazed at the tent's edge. Again at the changing of the guard, he heard the complaining voice of Bledso as he dressed for duty.

Just before dawn, as the night deepened into its darkest moment, hushing the world into silence, the shots rang out.

Bolting upright in his bed, his heart pounding, he searched in vain for his clothes in the darkness of the tent.

"Indians!" someone shouted from the trees.

Frantic, McReynolds scrambled for his boots while Sheets cursed on the other side of the tent. Both found their carbines and arrived at the flap at the same moment, struggling in confusion as they tried to exit.

Dawn broke, lighting the tops of the trees as they crouched at the side of the tent, searching the shadows for movement.

McReynolds saw Bledso first, cringing behind a rock.

"What is it?" he whispered.

"Indian," Bledso said, his voice shaking. "Over there. I think I kilt him. Heard the big son of a bitch fall in the branches but there might be more coming."

They inched forward toward the fallen Indian, the click of hammers being cocked behind them.

"Where?" Sheets whispered.

His hand shaking, Bledso pointed to the clump of skunk brush growing just beyond the clearing. They approached, carbines at the ready, pulling back the brush.

"It's my horse," Sheets said in astonishment, his face contorted. "He's shot my goddamn horse!"

"Your horse, sir?" Bledso's face ashened. "Couldn't be. It

was the biggest Indian I ever did see coming right out of those bushes."

"Shot him between the eyes," he said, looking at McReynolds in disbelief. "The best horse in the territory and he shot him right between the goddamn eyes."

Camp broke a little later than usual that morning, but moved west once more as it always did. On point were Renfro and his molly mule, leading the expedition as proud as any war chief ever led a war party.

Bledso, on foot, with two twenty-pound bags of shot tied around his neck, brought up the drag somewhere back in the dust.

Sixteen

The days turned into a week as the expedition sustained itself on brackish water, hackberries, and Indian bread, a carrot-like plant that Twobirds introduced. The plant clung to the packed earth and was distinguished from the other weeds by a fearless magenta blossom that rose into the heat and wind. The bitter root was manageable only when dipped in ample quantities of salt, but salt was as scarce as the water it took to quench the subsequent thirst.

Each night Bledso arrived into camp after dark, the ropes bloodied about his neck, eyes sunken, feet blistered and raw from the unforgiving terrain. Each night he arrived later and recurrently worse for the wear.

No attempt was made by Sheets to deprive him of either food or water, permitting McReynolds to administer whatever medical attention was necessary, protecting himself no doubt. But Bledso was issued neither horse nor mule, nor relieved of his onerous burden. Each night like clockwork Sheets inspected the bags to see that none of the shot had been removed.

It was the sixth night, or the seventh, he couldn't remember which, that Bledso failed to make camp. Rising at dawn, McReynolds retraced the trail for several miles, but there was still no sign of Bledso.

"Don't you think we should send someone?" he asked Sheets as he came out of the tent.

"It's not in the best interest of the expedition," Sheets said.

"I'll have to report it when we return to Fort Gibson, Lieutenant. It's my duty as medical officer."

"Of course, by all means report it," Sheets said, slipping on his gloves, mounting the bay. "Report also that Private Bledso killed the commander's horse, a deed that may have jeopardized the whole expedition. Also note that the punishment of Private Bledso was carried out according to Army regulations and at no time was he denied medical attention or rations. State as well that Private Bledso failed to report for duty and from this point hence must be presumed a deserter."

"Presumed dead," McReynolds said.

"Perhaps."

"Legal is not always moral, Lieutenant."

"Sympathy is for cowards and for women," Sheets said, kicking his horse in the ribs, "and for assistant surgeons it seems."

Two more days passed without game or water, and by noon the third day even the mules had begun to pale.

Despair mounted as they entered a small canyon promising rough going. But instead the trail dropped below the surface, the trees thickening, a majestic green curtain rising up the canyon walls, rooted in dark and secret streams beneath the baked crust of the earth.

A restoring breeze swept over them, laden with the smell of rotted wood and leaves. The blistering sun beat against the impenetrable ceiling of leaves and the locusts' drone gave way to the songs of birds. The men's spirits rose and once again laughter could be heard among them as they worked their way down the steep trail.

At the bottom of the canyon, a dry gulch ran at right angles to the column. Scouts were ordered out, thirty minutes in both directions, in search of water.

The others waited, leaning against trees or lying prone on the damp ground while their mounts stretched their necks to reach the succulent green leaves hanging overhead.

Within the hour the scouts were back, reporting water not three miles downstream, an artesian, they announced, gushing

from the base of the hill like God's own fountain, pooling, then
spilling over into a crack in the earth. The men cheered at the
news.

It was as glorious a sight as McReynolds had ever seen, water,
clean and cold, gushing from the earth so fast that its flow could
not be dented.

They held their heads under its stream, the icy water snatching away their breaths, rejoicing as their animals drank from
the crystal pool that gathered in the rocks, the mules twisting
ropes of water grass with prehensile lips and munching on the
squeaky stems.

"We'll make camp here," Sheets said, "a few days to hunt
and to repair equipment."

"Fill the canteens and go," Twobirds said, her arms crossed.
"This is not a place for camp."

"And why not?" Sheets asked. "What better than this?"

"It is a place of power," she said, "where the water spills
forth on its own."

Studying the area, Sheets turned, the undergrowth, the trees,
the column of water that hurled upward from the crevice.

"Indian magic," he said, "Make camp."

A black walnut tree soared fifty feet above McReynolds,
where he rested in its shade. At the far reaches of the tree a
squirrel dodged and darted, secure in its disguise and position.

A shot rang out within feet of where McReynolds lay, shattering the serenity. Vaulting to his feet, he threw up his arms,
prepared to fight for his life. Overhead the squirrel folded into
a furry ball, plummeting unchecked to the ground at his feet.

Holstering his side arm, Sheets picked up the squirrel, holding it out so the men could see.

"There," he said, "how hard can it be to turn up a little food
around here?"

Angered by Sheets's childish display, McReynolds made his
way to the spring. There were times it was all he could do to
remain silent.

Sand at the bottom of the spring churned as the water swelled in profusion, an open artery, a wound, a hemorrhage from the earth's heart. Shaking off the uneasiness that crawled down his spine, he thought of poor Bledso back there somewhere and how much he must need the water.

The men busied themselves making camp, gathering wood for the evening meal, enjoying their emancipation from the un-relenting trail. Many of them returned again and again to the spring and drank from it, more to reassure themselves that it was still there than to quench their thirst.

From across the clearing, Nurse Cromley approached Mc-Reynolds, her hair down in a provocative fall over her shoulders. Waiting at a distance was Twobirds, watching as Nurse Cromley made her way toward him.

"I have a favor to ask. Twobirds says I must not, but it's been so long."

"Certainly, if I can," he said, leaning against the rough bark of the tree.

"It's the water, you see. I've not had a bath in such a long time. If the men could leave after their meal, for even an hour?"

"Lieutenant Sheets would have to give that order, Nurse Cromley."

"If you would intervene, an hour, no more. It would be so grand."

"For you, we'll try," he smiled.

The tent flap was open, Sheets lying on his back, the map across his chest.

"Yes?" he said without looking up.

"It's Nurse Cromley, Lieutenant. She's asked for an hour's privacy after supper in order to bathe."

"Privacy?"

"Yes sir, for just an hour. It's difficult for the women. I'm certain the men wouldn't mind."

"I suppose," he said, standing, "for all they're worth. Look at this map, McReynolds, it's useless. We need a scout, someone who knows the country, knows the trails, like that Kiowa woman out there who wouldn't open her mouth if we were marching into the sea. For Christ's sake, McReynolds, doesn't she know we are doing her a favor? Look," he pointed to a large empty space on the map, "there must be a hundred square miles there without a single mark. How the hell are we going to find our way with nothing but this useless thing?"

"Maybe we'll find a scout among the Kiowa, Lieutenant, once we find them."

"If we find them, you mean?"

"Then it's alright, sir, if the men leave camp after supper?"

"I suppose, and afterwards we can have a church social. Alright, maybe it'll loosen that squaw's tongue," he said, "but I'm telling you, that Kiowa knows a hell of a lot more about this country than she lets on."

A dozen squirrels were cleaned for supper, and with more time than usual to prepare the meal, corn bread was made in iron skillets, burying them in the hot coals to brown.

A skirt full of muscadine grapes no larger than peas was shared by Twobirds and the whole affair·was topped off with quantities of cold water from the spring and boiled coffee. The aroma conjured up images of home and hearth.

After the men smoked their pipes and settled back to rest, Sheets gave the order.

"All right men, fall in. Time we figured a way out of this canyon with these wagons."

The men grumbled at leaving their fire but followed Sheets up the canyon like children at their mother's skirt.

Watching them go from her place by the wagon, Nurse Cromley smiled at McReynolds as he fell in behind the others.

"They've gone," she called to Twobirds, "and we've a whole hour to ourselves. Come now, we'll take a bath, a glorious bath. I can't remember how long it's been."

"It flows from the heart," Twobirds said, "a place of power."

"I'm taking a bath," Nurse Cromley said, unbuttoning her skirt, "and no man nor god is going to stop me." Slipping from her blouse, Cromley stood naked at the edge of the pool, sticking her toe into the chilling water, groaning. "Oh, mercy it's cold," she said, leaning over, breasts heavy, sensual, splashing water up her legs, slipping into the pool. "It's wonderful. You must come in."

Hesitating, Twobirds slipped from her clothes and into the water. Without a word she plunged beneath the surface, bursting from its depths like an otter.

Water glistened on her brown skin, her nipples erect from the cold, her eyes shining like ebony buttons. Across her stomach was a jagged scar.

"You've been wounded, Twobirds?" Cromley asked, touching the scar, studying its path.

"No," Twobirds shook her head. "From mourning the death of my father. It is the way of the Kiowa."

"To inflict pain on oneself?"

"To show the respect," she said.

"You have seen a lot of pain, haven't you, Twobirds? It's in your eyes."

"I have seen death," she said, as she turned in the water, letting it swirl around her breasts. "The Osage came and massacred my people, women, children, and old men. Our chief, Dohasan, and the other men were away stealing horses from the Texans. When the men came back, they found the heads of their children and wives in the cooking kettles that were traded from the Spanish. We were gathering wood when they came, or our heads would've been in kettles too."

"You must hate to return," she said, lifting the water between her hands, splashing it onto her face.

"No," Twobirds said, "we move much but we see much. We suffer sometimes and we die sometimes, but living and dying are of the same world.

"And we are a rich people with many horses, more than any other, and are the best riders of all. Our children are taught to sleep on horseback. The Kiowa man's leggings are too long for walking, and he must ride even the short distances. Among our men are the strongest and bravest and most generous.

"There is the Buffalo Doctor society, those who know the

ways of healing, and On-da, seven feet tall, living alone on the prairie without his people. It is said that he can run down a buffalo on foot and slay it with his knife."

"I'm sorry if I offended you, Twobirds," Cromley said, rising from the pool, drying herself off. "I guess it's hard for us to see sometimes."

"I am sorry too," Twobirds said, stripping the water from her skin with the edge of her hand, "for showing the pride."

Feeling fresh and clean and new, they sat on a rock and watched the sun set.

Finally Twobirds spoke. "It is forbidden among the Kiowa for a woman to sleep with a man who belongs to another. The punishment is harsh; the end of her nose is cut off so all will know her betrayal."

"That's horrible," she touched the end of her nose, "but why do you say that just now?"

"I've seen the way you've looked at the doctor, but yet you do not go to him. It must be that he's taken."

"I admire him as a doctor, that's all." She looked away. If Twobirds had noticed, how many others? "He's a fine man, a sad man too, I think. My religion teaches that we should care for others."

"Then he is not taken by another?"

"No, his wife is dead. He is not taken."

"Then why don't you go to him?"

"We don't . . . it's not that way," she flushed, flattening her bare feet against the warm rock. "I am his nurse, that's all. My religion prohibits such things."

Puzzled by these people who felt one way but acted another, Twobirds fell silent. They lacked honor, particularly in matters of lying and stealing.

"If he's not taken and you want him, then you should have him. It is the way of things," she said, dropping her head, letting her hair fall between her legs, running her fingers through it. "It's not the body that harms, but the heart. One must be careful of the heart."

"They'll be back soon," Cromley said, tucking her shoes under her arm, "Perhaps we should go."

The light faded above the canyon walls as they picked their way through the rocks. Approaching the area roped off for Renfro's mules, Nurse Cromley suddenly yelped, her hands trembling above her head as she looked at Twobirds in astonishment. Crouching, Twobirds searched the canyon wall for raiders, the frenzied rattle of the snake registering only after she spotted it squirming from Nurse Cromley's leg, its fangs moored securely in her calf.

Knowing from experience that where there was one rattler, there could be many, Twobirds watched her step. Even in the pale light, she could see the amber venom oozing from around the fangs.

Wrenching the snake loose, she snapped its head against a rock with a crack, a twisting grizzly knot, as death moved down its length.

Stunned, Nurse Cromley sat down on the rock and clutched her wound. Bloody tracks ran down her leg as she looked up at Twobirds, terror in her eyes.

"You must do something."

"It's bleeding as it should, but your fear is spreading the poison," she said, placing one hand on Cromley's throat, the other on the back of her neck.

Taking a deep breath, Nurse Cromley tried to slow her pounding heart.

"You must get Dr. McReynolds."

"Your Dr. McReynolds will be here soon, but he cannot take the poison away. It's best I stay with you."

Pulling Nurse Cromley's head to her breast, Twobirds's fingers lingered on her throat to test the beat of her heart. Under Twobirds's touch, her pulse began to slow.

Ten minutes passed, an eternity it seemed, before the men returned and found Nurse Cromley nearly asleep in Twobirds's lap.

The puncture wounds extruded like molehills from Nurse Cromley's leg, her eyes opening under McReynolds's touch.

"I'm to die, I think," she said, "and so far from my father and from my church. My soul will be lost in such a desolate place."

"You are not going to die, Mary," he said, squeezing her hand. "We're going to see to that."

But the words were hollow even to him. The snake was monstrous, its venom devastating, sufficient to fell a full-grown horse, and his heart sank at what lay ahead for Nurse Cromley.

They carried her to the tent where McReynolds rolled blankets, elevated her leg, tore strips of cloth to use as a tourniquet, binding her leg just above the knee.

"I'll watch her through the night," he said, looking at Twobirds, shaking his head. "There's laudanum that might help with the pain. Beyond that, there's little else to do."

Stooping at the end of the cot, Twobirds pulled from Nurse Cromley's bag a small crucifix, laying it beside her.

"It is your Tai-Me," she said, "so your spirit can find you."

By midnight Nurse Cromley's toes were strutted, the swelling migrating like a lava flow up her leg," her bed clothing wet with perspiration.

The laudanum helped, at least she slept, and McReynolds gave her as much as he dared. In the darkest of night the fire flickered beyond the tent, where Twobirds maintained a vigil.

Once in the early-morning hours Nurse Cromley called his name and he buried his face in his hands, awash in futility and despair.

At dawn, Twobirds came to the tent, kneeling at her cot, examining the swelling's path, the unforgiving tourniquet, the toes black and swollen beyond recognition. With her knife she cut the tourniquet free, Nurse Cromley groaning as flesh blood rushed past the wound.

"The beaver knows to build its dam before the flood, not during it," Twobirds said.

With neither the heart nor the confidence to argue the point, McReynolds let it pass, what harm now in any case?

Later, Twobirds came again. The swelling in Nurse Cromley's leg reached to her thigh, the skin from under her knee having torn from pressure, weeping a sticky pink fluid onto her bed.

"It's very bad," Twobirds said. "To camp at these waters was foolish. Such men as your Lieutenant Sheets are banned by the Kiowa, to live alone on the prairie."

"He lives alone among us," McReynolds said, shrugging his shoulders.

"Go," she said, pushing her fingers into her hair, "I'll watch till dark. You sleep."

But sleep was elusive for McReynolds. Daylight bled through the cracks in the tent and pierced his closed eyes. Cheerless and demented strangers walked through his dreams and mosquitoes whined death chants in his ears.

Still weary, he rose at dusk and made his way to the spring. Even the icy water failed to revive him from his black and dreadful temper. On the way back to camp he examined the rattler tossed upon the rocks, now little more than a shriveled and harmless shell.

Knowing too well the progression of such wounds, he dreaded seeing Nurse Cromley.

On his way to the tent, McReynolds happened upon Sheets, who was sitting on a fallen blackjack eating roasted squirrel. Sucking at his fingers, Sheets motioned him over.

"We're going to have to move on soon, Doctor. These things happen as we all know but the expedition can't be jeopardized for one individual."

"The swelling is bad," he said. "There is danger her kidneys will fail."

Wiping his fingers on his pants, Sheets poured a cup of coffee from the pot.

"Well, Doctor, you understand that we have a mission here. As commander I've a responsibility to complete that mission."

"She'll live or die within the next day or two, Lieutenant. Does that resolve your dilemma?"

"Yes," he said, "I believe it does."

Sitting on the floor at the foot of Nurse Cromley's cot was Twobirds, her legs crossed, her arms folded across her breasts. In her lap was a beaded satchel and in her hand a small figure, an animal, a squirrel, a bear perhaps, which she tucked from sight when McReynolds entered.

"How is she?" he asked.

"The swelling has moved upward," she said, "stopping her water. Without making water, she'll die from her own poisons soon."

Opening Cromley's gown, he probed her abdomen, distended, hard, resistant to pressure. Twobirds was right, renal failure was inevitable if things didn't change soon.

"Mary, can you hear me?" he said, placing his hand on her forehead. "How are you feeling?"

"Like a fish," she smiled, searching for his hand.

"It's the swelling, Mary. Do you need laudanum?"

"I feel nothing now and can't stand to look," she said, turning her head away. "Twobirds is right, I think. I've violated the gods and they have taken my life. What I need is a miracle, but only gods make miracles."

Standing, Twobirds spoke to McReynolds.

"It's time for your medicine society to make its most powerful medicine." There was anger in her dark eyes. "Is your society so useless it cannot heal a small snakebite?"

"This was hardly a small bite, Twobirds."

"She must make water soon. Already she speaks crazy and sees things in her sleep."

Shaking his head, McReynolds stepped through the tent flap, wiping roughly at his eyes. Nurse Cromley was going to die, as certainly as his wife died, and there was no magic, no science, no society, that would alter that fact.

Never had Twobirds seen such useless medicine men. The Buffalo Doctor society of her own village would never walk away from such a wound. There was always something to be done, always something.

Searching the tall grasses near the spring, she found what

she wanted. Holding the green stem of grass to the sky, a speck of moonlight illuminated its end. A chunk of fat from the roasted squirrel would serve her purpose.

Back at the tent Mary lay in delirium, demonic dreams, blazoned images, her breast heaving against the poison that seeped into her bloodstream.

Opening the satchel, Twobirds lay the Tai-Me next to the crucifix.

"Mary, it's Twobirds," she said, rocking her head to and fro until she opened her eyes, searching for the face above her. "It's the water," Twobirds said. "You must rid the water. Will you let me try?"

More despair than hope in her face, Mary nodded.

Greasing the stem of grass with the squirrel fat, Twobirds lifted Mary's gown, holding back her hand, exposing her frail beauty.

"It's all right," Twobirds said. "There's no need for shame. We must rid the water somehow and this is the only way that I know. Men cannot be depended on for such things. They care only for filling holes, not opening them."

Resigned, Cromley lay back as Twobirds probed with the grass stem, searching to save this white woman and somehow her own honor, rooting the stem into her body. Crying out with pain, Mary turned her head from side to side.

Beads of sweat gathered above Twobirds's lip.

"It's done," she said. "Something is done."

Stroking the Tai-Me, coaxing forth its power, she waited, watching the single stem of grass protruding from Mary's body, a sprouting seed from her fertile belly.

First a single drop of blood gathered at the end of the stem, a single drop, pure and cardinal in color, and then urine, golden urine no larger than a pinhead but followed again and again by other golden drops. The yellow stain on Mary's gown grew larger.

"It comes," Twobirds said. "We have found the well, I think."

At daybreak, Dr. McReynolds walked toward the tent. Not

only had he failed to be of any use to Mary, but he'd lacked the courage to watch her die.

Pausing at the tent flap before entering, he listened to the sounds of the morning. The canyon abounded with life, obscene life so oblivious to the death struggle inside.

What greeted him was indeed a miracle from the gods, Mary sitting upright drinking a cup of coffee, her abdomen no longer distended, the swelling dissipated, Twobirds sleeping in the corner of the tent.

"Dr. McReynolds," Mary smiled, "once again I've been spared. It seems you are stuck with me."

"But how?" he shook his head in bewilderment.

"A straw," she said, "and the medicine of Twobirds." Turning on her side, she pulled the Tai-Me from under the covers. "Oh, Joseph, I found this beside me. It's such a heathen thing. Do please get rid of it."

"But what about Twobirds?"

"Oh, dear, I don't know." She lay back, her arm across her forehead. "Give it to her then, but I don't want it about. You do understand, don't you, Joseph?"

Seventeen

Three days were all Sheets would extend departure. During that time, scouts were sent ahead to determine the best route west, while Renfro and a half dozen others went on daily hunting parties, bringing down a large number of buffalo that frequented the spring. The remaining men were put to work butchering and salting with what little salt reserves were left, Sheets having refused to wait for proper smoking of the meat.

The wounds on Nurse Cromley's calf changed, a circle of flesh the size of a fruit jar lid suppurating at the site, but gradually responding to the sulfa powders and hot compresses that McReynolds applied.

Even though McReynolds and Cromley spent long hours talking, their relationship had changed. It had been an ephemeral moment, lacking the harsh test of reality. Here on the trail it had failed and neither could revive it.

But for Twobirds, who waited at the mule pen, the path was never more clear, more certain. The moon illuminated the trees, casting shadows on the canyon walls as she plunged her fingers deep into the leaves and smelled their earthy smell. Cool moist air descended like water into the cracks and crannies of the canyon and an owl hooted from above. The mules tightened their circle.

It was Adam's way to return again and again to the mules, and it would be here that she would find him.

Even before his monumental shadow stretched up the rock

face, she sensed his presence, knew his charge, his smell, his vigor, and tonight would be theirs and nothing else would matter.

Lifting his molly's hoof into the light, Adam spoke, as a father speaks.

"Whoa, Molly girl, whoa."

The moon tipped his hair and darkened the crevices of his powerful shoulders.

Reaching to touch him, she retrieved her hand at the last moment. In the wilderness surprise came with risk, particularly with a man like Adam Renfro.

"Adam," she whispered, her voice trembling with excitement, his muscles snapping, eyes blazing in the soft glow of the moon. "It's Twobirds."

"Twobirds?" he crouched at the side of his molly. "Come into the light." Slipping from the shadows, she did as she was told, his power filling her as she moved into his arms. "I thought you'd never come," he said, "that maybe you didn't want to."

Encircling him with warm arms, she kissed him.

"Here," she said, "in this land, I am not yet Kiowa and you are no longer white. This is our place, the right place."

Unbuttoning her blouse, he touched her, his gentle hands exploring the secrets of her body, his lips hot against her breasts. As Adam forsook the uniform covering both body and soul, Twobirds lifted her neck to the moon's kiss and waited.

Trees pushed into the night sky above her, deep into the spectacle above, prodigious trunks plowing open the belly of heaven and spilling stars into the blackness of space.

Engulfed, swallowed, staved by his vanquishing passion, she knew that this must be all, that beyond this place, theirs was a doomed and forbidden love, that no man nor god would ever bless them.

In her silent way she held him. In her heart she cried for the scars on his back, for the things that lay ahead.

Eighteen

By departure day, Nurse Cromley was able to ride and McReynolds lifted her onto her horse.

"Keep the leg up as much as possible," he said, "and the wound clean. It wouldn't do for infection to set in. Tonight at camp we'll boil water and wash it thoroughly."

"I'm a nurse, remember," she said, leaning down from her horse, touching his hand, "but thank you anyway and thank you for sticking by me."

Tightening the cinch on her saddle, he avoided looking at her. Twice now he'd failed important people in his life.

"You have Twobirds to thank for that."

"A sweet girl. Think what the church could do with such a faithful soul," she said, rubbing her leg as she watched the soldiers move onto the trail. "Sometimes being out here is like falling into a dark tunnel, deeper and deeper with no way out and nothing at the end but disaster." She looked down at him. "I want to see my father again, you know. I want my church, the things of my church, the sounds, the smells, the rites that connect me to truth and to history. Here there is nothing but the present. This is such a lonely and frightful place."

"We're going to be alright, Mary," he said, pushing back his hat, looking up through the trees and into the sun. "It's only because we're heading west again that you feel this way. Things will be different once we turn around and start for home. We're well supplied now and we have Twobirds to help guide us. There's nothing to worry about."

"Yes," she said, "we have Twobirds, but I wonder how long Twobirds will have us." Pulling up her horse's head with the reins, she smiled. "Oh, you're right, of course. "I'm just feeling sorry for myself this morning. Perhaps it's the accident and coming so close to death for a second time. You go on now and I'll see you in camp tonight."

For several hours the column wound through the canyon, at times dismounting and leading their horses through the dense underbrush. Still, their spirits were high. There was fresh water in their canteens and the wagons were packed with ample supplies of meat.

The canyon opened onto a haze-shrouded vista, a welcome relief from the rocky trail in spite of the mounting heat.

Within a few miles, however, desert winds blasted from the southwest. Perspiration evaporated more quickly than it could be generated, salt crystals gathering anywhere leather met flesh.

That night in camp, McReynolds passed wagon wheel grease among the men to soothe their cracked and bleeding lips, boiling water for Nurse Cromley's wound, cleaning it carefully, in spite of her protests that she could do it herself, thank you.

The evening fire crackled as McReynolds looked on, Twobirds preparing the berries she'd gathered along the canyon trail, a beautiful woman, he decided, but distant, aloof, allowing no one to step into her world.

Later, Twobirds approached him as he inventoried medical supplies, bending at his side, head down.

"It's the meat," she said. "The salt is too thin."

Alarm bolted through McReynolds, knowing all too well now that nothing was more important than food and water, nothing.

"Have you told Lieutenant Sheets?"

"I told Corporal Renfro's molly mule," she said, "because she is more clever."

In spite of the seriousness of the situation, he chuckled.

"There's no need to tell the others just yet. Perhaps you are wrong."

"The best is behind and the worst ahead," she said. "The game is wary near the salt, for all creatures must come to the fields. Even the best hunters cannot stalk the buffalo there, and the warriors must hide their women and children in the brush for fear they will be killed by other tribes."

"We'll post guards," he said, in an attempt to convince himself.

"Trails lead to the salt from all directions," she said, clasping her knees. "There is no place more dangerous. The water is bitter. Only sage and mesquite grow and even the coyote's belly is slack from hunger. Your lieutenant is a foolish and small warrior on a hunt of his own, I think, and will lead you to your death. You must go back now."

"I'd like that just fine, Twobirds, if it only worked that way. We have our orders to deliver you to your people and to evaluate the worth of the saline fields. I'm afraid there is little I can do."

"And there is little I can do." She stood, the firelight dancing in her black eyes. "I am but a woman and cannot turn the events of men. Your lieutenant's heart is cold without courage and his spirit has fled. I do not understand how such a man could be your chief." So many words were unlike her. "It's foolish to think my people would change the old ways because of my return. No man," she paused, "nor woman would ever be more important than the tribe."

"I don't understand either, but power does not always fall in the hands of the wise," he said, touching her shoulder. "And thanks for whatever it was that you did for Nurse Cromley."

As the days passed, the column ascending onto the high plains of the territory, Twobirds's words of warning about the salted meat were to return again and again, a tribute to poor judgment and ignorance.

Torrid winds scalded their lungs and peeled the skin from their faces. Swirling sand wore the hide from their horses' ankles and flies swarmed at their wounds.

The earth heaved upward toward the Rockies as if gasping for a last breath and the red soil split open under the savage heat. What little grass there was sprang from the earth like hair and finally disappeared altogether.

Lizards with skin like pearl ran from rock to rock, their feet skimming the blistering earth. They sat motionless as the column passed, unalarmed by the despondent creatures who plodded through their domain. With hardened smiles they watched as the column marched into the sun.

Holding the stick with the chunk of buffalo hump on it at arm's length, Twobirds let McReynolds examine it. The meat moved with a life of its own as the maggots rooted about in the juices. His stomach lurched at the sight.

"Is it all this way?"

Maggots snapped like popcorn as she tossed the fetid meat into the coals.

"Yes," she said. "There is none fit to eat. We've still a little flour and lard, enough for a day or two, but we must have game soon."

"I'll tell Sheets," he said, "but he isn't going to like it."

"He'll like it less when his stomach shrivels," she spat into the fire, "like the bag between his legs."

Sheets first cursed the men who'd salted the meat, then McReynolds who dared tell him the news, and then the Army and the territory and the Indians who hid in the hills. And when he could think of no one else to curse, he sat on his bunk, his face red from anger.

"So what do we do?" McReynolds asked, as the tantrum subsided. "We can't go on without food. Perhaps we should turn back now. Twobirds says it's dangerous country and there's no game to be had."

"We'll find game," he said, unfolding the map. "We're too close now to turn back. People have trekked through this country for centuries, the Kiowa, the Spanish, and who knows who before them? By God, if they survived then we can too."

Leaving Sheets with his map, McReynolds searched out Renfro, finding him down the draw cutting grass with his knife to hand-feed his molly mule. Listening to McReynolds's account, he pushed back his hat and studied the sky.

"Well," he said, "I'm just a deserter and don't know the whereabouts of high decisions, but if I was something other than what I am, I'd think a man would be wise to listen to that Twobirds girl.

"Makes a lot of sense to turn back and hunt awhile before venturing too far down the road. It's a shame sure enough about the meat, but a man can't make salt where there is no salt and as far as I can tell it was the lieutenant hisself didn't want to wait for jerking.

"Mounts are already pulled down pretty hard." He readjusted his hat against the sun and rubbed at his chin. "With this heat and all. Another week of resting and grazing wouldn't hurt them none either."

"Logic has not been a compelling force on this expedition so far, Corporal." McReynolds shrugged.

"Guess we move on, then, sir, but men's bellies can outsmart their heads sometimes. Hope Lieutenant Sheets understands that."

The next morning they moved out as ordered. Before they'd gone a mile, buzzards circled high overhead in greedy anticipation of the carnage that had been dumped from the wagons.

By ten, hot winds swept in from the southwest, evaporating the remaining few puffs of clouds that raced overhead. By noon the heat bore down on their backs like an invisible weight. Its silence rang in their ears like the peal of bells, and they hunkered against its power and buried their thoughts deep within themselves. By the third day the rations were gone and they savored the last of the dough balls as if they were rare fare, and lay awake in the night, their bellies growling for food.

Four days and sixty grueling miles later, the lead supply

wagon dropped into a badger hole with a sickening crack. Examining the damage, Renfro scratched at his chin and looked up at Sheets, who stood over him, hands on his hips, awaiting the verdict.

"Two spokes gone, sir," Renfro said. "They'll have to be replaced. I saw a fair-sized mesquite back aways, could be shaved out for spokes. Going to take some time, though, and that rim's bent pretty bad. Take some doing to fix that, I reckon. Maybe have to forge it some."

"We don't have a forge, do we Corporal," Sheets said, "or are you suggesting we just walk on back to Fort Gibson and ask the smith to fix it?"

"Guess it ain't that hard to make a forge, if you can build a fire and make wind," he said, looking up at Sheets. "Seems to me these men been making wind ever since we left Fort Gibson."

"Fix it then," Sheets glared, "and see if you can't shoot something on the way back to that mesquite. Take some of these crack hunters with you."

"Yes sir," Renfro said, "but the closer we get to that salt, the more skittish the game, sir. Can't get within a mile of beast or bird. I think them buffalo got lookouts posted top ever' hill."

Three of the best shots were selected, McCasson, a feisty little Irishman with eye-watering breath, Brandywine, a kid from Vermont with a reptilian conscience and steady hands, as good a shot as McReynolds had ever seen, and Jesus Martinez, a Mexican half the size of any man in the company, with no past that he could recall and in all likelihood no future either. The men feared him, sensed in him a ferocity best left undisturbed.

Not enthused about another mealless camp, McReynolds approached Renfro.

"Mind if I ride along, Corporal? Perhaps I can be of some assistance. I am a fair hand with a knife."

"Happy to have you, sir. Bring your gear. These clear nights can get a tad chilly, and not likely we can get back before dark."

Within the hour they departed, Renfro and his molly in the lead, the shy wave of Nurse Cromley from back of the supply wagon. It pained McReynolds to think of her going hungry again tonight. If only they could find game, anything to fill the void in their stomachs.

The tree was farther back than Renfro remembered, and the sun was low by the time they spotted the mesquite clinging to the side of a hill. Flat rocks, like stones for a garden path, lay scattered at the bottom, left behind by the ravages of wind and time and the gradual melting of the hill.

"I swear, Corporal, how do you do it?" McReynolds asked, shaking his head. "Crossed half the Territory since morning and you remember a single mesquite big enough to repair the wagon."

"That size mesquite ain't nothing but a freak of nature," Renfro said. "Kind of big and unusual you might say. Remember thinking that as we passed her by; otherwise, I guess she'd have gone the way of the others. Sometimes standing out too far from the crowd can be costly." The mesquite bore a few pods in the upper limbs. "Enough there for a little pinole flour," Renfro said. "It's a land of surprises, ain't it, half dust, half rock, and all dry, yet there she sits as big and pretty as a Tennessee pine."

"Is it big enough for spokes, you think?" McReynolds asked.

"Should find a spoke in there somewhere. Better stake the horses, boys, 'cept Molly here. She don't take a step isn't required anyways.

"Get them busted spokes from the saddlebags, Martinez, and we'll use 'em for a measure. And keep a sharp eye out for anything that moves, hear? If it's alive and don't shoot back, we'll kill it and eat it." He grinned. "Even if it shoots back, we'll kill it and eat it. Hell, even if we don't kill it, we'll eat it and shoot anyone who tries to stop us."

"I'll take my carbine," Brandywine said, Renfro's humor lost on him, "case we spot something. Let the Mexican carry the ax and spade. Ain't apt to hit nothing with his carbine anyways."

Eyes flashing, Martinez picked up the tools without a word,

while McCasson walked ahead, his breath sour on the wind. Twenty minutes and considerable effort later, they were there. The hill was higher than they'd surmised, and the mesquite proportionately larger.

Walking the circumference of the tree once, Renfro then walked it again.

"Mesquite's as big underground as it is atop ground. Them roots would make the best spokes, I'd guess. They're hard as iron and more apt to take the punishment," he said, marking an X with his foot in the dirt. "Dig here, boys, and see if we can't find a nice big one to take home."

The first turn was taken by Martinez, digging steadily and with the endurance of Renfro's Molly, black hair dropping over his eyes, shirt growing wet with perspiration.

In the meantime Renfro walked further up the hill to look for game, stopping to check for tracks where the earth was soft.

When Martinez grew tired, McReynolds took his turn, Brandywine smiling to see an officer with a spade in his hand. The digging was hard, the root's resolute grip unshakable in the dry earth, but by the time Renfro returned, they all sat around the freed root, sweat dripping from the ends of their noses.

"Should be a couple in there," Renfro said, holding up the pattern, "maybe more, case we break down again." Rolling the root back and forth with his foot, he checked for level. "You boys split her into four with the ax while the lieutenant and I take a look at those tracks up yonder. Been a buffalo cow through here, I think. There's afterbirth dropped and signs where she's been laying about."

Straining to keep up, McReynolds followed Renfro through the jumble of rocks. When they were out of earshot, Renfro spoke.

"Something else I wanted to show you, Lieutenant. Course, I weren't lying about the buffalo cow, probably a breech calf by all signs. But there's something else mighty peculiar."

"What's that, Corporal?"

They climbed to the top of the hill where it opened onto a flat mesa before Renfro answered.

"Right there," he said. "Did you ever see anything like it?"

"Like what?" he asked, peering at the mesa.

"Right there. See them circles, sir? There's three of them right there next to each other, big as wagons they are, and perfect too."

"Maybe they're rock formations," he studied the faint lines of the circles, "or sinkholes, or even prairie dog holes."

"Hope we shoot one, sir," Renfro smiled. "Feed the troops and half the territory if we could load him in the wagon.

"No rain since time began," he ran his fingers into the dirt, "and in they go, easy as pie. Ain't nothing in nature makes a perfect circle," he said, wiping his hands on his pants, "except men, least as far as I know. Besides, I got a notion they're hollow. They sound hollow when you walk on 'em."

"What do you think they are, Corporal?"

"Can't be certain what without digging but I've heard tell that Indians sometimes bury their food in caches. Store it up for winter like ants. Could be that. Could just be a Goliath prairie dog," he said, walking the circle again.

"I ain't much to know about command decisions, but ever'thing aside, we could dig and see."

"We'd have to wait till daylight, Corporal. Sun's nearly down now."

The sun lay like a melon on the horizon, bulging with furious liquid, and Renfro's face shone against the darkening eastern sky, a much younger man than McReynolds realized. Many boys are never men but a few men are never boys and Corporal Renfro was most decidedly one of those men.

"They got no place to go till that wagon's fixed in any case, sir? We could make camp here for the night. Send someone on back with word for the company to backtrack come tomorrow. Can work them spokes down just as easy here as there."

Looking down the hill, he pointed to where McCasson, Brandywine, and Martinez were stretched out under the shade of the mesquite.

"Could send McCasson back, sir. Ain't too big on smelling that dog breath all night long anyway."

"Lieutenant Sheets isn't going to be pleased about the delay," McReynolds said, studying the circles.

"Begging your pardon, sir, but the lieutenant wouldn't be pleased with a gold pecker, stiff as a poker and worth a bottle of the finest whiskey, choices aplenty for most men."

Capitulating to his grin, McReynolds accepted the unlikely conversion of Renfro, nodding his approval, motioning for the others to come to the top of the hill. With careful instructions, the plan was laid out and McCasson was sent on his way, grumbling at the prospect of a night ride back to camp.

By the time the sun set, they'd brought the horses up to the circles and built a small fire, grinding the mesquite beans into pinole and mixing the handful of flour with water. There was little more than a mouthful for each of them, but it was satisfying and more than what the others were getting.

Later, as the night set in, they began work on the spokes, each man whittling at the coffee-colored wood, checking his work from time to time against the dimensions of the broken spoke. It was slow business and the results less than professional, but there was little doubt in McReynolds's mind that the spokes would serve their purpose.

They talked of home and of food and of women they'd known and huddled close about the tiny fire. They talked of the circles in the earth and what might lay beneath. As the night grew clear and cold they pulled their blankets about them and cursed their rocky beds.

Coyotes lifted their voices from the darkness of the night and the men spoke no more but awaited in silence the rising of the sun.

Nineteen

The men rose early and stood about with blankets over their shoulders while Renfro built the fire. When the morning sun broke, they turned their backs into it for warmth and waited for full light.

The decision was made to take turns, spelling one another until the job was done. So with empty bellies and considerable hope they began digging.

At mid morning, McReynolds began watching the horizon for signs of the company. Soon they hit a layer of rocks, the same flat rocks that lay scattered at the bottom of the hill. Renfro, sweeping away the dirt with a sage branch, looked up at McReynolds and winked.

"Guess this is it, sir. You boys get ready in case we have to fight. I don't want it said that Corporal Adam Renfro was kilt by no prairie dog, I don't care how big it is."

The men watched as Renfro slid back the first rock. Inside a grass-lined hole were three baskets. Lifting the lid of the first, Renfro found it full of mesquite beans. A shout went up among them. The second and third baskets were full of ears of corn, green from mold but corn nonetheless.

After heated discussion, they agreed to eat some of the corn, grinding a few ears into flour, mixing it with water, and cooking the dough balls on the end of a stick. Their strength and guilt returned as they sucked every morsel from the sticks.

"Amazing, ain't it," Renfro said, examining each ear to the

bottom of the basket. "I'll wager this corn's been in there for months, and every bit as good as the day it was put down. Bury something deep enough and even the bugs won't get it, 'cept two-legged ones maybe. When my time comes, hope they bury me deep and away from varmints, just like this."

Standing, his hands over his eyes, McReynolds scanned the horizon. "Wonder where they are, Corporal?"

"Should have been here two hours ago at the latest. Either McCasson didn't get there or something's happened to the company. Maybe got their horses stole or run off," Renfro said.

Encouraged by their find and strengthened by food, they finished unearthing the second cache within a couple of hours. Stacked in rows were four baskets of corn and a cake of fermented sand plum. Renfro scratched off the black surface and sampled the red sweet meat.

"Won't this go good on morning biscuits," he said.

They nearly missed a small urn of walnut meats that had been buried under one of the baskets. Finally, all sat on the edge of the cache and rested.

"It's McCasson, probably," Renfro said, "fallen asleep, or fell off his horse, or the buzzards smelled his breath and snatched him right out of the saddle."

Turning on his stomach, McReynolds let the weariness of his muscles drain into the soil.

"What do you figure we should do, Corporal?"

"Well, sir, now that you asked, I figure first thing is to dig that last cache. Can't walk away from food no matter the case. It ain't much food considering the size of the company but it's considerable more'n we had. Won't hurt none to travel in the dark. It's a straight shot back. Anyway, if something's happened, there ain't much to be done. We just as well finish our job here."

It was with increasing weariness that they started the third cache. Brandywine, examining the blisters on his hands, complained that a man of his shooting skills had no business on the end of a spade.

"Let the Mexican do it," he said. "What are Mexicans for, if it ain't for digging holes in the ground?"

Anger in the ring of his spade, Martinez dug on against the hard earth.

The sun was setting when Renfro swept clean the layer of rock, his spirit falling.

"It's empty," he said. "Wait, here's something."

Pulling a weathered parfleche from the bottom of the cache, he opened the flap. In it was a tea-colored bone necklace. At its center, strung on a deerskin thong, was a corroded medallion.

"Kiowa," Renfro said to McReynolds. "Seems a shame to dig this big hole for such a small thing. Few more baskets of corn would have been nice."

"Can't argue there, Corporal. Still, don't suppose it's the first time religion's taken precedence over food."

It took another hour to break camp, to carry the corn down to the horses, and to pack it for the trip back.

On their third and final trip, Renfro stopped, signaling them down with his hand, pointing to a draw running downwind of them, motioning for Brandywine to come forward with his carbine. Not until that moment did McReynolds see the buffalo cow, an amber-colored calf curled at her side.

Kneeling on one knee, Brandywine took aim. Ages passed as he sighted the cow and squeezed the trigger into the palm of his hand. A single shot rang out and the cow's head dropped. The calf never moved.

"Fine shooting," Renfro said. "That will feed them for awhile."

"Ain't no man better," Brandywine said, reloading his carbine, turning to Martinez. "I shot her, you skin her."

"Go to hell," Martinez said.

"Lazy Mexican," Brandywine snarled. "I might mistake you for a Kiowa someday."

So quick was Martinez's movement that McReynolds was not certain of the events, but in an instant the carbine was in Martinez's control and he fired straightaway into Brandywine's uplifted hands, the shot tearing away his wrist, exiting his palm in considerable disregard for his fingers.

A dark pool of blood gathered on the rocks at Brandywine's feet, a spray across the front of his shirt, fingers dangling like dead fish on a stringer.

"Oh," he said.

Tossing the carbine onto the ground with a clatter, Martinez walked off in the direction of the company.

Holding his hand in front of him, Brandywine stared at the white bone of his thumb, a piteous wail rising from his throat, the dual assault of pain and grief wrenching him into reality. Chills swept down McReynolds's spine but Martinez walked on, not looking back.

Using his belt as a tourniquet, McReynolds tightened it about Brandywine's arm.

"There's nothing left to save," he said, looking at Renfro.

"Best do it, Lieutenant," Renfro said. "Be a shame to shoot Martinez for murder without having to."

Steeling himself, McReynolds inspected the mangled hand once again.

"I left my bag at camp, no scalpel, no needle, nothing."

"Could use that skinning knife you been sharpening ever since we left the fort," Renfro said.

"You ain't cutting my shooting hand off," Brandywine trembled. "No son of a bitch going to cut off my hand with no skinning knife."

Circling behind him, Renfro spoke in a calm voice.

"Look at it this way, Brandywine, you'll have half the blisters you got now and won't ever pick up another spade."

No sooner had Renfro spoken, than he spun Brandywine around, securing the mutilated hand between his legs.

Mouth hot, McReynolds unsheathed his knife and drew it across the joint, skin opening like a melon, blood spilling over Renfro's fingers, Brandywine's scream rising in a crescendo as he lunged against Renfro's relentless hold.

Sweat broke across McReynolds's forehead as he thrust the

blade deep into the joint, renting it apart, listening for the un-hinging, for the telling and merciless crack as the joint separated.

When Brandywine passed into unconsciousness, McReynolds shouted with relief and with a final and deliberate blow severed the bloodied hand from its mooring.

Working quickly, before Brandywine regained consciousness, they bound the stump with cloth and tied his legs around Molly by running a rope under her stomach.

Double-checking the tautness of the rope, Renfro slapped Molly on the rear.

"Hope ole darlin' here don't blow up like she's prone, or Brandywine's feet will go the way of his hand."

Little more than a mile away, Martinez waited on a rock for them to arrive.

"He ain't dead," Renfro said, "although by morning I figure he'll wish he was and maybe you too by the time Sheets is done."

Martinez nodded, mounted his horse, and fell in behind McReynolds.

Night fell dark and complete in the absence of a moon, and they all followed Molly's white rump through the night.

Regaining consciousness, Brandywine set to moaning and pulling at the bloody wad of cloth.

They'd traveled only a few miles more when Renfro pulled up short.

"What's the matter?" McReynolds asked.

"Something there," he said in a hush, pointing to edge of the trail.

Circling their animals about them, they took some comfort in the heat and smell of their bodies.

"Where?" McReynolds asked.

"There yonder," be whispered, "just to the side. Do you see?"

"McCasson," McReynolds said, making out the faint figure on the ground.

Tying the mounts to a tree, they listened until their ears hurt for sounds of movement.

Approaching with caution, McReynolds knelt at McCasson's side, touching the cold hand, rolling him on his back. An arrow protruded from both sides of his neck, his swollen tongue lolling from his mouth. A circle of scalp the size of a biscuit was missing from his head, his skull shining through as white as a bar of soap.

Unfortunately, the arrow had missed the carotid arteries, the crushed and broken grass around him suggesting a long and torturous struggle.

"Guess we know why they didn't come," Renfro said, squatting next to McReynolds.

"Suppose the company's alright?"

"Suppose so," Renfro said, reaching down and snapping off the arrow quill. "Only one set of tracks in and one set out. Biggest damn feet I ever saw, though. Whoever got McCasson was traveling alone."

There was no room for the body without unloading the corn, so they determined to bury McCasson where he'd fallen.

"Get the shovel, Martinez," Renfro said. "Guess Brandywine gets out of this one."

Taking the shovel, Martinez began what was to be a shallow grave indeed. With little ceremony, they covered the body and made their way in the darkness toward the company.

They moved as if wounded, one dead and one near dead, dreading more than a little their encounter with Sheets. A red trail of blood from Brandywine's bandage dripped down Molly's side.

Exhausted, they pulled up for a moment's rest before pushing the last distance into camp. The stars fled as daylight broke, and even the horses trembled in the chill of dawn.

"Look there," McReynolds said, his heart sinking at the buffalo calf watching them from a distance, "piteous thing's followed us the whole night."

Lifting his carbine, Renfro fired without a word and the calf dropped.

Shocked, McReynolds whirled about, "What the hell!"

"Sorry, sir. I know it don't seem proper, but food's food. Back there in the commotion, you and me left that buffalo cow for the coyotes."

It was the first McReynolds had thought of the cow since the accident.

"Maybe we could send someone back."

"Nothing but bones by now, sir. It was a bad mistake and Sheets will probably have me at the drag for it. Still, what's worse, it might cost some lives 'fore we're done. That calf wouldn't have survived another day in any case."

Pushing back his hat, Renfro stood over the crumpled heap at his feet, unsheathing his skinning knife, checking the blade for sharpness.

"Now, just time to skin him out before Lieutenant Sheets gets here," he said.

Twenty

With only one hand across his chest, Brandywine looked odd lying there while Martinez worked, digging his fifth hole in two days. No one was certain when the blood stopped dripping or the moaning ceased, but by the time Sheets rode in from camp, Brandywine was dead.

Without emotion Sheets listened as McReynolds recounted the story of Brandywine's amputation, of McCasson's brutal death, but it was the fate of the buffalo cow that caused him to kick dirt into the air with the toe of his boot.

"We are doomed!" he yelled, pointing at Renfro, "because of your stupidity. On the verge of starvation, waiting for you to return, and you leave a whole buffalo cow for the coyotes." Stepping in close to Renfro's face, his eyes darkened. "Let me tell you, Corporal, this . . . this doctor didn't know any better, but you did. You've endangered the entire company and by damn you'll pay for it."

"Sorry, sir," Renfro said, "but we did get the corn and the spokes too, and this here calf, although a tad small."

"And you, Martinez," Sheets said, his voice dropping, "killing the best shot in the company. There's no one left could hit a buffalo if it stumbled into camp and lay down at his feet." Whirling about, he mounted his horse. "I'll deal with you later, Renfro, and you too, Martinez. You'll wish you'd carried that buffalo on your back by the time I'm through."

The others greeted them, grateful enough for the baskets of

corn, examining the feather from McCasson's fatal arrow and the necklace retrieved from the cache.

"On-da," Twobirds said in a hushed voice.

"Who is On-da?" McReynolds asked.

"On-da," she said again, turning the bloody feather between her fingers. "Once a Kiowa but now banned. Like a spider he lives alone, hunts alone, and kills even his own kind."

"Why was he banned?" Sheets approached, leaning close to Twobirds's face.

"For taking another's wife. Later he returned to steal her husband's horse for trade. No Kiowa since we came from the north many generations ago has hunted without a horse or alone and lived," she paused, "except On-da.

"With snow on the ground, he hid the stolen wife in the bushes to wait, but it was very cold and her clothes were thin. After stealing the husband's horse, On-da left without her, leaving her to freeze to death in the woods. Now he hunts alone. His strength is that of three men and he runs without tiring. No buffalo, no horse, no man can run longer."

"And this?" Sheets asked, picking up the necklace.

"I know nothing of this," Twobirds said.

"But this too is Kiowa, isn't it?"

"It is of no importance to you," she said.

"Nor the food either, I suppose. That's why you failed to mention the caches."

"The food gathered by others should not be taken."

"Well," he said, walking toward the tent, "if it weren't for the stupidity of our mule skinner, we'd all be eating buffalo hump for breakfast." Turning, he glared at Renfro. "Fix that wagon and break camp. We're moving out."

"But what about the forging, sir?" Renfro stood. "That rim's bent out of round and apt to bust again."

"Break camp, Corporal, and take the drag. Martinez, I'll see you at formation."

Later, as the sun rose hot in the eastern sky, Martinez steeled himself, looking straight ahead as Sheets tied the bags of shot about his neck. But as the order came to move out and the column rode past, there was little doubt as to the dread in his eyes and the fear in his heart.

Two days passed, but the salt fields were still nowhere in sight, food increasingly scarce, the marrow from the calf's bones providing the last thin soup.

Without horse or rations, Martinez had not made camp a single night. Hanging would have been a far more merciful punishment than the one Sheets dealt.

"Perhaps I should ride back and check on Martinez?" McReynolds asked Sheets. "You know what happened to Bledso."

"You do and I'll have you court-martialed for interfering with disciplinary procedures," he said, his eyes sweeping the horizon.

"But he'll surely starve without rations."

"The rations are the same, Doctor, for us and Martinez. All he has to do is show up and get them. Indeed, if Martinez and others of this command had exercised better judgment, we'd all be eating meat about now, wouldn't we?"

By the third day, the red soil deepened to rust and wind-eroded canyons opened suddenly in unexpected places, a clay frieze at their crowns like slashes of war paint. Mesas thrust from the prairie floor like bountiful and full breasts, while chunks of translucent mica set the hills alive in a frenzy of light.

The men talked among themselves, awed by the vastness, lured by the shade. But they pushed on, stupefied by the heat, oblivious even to the heel flies feeding at their veins, their bellies gorged with blood. The sun wrung the atmosphere dry and the distances opened before them.

At first McReynolds was uncertain of the movement on the horizon, but then it was there again, an animal, or a man perhaps, moving at a slow but steady pace, like a predator stalking prey. Sweat stung his eyes as he stared into the quivers of heat against the sky. And then there was nothing, nothing but the zing of locusts in the midday heat.

Pulling down his hat, he fixed his gaze on the synchronized thrust of Nurse Cromley's hips as she rode. Perhaps he was giddy from the heat. No human could keep pace with horses, not even under the best of conditions. In this heat, death from dehydration and exhaustion would come within a few short hours.

Still, what if there was someone back there? He'd failed Bledso, hadn't he? What if that was Martinez, dying of thirst, trying to keep up with the column? How could he let him die, and within shot of the camp?

When once again the wagon spoke splintered, the ill-fitting rim careened across the prairie, causing Sheets to throw his arms in the air.

"Have to shave another spoke, sir," Renfro said, studying the wheel, "and forge that rim or she'll not hold."

"Well, forge it, Corporal," Sheets yelled, his voice pitched and angry.

When the wheel was off, Renfro ordered a pit dug and a fire built of mesquite and buffalo dung. Watching on, Twobirds shelled the corn, the same corn she'd refused from the beginning to eat.

"A small fire to melt the iron," she said, "a big fire to cook the rabbit. I'll never understand the white man's ways."

"It's a small fire that can be the hottest," Renfro said. "Little thing like yourself ought to understand that."

Fashioning bellows from the calfskin, Renfro pumped the fire white hot, holding the wagon rim in the glowing coals, lifting it from the forge at the exact moment and onto a flat rock that had been carried to the fire. With careful and deliberate blows, he struck the rim until its symmetry was regained. McReynolds's respect for him grew with the masterful skill, the precision and finesse of the blows.

With the wagon repaired, corn was cooked over the forge fire and shared among them, Twobirds refusing her portion, brewing sage tea instead, passing it around for all to share, a remarkably pleasant and soothing concoction.

Shortly after supper Sheets retired to the tent while the others sipped their tea and huddled close to the fire. The hills loomed about them like Egyptian tombs and the mica winked in the soft orange light of sunset.

The flicker of the candle through the tent was a sure sign that Sheets was studying his worthless map.

"Lieutenant McReynolds," Sheets called from the tent, "I want to see you."

Poring over the map, Sheets looked up. Next to him lay the necklace taken from the cache.

"What is it, Lieutenant?"

"Know what this is?" Sheets asked, tossing the necklace to him.

"A Kiowa necklace, I believe, a medallion of some sort."

"Indeed, but take a closer look."

"What's your point?" McReynolds asked, turning the medallion in his hand.

"It's metal, silver in fact," Sheets said, rising, pacing the short distance in front of his cot.

"So it is. I wonder where the Kiowa attained silver?"

"Yes," he said, "exactly. Where did the Kiowa attain silver?" Taking the necklace, Sheets turned it against the light. "It's a silver coin to be precise, fashioned into one of those cryptic symbols so favored by our Kiowa friends.

"In thirty-two," he said, tossing the necklace on the cot irreverently, "twelve traders from Santa Fe transporting ten thousand dollars in silver specie disappeared without a trace as they made their way to Saint Louis. They came the southernmost route, not far from where we're now camped I should think. If you look closely at that medallion, you'll see that some Spanish markings remain."

"Still, there could be any number of explanations," McReynolds said, picking up the coin to examine it again.

"They didn't even know what they had," Sheets said. "If my

guess is right, it's still intact somewhere. Once they made their trinkets, the remainder was probably abandoned or hidden, too heavy to transport far. All we have to do is find out where, and I'd bet my commission that squaw out there knows exactly where."

"They could've traded for that coin, Lieutenant. Trading is their way of life."

"It wasn't right, you know," Sheets tucked his chin, "killing those traders like that, a crime, a crime of murder and thievery and it's our duty as representatives of the United States government to do all that we can to see that it's rectified."

"What are you suggesting?"

"Only that as soldiers we are obliged by our oath to protect the citizenry of this country, McReynolds, and that's exactly what I intend to do."

"This company is starving half the time and lost the other half, and you're suggesting we set off on some treasure hunt? That's the craziest thing I have ever heard. That's not our mission, Lieutenant, and you know it."

"I'm not suggesting it, Doctor, I'm ordering it. You'd do well to remember those poor souls had as much right crossing this country as us, and I intend to see that their deaths are avenged and their possessions recovered." He waved his hand in dismissal. "And in the future you would do equally well to remember who is commander of this expedition, Lieutenant."

Whether it was from malice, hatred, or simply retaliation for Sheets's irreverence, McReynolds stuck the medallion into his pocket.

Rank and power were the only things Sheets feared. As assistant surgeon, McReynolds's rank and power were sadly lacking. Today they still stood between him and Sheets's wrath.

Tomorrow could be a different story, however, because he was going back for Martinez and damn the cost.

Twenty-one

At first he determined to recruit Renfro to go back with him in search of Martinez but decided it was better to keep the responsibility to himself. Rank being what it was, Renfro had precious little protection from Sheets already.

Separating oneself from the others was on its face a dangerous thing and probably fruitless as well, certainly so in Bledso's case, but then perhaps if he'd been more determined, more persistent, things would've been different for Bledso.

This then was an act of vindication, of absolution for himself, a selfish act to ease his conscience and he had no right to involve anyone else. With a little luck he'd be back before morning and no one would be the wiser.

When the camp was asleep and Sheets's breathing was steady, McReynolds moved from the tent, waiting at the tree line until even the whippoorwill sang securely in the night. Leading his unsaddled horse a fair distance from camp, he mounted, and headed east to find Martinez.

Landmarks were hard enough to find in the daylight—a peculiarly shaped mesquite, a butte with the profile of a man, a rock jutting from a canyon wall. In the darkness his chances of recognition were small indeed, but come daybreak his course should be more clear.

The plan was to backtrack two hours, allowing two hours to return. If he found Martinez alive, he would leave him the horse and tell Sheets it had been stolen during the night. Even if

Sheets suspected the truth, there would be no proof and little choice but for him to take his word.

Both relief and anxiety set in when a full moon rose into the sky, his shadow skimming over the crevices and rocks like a ghostly companion. An hour had passed, maybe less, when he pulled up his horse and listened. One by one he separated the night sounds, categorized them, dismissed them.

When all was done, it was the singular and terrifying silence that caused his skin to prickle. The night knew what he did not, and his heart surged with adrenaline. At first it was but a fleeting specter and then a fearsome reality as he made out the red paint on On-da's throat glistening in the moonlight.

"You," he choked.

Rawhide muscles rippled through On-da's body. About his massive chest was an immense bois d'arc bow. Braids swept nearly to his waist, lengthened with horse tail hair and bound with ragged strips of deer hide. On foot he stood nearly as tall as McReynolds did on horseback, the largest man he'd ever seen. Instinctively he buried his heels into his horse's flanks and lunged blindly into the night.

Clinging to his horse's mane, McReynolds rode through the dark, head down, eyes closed, waiting for an arrow to speed through his body, praying to somehow miss the yawning canyons, the dry gulches, the prairie dog holes that could snap a horse's leg like dry tinder. Branches hidden in the dark whizzed overhead, capable of swift and efficient decapitation.

How far or in what direction he rode before he dared look back, McReynolds was not certain, but when he did, On-da was not to be seen. Even then McReynolds's pace did not slacken, determined as he was to get as much distance between him and On-da as possible. Better to be lost than dead, and so he rode until both him and his horse blowed with exhaustion. Dismounting, he led his horse to the top of a knoll and turned in a slow circle, studying for his life the moonlit terrain.

Without warning or sound an excruciating pain shot through his buttocks and raced up his back like a hot flame.

"Oh Christ!" he screamed. "Shot!"

Whirling about to face his assassin, the red-throated warrior, the giant with the horse's legs and the cougar's heart, his horse looked back, a satisfied glint in its eye, content that a good chomp on its rider's rear was fair revenge for the harsh treatment it had just endured.

Rubbing the tingle from his buttock, McReynolds smiled at his own foolishness. No man on foot could ever sustain such a pace, not even the infamous On-da.

A rock presented itself to lean on and he closed his eyes for a moment's rest.

First, it came like the soft and gentle rustle of leaves, but then more of a swishing sound, like the strong pace of a runner, and McReynolds's heart froze. On-da still came, a powerful and relentless stride, moving like a jackal moves, just behind, but always there within striking distance when its prey fell from exhaustion.

Panic-stricken, McReynolds grabbed for the horse's reins, but it threw its head high in the air and galloped off into the darkness.

"Whoa," he cried in desperation, "whoa, boy."

But his horse was gone and On-da was closing the distance. In total confusion and fear he ran from the swishing feet of On-da, running with all his strength, with all that was within him, until his lungs burned from the night air and his heart hammered in his chest.

When McReynolds could run no more, when his lungs raged with pain and he gulped for air like a dying fish, he fell to his knees. And in that brief reprieve the sound of On-da's feet beat in his ears like the beat of his own heart and fear drove him on.

In his own mind he never stopped running, but the cadence of On-da's feet belied what his mind believed, and the pungent smell of earth in his nostrils confirmed the deception and like the trembling fawn he awaited the predator's clutch.

With diminishing will McReynolds inched forward, elbows scraped and bleeding into the dust that would soon enough claim him. Cool air rose from the abyss and stopped him in his tracks. Peering over the edge, he shriveled inside.

Death waited behind as McReynolds rose to face him. Towering like a majestic red cedar, On-da stood, his body glistening, smelling of smoke and sage and sweat. In his hand was a knife and in his eyes the final mandate.

Whether of gods, of hollow logs, or of the stars themselves, McReynolds didn't know, but suddenly the medallion was there in his hand, an irrevocable shield between him and death.

Perhaps it was that split second of recognition, of confusion, of indecision, that caused On-da to reach for the medallion, plucking it from McReynolds's hand as he swept past into the infinite depths of the canyon like a mute and helpless giant.

Exhausted, McReynolds collapsed onto the ground. Tomorrow he would find his way, his horse, his camp. Tomorrow he would find On-da's body because he wanted to know that he was forever dead. Tomorrow he would search again for Martinez and indulge himself in despair and complain of hunger and fatigue and pray for deliverance.

But for now, at this moment, there was only sleep and the welcome earth beneath him.

Twenty-two

The morning sun rose bright but cold as McReynolds awakened, rubbing at his muscles, knotted and aching from the night's desperate chase. As light fell across the canyon wall and then into its profound depths, there splayed on the rocks below lay the body of On-da.

Determined to see it through, whatever it took, McReynolds began the descent. Never again did he want to hear the sound of On-da's feet behind him.

An hour later he dropped the last ten feet onto the canyon floor and stood over the gigantic figure. The fall had been cruel, his large torso ruptured on the rocks, his distended abdomen pregnant from the morning heat.

McReynolds knelt next to the body, the chalky stare, the anemic buzz of flies, the bloody drool of On-da's lips, and the enormous hands curled like a hawk's claws, still clutching the medallion.

Tied about On-da's waist was a deer hide belt and from it a half-dozen dusty and tattered scalps. When he saw the two freshest additions, McReynolds's throat tightened, the flame of Irish red, the inky black of Martinez's straight hair.

Tucked under On-da's belt was the shot bag, empty now except for a few strips of jerky. Tearing off a piece of the tough hide still damp from On-da's sweat, he chewed hungrily. There was a rush of energy and life renewed.

* * *

By noon he was clear of the canyon and had located the tracks leading back to the camp, at least that was his hope. They could just as easily be leading in the opposite direction. Still, the tracks moved into the sun and in the general direction of the expedition, and for that he was grateful.

By mid afternoon his progress slowed and his confidence waned, struggling with indecision, with the fear of abandonment in this torrid and barren land.

Thirst came suddenly, an uncompromising craving, intensified by the salt and smoke of the jerky and the scorching sun, lips cracking into a bloody mosaic.

At sunset he found the deserted camp and despaired as he knelt at the cold fire, wanting to cry, like a child, like the day his father left him at school to face the world alone.

But then he saw the canteen, hanging there in the mesquite and his spirits soared, drinking deeply of the warm water and giving thanks to his unknown champion.

That night, alone and cold, he shivered under the star-filled sky, abandoned and forgotten in this perilous land.

This much was certain: The column would move at sunup as it always did and there was little chance of overcoming them on foot. To walk longer at the beginning and end of his day while the column was idle was his only hope. Decision made, he curled up on the ground and slept the few remaining hours.

The plan was flawed, as McReynolds soon discovered. By leaving before daylight, he could no longer see the wagon tracks and was soon lost. At sunup he simply turned west, following the sun's track across the sky.

At noon he rested and ate a piece of On-da's jerky and took a pull from the canteen. Immense blisters had developed on his feet, thin water-filled membranes wrapping both heels. There was little to be done but suffer them.

By late afternoon he was near exhaustion, taking shade under a small mesquite for a moment's rest. Something caused him to sit up, a change in sound perhaps, but the prairie answered in a familiar voice. It was a slow but certain realization, smell not sound, the indisputable scent of burning wood. There at a distance the curl of smoke, and he ran toward it, blisters be damned.

Stoking the fire like nothing had happened was Renfro.

"Thought you'd never get here," he said.

"Decided to have myself a little walk," McReynolds said, "like a couple hundred miles with an Indian the size of that molly bent on taking my scalp."

"Figured something like that," Renfro said, pumping on the bellows. "Your horse came in the next morning all lathered up and looking for the world like things gone wrong."

"Found this," McReynolds said, tossing him the shot bag, "and the two fresh scalps."

"Shame," Renfro said, poking at the fire, "good boys, both of them." After what seemed a considerable time, he looked up at McReynolds. "That On-da feller ain't still coming is he, sir?"

"Not this time, Corporal, and I can't tell you what a relief I find that to be."

"Yes sir," he grinned. "Guess you'll be a legend after this."

"Long as I get some rest and grub, Corporal, I'll be a legend or anything else." He looked around. "Where are the others?"

"Well, sir, this here wagon wheel came off. Seems I failed to tighten the hub nut and the lieutenant was a tad upset. I figured I was bringing up the drag anyways, so I volunteered to stay behind and fix it."

"Lucky for me, I guess," McReynolds said. "Don't think I could have held out much longer."

"No sir," he said.

"Never knew you to make a mistake like that before," McReynolds said, pulling off his boots to examine the ruptured blisters, "not tightening the hub nut and then leaving your canteen behind too."

"Old age and moonshine," he grinned, "and riding that mule over half God's creation."

"There's jerky in that shot bag, Corporal. It taste like harness leather and lord knows what it is, but it beats an empty stomach."

Walking to the wagon, Renfro lifted out a jack by its ears.

"Got curious while I was fixing that wheel there and I beaned him with the hub wrench. Guess he'll be joining us for dinner.

"Hope the others are getting something too. Shouldn't have left that cow like that. Just a bad mistake all around," he said, turning his hand to the fire. "Well, things done are done and there's never any changing 'em, is there, sir?"

"It could have happened to anybody, Corporal. There were considerable distractions as I recall."

"Yes sir," he said, "considerable, and we got camp to make. With an early start we should pick up the others by noon tomorrow.

"Here, sir," he handed McReynolds the jackrabbit, "guess the surgeon gets to use the knife. Tonight," he grinned, "I'm sleeping indoors like a human being. The lieutenant's tent is in the wagon. Guess he forgot to take it out. Hope he don't get cold or snakebit sleeping on the ground."

The sun set in a blaze of color, a spray of orange ascending to the clouds, painting their tips like toasted meringue. The aroma of flying rabbit engulfed McReynolds, overwhelming his hunger, and he ate ravenously. Afterward, sage tea was boiled and socks were hung to dry next to the dying fire.

Sharpening a stick, Renfro picked at his teeth and then spoke in a soft and easy voice, like the night itself.

"It's a strange and mysterious country, ain't it, sir, unpredictable like a woman, sometimes all full of anger and heat, other times soft and gentle as a winter snow."

"It's a mystery, all right."

"You know, sir, that nurse was surely concerned about your well-being."

"Nurse Cromley?"

"Yes sir, that one," he smiled.

"Well," McReynolds shifted his weight, "we've been together for some time now. I guess she's grown fond."

"Yes sir. Course, a man ought to have someone who cares whether he lives or dies. Without that, nothing else matters."

"That's a fact, Corporal."

"Seems a tad troubled to me, sir, like things working at her mind and such."

Nodding, McReynolds didn't answer, for truth needed no answer.

With pearl moon rising he fell exhausted into the luxury of his cot, sweet surrender to consuming fatigue. Tomorrow they would march again.

For the briefest moment as he fell asleep, he thought he heard the swish of On-da's feet running in the night.

Twenty-three

"Well, Dr. McReynolds," Sheets said, "been on a little missionary work have we?"

"Just doing what I had to do, Lieutenant."

"A bit impetuous, don't you think? Been one of the men here, you'd be carrying shot on drag."

"I'm not one of your men, Lieutenant," McReynolds stared back with bravado, knowing full well this was not the time to back down. "I'm a medical officer with every right, responsibility, to check on the well-being of prisoners."

"And I am the commander, Doctor, with the responsibility of the entire expedition. I'll not have my orders disobeyed."

"Your orders have killed two of our men," he said, throwing the scalp locks at Sheets's feet. "And keep this in mind, Lieutenant: If nothing else, you and these other men here may well need my services before this expedition is over."

Thumbing the hammer of his side arm, Sheets looked about.

"Hadn't been for Corporal Renfro's inept blacksmithing, you'd never have made it," he said. "You think about that next time you decide to take things into your own hands. All right, let's move out."

They marched two full days at breakneck speed, Sheets more driven than ever, complaining bitterly at the slightest delays. Even the heat did not deter him, the suffocating, blistering heat that sapped their energy and undermined their morale.

The horses scrubbed for pasture in the few short hours of

daylight left to them at the end of each day but found precious little to eat. They grew lank and reluctant, requiring constant coaxing to move forward. The only redeeming matter in the whole exasperating drive was the sudden and complete absence of insects.

"Ain't no life for a bug," Renfro said. "Water table dips ever time one of 'em takes a drink."

But McReynolds perceived a more ominous change, the thin, dry air, the ragged landscape, the deceiving distances. They were nearing the desert and he sensed its unforgiving nature. To the west and north the vast prairie rose to the snow-covered peaks of the Rockies, to the south and west the green and up-stretched arms of the saguaro cactus, but here only the primeval survived, a torpid, reptilian world that dulled the brain, baked hope away, choked faith into aching despair.

Camp was a miserable affair as they scratched for scraps like chickens in a pen, paddle cactus buds, mesquite pods, hackberries that caught in their teeth and scoured their bowels.

On the third day they found water, a shallow puddle smelling of gypsum and buffalo dung, a precarious green moss covering its surface. Swishing the slime back with decided flips of her nose, Molly drank reluctantly. The men followed suit, holding the sludge back with sticks as they filled their canteens.

"Ain't pure," Renfro said, "but ain't poison neither."

All had begun to weaken from their grueling circumstances but nowhere was it more apparent than with Nurse Cromley, who spent most of the days huddled in the back of the supply wagon.

McReynolds tried his best to cheer her but she would only look from under her blanket with large and sad eyes. Finally she stopped talking altogether and then stopped praying, her crucifix bouncing unattended in the floor of the wagon.

If food was not found soon, they would surely die or become so addled as not to be able to protect themselves or find their way.

And then suddenly it was there, a white sea of salt stretching down the canyon and into the horizon. Heat shimmered from its expanse, an ebb and flow of iridescent light. Through its center meandered a wide but shallow river no more than a few inches deep, moving so slowly as to be caught in time.

Across from their position and on the other side of the saline field rose a blood-red bank capped with a colossal table of alabaster. It was the mirror image of the bank on which they stood. Walking to the edge, McReynolds looked across its breadth and felt its spirit.

"The Grand Saline," Sheets said, "but bigger, much bigger than I ever dreamed."

Kneeling, Twobirds pointed. "There, there, and there, are trails that lead in like the spokes of your wagon. Everything comes here sooner or later for the salt, everything," she said, her dark eyes melting in the sun like drops of liquid wax. "All must take their salt and leave. It is the way."

"We'll camp here," Sheets said, "and find a way down tomorrow. Renfro, dispatch a hunting party. You're in charge. If all animals come here, then even you should be able to shoot something."

"It's not for hunting," she said, casting a glance at Renfro.

"Do as you're ordered, Corporal."

"Yes sir, as you say," he nodded

They made camp as Renfro set off in a northerly course with three of the best shots. Wood for fire was scarce but buffalo droppings cured by the sun were ample, burning with an incandescent red glow, a blue and pure flame dancing in the air.

The view itself captured them, held them at the edge of the canyon, dark green cedars twisting and knurled, sprouting from high on the caprock as if planted there by an ancient gardener, the smell of salt on the wind like the high seas.

Staring at the fire, her mind lost in thought, Nurse Cromley bobbed her foot. The scar of the snakebite reminded McReynolds of her courage, her strong and confident way, but here her spirits were broken, her courage gone. This country took from her, sapped her of life and gave her nothing in return. His attempts to cheer her were futile, smiling, then retreating again, her blanket pulled about her head against a place too cruel to bear.

Walking from his tent, map in hand, Sheets approached Two-birds as she tended the fire.

Shifting uneasily at his presence, she rose to leave.

"Just a minute," he said. "I want to talk to you."

"Talk?" she said, folding her arms.

"The Kiowa medallion is missing."

"I know nothing of this."

"You know very little it seems." Sheets said. "So what does it mean, this medallion?"

"It is the symbol of Koitsenko, a society of honor for Kiowa warriors."

"It was taken from an innocent caravan on its way to Saint Louis, wasn't it? They were never heard of again. Tell me you know nothing of this either, Twobirds."

"I know nothing of this," she said.

Pacing back and forth in front of the fire, he clenched his hands behind him.

"Ten thousand in specie and never heard of again. It's the duty of every person in this expedition to see that this deed is avenged and the silver recovered."

"I do not know of any silver," she said, her black hair shinning in the setting sun.

"Look you," his voice trembled, "you've eaten our food, drunk our water, ridden our horses. Every man in this outfit has risked his life to get you back to your people and how do you repay that kindness? By lying about the food caches, by not lifting a finger to help us, and now, this. Well, maybe I'll just leave you here. Maybe an Osage hunting party, or the Pawnee comes by and finds a Kiowa girl alone out here."

"When a Kiowa child cries, his cradle is placed in the woods until he cries no more," she said.

"That's enough, Lieutenant," McReynolds said. "She's said she knows nothing of the silver."

"Lieutenant's right," Renfro said, stepping from the shadows, his voice cold, deliberate.

Momentarily frozen by the menace in Renfro's voice, Sheets turned.

"I'll not tolerate insubordination, Corporal." Slipping past them both, Twobirds defused the confrontation with her absence. "And I suppose you came back empty-handed?"

"Just a rabbit too skinny to run or shoot, sir."

"This expedition is a sham and calamity," Sheets said, his mouth drawing into a thin line. "Can't hunt, can't forge, can't, for chrisake, find north on a map. We got a mission here, a duty, but we got to eat or there won't be anything left but empty uniforms and rusted guns when they find us." Picking up the map, he folded it along the well-defined seams. "I'm holding you personally responsible for our situation, Renfro, you and that Kiowa squaw. Whatever happens rests entirely on your shoulders."

After he was gone, Renfro pushed back his hat and scratched at his head.

"Something spoiled his day," he said.

"Smelling all that silver," McReynolds smiled.

"Course, he's right, you know. My fault about that cow. Guess we'd be that much better off if I'd minded the store."

"No one's faulting you, Corporal, except Sheets, and if he doesn't fault you, that leaves only himself and he's certain that's not a possibility."

"It's a calamity, sure," Renfro said, pulling off a boot and rubbing at his foot, "and that little nurse ain't faring too well either, kind of downhearted and lonesome like she'd been orphaned." He examined his toe protruding from a hole in his sock. "Some folk ain't cut out for the wilderness, needing finer and gentler things to rebuild their souls. They can't find it in the smell of sage, or the marbled sunset, nor in the lonesome call of the coyote. It's got to be dolled up with churches and organs and stained glass."

"I've seen her face things that would make most men cringe, Corporal."

"Yes sir, it's a funny thing, the wilderness. All in how you see it, I suppose. I always figured there was nothing in this creation I had to fear, except man maybe, and in all the places I been there's less chance of meeting up with him here than anywhere else." He pulled off the other boot and began the same treatment on the other foot. "Course, I didn't know that the lieutenant was going to be one of those men or me and Molly might have moved to Saint Louis."

From the corrals the horses and mules stirred, snorting, biting each other's rumps, the smell of dust in the air from their hooves. They too were hungry and in need of a few days' rest. Jaded horses dimmed their chances of survival and it was bad policy all around to push them too hard.

The men busied themselves playing cards and tending the fire, a fire more for their spirits than for the cold. Legs folded back, Nurse Cromley watched on. They were fine legs, browned from the sun, firm, warm, and McReynolds remembered their trembling passion. If only there was something he could do for her.

Her hands full of Indian bread, Twobirds joined them at the fire and began preparing the unpalatable root into a paste.

The shot breached the evening, renting the air, a hot and deadly whine. Spinning about, Renfro tried to determine its source, Twobirds crouching at his side, her eyes searching the shadows. Fingers tingling, McReynolds picked up his carbine and awaited what was surely the coup de grâce, the end of a rather brief and undistinguished medical career.

Listening, his carbine against the curve of his shoulder, Renfro pointed to where the horses were staked, motioning them forward with his hand. Like ducks in a row they waddled toward the horses, Cromley sobbing from behind.

Molly lay on the ground, Sheets's foot propped on her enormous white belly, his rifle slung over his arm.

Chills raced down McReynolds's back as Renfro fell at

Molly's side, holding her head in his arms, grieving at the death of his friend.

"Tonight we eat," Sheets said.

Rotating a half turn, Renfro drew down squarely between Sheets's eyes and squeezed the trigger.

"Wait!" McReynolds yelled, bringing the barrel of his carbine across Renfro's ear, dropping him as if shot.

"He's mine," Sheets howled, "drawing on an officer. You saw it." Bending at the waist like an old lady, he examined the trickle of blood that oozed from Renfro's ear. "I want him secured, you hear? I want him tied to the wagon till morning." Moving around Renfro, he studied him like a kid with a snake. "No one draws down on me, no one. There's a lesson to be taught here and I'm just the one to do it. I'll have him shot, by God, come daylight." The others now gathered around. "Well, secure him," he ordered. "Do as I say."

The men dragged the fallen corporal by his arms and tied him to the wagon wheel. The molly was butchered, legs spread immodestly on a singletree, hauled up a mesquite, and belly spilled onto the ground.

Turning away at the sight, Twobirds sought solace alone on the prairie.

The night dropped about them in blackness that matched the blackness of their souls, heat rising from the salt and the day's sun, a stifling heat, a damning and incriminating heat.

From the wagon wheel, Renfro watched on, hatred in his eyes penetrating the darkness as the spit turned over the fire, the smell of roasting meat tempting them beyond endurance, an elixir for their grinding hunger and pain.

And so they ate as they turned their backs to Renfro, to the last man, and hated themselves for the doing, an abdication of the spirit, relinquishment to the primal forces within them.

Sometime in the still of the morning hours, McReynolds awakened to voices beyond the tent.

"It's not possible," Sheets said. "To let him go would endanger the whole expedition. You think I can let an attempt on my life pass?"

"I know he can't be freed now," Twobirds answered, "he is full of anger and would surely take his revenge. But you must spare his life."

"Why?" Sheets snorted. "He's proven his intent. As commander I had every right to shoot that worthless mule. Government property, isn't she, and mine to dispose of as I wish. It was for the good of the company. That's my right as commander and I exercised it."

"Yes," she said, "it is the right of a chief but there were many animals to choose from, some too weak to carry a load. Wouldn't they have served better?"

"There is nothing I can do."

"Then you will never find what it is you desire."

There was silence and McReynolds turned his ear into the darkness to hear.

"What do you mean?" Sheets finally asked.

"The silver."

"Yes, I thought so all along. You would've let us march right on by, I suppose."

"I will take you to it but in return you must spare his life."

"Where? Tell me where."

"In a cave beyond the salt, a cave of alabaster that reaches deep into the earth. It is there that the silver lies and the bodies of those who brought it."

"I thought so, didn't I?" he said, his voice giddy. "I thought so all along. Buried in a cave. Didn't even know what they had."

"Then you will spare his life if I take you to the cave?"

"Sure," he said, "why not? We can let the courts decide the corporal's fate."

"No," she said, "when the time comes, he must be set free to go with me."

"With you?"

"Yes, that's the way it must be. You would never find the cave alone. If you want the silver, that's the way it must be."

"I see," he said.

"He must go with me when the time comes. You must let him free and I will take you to the silver, that I promise."

"Well," he said, "perhaps something can be worked out. Course, he'll have to be secured until then. You must be something special," he said huskily. "I could make things a lot easier, you know."

"It is the silver I've promised," she said, "nothing else."

"The silver, then," he said, "and you are to tell no one."

Making his way back to the tent, Sheets was soon asleep. But McReynolds was not so lucky, lying awake until daylight, his body racked with fatigue.

What would happen when Sheets got his silver? At that point no one was safe, not Renfro, not Twobirds, not the good doctor himself.

Twenty-four

With trepidation they moved into the Grand Saline, edging forward like ants in a flour bin, stopping, listening, watching in fascination at the glimmering expanse of salt.

History recorded Coronado's having passed this way, searching for the seven cities of Cíbola. Perhaps he had stood at the same place, known the same beauty and terror that the Grand Saline struck in their own souls at this moment.

As far as the eye could see there was but salt, blowing and moving like a thing alive, swirling before the southwest wind and lifting into the morning air like fog. Their eyes watered as they stared into the stinging haze.

Channels cut through the expanse like silver threads and immense selenite crystals glittered like shattered diamonds, beams of light scattering and skittering into the white sky. And placed about here and there as if by design great columns of water boiled from deep within the earth, carrying the salt from ancient seas and disbursing it on the plain to evaporate.

This was the heart and soul of this noble land, the place where all life must finally come. That made it a special and rare place; that made it a dangerous and perilous place where the odds of encounter and death were compounded.

Renfro rode in the wagon with Nurse Cromley, his hands bound to the side boards, bags of shot tied to his legs. The red slash of McReynolds's blow was still visible across his ear. When Renfro was escorted to a distance to relieve himself, he shuffled his feet like an arthritic old man, an ignoble and disturbing sight for them all.

Like the others, McReynolds avoided Renfro, having eaten the meat from his molly. Letting the meat waste would have been foolish, but his shame was irreconcilable.

The treacherous salt bed made travel slow, inclined as it was to give away unexpectedly, dropping the wagons onto their axles with a heavy and discouraging thud.

An extra team and all hands would rock the wagons free, only for the whole thing to be repeated again, sometimes within a few short minutes. From his perch on the wagon Renfro watched Sheets, his eyes seething with anger.

It was high noon when they spotted the buffalo herd, a veritable sea of life moving like a single entity, first one direction and then another and then back again in the same direction, their tails switching and twisting, synchronized by evolutionary time. The salt crust trembled under the men's feet, the thunder from the buffalo hooves pooling in their souls.

"First Sergeant Lansdown," Sheets said in hushed voice, holding up his hand for the column to halt, "take ten men and see if you can't bring some of them down."

"Yes sir," he said. "What about Renfro, sir? He's our best shot."

"No," Sheets said.

"The salt must be for all," Twobirds said, her jaw clenched.

"Do as you're ordered," Sheets snapped at the first sergeant.

The men split into two groups and began a slow and deliberate approach from opposite sides of the herd. With a signal from the first sergeant they charged, carbines blazing, firing within a few feet of their targets.

The buffalo circled and churned, a cloud of salt rising like mist above them. The men screamed and yelled and rode their horses at full gallop, firing with abandon. When all was done, nearly a dozen buffalo lay dying on the plain, their robes frosted white from the salt.

The column camped among the kill and began the butchering, exercising great care in the salting.

With Twobirds at his side, McReynolds carved the choice cuts from a fallen bull. Crimson rivers cut through the salt, the warm and fetid smell of blood about them. They worked until they were exhausted, their arms bloodied to the elbows, rubbing the salt deep into the meat, working it into the soft red meat with their fingers and stacking the slabs one upon the other in the wagon beds.

As evening set, the Grand Saline fell silent, all life fleeing even to the last, to the protection beyond the salt. Only the company huddled in the open, a hot and endless night, the moon watching on from the horizon like a bloody eye.

There was no wood nor dry dung for fire nor the whippoor-will's song nor even the coyote's dirge to set their place, to find their center, to define them and separate them from the wilderness. They were swept by the darkness and the ancient salt, swept into a bottomless sea and each man knew its desolation.

With a thin and well-salted cut of meat on the plate, McReynolds searched Twobirds out, finding her resting alone beyond the others.

"Twobirds," he said, "I've brought you meat. It's raw, I'm afraid, but you really should eat."

"It is good," she said, chewing the meat, nodding in approval, "and well salted."

"I've something to confess," he said.

"It is the way of white men to confess," she said, the moonlight shimmering in her ebony hair.

"Yes, well, that's true, I suppose. But before the confession, I would like to apologize about what I did to Corporal Renfro, hitting him like that. I just want you to understand my reasons."

"I know the reasons, Lieutenant."

"Well, the other thing," he said, picking up a handful of salt, letting it run through his fingers, "less honorable perhaps, is that I overheard, you see. I overheard you talking to Lieutenant Sheets." Her eyes fell. "It's all right, you know. I'm all for you getting the corporal free, but Sheets is an angry and dangerous man. You must be careful, very careful."

"I've known such men before," Twobirds said.

"I just want you to understand that I hope things work out. If the lieutenant has his way, I'm afraid it will be bad for the corporal. But you must be careful. When there is nothing left to bargain for, he will be a dangerous man."

"Beyond, in the center of the Grand Saline, there stands a lone cedar," she said. "It is a holy place for the Osage, for no other tree grows in the salt. There are often Osage here to gather the salt for their meat. It is swept into wooden troughs with turkey wings and boiled clean for use. Your lieutenant would be wise to leave this place, for the Osage are to be feared beyond all else."

"And what about you, Twobirds? What about your people?"

"As the buffalo moves so they move, but all come to the salt." Dusting her hands, she chewed the last of the meat. "But the Kiowa hide their women and children at a distance. The Grand Saline is too dangerous."

"Will we find them soon?"

"Soon, I think."

"But where?"

"Wherever they are," she smiled at the question.

"Yes," he said, "I suppose so."

"The Sun Dance is soon and all Kiowa gather beyond the alabaster cave. It is a holy time, a safe time without war. A lodge pole of cottonwood is raised and the white buffalo hunted so that its hide may be hoisted on the pole."

"A celebration," he smiled.

"More," she said, "the end of grief, the end of dispute, the renewal of life. The Sun Dance closes the circle."

"All Kiowa people come?"

She nodded. "If all is well, and they will wear yellow and blue like the birds and the warriors will tie sinew through their muscles and pull buffalo skulls about the camp to show their bravery and the women will cut off fingers at the joint to grieve for dead husbands."

"And what happens when we find them, Twobirds? What happens then, to you, to Corporal Renfro?"

Rising, she brushed the salt from her skirt. Several moments passed before she spoke.

"My mind is not clear on this. He would be unhappy in the Kiowa camp as I am unhappy in his camp." Looking up into the moon, her brown face was illuminated in its light, the vision of ages there in her face. "He is life to me so it is his life which I must not destroy. I shall not let that happen."

"You are a brave woman," he said.

"Your Nurse Cromley is sick at heart since the snakebite," she said, looking down at him, the clear and soft moon at her back. "I think her spirit is poisoned. Now she mourns for all her loss and fears greatly the land, like a bird held captive too long, seeking only the safety of its cage."

"She should never have come. It was a foolish decision from the beginning, but there have been many foolish decisions on this expedition. I wonder how many we can survive?"

Twenty-five

The explanation as to how seven of their best horses and three mules could have disappeared overnight fell to Private Haulton, who stammered under the glare of Lieutenant Sheets.

Horse tracks from the raiding party led directly across the salt, straight to their camp, where the best mounts had been selected and ridden away without anyone the wiser.

Finger quivering in the air, Sheets condemned Haulton to the drag until the gates of hell, or Fort Gibson, whichever one came first, swung open for their arrival.

"Where were you," he screamed, "when they came to cull the herd?"

Looking at his feet, Haulton shook under Sheets's interrogation.

"Sick, sir, too much raw meat and salt."

"You were sick?" Sheets's brow peaked. "So why didn't you awaken the first sergeant, Haulton? Didn't it occur to you that the whole expedition was endangered without a sentry posted?"

"No sir," he said. "I mean it didn't occur to me to stir the first sergeant, sir. He ain't a pleasant man to awaken in the middle of the night, if I might be permitted to say so, sir."

Except for his boots, Haulton was in full uniform, his little toe springing off to one side, leaving a peculiar track in the salt like a turkey claw.

"So you just lay down, took a little rest, I suppose? Let me tell you, Private, just in case it's slipped your mind, sleeping on sentry duty is a court-martial offense. Men have been shot for less."

"Oh, I weren't sleeping, sir. I was sick-like, you know, so I walked off a piece to relieve myself."

"And you didn't hear half the Indian nation ride in here and steal our horses?" Sheets asked, leaning in, locking his eyes on Haulton's eyes.

"No sir," he said, avoiding Sheets's stare, "I walked quite a spell, sir. There ain't no tree or even a rock to squat behind, and I didn't want no women to see."

The whole company had gathered in a circle about Sheets and Haulton.

"Well," Sheets said, "that just about clears it up then. The private here was just modest, he says, afraid the ladies would be interested in seeing his scrawny ass, he says. Maybe that's why they call you 'Private' Haulton, because of your everlasting modesty." Anger smoldering in his eyes, he whirled about. "Well you aren't a private any longer, soldier. From this moment forward you aren't even a member of the human species."

"Yes sir," Haulton said, snapping to attention.

"Then take them off," Sheets said.

"Take them off, sir?"

"That's right, Haulton, take off the britches. You are no longer a member of the human species; therefore, it would be improper and illogical for you to continue to wear britches."

A flush spilled across Haulton's neck and rose into his ears.

"You mean here, sir? Now?"

"That's right, Haulton, now."

Casting about for help, Haulton laughed anxiously.

"But the ladies, sir, I mean, that wouldn't be a right thing."

"Punish him if you must, Lieutenant," McReynolds said, stepping forward, "but with protocol at least."

"Protocol? I could have this trash shot right here and be within my rights. Take 'em off, by God, Haulton, or so help me I'll leave you for the buzzards."

Fumbling at his buttons, Haulton dropped his pants into the

salt about his ankles, skinny white legs trembling in the morning cold.

"All of them," Sheets said.

Fear and mortification swept Haulton's face as he pulled off the ragged shorts, trying to cover himself with his hands, his head lowered in shame. Twobirds turned her back, walking away.

"It ain't right," Haulton mumbled, and all knew that what he said was true.

Looking forlorn and pitiful, Haulton soon disappeared behind the wagons, the only thing between him and the blistering sun, the two heavy bags of shot hanging about his neck.

The Grand Saline was painful and excruciating for them all, the lack of mounts, the heavy loads of meat, the bottomless bogs that foiled their wagons. Men and stock crept across the white salt and into the unimaginable heat.

Occasionally Haulton would be spotted, squatting on the distant horizon, waiting for the column to move, but soon he was gone and not seen again.

Tracking the raiding party proved to be useless as well, all signs of life soon swept away by the shifting salt.

Attempts by McReynolds to engage Nurse Cromley failed as she peeked despondently from under her blanket. Later that afternoon he dropped back to the second wagon where Renfro rode, his shoulders pushed tight against the side boards to reduce the jostling from the wagon.

"How you doing, Corporal?" he asked, tipping his hat.

"My rear's a bit sore from this here wagon bed and I'm a tad randy too, I reckon. Aside from that, just don't know where I'd rather be."

"Sorry about the molly, Corporal," he said, handing him his canteen. "Everyone is sorry about the molly. Not a man here doesn't regret it happening."

"I reckon I know that, sir. Ain't but one truly responsible.

Every man has some justice before it's done, even fine officers with polished boots and sleeping tents."

"Take it easy, Corporal. You weren't but a breath from being shot. Something happens to you, no telling about that Indian girl."

Hanging his bound hands over the sideboard, Renfro sat up straight.

"What do you mean by that, sir?"

"Just that maybe she's the one standing between you and a bullet, Renfro, so be careful what you do or say."

"Thank you for that information, sir. I'll keep that in mind, certain."

They rode on in silence, the crunch of the wagon wheels on the salt like the squeak of a rocking chair on the front porch.

"You know, Corporal," McReynolds said, "I've been feeling jumpy all day. It's so damn quiet out here, not a bird, jack, or fly to be seen."

"From eaten molly meat, sir, makes a man edgy they say."

"Sorry about that, Renfro. Just seemed a waste not to."

"Couldn't agree with you more, Doctor. That's the way Molly would've had it." Pointing toward the horizon, he said, "Look back there, sir, just off to the south."

In the distance McReynolds could see black specks moving imperceptibly across the white salt.

"What is it, Corporal?"

"I can only guess, sir, but I'd say it's that raiding party that took our horses last night."

"Does Lieutenant Sheets know?" he asked, his stomach tightening.

"Well sir, that I don't know since he ain't been by the wagon for a morning conference yet."

Finding Sheets to the front of the column, McReynolds pointed to the specks. Standing high in his stirrups, Sheets scanned the horizon.

"Damn it all," he said, "those brazen bastards are following us. Waiting for dark, I suppose, to carry off more of our horses. Well, this time we'll be ready for them."

Two hours later the figures had moved closer, apparently unconcerned about detection.

Holding up his hand to halt the column, Sheets pointed off to the east.

"I'll be damned," he said, "if it isn't a tree growing right out of the salt. I've never seen anything like it."

A blue-green cedar perhaps forty feet high rose out of the white plain, its trunk twisted and worn from the harsh climate.

"Would you look at that," McReynolds said. "Must reach down to pure water to grow out here."

"We'll camp," Sheets said, "and wait for our friends."

Adjusting his hat against the burning sun, McReynolds could see their horses still moving steadily toward them.

"Twobirds says the tree that grows from the salt is considered a sacred place for the Osage, Lieutenant Sheets. Do you think it wise to make camp under it, seeing as how they might be headed this way?"

"Attend to the medical needs of this expedition and leave the choice of campsites to me, Doctor."

"Sorry, Lieutenant, but those could be Osage behind us. Just doesn't make sense to upset them any more than necessary."

Camp was pitched under the majestic cedar, its shade a welcome relief against the brutal sun. Guards were posted around the perimeter and wagons moved on opposite sides for cover. A small fire was built from fallen limbs and for the first time in days, the aroma of cooking meat drifted through the camp.

With their backs against the tree, their eyes on the horizon, they sat down to their first good meal in weeks as the raiding party moved ever closer toward them.

Everyone but Renfro was armed, his hands and feet still bound. With his mouth open like an infant, he took the small pieces of meat from Twobirds's hand.

Leaning against the wagon, Sheets watched as the party approached.

"Who do you suppose it is?" McReynolds asked, squatting next to Twobirds and Renfro.

Popping the last piece of meat into Renfro's mouth, Twobirds wiped her hands across her lap.

"Osage," she said.

Chewing, Renfro looked up at McReynolds and shrugged.

"If she says they're Osage, sir, then they're Osage. I'd bet a month's wages she's not wrong."

"But what would they want from us?" McReynolds asked.

This time it was Twobirds who shrugged her shoulders.

"We will know soon," she said.

As the party drew near, McReynolds joined Sheets at the wagon. It was the first time he'd seen Indians, besides Twobirds and On-da that is, the first time in broad daylight and approaching larger than life.

There were but ten or twelve of them and they rode with grace and stealth, their horses dancing, their bows about their shoulders, their muscles rippling in the afternoon heat. Led behind them was a string of horses and mules.

"By God!" Sheets said, surprise on his face, "will you look at that. They're bringing our horses back. Who would have thought those bloody savages would be bringing back our stock."

The party stopped just beyond the wagons. The leader of the party grinned, holding up his hand as if in peace. Sheets motioned for Twobirds.

"Can you understand them?" he asked.

"Some, for trade, but little more," she said.

"Well, ask him who he is and what he wants."

Head down, eyes averted, Twobirds spoke slowly and precisely.

The leader rode forward, scanning the soldiers, noting every detail with his black and piercing eyes. A savage scar began in his hairline and ran across one eye, causing the eyelid to droop curiously.

When he answered, he did so directly to Sheets.

After he was finished, Twobirds began a halting translation.

"He says his name is To,wan,ga,ha and that he smelled the buffalo cooking and came to join us for dinner, which is the custom of all who come to the Grand Saline. He says that he has horses and mules to trade for buffalo meat, that they are fine horses and are only scarred a little."

"By God, the audacity," Sheets said. "Those are our stock, stolen last night, and those are our brands, not scars."

"It is but a small matter," Twobirds said, looking at McReynolds, "and not worth your lives."

"She's right, Lieutenant. Share the meat."

"But that's our stock," Sheets said. "They want to sell our horses back to us."

"Guess that's not the way they see it," McReynolds said. "Once they stole those horses, they were no longer yours but theirs."

"All right," Sheets said to Twobirds, "tell them they are welcome to our camp and that they should help themselves to supper. We will talk then about the horses."

To,wan,ga,ha grinned again and motioned for his warriors to move into camp. Without further encouragement they gathered about the fire and ate, discarding the bones and scraps over their shoulders and taking long pulls from the soldiers' canteens. Watching Renfro, To,wan,ga,ha spoke to Sheets.

"He wants to know if the one tied up is a crazy man." Twobirds interpreted.

"Tell him that it is so," Sheets said, looking at Renfro, "that this one tried to kill the chief and must now be punished. Tell him that to kill a white chief is a very serious matter." Twobirds translated, and To,wan,ga,ha responded with a smile.

"He says that the white people must have many crazy men, like the one they saw on the salt yesterday with bags over his shoulders and without clothes, chasing a sand rat. His toe stuck out like a bird's and he was crazy in the eyes."

To,wan,ga,ha looked at his warriors and said something in a deep guttural voice. They all nodded their heads in agreement.

"What did he say?" Sheets demanded.

"It is nothing," said Twobirds.

"I want to know exactly what they're saying," he said.

"That the naked crazy man had little to offer his squaws anyway."

"Yes, well," Sheets cleared his throat, "he was a poor soldier, letting someone steal our horses right out from under our noses, an awfully lot like the horses you have there in fact."

"To,wan,ga,ha says they are fine horses and that he will trade them for the buffalo meat in the wagons, that his people have many horses and that they will sacrifice these for the white man who is so brave to come to the Grand Saline."

Walking to the horses, Sheets looked at the U.S. Army brand on their hips.

"Tell him I will trade half the meat for the horses and will expect no more visits from his warriors in the night."

"He wants to know if you have a medicine man." Twobirds said.

"Tell him that's exactly what we have, a medicine man."

"He says his camp is less than a day's ride from here and that many of his people were very ill when the hunting party left eight days ago, that they had many sores on their bodies. He wants the squaw and the medicine man to ride ahead with them in the morning."

"Tell him we'll send the medicine man and the squaw, that we'll also send the medicine man's nurse and that we'll be along in a couple of days. Tell him also that he is to leave his best warrior to guide us and to make certain that our medicine man comes to no harm. Tell him we will give him one-third of the meat and the medicine man's services for the horses."

To,wan,ga,ha nodded his approval and turned satisfied to his supper.

"Knew your medical learning would come in handy sooner or later, sir," Renfro winked at McReynolds.

"Yeah, thanks," McReynolds said. "Riding off with an Osage hunting party is just what I've been wanting to do."

When To,wan,ga,ha had finished his meal, he dispatched his

warriors to pitch camp just beyond the tree and they too built a small fire. When this was done, To,wan,ga,ha returned and motioned for Sheets and McReynolds to come. Twobirds followed a few steps behind to interpret.

They'd walked only a few yards when To,wan,ga,ha stopped, squatting on his haunches. With cupped hand he began sweeping the salt into a heap as he talked in a slow and guttural tone.

"For our people," he said, scraping at the salt without looking up, "the tree that grows from the salt is a sacred place. It is a place where life springs from death and it is here that the grandfather of our people lives forever. It is here that life and death are one like the big cedar."

Fanning at the salt with the edge of his hand, he swept away the finest grains, and then, there before them the bloodless face of antiquity, the dehydrated remains of an ancient and primal man, mummified so completely as to be the envy of the most opulent and powerful pharaoh.

Around its neck was a tarnished silver crest of Spanish origin, an eagle lifting into the sky, prey dangling from its talons. It was, even to the untrained eye, an exquisite piece of art. Perhaps Coronado had in fact preceded them to this very place.

"By God," Sheets exclaimed, "will you look at that. Looks like he could've died yesterday."

To,wan,ga,ha pushed the salt back over the pallid stare of the dead warrior.

"It is as I say," he nodded. "Our grandfather lives here forever like the cedar." The look on To,wan,ga,ha's face hardened and his eyes cooled in the fading sunlight. "I show you this because it is a place of great importance and no man must disturb it. No man."

"Yes, well," Sheets said, "we have no intention of digging up your grandfather, no intention at all. We'll just be on our way as soon as possible. Our mission is to return this poor girl to her people with haste."

Rising, To,wan,ga,ha nodded his head, and walked into the darkness toward his camp.

Twenty-six

The Osage band moved as one, tirelessly forward until they exited the Grand Saline and at last watered their horses at a small stream. Running red with iron, the water smelled of mud and frogs.

Without dismounting, they watered their horses, pushing west once again even before they were filled. By midday they'd traveled more miles than the expedition would normally cover in two full days. Weariness knotted between McReynolds's shoulders, and his crotch burned from the pummeling of the saddle.

Following behind the band was Twobirds on an army horse, leading the mule that carried Nurse Cromley, who had agreed to come, or more accurately, had failed to refuse. Clinging to her saddle horn, she bobbed against the rough trek and the uncoupling gait of her mule.

By afternoon the Grand Saline was far behind, not more than a white haze low on the horizon. As the band topped a small knoll, nestled among the rocks and trees below were half a dozen hide tents. A half-starved camp dog greeted them, yapping at the end of his tether. Beyond that there was no sign of life, only the unnerving silence of the prairie.

"How are you doing?" McReynolds asked, lifting Cromley from her mule.

Dark and brooding eyes watched him from under the blanket, but there was no response.

First off his mount was To,wan,ga,ha, dropping easily onto the ground, ducking into the first tepee. Cold campfires were everywhere, vessels lying empty on their sides, the disturbing absence of life.

Huddled clumps of humanity began to move along the perimeters of the camp, clinging to each other in the brush, their bodies devastated with sores. Like specters from hell they moaned and cried in anguish under the consuming pox.

"Bring my medical bag," McReynolds said to Cromley. Sad round eyes watched him from under the cover. "Get water for them to drink and then clean those lesions," he said, taking hold of her arm. "Do what I say, Nurse, or I'll have you court-martialed for neglect of duty. Do I make myself clear?"

"Yes, Doctor," she said, her eyes tearing.

"Good then. Now, get these people water. They're suffering from dehydration and fever. Twobirds," he said, walking to the edge of the clearing, "you and the others begin a search. They're scattered about like cordwood, and tell To,wan,ga,ha to get those warriors off their horses to help."

"It is not for warriors to work," she said, fear in her eyes.

"Tell him, by God, that if he doesn't help, neither do I."

Looking about at the dying people, To,wan,ga,ha motioned for the warriors to dismount.

Within an hour forty people, mostly women and children, were carried from the surrounding area and laid about the camp, a pitiful lot they were too, some so advanced with the disease that not a single inch of their bodies was left uncorrupted. The children lay limp, too sick to cry, their lips cherry-red from raging fever.

Whenever moved or touched, great care had to be exercised not to tear their ravaged skin. Some lay naked on logs or rocks to cool themselves. When they were moved, sheets of skin remained attached to their makeshift beds. Others lay quietly, their eyes blank with despair and impending death.

"It is all we can find," Twobirds said. "There are others out there but they no longer need our help. There is a small hunting party north, they say, but they have been gone many weeks now. Who knows what's become of them."

Into the dark and cold night they worked, cleaning, sterilizing, soaking the festering scabs, moistening blistered and cracked lips. But it was a hopeless struggle, their medicine sadly lacking against the catastrophic disease. One by one death took them and by midnight nearly a dozen more had died.

Lowering his head in resignation, To,wan,ga,ha signaled for his warriors to follow. On the edge of camp they built a small fire and the beat of a singular and distant drum charged the night and conceded the enigmatic hand of death.

In the face of disaster Nurse Cromley's energy abounded, working into the night, stopping for neither food nor rest. The dying clung to her dress, cried for her touch, begged for her solace and she moved among them undiminished by their pain and privation.

Through the night McReynolds watched her labor, stroking their cheeks, cooling their feverish brows, holding their hands in the throes of death. Their need fulfilled her, completed her, gave reason to her life, and she flourished under the toil.

Two days passed as if an hour, and before all was done, only seven of the camp remained alive. Two of To,wan,ga,ha's warriors also fell ill and the hillside to the south of camp was littered with bodies rolled in blankets. The smell of sickness and death hung in the camp and neither red nor white any longer found the strength to mourn.

It was the creak of the wagon wheel that reached them first, leaning precariously, flopping on its axle, smelling of hot grease and dust. Like guests at a family picnic the expedition rode into camp.

"Looks like your medicine was not so powerful, Doctor," Sheets said as he turned in his saddle.

"We had no vaccine, Lieutenant. Probably didn't matter at this point in any event."

"And where's the good chief, out stealing more horses?"

"Building a funeral pyre. Wouldn't do to leave all these bodies about. Have half the territory infected within a week."

"Well, we'll make camp and move out in the morning."

"But what about these others, Lieutenant?"

Sheets stood in his stirrups, looking about at the pitiful lot. "What about them?"

"We can't just leave them. Without help they have no chance at all."

"Look, Doctor, we've kept our end of the bargain and paid for our horses twice in the process. They can take care of their own from here on out."

"It's your expedition, Lieutenant, but these people don't have a chance without proper attention. Their lives are in your hands."

Sliding from his horse, Sheets walked through the ruin and devastation of the camp and then back to McReynolds.

"As you say, Doctor, it's my expedition. Now I'll take this first tepee for the night since it is obviously unoccupied and we leave first thing in the morning."

Dark clouds gathered on the horizon as the sun set, dust rolling before the storm, burning a brilliant orange. Thunder rumbled in the distance and the smell of rain filled the air.

On the knoll above the camp To,wan,ga,ha and his men lit the mound of wood that had been stacked to burn the bodies. Three times they tried, but each time the flame fluttered and went out, refusing its onerous burden. On the fourth try smoke curled into the night like an ascending spirit.

Soon flames licked and lapped and crackled hungrily at the humanity above. Within moments the fire roared into the darkening sky, the doors to hell open as blackened bodies twisted dervishly in the howling blaze.

Their drums beat the beat of death, a final and lonely salute to those they would never know again. Rain splattered and hissed into the raging fire, lightning crashing about, but none feared it. Already they knew the worst this world had to give.

Morning approached with the smell of smoke and death hanging in the valley as the men gathered in formation, waiting for Sheets. To,wan,ga,ha and his warriors stood about the smoldering fire, the whole of their lives now but ashes at their feet. Dawn lit the quilted clouds, puffed and tucked like pink baby blankets on the horizon.

Horses stomped and complained as cinches were drawn tight. Still chained to the wagon wheel, Renfro drank from Twobirds's canteen, smiling at her from under his hat.

The great pride and strength of To,wan,ga,ha's band was gone as they walked to where the soldiers gathered.

Stepping from the tepee, Sheets's eyes darted about, shoes shining, uniform buttoned and smart, revolver slung low on his hip. Over his shoulder were the saddlebags in which his precious maps were kept.

"Where's Twobirds?" he asked. Standing, Twobirds approached, her eyes cast down. "Tell the chief here that we're moving on now," he said, "that we've big business with the Kiowa and cannot tarry further." To,wan,ga,ha only nodded as the information was translated. "Mount up," Sheets ordered. Suddenly he stopped and turned in a slow, deliberate circle. "Where's Nurse Cromley?"

Ducking from under a tepee flap, Nurse Cromley approached. In her eyes was a light that McReynolds had not seen for many days, and about her neck was the abandoned crucifix.

"I'm here, Lieutenant," she said.

"So I see. Get mounted, Nurse Cromley. We've wasted quite enough time already."

Lifting her chin defiantly, she looked first at McReynolds, then at Sheets.

"I'm not going," she said.

"The hell," Sheets snorted.

"I'm not going, Lieutenant. These people need me. I'm a nurse, you know, and this is my job."

"They'll hang you up by your heels and gut you like a deer

before we clear that knoll," Sheets said, his mouth curling at the corners.

"He's right, Mary," McReynolds said. "It's too dangerous and there's no way to get back."

"I can't let these people just die, not when there's a chance."

"So be it then," Sheets shrugged, "but I refuse to take responsibility for your actions. Is that clear, Nurse Cromley?"

"Clear enough."

"Mary, no," McReynolds said, taking hold of her arm.

"I've made up my mind." She pulled away. "This is where I'm needed."

"Twobirds," Sheets said, whirling about, "tell the chief here that we're leaving our nurse to take care of the children. Tell him this proves the generosity of the U.S. Army, that Nurse Cromley has great medicine to offer his people."

Before Twobirds could reply, Sheets tossed his saddlebags over the rump of his mount. Maps and drawings spilled onto the ground from an untied bag.

An object rolled from the bag, partially exposing its burnished surface and the outstretched wings of an eagle. Recognizing it as the Spanish crest from the mummy's neck, McReynolds's heart froze.

At that very moment To,wan,ga,ha's anguished cry caused the hair on McReynolds's neck to stand erect. Dropping to one knee, To,wan,ga,ha tried to string an arrow from his quiver, but Sheets's side arm exploded point-blank into his face, the bullet exiting in a spray of blood and bone, his big frame toppling forward into the dirt, eyes open, one lid forever stilled in its curious droop.

The morning quiet erupted in a volley of gunfire as the soldiers opened up on the remaining warriors. Beyond the cloud of smoke, Renfro cursed as bodies convulsed on the ground from mortal wounds.

"Mount up," Sheets said, turning to assess the gravity of the situation. "And take their horses too. I think they'll not have much use for them now."

"I'm not going," Nurse Cromley said again, picking grass from her front. "God forgive you, Lieutenant."

"Stay then. What use are you to this expedition, hiding behind your blanket like a frightened kitten?"

"I'm staying, too," McReynolds said.

"That won't be possible." Sheets's eyes narrowed. "We may need you before this expedition is over. Your duty is to these men."

"Go on, Dr. McReynolds," Nurse Cromley said, "I'll be all right here. These people need me. This is the way it must be."

To leave her behind was tantamount to a death sentence and everything in McReynolds resisted. But with Sheets's revolver at his back he had little choice but to ride away, watching her as long as he could, returning her shy wave as they topped the knoll and disappeared from sight.

As they rode west he remembered the way she squeezed shut her eyes when she prayed, the way she had come to him in the storm, her fervor, her passion and spiritual appetite.

In the distance the camp dogs yapped. Mary's decision to stay with the Osage was filled with peril but then so too was traveling with Lieutenant Sheets, and there was naught ahead but his greed and fury and the silver that fed it.

Twenty-seven

The bindings on Renfro's wrists were nearly covered by swollen flesh before McReynolds noticed. While pulling at his canteen, Sheets listened to McReynolds file his complaint. Water dribbled from his chin and he wiped it away with the sleeve of his shirt.

"The bindings stay, Doctor. He's a prisoner and he's dangerous."

"I must protest," McReynolds said, kicking at the wagon wheel with the toe of his boot. "Gangrene could set in and he'd lose those hands. The bindings are too tight."

"Protest then," Sheets sucked at his tooth with indifference, "but the bindings stay." Pushing back his hat, his eyes bore down on McReynolds. "Look, there's no quarter for renegades in this outfit. Any man comes for me better understand that sooner or later he'll pay dearly for his mistake. It's as certain as the stink of mules and the retribution of hell, and every man in this expedition will know it. Do we understand each other?"

"Then at least let me try to clean around them."

"Medical attention is not denied, Doctor, but the bindings stay."

Cleaning the corruption from around the bindings was both painful and slow but Renfro bore it without complaint.

"Can't do much but pray," he said, "with my hands tied together, and can't think of anything to pray for 'cept the slow and deliberate death of my enemies."

"It's a sad day, Corporal, when a man is treated in such a way. It's my full intention to report Lieutenant Sheets for abuse of power when we return to Fort Gibson."

"Well, sir," he said, his eyes flickering with pain, "I appreciate that, but by the time we get back to Fort Gibson, I ain't going to have nothing left here but a couple of ivory stumps, and even praying's going to be out of the question." Turning his wrists, he looked at McReynolds. "Don't suppose you could do something in the meanwhile? How's a man to tie his shoes without hands?"

The sun warmed McReynolds's face as he looked into the blue sky.

"I've got to figure what to do, Corporal. It can't go on this way much longer."

"Yes sir," he said, pulling his knees up and sliding back against the side board, "sure hope you come up with a solution real soon. The lieutenant already took more lives than the entire Indian Nation has, and we ain't turned homeward yet." Bracing himself into the corner of the wagon, he pulled down his hat. "I figure the only thing's keeping me alive is this here busted wagon wheel, and I don't know how many more times I can fix it wrong."

At midday, First Sergeant Lansdown brought down a large buck that was sampling paddle cactus buds, and dressed him out on the spot. Fresh meat would be a welcome relief to the buffalo roasts that had grown prodigious with salt. A twinge of guilt shot through McReynolds as he thought of Nurse Cromley and the fare she would be eating tonight.

By late afternoon the land started to change, an impoverished landscape that bulged and rose and dropped unexpectedly into imposing red canyons. The blood-colored earth throbbed under the sun and turkey buzzards circled high in the sky, their wings warping and furling in the invisible columns of heated air.

Spirits rose from the ancient seabed, hovered among the men, flew above them, watched them from the buzzards' crafty eyes. Each man knew his own mortality and the column tightened in mutual need of humanity.

At the lead was Sheets, his thin legs wrapped about his mount, the anger in his soul riding there on his stooped shoulders. Just behind the supply wagon was Twobirds, the facile thrust of her hips in harmony with her world, a triangle of sweat between her shoulders.

To her right and two lengths behind rode the boy with the crooked pelvis McReynolds had seen at Renfro's punishment, his riding grace distinct from his misshapen walk.

Suddenly Sheets held up his hand to halt the column, standing in his stirrups, pointing westward.

"There," he said excitedly, "there it is."

"There is what?" McReynolds asked, riding up beside Sheets.

"Chimney Rock, by God, just like it says on the map." He looked over at Twobirds, who had ridden up beside them. "There," he turned to Twobirds, "in that direction?"

"Just beyond," she said quietly.

"We'll camp at Chimney Rock tonight," he said.

"It is another day's ride," Twobirds said. "The rock is as large as the distance."

"We'll ride late," he insisted.

"Look at the wagon wheel," Twobirds said, shaking her head. "It must be fixed soon."

The wheel leaned at a distorted angle, axle grease black as tar dripping from the hub.

"Damnation," he fumed, "I'm surrounded by idiots."

"It is only the corporal who can make the wagon right," Twobirds said, looking at Sheets. "He'll have to be freed."

"Over my dead body," he snorted.

The look in Twobirds's eyes left little doubt as to her lack of objection.

"He must be freed if you wish me to lead you farther," she said.

"She's right," McReynolds said, smiling inwardly. "We're going to need him unless you want to leave the supply wagon behind."

"Cut him loose, but understand this: the first wrong move he makes, he's dead." Dismounting, he drew his pistol, checking the chamber. "We'll camp here and repair the wagon. Tomorrow, it's an early start and Chimney Rock by day's end."

Without a word, Twobirds walked directly to the wagon and cut Renfro's bindings.

Winking at her, he examined his wrists.

"I was hoping you'd be interested in saving these here mitts."

His eyes turned to Sheets, who stood at a distance, his hand resting on the butt of his pistol.

"Not now," Twobirds whispered. "There is time. Fix the wagon so that the lieutenant may reach the end of his journey soon."

"For you, wild thing, I'd do anything," he smiled.

With swollen fingers he turned to the task and by the time camp was made the wheel was perfectly straightened.

That night McReynolds cleaned Renfro's wounds and heated the tip of his knife in the campfire until it reddened. With precise and skillful application he seared the wound closed, Renfro whistling quietly all the while. When finished, Renfro grinned and blew on the seared flesh.

"Hope these boys don't get a smell of this cooked meat, Lieutenant, or I might go the way of my molly."

"Too old and gamey," McReynolds said, "even for starving men."

The decision to move out of the officers' tent came suddenly for McReynolds. Perhaps it had been there in the back of his mind all along, the inequity, the injustice, sleeping in the comfort of the tent while others suffered unprotected under the elements. But it was with a certain foreboding that he approached Sheets.

"No," Sheets said. "Officers do not quarter with enlisted."

"There's no such regulation and you know it, not while on expedition." Gathering his gear into his arms, he stood at the tent opening. "I can no longer separate myself like this. Do what you must, but I'm moving out."

Beyond the tent the men laughed with each other and their voices rose in exchange.

Pulling on his boots, Sheets stood, adjusting his side arm.

"All right, Lieutenant, if you're determined to align yourself with them, than that's the way it will be." A gust of wind swept through the tent opening, blowing back the blanket on Sheets's bunk. "I've had my doubts about you from the beginning, McReynolds. You're not officer material, do not understand the exercise of power and leadership. Perhaps sleeping on the ground with the enlisted is just the place for you."

"It's not a matter of aligning myself with anyone, Lieutenant, but a matter of fairness, that's all."

"Go then," he scoffed. "I'll lead this command with or without your help. I stand alone as I always have and require nothing from any man. But know this, McReynolds, your choice has been made and it's final. Don't come crawling back to me for help."

That night McReynolds made his bed in the open with the others.

"Hate to think of you deprived of Lieutenant Sheets's company, sir," Renfro said, "but it's a fine thing you did and every man here knows it, I guess. Just don't put your bed under a tree," he grinned. "Ain't nothing between you and a bird's butt except twenty feet of open air."

Soon the smell of fresh venison cooking on the spit filled the evening. Sitting by the fire, Twobirds crossed her legs and watched Renfro as he rubbed at his swollen hands.

Private Richards, a timid and backward boy, pulled at McReynolds's sleeve.

"Could you come, sir? Private Fielding needs some medical attention."

"Exactly what does he need?"

"I'd rather not exactly say, sir, not in front of the others."

"I'll go with you," Renfro said, brushing the red dirt from the seat of his britches. "Fielding's likely to have done 'bout anything can occur to you."

The two of them followed Richards into a small brake where the horses were tied. Sitting on a rock, head down, arms holding his knees into his chest, was Private Fielding.

"What seems to be the problem?" McReynolds asked, setting his medical bag on the rock.

"I thought I told you the doctor only," Fielding snapped at Richards, pain registering on his face.

"Take it easy, Private," Renfro said, putting his foot up on the rock. "You got a problem, it's Army business. Tell the lieutenant here where you're sick."

"It's that dang mule," he said, standing, half bent with pain. "That one over there with the splotch on his head. He near bit my dong off."

"Bit what off?" McReynolds asked, his brow furrowing.

"Well I'll be dogged," Renfro grinned, "I never heard that one before."

"Well let's see," McReynolds said.

"Oh, no sir," he shook his head, "what with everyone looking on?"

"Guess we've seen one before, Fielding, so stop being so modest."

Opening his britches, he rolled his eyes to the heavens. All three of them, McReynolds, Renfro, and Private Richards, leaned over and scrutinized the damage to Private Fielding's privates. Two enormous teeth marks adorned the swollen and bruised appendage.

"My God, Fielding," McReynolds said in dismay.

Pushing back his hat, a grin pulled at the corners of Renfro's mouth.

"How'd that mule get so close?"

"I was just making water and all of a sudden he took a chomp. It hurt something awful, too."

"Maybe he thought it was an ear of corn or a milkweed stalk. Mules favor milkweed stalk," Renfro said, winking at McReynolds.

"It's sure throbbin', sir, like it might fall off."

"Can you urinate, Fielding?" McReynolds ask.

"I don't know, sir. It hurts too bad to try."

"Well there isn't much I can do here, Fielding. My best advice is to choose more carefully where you relieve yourself. If you have trouble urinating, let me know."

"Yes sir," he said, buttoning his britches.

"Keep an eye out for crazed mules looking for milkweed stalk, boy," Renfro said, slapping him on the back. "You gotta be careful what you share, even with a mule."

As they walked silently back, the campfire winked like a guiding light beyond in darkness. Like old friends they listened to the night sounds and let the silence seal the bond. It was Renfro who finally spoke.

"Ain't it a sight," he said, "the mystery of life? One minute everything's going just hunky dory and the next minute a mule charges over and bites off your dong."

"Good night, Corporal," McReynolds said.

"Good night, sir."

Twenty-eight

Up before dawn, Sheets threatened to tie Renfro's hands and drag him to Chimney Rock if he didn't get things on the move, but he let him ride free on one of the pack mules, and for this McReynolds was grateful.

By noon they'd stopped only long enough to eat cold venison and take water. Chimney Rock rose in the west, its potent outline arching into the deep sky, but the distance was deceptive and another six hours passed before they approached the outcropping.

Every man fell exhausted on the ground to rest, except Sheets who paced the area ordering this and that and being generally disagreeable.

"Ain't it special," Renfro said, lying on his back and looking up the full length of Chimney Rock, "how it reaches straight to the heavens? It's a wondrous place and nothing to explain it but God's touch, I reckon."

Leaning back, McReynolds watched the clouds race past the pinnacle, his head whirling unexpectedly.

"It's a fair sight to be sure, Corporal."

Climbing the embankment, Sheets approached Renfro and McReynolds.

"First light I'm taking out a detachment. I want Twobirds and you two to go along. We're getting close to the Kiowa, I think, and we've got to be certain that we'll not be overpowered."

"No sign of Kiowa, sir," Renfro sat up, scratching at his chin, "not this close to the Osage for certain."

"A detachment, first light, if you please, Corporal."

"Yes sir," Renfro said, "but if you don't mind me asking, why would you want me to go along? Just recently as I recall I was tied like a pig and throwed in the back of the wagon for fear I'd cut your throat."

"You'd still be there if I found it to my liking, Renfro," his hand moved to his pistol, "but we're taking the wagon and the mules and I need a driver."

"I see, sir, but what I don't understand is why you'd need a wagon for a scoutin' party."

"I guess you don't need to understand, Corporal. That's why we have officers, to do your thinking for you."

Spinning on his heel, Sheets headed back down the embankment.

"Seems an odd scoutin' party to me," Renfro said, pulling his hat over his eyes. "Wonder if it ain't possible he's looking for something other than Kiowa."

That night McReynolds seriously questioned his decision to sleep in the open with the troops. It rained, not just a little, nor even a lot. It rained in memory of Noah, a toad-strangler that threatened to wash them all into a gully that foamed and churned with red water. Lightning danced above them and the air filled with electricity. The hair stood erect on their arms and their bodies tingled and tempted the bolts of lightning.

Huddling under his blanket, McReynolds trembled from the cold. It was an unsatisfactory shelter whipping around his neck, cold water racing down his britches. Thunder crashed about in terrifying volleys and in the bursts of lightning they could see Chimney Rock vanishing into the black clouds that boiled above them.

It was dawn before the rain stopped and a chilling northwest wind rushed in from the Rockies and set them to shaking.

Light broke gray, clouds racing across the sky with courses set. The smoldering fire did little to warm McReynolds as he stood in its smoke, cursing the army and the territory and all God's living creatures.

Whistling, Renfro snapped small limbs and lay them across the fire. Soon it began to crackle and its warmth embraced them as they stood around it. What a pitiful and worn lot they were, good for nothing but bait and prey.

Squatting next to the fire, Renfro set the blackened pot on for sage tea.

"Ain't so bad, sir," he said, "least you got a good fire here and a commander that loves you dear."

Holding his blanket to the fire, McReynolds watched the steam rise into the morning cold. Whenever things were at their worst, Renfro's words were like a helping hand lifting him up from the depths.

"Right, Corporal, and a mule driver at my back that smells as if he spent the night in the corral."

The sprigs of sage floated to the top of the cup as Renfro poured the hot water over them.

"It's this here tea, sir, that's what it is. Makes the hair fall right right out of your nose."

Rolling a rock to the edge of the fire, McReynolds sat down, swinging the warmed blanket over his shoulders. Below, Twobirds climbed the hill, a venison roast under her arm. There was never complaint from her lips, not of the heat, nor of misery, nor of the foul and cantankerous men with whom she rode.

"Looks like breakfast coming up the hill, Corporal."

"Yes sir," he said, "bore by the hands of an angel, too."

Together they sipped their tea and watched as Twobirds approached. Without a word she sliced steaks from the roast and skewed them on a stick. Soon the smell of cooking meat filled the air.

At the bottom of the hill the other men stirred, coming from under their blankets like caterpillars from their cocoons.

"He'll be here soon," Twobirds said.

"That he will, and we're off to the strangest scoutin' I ever did," Renfro said, scraping at the red mud that clung to the bottom of his boot. "Never heard of taking no wagon on a detachment, not for a quick out at least. Not that I mind going for a ride and seeing the country and all, but guess I'd feel better if I was armed, in case we ran into trouble. I ain't got that much confidence in the lieutenant's shooting skills nor yours either, sir, if you don't mind me saying so."

"Can't understand why," McReynolds smiled.

There was little time to consider it further because Sheets climbed the hill once again.

"Time to move out, and no need for provisions. We'll not be going out that far." Walking over to Renfro, he draped his hand over the butt of his side arm. "You ride in the wagon with the doctor, Corporal. The squaw will ride with me." When there was no reaction from Renfro, he leaned close to his face. "And don't try any of your clever stuff. You're still under arrest and I'm within my rights to use this weapon if I need."

"Yes sir," Renfro said, "I guess you'd do just that, but what I can't figure, sir, is why you'd take a wagon."

"I owe you no explanations, Corporal, but I've sound evidence that the bodies of a lost trading party are within a day's ride. I think it's my duty both as an officer and as a citizen to recover those souls, to let their families bring to an end their uncertainty and to recover any valuables for the U.S. government. It's our business to let the savages that killed them know that we take care of our own. Now, I know you might find that difficult to understand, Corporal, but then that's why I'm in charge, isn't it?"

"Yes sir, guess that's true enough, and I can't tell you how keen I am about your patriotism and caring nature, sir. I guess I'd be the first to recognize the ignorance of the rank and file too, sir, what with their sleeping on the cold ground like common animals and carrying bags of shot in the hot sun, and stickin' their dongs up mule noses like they got no sense what God spared them."

"Yes, well," Sheets looked at him puzzled, "just see you keep

that wagon coming along, Corporal. Might need it to carry back
evidence of this crime on nature."

"Wouldn't be for the valuables, sir, like silver or gold or
such?"

"Now how would I know that, Corporal, and even if there
is, it's our duty to see it recovered."

"Yes sir, that's what I had figured."

"Be ready within the half hour. It's past late for starting already."

"Just one other thing," Renfro said, stepping forward.

"What's that, Corporal?"

"Seems I recall it raining some last night. Every creek's going
to be belly full and the ground's got no bottom. I'd think a day
or two wait would make things a tad easier."

"You're right about the rank and file, Corporal. They've got
no taste for the challenge. Now, get ready to move out."

The camp had no sooner disappeared from sight than the
grass thinned and the terrain turned to a red and barren flat
nearly void of all vegetation. There was no cactus, no mesquite,
not even the invincible sage and the soil was a red clay, a slick
and greasy goo that built up on the wagon wheels, causing them
to slide forward into the mules' heels.

From over his shoulder Sheets watched as the wagon fell
farther and farther behind, his hands lifted above his head in
frustration.

By mid afternoon the sun broke and steam rose from the
saturated earth, a sweltering and suffocating vapor pressing
down on them. Perspiration dripped from the ends of their noses
and the mules frothed between their legs and under their tails
as they pulled the mud-laden supply wagon.

As they climbed from the flat onto a higher plain where the
air was clearer and brighter, Renfro pulled the team to a halt.

"Why are you stopping?" McReynolds asked.

"For a spell, sir. Ain't right to work animals like this without
a spell."

"Well, here he comes, Corporal," McReynolds said, as Sheets headed toward them full gallop.

Holding the reins between his legs, Renfro waited, watching from under the brim of his hat.

"Ain't it so, and with full head like there's no tomorrow."

The front feet of Sheets's horse plowed furrows in the mud as it tried to stop. From a distance Twobirds watched, a yellow band the color of a canary around her hair.

"What?" Sheets screamed.

"Just spellin'," Renfro said, not looking up. "Can't be working animals all day without a spell."

"Move out now, Corporal," he ordered. "You think the Army's got time to set around here all afternoon for your spelling?"

"They'll be ready in ten minutes or so, sir. Mules don't take as much spellin' as horses, but what they got coming they aim to take and they ain't got much concern here nor there for bars on your shoulders or a pistol on your hip."

In exasperation Sheets threw his hands in the air, mounted his horse, and rode back to where Twobirds waited.

When the full ten minutes were up, and then some, McReynolds thought, Renfro snapped the reins and the wagon was on its way once again.

The going was easier as they left the red mud behind and rode into a sea of tightly knit buffalo grass. In the distance Chimney Rock was still visible and a comfort somehow. Two hours they rode without stopping, making good time across the plateau, then Twobirds suddenly held up her hand, pointing to a chasm ahead that ripped open the land like a giant scar. Lush trees rose from the bottom of the canyon, their green tops in stark contrast to the brown and nappy buffalo grass. The four of them stood at its edge. Even the mules craned their necks to peer into the gorge.

"This is it?" Sheets asked.

"Halfway down is the cave opening," Twobirds said. "In it you will find the bodies of the traders and the silver you seek."

"Just lying there in a cave. Didn't even know what they had."

"And then you will set him free," she said.

"After we find what we're looking for."

"You striking bargains on my account, Twobirds?" Renfro asked, rubbing at the forehead of his lead mule.

"Yes, Adam," she said, averting her eyes.

It was the first time McReynolds had heard her or anyone else use the corporal's first name.

"Well, you're a fine and generous girl to do such but it takes two for a bargain nearly always."

"Let's go," Sheets said. "We're wasting time."

"I can understand your rush," Renfro said, "all those poor souls to be rescued, but these animals can't go down that trail and they can't be left harnessed to this wagon. They'll have to be unhitched and hobbled up so's they can graze and rest while we're down there scratching around in the dark."

Seeing the futility in rushing Renfro, Sheets shrugged his shoulders and waited while Renfro hobbled the animals. The others searched the canyon wall for torch material. A few yards down the trail they found a bog spring with sufficient cattail for torches and ample cedar resin to fire them, and all too soon they were making their way down the winding path toward the cave.

The entrance was unexpected, an unassuming recess in the canyon wall that most would have passed without notice. Cedar trees clung to the gypsum rock and tangled skunk brush clogged the opening. The only indication of what lay below was the cool air that bled from the cavern like a cold breath from the grave.

The cattails were difficult to light, the night rains having dampened them to the point where only acrid smoke curled from the smoldering ends. Not until they built a fire and dried the cattails did they burn in a satisfactory manner.

A single torch was lit and carried by Twobirds as she began the descent, followed by Sheets, then McReynolds, and finally Renfro. Once through the entrance, the path opened into an imposing chamber that dwarfed the tiny party. Their voices echoed, small, brittle, narrow in the chamber's enormity.

As she worked her way down, Twobirds's torch flickered in the overwhelming darkness.

"How much farther?" Sheets asked.

"Through there," she said, pointing to a small break at the edge of the chamber, "and on to the spring that comes from the heart of the earth."

High above in the carved dome of the cavern came the whir of countless bats, black voices, folded arms, needled teeth, the ceiling alive with twisting, preening bodies. Guano showered about them from the darkness in a soft murmur.

The men watched Twobirds's steps, placed their feet in her tracks as they crept across the chamber floor.

"Here," she said, "this is where we must go."

"We can't go through that," McReynolds said, his throat constricting.

"Sure we can, Lieutenant," Renfro said. "Ain't no more than slipping under the covers."

The narrow breach was two foot square, maybe less, through a million tons of rock within an inch of their faces. Perspiration broke out across McReynolds's upper lip, his stomach knotting, his body separating into a thousand pieces.

"It's not so far," Twobirds said, her torch flickering in her eyes, "the length of two bodies, no more. It is safe. My people have been coming here for generations and the rock has never fallen."

"It's been waiting for a white doctor with big hips," McReynolds said.

"What are we waiting for?" Sheets asked.

Sliding her torch through the hole ahead of her, Twobirds lay flat on her back and squirmed into the cavity, legs disappearing in small, measured increments as she inched from sight.

Next, Sheets followed, his pistol tucked in his belt on his stomach, moving into the passage like a snake, his thin hips and narrow shoulders at last an asset.

And then it was McReynolds's turn, and panic seized him, splitting the length of his body, nerves throbbing, exposed and defenseless for Renfro to see as he steadied himself against the damp wall of the cave.

"I don't think I can go in there," he said at last. "I'm very sorry."

"Yes sir," Renfro said, "know exactly how you feel. Caught my finger in a whiskey bottle once and near tore it off getting it loose. Course, it came right out and weren't but little chance I'd have to wear that whiskey bottle on my finger for the rest my life, but for a split second I was sure convinced otherwise." Leaning over, he looked into the passageway. "That hole there ain't nothing but a hole that has an end to it," he said, motioning for McReynolds to look. "See there, that light at the end. That's Twobirds's torch burning now, and she's through just fine. Ain't nothing to me, sir, if you stay or go, 'cept that Lieutenant Sheets went through and he ain't the man you are."

"Okay, Corporal," he said with bravado, "let's go."

So close was the roof of the passageway that his breath came back to him hot and void of oxygen, squirming, inching forward with no more than the tips of his fingers, the push of his heels, and the compelling need to reach the other end. There was no turning back, a cruel truth, and he prayed for the end of the tunnel or the end of his life, just as long as there was an end.

And then, as if his prayer were answered, the warm and strong hands of Twobirds pulled him free. It was as if the sky had opened and he filled his lungs in relief. Crawling from the passageway, Renfro slapped him on the shoulder.

Another torch was struck, illuminating the walls of a much smaller chamber. The swirl of an ancient river was carved into the alabaster walls, tumerous growths of gypsum sprouting like cauliflowers, vertical slabs of isening glass cleaving the chamber walls, veins rupturing into the supple alabaster flesh, spidery bursts of red like a woman's flush.

"Now where?" Sheets asked, shifting his pistol back to his side.

"This way," she said, pointing to a narrow path that descended in a dizzying spiral.

And so they followed this ancient woman, the three of them, down ever deeper to the core of the cave, to the black tomb of the traders. As they drew closer, Sheets grew anxious, watching Renfro, casting furtive glances over his shoulder, checking the whereabouts of his revolver from time to time.

And when McReynolds thought the descent would never stop, it opened into a room, a cathedral of alabaster, myriad splashes of pink, great chunks of black, white dollops bulging from the earth the color of goose down, and a spell was cast upon them. A pool in the center of the room mirrored the torchlight like a mounted jewel, clear and still.

"Here is the place," Twobirds said, standing at its rim.

"What?" Sheets said, checking the whereabouts of Renfro. "There's no place."

"Down there," she said, walking to the opposite side of the pool, "all that you asked."

Pulling his pistol, Sheets cocked it, the metallic click, invasive, sacrilege.

"Is this some kind of hoax?" he said, his voice frosty.

"There," she said, "the Spaniards and their silver."

Leaning over the rim, Sheets peered into his own reflection.

"You bloody wolf bitch," he cried, "they're fifty feet under water."

In that narrow moment Renfro lunged for the pistol, but Sheets was ready, sidestepping, throwing himself backward from Renfro's reach, fanning the hammer with the butt of his hand in a deafening assault as he fell to the floor of the cavern.

Instinctively Twobirds flung the torch at the blazing muzzle of Sheets's revolver and darkness fell about them as complete and absolute as death itself.

The sound of Corporal Renfro pitching into the frigid pool broke Sheets's cursing, and the hearts of those who waited. Like blind fish they groped in the blackness. Minutes passed, hours it seemed, before the torch flickered to life once again in Sheets's trembling hand.

Ears still ringing, they gathered at the pool's edge and held the torch high, poor Renfro and the silver now lost from sight below the bloodied water.

Some time passed before anyone spoke. When they did, it was the damning voice of Lieutenant Sheets.

"It's a pity," he said, "that he can't be had, because I was figuring on hanging the son of a bitch the minute we got back to Fort Gibson."

The trip out of the cave, the suffocating course beneath the rock, the silent enmity of Twobirds was of a distant and vague memory in McReynolds's mind. Only once did they stop, Twobirds grabbing his arm.

"Did you hear?" she whispered.

They held each other, straining to hear above Sheets's steps from behind.

"Hear what?" McReynolds whispered back.

But she did not answer and it was the sweet and fragrant air of the outside world as they exited the cave that wrenched them into reality.

Sheets had killed Adam Renfro with detachment, a chilling and definitive fact that burned in their minds as they climbed back up to the ridge that day.

Only a Kiowa girl, Lieutenant Sheets, and he, Joseph McReynolds, Assistant Surgeon, remained to lead this ill-fated command into the territory.

Twenty-nine

To what extent Twobirds mourned Renfro's death McReynolds could only surmise, because there was little outward evidence, only a deep and brooding silence as she moved into herself, layer upon layer of silence that drove them all ever farther away.

Even Sheets kept his distance, detecting something volatile in her. Like a hyena stalking its prey, he knew when to fall back, when to wait.

Riding at the back of the column, Twobirds refused food, taking water only when no one was around.

As for McReynolds, Renfro's death was desolating. Not only had he liked and respected him but depended on his pragmatic wisdom more than he dared admit. The prairie was now a more menacing place, a more raw and coarse place in the absence of his friend.

And then there was the never-ending heat, the monotony, the boredom that wore away one's strength and determination. Even the strongest faltered under the tedium.

Like Twobirds, he too turned inward. It was after all the only course, inward into memories, into images, into the past. In his dreams he touched the cool rain on Nurse Cromley's body, heard the pounding feet of On-da, watched the convulsive throes of Renfro's molly. The days were as aimless and empty as the story of his own life, the struggle for recognition, the futile studies, the death of Alison.

A week they rode, twisting and turning like water seeking its level. At night Sheets studied his map, held it to the campfire light, scrutinized its every detail. There was little doubt in anybody's mind, except Sheets's perhaps, that they were irretrievably lost and that only Twobirds could save them.

Their camps were cold and silent affairs, their food supply dwindling quickly. The men avoided Sheets whenever possible, each knowing who was responsible for Renfro's death, although neither McReynolds nor Twobirds had challenged Sheets's version of the incident, a story of innuendo and half truths, a story painting Renfro as a black-hearted aggressor who would have ruined them all if not for Sheets's quick action. No one believed it, not from the start.

That evening they camped within sight of a majestic mesa that rose from the prairie floor, standing alone, thrusting upward from the center of the earth, towering above them with a singular and powerful presence. Turkey buzzards rose and dipped high above the caprock. Here and there great sheets of red earth slipped down the mesa and massive boulders lay tumbled at the bottom from their tumultuous ride.

The moon rose full, a silver night, calming even the prairie winds. In the darkness, his map rolled and clamped under his arm, Sheets sought McReynolds out.

"It's this map," he said, "it's useless. We've got to do something or we will all die among these savages."

"Perhaps if the corporal were still alive," McReynolds's temper flared, "we wouldn't be in such a predicament."

"Perhaps," he said, his fierce eyes glinting in the moonlight, "but it was Renfro who elected to attack an officer. It was his decision, albeit a bad one." Rolling up the map, he slapped his leg with it and then began to pace. "We need a guide," he said, "someone who can get us to the Kiowa. Twobirds could do that if she'd cooperate."

"There's precious little she owes any of us," McReynolds said.

"Yes," he said, ignoring McReynolds's remark, "I always sus-

pected her and Renfro, a handsome woman all right, but stub-
born as those army mules. Well, in any case this expedition
must not be jeopardized by a Kiowa girl." Squinting up at the
moon, he fell silent for a moment before pushing back his hat,
decision made. "I want you to talk to her, McReynolds. I can
see that you have some influence and it is your duty to convince
her to help."

"You shot the one man who could've gotten us out of this,
the one man she happened to love, and now you want her to
save your hide?"

"I don't expect you to understand the difficulties of leadership, Doctor. Your course is quite clear, mine less so. There are
times one must do difficult things for the sake of the command.
Even if you don't feel any loyalty to me as your leader, you
must feel some responsibility for these other poor souls. They
will surely perish if we don't find direction soon."

In the distance an army mule brayed. The mesa was awash
in the moonlight, wisps of clouds racing across the prairie sky,
turning, basking in its glow.

A faraway figure worked its way to the top of the mesa,
climbing, stopping, climbing again. Only Twobirds moved with
such grace and agility.

"I'll try," McReynolds said, "for all of the poor souls who
share this forsaken command."

"Good," he smiled, "good."

Just as the figure reached the summit, McReynolds struck
out. The night was still and tranquil about him as he walked.
Expeditions were clamorous affairs, the perpetual yammer of
men, the complaining, the endless ribbing and vulgarity. A moment of privacy was rare enough indeed, and the pleasure of
solitude had nearly been forgotten by him.

With some uneasiness he began the ascent. Placing his feet
strategically among the rocks, he began an oblique track to the
summit.

Gypsum boulders, pocked and worn from the wind, emitted
the day's heat. Iridescent lizards scurried across the rocks and

grasshoppers vaulted from the tufts of grass, tacking away from his feet as he climbed. Night fell, and below him the campfires flickered like fireflies on the wind, tiny points of light in a vast sea. Stopping for a rest, he leaned against a boulder and let its warmth enter his muscles.

Gasping for breath, he pulled himself to the top of the caprock and lay on his back. Overhead, stars spilled across the sky in a dazzling display.

And then he saw her standing on the highest point of the caprock, her arms lifted to the sky, her black hair shimmering in the light of the moon. A cry rose from her throat, a mournful and anguishing cry like that of the lone coyote, a cry of the damned and meant for no man's ears. Chills raced down McReynolds's back at the deep and unfathomable grief. With trembling hands she tore at her clothes and pulled at her hair.

Spellbound, riveted by what he saw, by the enormity of her agony and the beauty of her body, he watched in fascination. Picking up a jagged rock, she slashed at her arms, stomach, breasts. Again and again she rent her flesh with willful and deliberate slashes, severing the pain that threatened her life, her soul.

Stomach heaving, McReynolds's rushed toward her, to stop her somehow, to stop the destruction and desolation.

"No," he cried, sweeping her into his arms, the warmth of her blood through his shirt, her black eyes searching his face, struggling, incredulous.

"Adam," she sobbed.

"No," he said, lifting her face into the light, "It's Dr. McReynolds. You must stop this, you hear? You must not do this."

"Why are you here?" she cried, pushing him away. "Why have you followed me?"

"I didn't follow you," he said, pulling her torn blouse about her. "I mean, I didn't come up here with the intention of intruding, but I'm glad I did. What would you have done?" Pushing her hair from her face, Twobirds sat down on the rock, pulling her knees into her arms, and did not answer. "I really didn't mean to intrude. I'm sorry."

"Why then are you here?" she asked.

"Sheets asked me to come."

"He's lost and wants my help," she said, her voice hardening.

"Quite lost, I'm afraid."

"Yes, for many days now we have circled the prairie like buzzards searching for the dead. Hatred lives in your lieutenant's heart and evil burns from his eyes like the viper and each night I cry to spill his belly onto the ground." Rocking to and fro, she moaned and held her face between her hands. "Soon enough the ants will shine his bones."

"And the others as well, Twobirds, including me, if we are not helped."

"The hatred smothers me," she said, burying her bloody hands in her lap. "I don't know if I can do this thing that you ask."

"You must understand that we're not all Lieutenant Sheets, no more than you are all of your people. I miss Adam too and want his death avenged, but we're all condemned without your help."

Below, the red glow of the campfires was barely visible now.

"You were Adam's friend," she said, "helping him when he was punished by the lieutenant. I wish no harm for you. What is it that you want from me?"

"To get us to your people and then to obtain a guide so that we may get back to the fort."

"But it is you who are returning me to my people."

"I know," he said, "ridiculous, isn't it."

"It is the silver he wants," she said. "He will be back with others."

"I plan to file a complaint in hopes of a court-martial when we return. The others will support me I'm certain."

"The Kiowa will not enter the Cross Timbers. You must go alone from there."

"You get us to the Cross Timbers," he said, stepping to her

side, "and I'll ask no more of you. And you have my solemn promise that Sheets will get his due."

"I do it for Adam and for you, his friend. Only for Adam and for you," she said, dropping to her hands and slipping over the edge of the caprock.

Within a day all had changed. Not only had they spotted game, but First Sergeant Lansdown had brought down a bull buffalo nearly seven feet high. Gorging themselves in celebration, they gathered about Twobirds, patting her on the back, carrying sage tea to her, all knowing full well that it was her keen instincts that had made it happen.

With the aid of her cunning sense of direction, no longer did they find themselves wandering aimlessly, backtracking, or fording the same stream several times in a single day.

Even Twobirds's spirit lightened and she began to talk to McReynolds as they rode at the head of the column, her conversation satisfying and wise, filling a need within him left by Renfro's death. There were times when her English failed and she would shrug her shoulders and smile.

Three days passed as they moved west, due west into the sun. The landscape changed, deepening into a rust color with a decided thinning of mesquite. Small barrel cactus bubbled from rock crevices while magenta blossoms sprung like trumpets from their tops and black and gold bumblebees hummed about them. The heat was numbing but they moved ever forward because there was no retreat now, no turning back.

Riding ahead of the expedition, Twobirds and McReynolds scouted the best passage. An hour out, they tied their horses under the sparse shade of a mesquite while Twobirds surveyed the area. Satisfied with her decision, she turned to him.

"There is something I must say."

Leaning against his horse, McReynolds slung his arms over the saddle and watched a hawk skim the landscape.

"And what might that be, Twobirds?"

"I think your Nurse Cromley is dead," she said, her eyes clear and black as obsidian.

"You don't know this," he said, his heart stalling, starting again.

"It must be," she said, untying the reins of her horse.

"Why do you say this thing, Twobirds?"

"You must not hold the dead in your heart. The Kiowa know this. The living must grieve until there is nothing left but life."

"But she stayed to help. They will take care of her."

"She was nothing to them," she said, mounting her horse.

"She shouldn't have stayed," he said. "I should have insisted that she come."

"Your woman was brave in her way and she loved her gods, but she was foolish." Hooking her toe in the stirrup, Twobirds mounted her horse. "Like the butterfly, the foolish live but a day in this land."

Reining her horse toward the column, she kicked it into a gallop as McReynolds watched her move into the horizon, her black hair surging with the rise and fall of her horse.

There was no certainty of what she said, no way anyone could know Mary's fate.

Mounting his own horse, he kicked him into a canter, wiping away the salty taste of blood from his lip with the sleeve of his shirt.

Thirty

For two days they rode, making slow progress in the oppressive heat. On the third day they came upon a river, the far bank barely visible across the vast expanse of the bed, a thin sheet of water moving imperceptibly down its center. It was too salty to drink and smelled of gypsum.

Studying his map, Sheets concluded that it must be the Cimarron or the Salt Fork or maybe the upper reaches of the White Horse, he couldn't be sure. Bemused, Twobirds shrugged at Sheets's need to study a piece of paper at everything he came across.

They followed the river south, making time across the flat terrain, but by late afternoon they found themselves in bald dunes that rolled across the horizon like a great tidal wave.

Wagons bogged into the bottomless sand, horses lunging again and again against its hold, but the sand poured from above, ever down over itself and over the wheels of the wagon. Like water it pooled about them and sucked at their legs.

Soon enough the horses were jaded, heads down, nostrils flaring as they gasped for air. Nothing grew in the sand but an occasional sprig of river grass, leaves so wiry that even the grasshoppers left it untouched. The tenacious grass clung to life on the northern side of the dunes, sharp green blades capable of slashing one's skin.

Rivulets of sand sped from Sheets's heels in a downward rush as he pawed his way to the top of the dune. Perspiration beaded on his forehead and dripped from the end of his nose as he took off his hat and turned like a weather vane on a calm day.

"Now what," he said, "the bloody desert?"

Resting in the shade of the wagon, Twobirds spoke without looking at Sheets.

"It is but the ancient bed of the river," she said, "left here as it moved westward toward the mesas. The distance is not great." Lifting a handful of the sand, she poured it through her fingers into a golden mound. Left in her palm were the bleached fragments of tiny water snails. "See," she said, "the water once passed this way."

"And where are your people? Where are the mighty Kiowa now?"

"I cannot know where they are," she said, blowing the sand from her palm. "I can only know where they have been. It is the custom to come to this river at this time. The plums will soon ripen and the buffalo move south through the great flat. There is food to be found and the winds blow up the riverbed. It is where my people have come for the Sun Dance and perhaps they will come again."

"Your people, your people," he said, "wandering around this godforsaken country without maps, without calendars, without the slightest notion of where they are going or what they are going to do. How they've managed to survive, I'll never know."

"It is not my people who are lost," she said, her hands clenched. "And we had calendars even before the white man. It was the warrior Anko who made the Kiowa calendar. It does not keep the days as your calendar, but what do the days matter? Days do not make lives."

In disdain Sheets threw his head back and laughed. When he turned to leave, Twobirds stood.

"Sheets!" she said, her voice filled with the hatred and bitterness that had accrued over the weeks.

"What is it, squaw?" Sheets said, dropping his hand to his revolver.

"I'm not a squaw," she said, "and you will never speak of my people in this way again."

"Or?"

"Or I'll let you starve," she said, "until you crawl on your belly in search of insects, until you eat the blades of grass and your bowels drop into the sand, until the salt turns your water to blood and your life passes from between your fingers."

"What happens to us, happens to you . . ." He started to say *squaw*, but changed his mind.

"Yes," she said, "and it will be so."

"Get these wagons moving," he ordered, but said not a word to Twobirds as he stomped past her.

As Twobirds had said, the sand was but a short distance, and by late afternoon they stepped onto solid earth once again. From a seep in a red bank Twobirds collected water while the men hand-cut pigweed for the horses, now nearly too exhausted to graze. Rubbing the froth from their backs with burlap, they hugged their great strong necks in respect.

With instructions from the men to guard against mules looking for milkweed stalk, Private Fielding was assigned watch over the animals. Tending the fires as usual was Twobirds, and soon the winds fell silent for the evening. Mourning doves cooed from the sunset and quieted the souls of all.

Searching out McReynolds, Twobirds lay her bed next to his, having drawn closer to him since Renfro's death, riding often at his side, eating her meals next to him in silence.

It was with some consternation and guilt that he found this development pleasurable, her strong brown arms, her back like a finely carved violin.

"Twobirds," he said.

"Yes."

"Did you mean what you said to Sheets?"

Drawing her skirt above her knees, she crossed her legs, a fine and strong thigh, the beauty of her body causing him to look away.

"Yes," she said, leaning forward until her elbows rested on

her knees, the weight of her breasts, the curve of her throat, the chiseled cut of her chin. "I cannot let my people be shamed by him."

Kneeling at her side, he could smell the salt of her skin and feel the heat of her body.

"He's afraid of you."

"Fear burns within him like the prairie fire until there is nothing left but his own dark spirit. This he fears the most."

Touching her hair, his fingers tingled and she reached for his hand, cool and gentle against his skin.

"Come with me," she said. "There is a place I want you to see."

A path worn deep by the hooves of buffalo twisted along the banks of the river. The sun lay low on the horizon, their shadows following in the dusk behind them. In the distance the laughter of the men rose and the smell of smoke drifted on the breeze. Soon the sun dropped below the horizon and all grew quiet except the sound of their feet along the path, the zing of crickets, the distant yip of coyotes.

At the water's edge, a rock jutted over the embankment, flat and worn by the wind, white from the gypsum, warmed from the day's heat. Below them the river slipped past and the moon rose above and soon the river shimmered in its light.

"This is a beautiful place," he said.

"Yes," she said. "I came here often as a child."

Looking out onto the water, he smiled. For some reason he had not thought of her as a child, not out here like this.

"A lonely place for a child."

"Of all that I ever felt here, Joseph, it was never loneliness."

His name fell sweet from her lips and he touched her hand as she leaned into him, her shoulder against his. From somewhere in the salt sage along the river's edge, an owl hooted in soft and muted tones.

"I'm sorry for what they did to you, Twobirds, for what they did to Adam. Maybe there was something that I could've done. Maybe I could've been more courageous."

"Do not speak the names of the dead," she said, touching his lips. "They are no longer of our world and do not want to be bothered by us."

Pulling her into his arms, he searched hungrily for her mouth, her black hair like a velvet curtain between them and the uncharitable world beyond.

Holding her face between his hands, he kissed her eyes, the upturned corners of her mouth, the golden crest of her throat, a moan emanating from deep within her, passion, love, grief, neither knowing nor caring as the boundaries fell away.

With trembling fingers he unfastened her blouse and lay her back on the warmth of the rock, the heave and fall of her breasts, the smell of the desert night, the salacious lift of her hips as he traced the mound of her stomach and lay his head in the crevice of her thigh.

As the moon rose over his shoulder, its silver light warmed her face.

"Are you certain?" he asked, knowing that at that moment there was nothing that could stop him, not the memory of his wife nor the spirit of Nurse Cromley nor the friendship of Adam Renfro. This wild and beautiful creature was to be his, to fill her with his love, to take from her a small part of what she was.

With strong hands she guided him, touching, leading him as from the beginning, her raven eyes radiant, seductive.

All that was soft and gentle and loving was surrendered as he flew in anguish to the mesa tops, to drive away the deep suffering of the living for the dead. And she took this to herself, shuddering under his passion, his pain flooding her, drowning her in its profusion.

Afterward, they lay in each other's arms, the night deepening as the moon climbed high into the sky. They had loved when all was against it and it had changed them.

A new world was created between them, a world that was neither his nor hers, an imperiled world even in its infancy because soon Twobirds would be reunited with her own people. All that was familiar and welcome would be alien to him. And all that was splendid and worthy about this night would be acceptable to no man.

But for now they clung to each other, them against the world, and waited for dawn and the dangers that lay beyond.

Thirty-one

For three days they worked their way down the river without a sign of the Kiowa. The going was slow, complicated by winding tributaries feeding into the river like veins into a body, small but deep enough to snare a passing wagon wheel.

Each time it happened there was a frustrating search for bridging material, the rounding up of all hands to heave against the wagon until it was freed, maddening work souring everyone's temperament.

Large game disappeared altogether but there were ample quail that squatted beneath the clumps of sage along the river's edge, their tiny tracks a dead giveaway. The men stalked them with the intensity of hunting buffalo, with deafening volleys as they potshot into the tangled underbrush, often little but feathers and beaks remaining from the massive assault.

As he studied his infernal maps, now little more than tattered rags, Sheets questioned Twobirds about their course, how much farther, how many warriors, how far from the cave of silver?

"A few more days," she said.

"And what if it isn't a few more days?" he said, flinging his map to the ground.

"Then there is only forward. The days are beginning to shorten," she said, holding her hand over her eyes to examine the position of the sun. "The Kiowa will begin moving soon toward the mountains of the eagles. It is warmer there for the winter and in the great rocks are many caves for protection from the winds." She paused. "But it is ever farther from the cave of silver."

"Perhaps we'll return to the fort without having found your people. Perhaps you'll never see your people again," he said.

"Your commander wishes otherwise. Without my return the Kiowa will never welcome the tribes from the east. Neither you nor your commander will be honored by your people. Your failure will be carved in the stone that marks your grave."

"Mount up," he said.

Just as Twobirds predicted, the weather took a decided turn, nights cooler, mornings crisp, the smell of fall in the air. The cool was a welcome relief from the relentless heat, but all knew, including Sheets, that to be caught on the plain by winter would spell disaster. Without feed for their horses and supplies for themselves, they would all perish.

The river swept eastward, bounded on the west by vertical red cliffs, columns rising from the river like gothic cathedrals.

Dwarfed by the immensity of the landscape, the men made their way along the base of the cliffs and the water's edge, a tiny procession, single file and silent. Small caves watched with sunken eyes from the crest line, some deep, some shallow, some too foreboding to look, swept smooth by floods, rounded and slick from churning waters.

At first McReynolds thought it was a bird, a killdeer faking an injury to distract them from its nest, but then he was not certain.

Reining up, he let the others pass, listening again.

"What is it?" Twobirds asked, riding back to where he waited.

"I heard a cry."

"Where?"

"Up there, I think," he said, dismounting, pointing to the shallow cave above them.

"It is not our business," she said. "Let's go before we are missed."

"No, no," he shook his head, "there is someone up there, I'm sure of it."

Without waiting, he began to climb, picking his way through the rocks, cognizant of the irritable rattlers who often sunned themselves in such places. Nearly to the cave, he turned to find Twobirds making her way behind him.

On hands and knees he leaned into the entrance of the small cave.

"Hello?" he called.

"There is no one," she said, touching his arm. "We should catch up with the others."

Then it came again, a cry just as he'd thought, and his heart quickened.

"There," he said, "someone's in there. I'm going in."

"No, Joseph," she said, gripping his arm, "this is a place for the dying. There is nothing to be done here."

Angered at her indifference, he pulled his arm away.

"That's ridiculous. If there's someone in there who needs help, I intend to give it to him." Waiting for his eyes to adjust to the dark, he moved into the cave. In the far corner lay a bundle of rags, something or someone huddled against the wall, a figure that he couldn't quite make out. "There's someone here," he said.

"No, Joseph. Please come now."

"How can you say that?" his temper flared. "Do you think I'm just going to walk away without knowing who it is, without trying to help? That's not the way it is, Twobirds, not in the civilized world."

"I know who it is, Joseph. Please come now."

Pushing her away, McReynolds reached for the bundle. A small shriveled hand grasped his as he opened the blanket. An Indian woman looked up at him, face so swollen and distorted that it was difficult to tell her age, in her eyes a flicker of recognition.

"My God," he whispered, "who is she?"

"She is Kiowa, a 'throwaway wife,' and her name no longer matters. I knew her as a child."

Turning the old woman's head, McReynolds examined her as

best he could in the darkness of the cave. Pus drained from her ear, the swelling extending into her jaw and under her eye, probably an abscessed tooth, or had begun that way. Now much of the jaw was putrefied and the infection raged throughout her body.

"A throwaway wife? What does that mean?"

"She is dying," she said, folding her arms, "as you see. The people must not be stopped from their journey south, so her husband has thrown her away."

The old woman's emaciated body was fouled from waste and her bones protruded through her skin.

"What kind of people would do such a thing?" he asked.

"She is dying."

"In all likelihood, yes, but that doesn't give anyone the right to just throw her away."

"If the people wait for her, they too might die. The people cannot wait for the sick. It is the way of all creatures. The Kiowa know that a man alone is small and weak and will soon perish, but together the people are as a giant with great strength. It is only together that the Kiowa survive." Turning her back to the old woman, she looked down on the river below. "It is a lesson your Lieutenant Sheets has not learned, and someday it will cost him his life," she turned, "and perhaps your own life as well. You see how foolish it is to believe that my return will make a difference."

"Well, it's not my way and I'll not be a party to it. I'm a doctor sworn to help the sick no matter what." Resignation in her eyes, Twobirds started to leave when McReynolds grabbed her arm. "What if it were me in here, or you?"

"It would be the same," she said, pushing her hair from her face, studying him in the turbid light, "for me or for you. It is not your right or hers to endanger the people. This she knows. It is you who make it harder."

"I can't leave her here to just die, without even water to drink."

"Among my people it is not for a woman to make a man's decision. You will do what you must."

With great effort the Indian woman lifted her hand, pointing to the entrance, motioning for him to leave with Twobirds.

"No," he said, "I'm staying. Tell Sheets I'll catch up later."

"Don't die as your woman did, Joseph, for something you don't understand. There are reasons for the ways of the Kiowa. Here it is life and death that rule, not the words of men."

And then she was gone, the sound of her footsteps disappearing down the embankment.

Doubt swept him. What if he were unable to find the company on his own? The old woman was dying, wanted to die, and there was precious little he could do to stop it in any case.

What if the Kiowa came back and found him here alone, and what about Sheets? There could be punishment, perhaps even desertion charges or bags of shot.

For awhile he waited for Twobirds's return, listened for her steps climbing up the embankment, but as the sun dropped and the cave darkened, the full impact of his situation came home. If nothing else, Twobirds was practical, her decisions being based on reality. She would not be back. The likelihood of Sheets backtracking was equally doubtful. There was little to gain and much to lose and Sheets always played his own game.

Martialing his courage, McReynolds searched the steep embankment for wood. There was precious little to be found, only the decayed stump of a red cedar that had fallen from the top of the canyon. Breaking it into pieces, he built a small fire.

With sad and curious eyes the Indian woman watched, bearing with valiance what had to be excruciating pain. Even cleaning the wound turned out to be impossible and so he settled for covering her as best he could, moving her close to the fire for warmth.

As night fell the tiny fire flickered, illuminating little more than the arched entrance of the cave itself. Soon her fever soared and she trembled under her bundle of blankets.

Water dribbled from her lips and into her blanket as he tipped his canteen for her to drink. In the dim light he could see her rugged beauty and wondered of the husband who had left her to die alone in this place.

Once she spoke a name and then turned her face to the wall in silence.

The night deepened beyond the cave, no stars or moonlight to comfort them, dark clouds draping the sky like a shroud. The pungent smell of damp earth rose from the river below, the stench of death and loneliness.

The dampness moved along the floor of the little cave, swirling about them, clutching their bodies with its cold fingers, beyond, the river slinking and withering in the silent darkness, filling the canyon, rushing the cave in a suffocating torrent.

Stoking the fire, he drew a deep breath and shook it off.

And then he heard them high above on the cliff, the thin yelp of the coyote bitches as they gathered at the cliff's edge, their noses skimming the ground, their tails curled over their backs. The hair on his neck crawled and he pulled his knees into his chest. "God's dogs," Twobirds called them, knew the future, she said. Tonight they sensed death, of that he was certain.

Adding the last of the wood to the fire, McReynolds rested, the old woman moaning, eyes searching, reaching for unseen spirits, the hand of death.

Once more he stirred the fire, mopping the perspiration from her forehead. There was too little wood and it burned too quickly, but for now at least death was at bay.

Placing his back against the wall, he fell into a fitful sleep, of running, of cold steel, of intestines stringing in the dirt.

Trembling, he awoke, perspiration beading across his forehead. The dying coals sputtered against the darkness as he stretched the ache from his legs, pushing his back against the cold wall of the cave, sleeping again, beyond the dreams and time. Sitting upright, he groped his way in the darkness, his heart pounding in the pitch dark of the cave, smoke from the dying fire burning his nostrils.

Listening for the breathing of the old woman, his own anxious gulps rebounded in his ears. If only there was a sound, even the yap of the coyote, waiting for it, wishing for it, but there was only the silence and the loneliness of the vast prairie.

Perhaps she'd died while he slept or perhaps the Kiowa came in the night and stole her away. Perhaps it was nothing, his imagination running amuck in the darkness, like a kid having a bad dream in the middle of the night.

Rocking to and fro, he wrapped his arms about himself, infantile and paralyzed in his isolation, searching for the courage he needed. Rising at last, he made his way along the icy wall of the cave toward the entrance and the evils beyond.

Dawn broke on the horizon, a pale and cold dawn the color of water and blood, a thin fog drifting over the river below.

About his feet were a thousand tracks and the horrifying reality of the night's course, the events unfolding before him, the splatters of blood, the trampled grass leading into the rocks below, the gamy smell of butchery.

With dread he peered into the bloodied rags that lay scattered among the rocks, the shined and delicate bones of the Indian woman, his own soul giving way to the terrible forces about him, crushed by the inhumanity and the courage of her silence as the coyotes had stripped away her flesh.

With the evil at his back, McReynolds hurled down the embankment and ran southward, river mud sucking at his feet, heart thundering in his ears, his own cries of anguish dwarfed in the measureless prairie.

Once the column left the river, he would be lost, as forsaken and hopeless as the bones back there among the rocks.

With lungs aching he ran on, just penance for the suffering his ignorance had caused.

Thirty-two

"Not two miles up river from here," Richards said, as Sheets circled the morning campfire, "huddled down in a ravine like a covey of quail. There must be a hundret or so, sir. I smelled their morning fire first and crept up over the ridge and there they was. My heart near flopped out of my chest."

Sipping at the steaming coffee, McReynolds tried to steady his hand. Fate and Sheets's decision for an early camp had saved him. In their weariness the column had stopped less than a mile upstream and no one had even missed him. He'd simply walked into camp at dawn's break without a stir. Never again did he want to be alone.

From the periphery, Twobirds looked on, her chin set at the news Richards was breaking. Not yet ready to face Twobirds, McReynolds moved closer to the fire to drive away the chill.

"Are you sure they're Kiowa?" Sheets asked.

"No sir," Richards said, looking over his shoulder at Twobirds, "but I'm sure they're Indians, sir, and figure they're Kiowa."

"Well?" Sheets asked, turning to Twobirds.

"Yes," she said, "Kiowa."

"Good," he said. "Very good."

"They looked mighty fearsome to me," Richards said, "and ready for a fight. There were sentries posted and camp dogs everywhere. I was plain lucky they didn't spot me. Wouldn't do to just ride in, not in our condition."

"We'll ride in all right," Sheets said, looking at McReynolds's soiled clothes, "like soldiers. It's time we shaped this outfit up."

"Fell in the river this morning," McReynolds said, scraping at the dried mud on his britches, "right down the bank into the muck."

"This is still the army and we're riding in, full dress. That's an order."

"Full dress, Lieutenant?" McReynolds asked.

"And buttons buttoned. You'll go in first, Twobirds, and prepare the way. We'll come at high noon, the 7th in its glory and Lieutenant McReynolds at my side, lest there be trouble."

Following Twobirds to where the horses were corralled in the grove of shittim, McReynolds waited as she saddled her mount and snugged tight the cinch. Sensing his presence, she spoke without turning.

"Are you here to apologize once more, Joseph?"

Snapping a twig from the tree, he worked at his fingernails with the sharp end. Already the leaves were falling in the shittum grove and lay about like a golden blanket.

"It was a stupid thing for me to do, but I did it for good reasons. I'll have to live with the knowledge of the pain I caused that poor woman. I guess I've lots to learn about how things work out here."

"Do not let the lieutenant get you killed," she said, mounting her horse.

"Now that we're here, with your people, I'm afraid I might lose you."

Straightening her back, she looked toward the horizon.

"I've not seen them for so long now, I too am frightened."

Kicking her horse into a trot, she rode off along the bank of the river until she disappeared from sight at the bend.

Back at camp, McReynolds found the men grumbling as they put on the woolen uniforms, shirts wrinkled beyond repair, smelling of mildew and horse sweat. Some were missing buttons, traded to the Osage for goods. Others stuck their fingers through holes in the clothing, eaten through by unidentified varmints. All in all they were a sad lot, with sunburned faces, scraggly beards, and long hair.

Two abreast they lined up in an unsuccessful attempt to appear larger in number, and as ordered McReynolds rode at Sheets's side. With bravado they moved out to the Kiowa encampment, a pathetic collection of jaded horses and half-starved men exhausted from the relentless travel. Even with grass, there was little time for their horses to graze, a miserable existence of too little food and too few hours of rest.

As they came within sight of the camp, Sheets ordered the column into a canter, but even with the men whooping and hollering, the horses could not sustain the pace for more than a few hundred yards before falling into a lumber once more, heads down, ears drooping, pathetic bags of hide and bone.

When the column topped the ridge, the men fell silent. The Kiowa horses danced and pranced below them, tossing their heads against the bridled strength of their masters. The warriors moved as one with their mounts, ancient centaurs, both horse and human, their colors flashing in the noon sun, their bodies glistening with sweat.

On foot and at the back were the Kiowa women, a single line as quiet and still as the desert dawn. At first McReynolds didn't recognize Twobirds standing at the end of the line.

She was in full buckskin, amber in color and soft as silk. On the front of her dress was an intricate beadwork design, on her feet, gray legging moccasins. Like black strands of rope her hair lay over her shoulders, her breathtaking beauty wiping away his fear.

"My God," Sheets said when he saw the Kiowa warriors.

As if by signal, the warrior at front and center held up his lance and Twobirds moved to his side.

"I think he wants to talk," McReynolds said.

"Yes," Sheets said, clearing his throat, "that seems to be the case. You're to ride up with me, Doctor."

"I wouldn't have it any other way," McReynolds said.

The smell of smoke from the Kiowa campfires and the barking of their dogs from the tepees were familiar sounds as they moved forward.

The chief was a powerful figure, not young by any measure, but still strong and imposing, his voice rumbling through his chest as he talked.

"My name is Dohasan," he said, "chief here among these warriors. We are grateful for the return of our daughter, Twobirds." Interpreting, Twobirds looked at her feet. "We are grateful for the return of our daughter and for the Tai-Me. It is only now with its return that we can have our Sun Dance. For the return of these things we have brought horses and food and welcome you to our camp."

"It is an honor for us to be here," Sheets said, "and to return Twobirds to her people. It is the kindness of the white chief in Washington that has brought us all this way to return her. We seek nothing from you, only to see her home at last and for you to welcome tribes who are removed from the south and into this land."

Waiting for the translation, Dohasan showed no expression, his horse prancing under him, his shield at the ready, canary yellow with a warlock wrapped in red cloth hanging from its center. On each side of the warlock was an eagle feather attached by short strands of leather. Leather fringe dangled from the shoulders of his buckskin shirt and a rectangular patchwork of beads, blue moons woven intricately around its border, adorned the front. Leggings reached to his knees, silver medallions spanning their length.

"Your chief wants our hunting grounds in trade for this woman, Twobirds?" Dohasan asked.

"No, no," Sheets said, "not a trade."

"I trade three squaws to your chief for the land beyond the Cross Timbers," Dohasan grinned, as his warriors lifted their lances.

"No, no," Sheets said.

"Four squaws," Dohasan said.

"No, no," Sheets said, exasperated. "He does not want to trade. He wants nothing from you."

"Nothing?"

"Nothing," Sheets said. "It is enough to see the great happiness we bring to the Kiowa."

"Then we will not offend your chief with gifts of horses," he said, turning on his mount to look at his warriors, "but instead will give you counsel from our forefathers, who learned these wise things in turn from their forefathers."

"We would be honored," Sheets said, taking a quick look at McReynolds, "to know the secrets of the great Kiowa."

"It is best to wear buffalo robes in the winter when the ground is white with snow, not in the summer when the sun is high overhead."

His jaw rippling, Sheets stood in his stirrups and looked at the column, sweat dripping from their noses, large circles spreading from under their arms, faces scarlet under the noonday sun.

"Well, it is regulation," he said to Dohasan. "The army has certain rules."

"And in the winter, do your warriors wear loincloths and sleep naked in the snow?"

"Of course not," Sheets said, his face reddening.

"Your chief has many strange ways. He wants our hunting grounds for a single woman but he takes no gift of horses when they're offered. He does not know summer from winter and thinks of sending strangers to my land. Your chief has much to learn."

"The great white chief lives very far from here," Sheets said, trying to control himself. "Sometimes he doesn't always understand the ways of the prairie."

"Yes," Dohasan said, "it is best to ride with the warriors you lead. Come to our camp. Tonight we will feast and rejoice in Twobirds's return. You will stay until your horses are strong and your men rested. And then you will return and tell your chief that the Kiowa hunting grounds are not for trade, not for many women."

When Sheets started to protest, Twobirds shook her head. The long-awaited negotiations were over.

Not until Dohasan was out of hearing did Sheets order the men out of full dress. There was a great flurry as woolen coats were shed and stuffed into saddlebags.

But not a word was said, not by the highest nor the lowest, for each man knew that it was only Dohasan and the great Kiowa tribe that protected them from the wrath of Sheets.

Thirty-three

The world of Twobirds was soft and round, full of color and life. The tepees faced the east, their backs to the prevailing westerly wind, soft and gentle domiciles thrusting up from the prairie grass like women's breasts, fastened with lacing pins, smoke flaps folded back like shirt collars. Motifs of blues and reds and yellows adorned the three-poled tepees. Some were horses with great phalluses thrusting forward from their bellies, colored ears and manes, legs stiff and rigid like wooden toys.

Camp dogs roamed at will, sniffing under upturned tails, trotting from tent to tent in search of food. Children laughed and scrambled about like children do everywhere and the women worked at their food and prepared for the evening's event, eyeing the soldiers curiously from a distance.

The soldiers pitched camp at the edge of the Indian encampment and unarmed guards were posted about. Horses and mules were hobbled and turned out on the plentiful buffalo grass that carpeted the valley floor.

Soon slabs of smoked buffalo meat and pemmican began appearing at the edge of their camp. Buffalo robes, baskets of berries, roots, and all manner of trinkets were left for them by the generous Kiowa. The soldiers soon rallied, and laughter filled their camp for the first time in many weeks.

While Twobirds reacquainted herself with her people, McReynolds cleaned his gear and himself. A careful inventory of his medicines indicated very little of value remaining, insect ointments, surgical instruments, some rusted beyond use from rain and dirt.

Evening fell and the winds quieted as the prairie began its song, a symphony spreading to the horizon and filling the air about them. High overhead, geese winged their way southward, their plaintive honks touching the souls of the men in this alien land.

The sun dropped to the horizon and the sky exploded in oranges, golds, pinks, clouds churning with color, boiling into the darkening sky, cauldrons of molten, spewing lava, and the men gathered at the camp's edge and watched as night squeezed the day into a brilliant swirling mass and pushed it over the edge of the earth.

Like the quiet beat of a heart, the sound of the drum beckoned them and they circled about and awaited the warriors. Firelight danced in the drummers' faces, ancient black eyes, slashes of color across their cheeks like open wounds.

Dropping to his side, Twobirds put her hand on McReynolds's arm. About her neck was a necklace and in her ears were rings of silver, the smell of fire smoke in her hair.

"They do you honor," she said, "for my return and the return of the Tai-Me."

"There never was a Sun Dance, was there," he asked, "without the Tai-Me?"

"No," she said.

"You figured to let Sheets starve out here looking for your people, me too maybe, all of us even?"

"I would not do you harm, Joseph."

"And why didn't you leave us, Twobirds?"

In perfect unison, the drummers worked at the huge drum. Through the flames McReynolds could see Sheets watching them.

"It was the throwaway wife," she said. "I thought my people were several days ahead. All the signs led to that. But they had stopped, waiting to see if the ill woman could go farther. It was at the cave where she lay dying that I knew we had found them."

Folding her legs in Kiowa custom, she studied Sheets through the flames. "I told the lieutenant that night that we must not go farther, that there was little wood ahead for fire.

"Once, he called for you, to puncture blisters on a soldier's feet. I told him that your horse had pulled up lame a few miles back and that you were walking in. He never asked more." She shrugged her shoulders. "We found the Kiowa by chance."

The beat of the drum grew bright, an intense crescendo causing chills to race down McReynolds's back. From the darkness spun a whirling dervish of feathers and paint, his face white as milk, his body rippling, dipping, gyrating like a wild animal. As a spirit he moved through space, above and apart from those who watched, a specter floating and spinning and yelping, the whites of his eyes glowing in the light of the fire.

And from the darkness other warriors joined in, some old with twisted and worn faces, others young and fierce with piercing eyes, and the drum grew louder, thundering now through the night, crashing through the night, deafening, raging, driving the fearsome prairie from their backs.

From the far side of the circle the Kiowa women joined the dance, their knees bending to the beat of the drum, rising and falling to the count of the drum, the line twisting, turning, ever forward like an enormous reptile. They were a fine and perfect people, fulsome, bronzed amazons, and the final link in the circle.

"It's spectacular," he said, looking into Twobirds's eyes.

Pleased at his acceptance of her people, she smiled and pointed to the warrior whose body was painted red from head to toe, pulsing with the beat of the drum and in his face the sign of grief.

"He is the husband of the throwaway wife," she said.

Dancing close to the fire, the warrior's moccasins scattered embers into the blackness and McReynolds knew this warrior's pain, for he too bore the blood of his wife.

"I hope he never knows how she died," McReynolds said.

"She died as she should," Twobirds said, her eyes locked on

Sheets through the roaring flames, "without shame to her husband or to her people."

As the drums quieted, an old man entered the circle of dancers, the hardship of the prairie engraved on his face, and in his hands was the Tai-Me, in his eyes the wisdom of the ages. Holding the unpretentious bundle high, he walked the circle of warriors.

Even at that moment, McReynolds understood the naïveté, the inherent gullibility of such rites. The world was round not flat, but the feelings he had could not be explained and they rose up in him like a great tidal wave.

Circling the fire, the old man lifted the Tai-Me over his head and all knew in that circle that this was a special and divine moment, and then he was gone.

Like cryptic spirits, Indian boys slipped from the darkness piling log upon log onto the fire and it rose into the night, its heat driving them back as the drummers worked the drum, possessed by its voice and breath. At that moment, McReynolds knew no fear, not from the prairie, not from place nor past, for nothing dared enter this circle nor cleave its accord.

"What is it?" he asked.

But Twobirds did not answer, bending now to the rhythm of the drum, her body as one with the beat of the drum, turning away from all that was alien now to the heart of the drum.

"They honor the warrior that has taken the head of an Osage," she said, "and the soldiers who have returned the Tai-Me."

The lance pierced the earth, swaying under the weight of the head atop it, eyes sunken, mouth taut, earrings swaying to the throb of the drum.

Lifting the lance, the red warrior held the head high above him, tipping the lance in honor as he came to each man, the hair undulating to the beat of the drum.

Eyes wide, Sheets stared at the approaching head. No one heard the name he uttered, but "Swinkoe" formed on his lips and rose from his past and stood in the darkness at the edge of the circle.

With bitter anticipation, McReynolds awaited his turn, tasting the sweetness of revenge, crying out the war chant, railing against the boundless prairie that would surely swallow them all.

In all its terror the lance rose above him, the severed head, the peering dead eyes, the crucifix of Nurse Cromley swinging about its ragged neck.

Transfixed, he moved to the throb of the drum, joining those who were as he, one with him and against all others, dancing for those who went before, for McCasson and Martinez, for his wife on the table, for the unspeakable fate of his own sweet Mary.

Thirty-four

An altercation between blue jays in the tree above the tent awakened McReynolds. Folded over the leather thong laced about the circumference of the tent was Twobirds's buckskin, but she was nowhere in sight.

Pushing back the tepee flap, he let in the cool morning air. Camp smoke hung in the Indian village, children laughing, scampering about like kittens. In the distance smoke rose from the soldiers' camp.

Stretching, McReynolds rubbed at the stubble on his chin and examined his hands. Once nimble fingers were cracked and worn from the heat and the constant tugging of the reins, fingernails split and ever in need of cleaning. The neat and starchy existence of his surgical days were far away and remote at this moment. Still, there was something gratifying about this place.

Yawning, he watched the smoke from last night's fire curl into the morning sky, his soul cleansed, his spirits gay. From across the camp, Twobirds approached, a steaming helping of corn pone and buffalo meat in her hands.

"I'm going with the women to gather food," she said. "The hunting party left at dawn. It is for you to rest until my return."

"This is an assignment I don't mind doing," he said.

Laughing and carefree, she left with the other women, different here, no longer the solitary figure who rode with the soldiers, but complete now, fulfilled. Happiness should be hers;

he wanted it for her, but his feelings were ambivalent, diminished by the possibility that he might lose her.

Mopping up the juices from his plate, he finished his meal and dressed for the day. The morning sun, now void of its sting as it drifted southward for the winter, warmed his face with a soft and gentle touch. Squatting near the fire, he held his hands to its warmth.

An old squaw exited from the tepee from across the camp, her massive skirt hanging from her girth. In one hand was a basket of biscuits and in the other a walking stick. Shuffling her way backward with waddling hips, she dropped a biscuit, a few more steps, and then another.

Tail curled above its back, a camp dog approached, looking first to the left and then to the right before gulping down the biscuit. Each time it repeated the same process, surveying the area for danger, then wolfing down the next biscuit.

Working her way across the camp in such a fashion, the squaw dropped each biscuit until all were gone, ignoring the dog, which now watched her from a distance as she disappeared into her tepee.

The encampment was a place for living, no end of joviality and laughter. As he passed, the women dropped their eyes and worked at their duties. Some dressed skins with tools, scraped at the fat with precise and skillful thrusts. About their necks and wrists were brightly colored necklaces, rings of all degrees dangling from their ears, laughing at the antics that never seemed to end.

Rules were implicit but for the most part obeyed, and the camp bubbled with life. Basking in its peace, McReynolds relished the escape from the hard and humorless trail, and was surprised to soon discover the afternoon gone.

Like an animal to its den he returned to Twobirds's tepee, tanned buffalo skins carpeting the floor, light penetrating the walls, nebulous, opaque, filling the quiet world with warmth. For the first time in many weeks he slept a restful sleep and healed the wounds of body and mind.

When he awoke, the light was gone, the campfire sputtering and spitting under a rain that murmured against the drawn skin of the tent. Stretching his arms into the darkness of the tepee, he realized that she was next to him, her delicate hand on his chest. Tracing its cool edges, he surrendered to its structure, its design.

"I've come back," she whispered.

Rain swept against the tepee as the wind raced in from the north, her body an ember against him, the curve of her mouth, the smell of her earthy skin.

"I need you," he said.

And she was his, her passion and love, her courage, his alone at that moment but for how long, only the gods could say.

Wet and warm and wrapped in buffalo skins they lay in each other's arms, sleeping as one, the storm fading with the night.

Three days passed and upon each rising McReynolds watched the old squaw from across the way exit her tepee with her basket of biscuits.

Like clockwork the spotted dog entered, looking first this way and then that before gobbling down his fare. With each biscuit he took less time, grew more reckless, the old squaw leaning on her stick watching, hobbling back to her tepee.

On the morning of the fourth day the hunting party returned with packing horses swaying under the weight of a half dozen gutted buffalo carcasses. Soldiers and warriors alike gathered to watch the women butcher the buffalo and soon the smell of smoking meat drifted through the valley. Within hours, strips of buffalo meat hung drying on racks throughout the camp. Only then did the warriors sleep, secure with food awhile longer.

With each passing day McReynolds found himself growing stronger, happier, walking in the prairie, often for miles, relishing the rugged beauty of the country. Mesas stretched like an ancient wall across the western horizon. Sometimes he would just sit in the swaying grass and listen to the prairie sounds about him.

Each morning upon rising McReynolds watched the old squaw feed the spotted dog, admiring her tenacity, her compassion, and even in these few short days he could see that the dog had gained weight, its coat glistening from the attention.

On this particular morning the old squaw dropped the biscuits closer together and with deliberate care, the dog waiting in anticipation. Leaning on her stick, she sucked at her lips, enticing the dog. Unable to resist longer, it stepped in for the biscuit at her feet and with lightning speed she clipped it between the ears with her walking stick. Yelping once, the dog flipped on its side and died. Lifting it by its tail, she smiled at its condition and weight for her pot.

Shaking his head, McReynolds turned away. Nothing in this wilderness was ever what it seemed.

Like the other women of the tribe, Twobirds avoided contact with him during the day, keeping to herself or working at her duties. But at night and in the privacy of the tepee she came to him, often only talking, laughing, walking sometimes in the night. Layer upon layer her rich life was revealed to him, the kinships, the loyalty, the depths of her beliefs.

The days grew cooler, somber, gray, laden with moisture from distant oceans, the smell of winter in the wind. And with each day Sheets's agitation grew, long rides into the prairie were ever more frequent, marching the men at times beyond the encampment, tattered and unrespectable as they were, back and forth through the prairie grass like ducks in a field.

On a black and moonless night the north wind blasted full-gale into the encampment, tepees flapping, fires flaring in the wind. All knew that soon the decision to leave must be made, the Kiowa to their winter camp in the mountains to the south, the soldiers to the Cross Timbers and beyond.

Pulling the blanket over her shoulders, Twobirds held her hands to the fire.

"Your lieutenant does not know the bitterness of the winters here. The soldiers would not survive and soon the Kiowa will move on."

Surely he will decide soon," McReynolds said. "But then what happens to us?"

The night darkened and the wind howled from the north as Twobirds lowered her eyes. The warriors smoked and stood about the fire in silence. In the distance McReynolds could see the firelights of the soldiers camp and knew how unprepared they were for this night and for the nights to come.

A young Indian girl knelt at Twobirds's feet, in her arms a papoose. Speaking in hushed tones, she pleaded with Twobirds.

"What is it?" McReynolds asked.

"Her child is ill," Twobirds said, "does not suckle and is hot to the touch. She has heard of your medicine and asks that you look at her child."

Without a word she lay the papoose on the ground and unwrapped it, a boy child, thin, emaciated, burning with fever. Turning the infant's head to the firelight, McReynolds opened his mouth. White abscesses the size of coins covered his throat and his breathing was labored, heavy. He lay the child between them and shook his head.

"He's dying, I think," he said, more to himself than to anyone else.

Through the firelight McReynolds could see Private Fielding standing at the edge of the encampment, signaling for him to come.

The wind blew through the camp, embers spiraling from the fire and into the night, blinking away in the black sky as surely as the child's life would blink away.

"Sir," Fielding stepped closer.

Turning, the warriors stared at Fielding. Without Twobirds's consent no soldier was welcome here, not even McReynolds himself.

Holding up his hand, McReynolds tried to stop Fielding, but the scarf wrapped over his ears prevented him from hearing.

"Stop," McReynolds said.

Alarm registered on the warriors' faces as Fielding approached. The husband of the throwaway wife, circled the fire, red paint still on his body, eyes fierce and angry. Things were going awry here, going very wrong.

Walking toward him, Fielding grinned, proud of his assignment to fetch the doctor.

"Wait," McReynolds said, waving his hands in the air, but Fielding only waved back, stepping over the infant who lay uncovered on the ground.

Voices rose in disbelief. Grinning, Fielding looked about at the attention his presence had aroused.

"What is it?" McReynolds asked Twobirds in alarm.

"He has stepped over the child's body. He will surely die now."

"No, that's ridiculous."

But even as he spoke, the child's breathing ceased, his small hands curling in death.

What happened next happened so quickly that McReynolds could only watch as the red warrior stepped between them, pulling Fielding forward in a deadly embrace, the upward thrust of his knife, the dreadful sound.

Lurching forward, poor Fielding fell, his open cavity steaming in the night air. Just as quickly the red warrior was gone, the north wind riding through the encampment, leaves clinging to the pool of blood gathering at Fieldings' side.

Untying the scarf from under his chin, McReynolds lifted Fielding's head.

"You won't tell my kin 'bout the mule, will you, sir?" he said. "I wouldn't want them laughing none."

"No, I won't tell," McReynolds said.

"Sir?" he said in a whisper.

"Take it easy, Private."

"I forgot to give you the message."

"What message?" McReynolds asked, bending low to hear.

"Lieutenant Sheets," he said, "gone. First sergeant, mules, too."

"Gone where?"

But Fielding would never answer that question, not that it mattered, not for Fielding, not for McReynolds either, because he knew exactly where Sheets had gone.

Thirty-five

Prudence, along with Twobirds's insistence, convinced McReynolds to flee to the camp forthwith, but what struck terror in his heart more than anything was that he would now be the officer in charge. As a leader of soldiers, he was a hell of a good doctor. For all of Sheets's faults he at least had the confidence to make decisions.

From around the fire the men watched as McReynolds walked in from the encampment, horse in tow, Fielding tied over its back like a sack of feed. Doubt was in their eyes as they carried Fielding to the edge of the camp, where he was buried without ceremony. Even as the soldiers covered his grave, the smell of earth in their nostrils, the Kiowa drums mourned the death of the infant child.

"Go," Twobirds had said without explanation, and so had he done. Well, here he was and without a notion as to what to do next.

"Why did they do it, sir?" Richards asked when he returned from dressing the grave. "Fielding never hurt no one in his life and they gutted him like a shot buffalo."

"I don't know why, Richards, not for certain. Things just got out of hand and it happened."

"Well, something ought to be done 'bout it," he said, pulling his hat down, wrapping his arms about himself against the north wind. "They shouldn't be allowed to just butcher us when they take a notion like that, never hurt no one in his whole life, not no one. Why, he was the only one of us didn't eat Renfro's molly like a pack of hungry dogs. We did, sir, but not Fielding. He wouldn't hurt a soul."

Kicking at the fire, Richards listened to the thump of the Kiowa drum. "Didn't matter his stomach was squeaking from hunger, didn't matter everyone else was filling their gut, didn't matter it was just an ole plug-headed mule, he didn't eat a bit of it cause he knew it was the wrong thing to do. Now look what they done to him."

The other men had gathered about, seeing the hurt in Richards's eyes, feeling his pain, waiting for McReynolds, for an answer.

"Take it easy, Richards. We can't do anything rash here, much as we'd all like to."

"And what about Lieutenant Sheets, sir? Where's he gone and why did he leave us here like this? What's to keep them Kiowa from coming in here during the night and gutting us all out just like they did poor Fielding there?"

The men looked at each other and whispered among themselves. In the distance the Kiowa drum labored and McReynolds knew they must be dancing now, the red warrior spinning and spiraling, his muscled body shining with sweat.

"I don't know where he is, Richards, nor is it my function to question where he is. Perhaps it's yours?"

"No sir," he looked at his feet, "I didn't mean to question you, sir, but it sure seems like we've been left to fend for ourselves and with mighty slim odds."

Screwing up his courage, McReynolds lifted his chin.

"Well, that's not for you to decide, is it? I'm in charge here. I'm next in line and it's my intention to do my job."

The men looked at each other with skepticism. He hardly blamed them. Following him anywhere seemed a cruel and dark joke.

From the far corner stepped a small and unassuming soldier. Matted hair stuck from under his hat and he was badly in need of a shave, nose bent on the end like a fire poke and, in spite of his youth, walking in a peculiar stance, looking for the world like an old man.

His sleeve was slick and McReynolds remembered him as the soldier who saluted and broke ranks at Renfro's lashing. Slick sleeves suffered greatly and bore the worst possible indignities in the 7th, even from the other enlisted men.

"Sir," he said.

"What is it, soldier?" McReynolds's commander's voice sounded thin and weak even to himself.

"Sir," he said, "I ain't much around here as you can see, Lieutenant Sheets saw to that, but I'll do whatever you need."

"What's your name, soldier?"

"Number, sir, Paul Number, although I don't count for all that much."

"And what was your rank—before, I mean?"

There was a pained look in Number's eyes.

"Corporal, sir, and a damn good one. Worked at it long and hard and it was gone in a flash for spittin' on the lieutenant's horse, sir."

"Why would you do a thing like that, Number?"

"Don't know, sir. The lieutenant told me to take care his horse was clean 'fore I saddled him up. Said he didn't want no horse dung smellin' up his mount during the heat of the day. So I just lifted that horse's tail and spit right in its eye. Shined it up with my sleeve and said, 'Here's the cleanest horse's ass in the command, sir,' but the lieutenant didn't take it too light, sir, being a tad shy on humor, if you don't mind me saying so."

"Well, consider yourself a corporal again, soldier. I'm going to need loyal and true fellows and you strike me as one."

The others looked at each other in disbelief as they hunkered against the wind. After considerable consultation, Richards was appointed to step forward.

"We're with you too, sir. Just tell us what's to be done."

Something had to be done, Richards was right, even if it was of little worth.

"Break camp," he ordered with bravado. "We're moving

south. If they're going to cut our throats, they'll at least have to ride a piece to do it."

And so they broke camp, pulling reluctant mules from their sleep, harnessing teams, and loading supplies. Breaking camp was an arduous task at best, but with so many things having been unpacked for the extended stay, and in the dark to boot, it was especially difficult and slow. First, the men cursed the night, and then the animals, and then each other as they stumbled and struggled about in the darkness.

The first glow of light rose in the east before all was ready and the men were mounted. None believed for an instant that moving a few miles closer to home changed their situation, but they felt better somehow, mounted and ready to ride.

Riding at the front of the column was McReynolds, self-conscious and pretentious in his new role, at his back, Corporal Number with his head high. Somehow, even in the turmoil of breaking camp, Number had managed to sew back on his stripes.

With all the poise he could muster, McReynolds looked over his shoulder at the column of men who awaited his command and called out the order.

"Forward, ho!"

And to his surprise the column moved, and for the first time he knew the slightest confidence.

"Sir?" Number rode up.

Pushing back his hat, McReynolds stood in his stirrups and looked at the column of men following him.

"What is it, Corporal Number?"

"Sir, I thought you said we were moving south."

"That's right, Corporal, south. Moving north would put us smack into the Kiowa camp."

"But sir, we're going north."

"What!"

"Yes sir, due north, straight into Dohasan's tepee."

"Oh for Chrisake!" McReynolds yelled. "How the hell do you get them stopped?"

"Column, halt," Number said, lifting himself on his saddle-horn, "God almighty, column halt, sir!"

"Column halt! Column halt!" McReynolds yelled, waving his arms.

As the column halted the men shook their heads.

"Now what, Number? Now what do we do?"

"About-face, sir. Head them south before the Kiowa think we're dumb enough to attack."

"About-face!" he ordered, and there was a great scurry and rattling of gear as they turned their horses in the opposite direction.

"There, sir," Number said, "now we're headed the right way."

Heat rose in McReynolds's face as they made their way to the head of the column, but the men were too anxious to laugh and for that he was grateful.

When at last he took his place at lead, they rode south and soon hit the river, following its meandering course across the valley floor. The sun was high in the sky and warmed their shoulders as the wind gave way to a beautiful autumn day. Here and there bright splashes of flowers, the deep maroons and yellows of autumn, bloomed in wide sweeps as if broadcast by a giant's hand. If it had been any other day, all would have rejoiced in its beauty, but today there was only poor Fielding lying in his grave and the Kiowa at their backs.

"Up there," Number said, pointing to a break in the riverbed, "we could see a far distance, at least in the daytime, and there's wood to be had and river water if it came to that. We could make camp, at least long enough to see if Sheets is gone for good. If the Kiowa figure on doing us in, it might just as well be here as anywhere, sir." Checking McReynolds's face, he fell silent to see if he'd overstepped his bounds. "Course, I wouldn't for a minute tell a lieutenant what to do, sir, not for a minute."

"And you wouldn't spit up my horse's tail either, I suppose."

"Oh, no sir," he grinned. "I figure on keeping these stripes right where they are."

Calling the column to a halt, McReynolds slid from his saddle and walked around on the other side of Number's horse, where no one could see him.

"Look, Corporal Number, there's no need for me to pretend about this. I'm a doctor not a soldier and I haven't the slightest notion how to lead a command. If you say this is a good spot to camp, then let's camp."

"Well," Number smiled, "back there for awhile I thought we were in full attack against Dohasan himself. Wouldn't he have been surprised, ragged bunch like us riding full-bent right up his nose?"

"Not half as surprised as me, Corporal, I can guarantee you that. If there's anything you can do to help me, it would be appreciated."

"Well, there is just one thing, sir."

"What's that, Corporal?"

"Well, sir, if you ever want your horse shined up, I'm just the man for it."

"Can see why you had trouble hanging on to those stripes," McReynolds smiled.

"Yes sir," he said, "I get your drift. But seriously, sir, there is one thing."

"What's that?"

"I figure there's only one reason we are still alive and her name is Twobirds. I'd sure think twice before having a spat with her, sir."

"I think I get your drift too, Corporal. Now see that camp is set up like it should be and that guards are posted around the clock."

"And the horses tied inside the camp, sir. They're the most likely to come up missing, and we're as dead as dead without them."

"Stake 'em close, Corporal. I've got some thinking to do now."

Saluting, Corporal Number ordered the men to action, his new stripes askew from having been tacked on in the darkness.

By late afternoon, camp was made, horses staked in the center of camp, guards posted in strategic positions on the perimeter. A small hunting party was sent out under Number's suggestion and wood was gathered for the night fire.

The autumn sun was hot through the thin air and pungent odors from the river sometimes rode in on the wind. The Kiowa drums had faded and the whole episode seemed distant and long ago now.

A small knoll lay to the north of the camp and McReynolds climbed to its peak, which offered a panoramic view of the terrain. At the summit he leaned against the caprock, held his hands over his eyes. To the distant north wisps of smoke rose from the Kiowa camp.

Beyond that somewhere, farther north where the blue sky curved downward and touched against the horizon, was the alabaster cave, where the silver lay scattered at the pool's bottom, where the bodies stared upward through the icy water forever caught in time, where the darkness was absolute, suffocating and final.

Somewhere out there was Sheets searching for his silver. How at that moment he wished him dead, lying with Renfro in his watery grave, with Bledso, Brandywine, McCasson, and the Mexican boy, whose name he'd already forgotten, how he wished at that moment all the pain and anger and grief of the last months would bear down and reach across the prairie and strike at the black heart of Sheets.

Swept by abandonment, his deepest fears and self-loathing mounted within him, but from it came an unexpected strength. The bottom had been reached and in there was the truth and the courage that he needed. In him no less than in Renfro, On-da, even Twobirds herself, was the legacy of human courage.

He turned and walked back to camp.

Thirty-six

The hunting party returned with three jacks and half a dozen quail, a meager take at best, but it flavored the cornmeal and filled their empty stomachs. A large fire secured them as night fell.

Before taking his place by the fire, Corporal Number double-checked the sentries and the horses, reporting all well.

Night fell clear and cold and the wind swept down from the north, driving through their unprotected camp atop the hill. Shivering, they huddled near the fire, arms wrapped about themselves, heads bundled in all manner of clothing. Feet burning against the fire, backs freezing against the wind, they tried to sleep, waiting and hoping for dawn because dawn would surely bring more than the bleak and freezing night.

But dawn rose bitter and frost glistened on the buffalo grass like broken shards of glass and steam rose from the backs of the horses and the men quivered under the icy wind as they boiled water for tea.

Sipping at the hot edge of the tin cup, McReynolds took stock of the men's condition. Without meat from the Kiowa they would soon be in trouble.

Even before the guard alerted them, McReynolds saw them on the northern horizon, Dohasan at center, his signature shield held high in front of him. To his right was the red warrior, his cardinal skin shining in the cold dawn, his knife lashed to his side. To the left was Twobirds and about her shoulders was a buffalo robe. Across the horizon were Dohasan's warriors, steam blowing from their horses' nostrils.

Lifting their lances, the Kiowa moved forward, horses snorting, prancing against their reins, a formidable and fearsome sight as they came toward them.

Just feet from the camp and under the full bore of the soldiers' guns, Dohasan stopped, Twobirds moving forward to interpret, but it was the red warrior whose face was filled with danger and whose horse danced beyond the others.

"This warrior no longer has a wife," Dohasan spoke, pointing to the red warrior, "and is in need of a woman. He is of the Koitsenko, the honorific society, and is known for his bravery in battle. It is the woman Twobirds he has chosen."

Her voice dropping, Twobirds chanced a look at McReynolds as the red warrior rode a tight circle around the fire, his horse shying against the flame.

"It is you who sleeps in her tepee and it is you he must fight," Dohasan said to McReynolds, looking down the line of warriors, pointing first to his left and then to his right with his lance, "or you may give her away, for she is only a woman and not of your kind."

Something in McReynolds broke, no longer caring about the consequences.

"I do not give her away," he said.

With a nimble leap, the red warrior was on the ground, his hand on the knife that had taken Fielding's life.

"Don't do it," Number said, stepping forward. "No one here expects you to do it."

Battle with a Kiowa warrior was a long way from surgery, and McReynolds knew how precarious was his situation, the warrior trained for killing, he for healing.

In muted tones Twobirds spoke to the red warrior, concern in her eyes at his response.

"One of you must die," she said.

Pulling his knife from its sheath, the red warrior held it high in the cold morning light.

"Must I use the inferior weapon of the Kiowa warrior?" McReynolds said, waiting for the interpretation.

The red warrior's eyes blazed as he answered.

"You may use any weapon that you choose. It is the warrior's courage that defeats his enemy, not his weapon." Twobirds said, hesitating, "There is no better warrior. Turn me to him and we will leave."

"Go get my bag, Corporal."

"Bag, sir?"

"My black bag. Go get it, Corporal, or do you want to lose those stripes again?"

"No sir," he shrugged, "I surely don't want that. Where is it, sir?"

"Back of the supply wagon, and hurry it up, Corporal. We don't want these gentlemen freezing."

As they waited for Number's return, Dohasan's horse plopped dumplings onto the ground with consummate disinterest, steam rising into the cold air.

Handing him the bag, Corporal Number stepped back among the soldiers as McReynolds dug through its contents.

Holding up the scalpel, its unassuming blade less than an inch long, he gave the red warrior his most fierce stare.

Smiling, the red warrior dropped into the attack position.

Eyes tearing in the wind, McReynolds followed suit, knowing well the facility of his modest blade, an extension of hand and mind, its keen edge so fine that flesh sometimes failed to bleed. In thirty seconds he could amputate an arm, a leg in forty-five. This was his territory.

The red warrior's knife whistled through the air, singing past McReynolds's ear. Such strength and speed were capable of decapitation if the mark was found. But in its power was a price, total commitment. Once initiated there was no recanting and there in the follow-through, the briefest moment when the red warrior's shoulder was vulnerable.

"Kill him, Lieutenant!" Richards yelled, jumping into the air, "for us and poor Fielding!"

Both soldiers and warriors tightened the circle as the combatants moved eye to eye about the camp. With a thud McReynolds fell backward as the red warrior swept his legs from under him, air rushing from his lungs, ears ringing, blackness falling as the red warrior's hand held his throat in a vice grip. With heroic effort he brought his knee upward into the warrior's tailbone, the vice falling away, blessed air filling his lungs.

Before him on the ground was the red warrior, his back covered with the dung from Dohasan's horse. But not for long, as he bounded to his feet, his battle cry charged with broken pride and hatred for this white man. Like dogs they stalked, circling, waiting for advantage.

In a show of arrogance the warrior spun, translating the spin into the force of his knife as he came about in a driving blow, but McReynolds was ready, sidestepping the fraction of an inch needed for the knife to miss its mark.

And there, as he thought, prayed for, the warrior's arm exposed from the follow-through. Leaning in, scalpel, mind, speed all integrated, he pared the leader with a snap, the red warrior's hand dropping useless at his side, his knife clattering into the rocks that circled the fire. Coming about and under his neck, McReynolds pulled him off balance, searching for that notch, for that small opening between the vertebrae, that fragile lifeline between mind and body. And even as he found it, the warrior's good arm encircled McReynolds's head, lifting him off the ground and onto his powerful back.

Feet dangling in the air like a puppet, McReynolds inserted the scalpel and the red warrior, Koitsenko, killer of poor Fielding, collapsed beneath him in a heap, with a wistful blink of his eyes. A merciful flick of his scalpel opened the carotid artery and he waited for the red warrior's life to pump away.

Both soldiers and warriors were silent as Dohasan moved forward on his mount.

"You will be called Little Knife," he said, "and the woman, Twobirds, is yours." Shading his eyes, Dohasan looked down at the slain warrior and then scanned the horizon. "The sky is white and it's time for the Kiowa to go. Even the geese have flown toward the sun. The snows will soon cover the horses' backs."

"Will you come with us," McReynolds turned to Twobirds, "so that we may get home?"

The north wind whipped the ashes about the red warrior and into the eyes of those who awaited her response.

"I'm yours to do with as you wish, as Dohasan has said."

"But I want it to be your choice."

"I will go with Little Knife," she said.

"We ask Little Knife to let us take our slain brother," Dohasan said, "to honor his bravery."

Nodding, McReynolds watched as they lifted the red warrior onto his horse. A more certain and true kinship he'd never felt.

As the Kiowa rode away toward the river and out of sight, Twobirds watched from his side, accepting what was, defeat or victory, with equanimity.

How humbled he was by her decision to stay and he wanted to tell her of his love, of his admiration, of his appreciation.

But Twobirds had turned away, her eyes fixed on Lieutenant Sheets standing half frozen at the camp's edge.

Thirty-seven

Next to Sheets, First Sergeant Lansdown stood with his head down. The men's clothes were dirty, faces drawn, frozen from the cold.

"Why have these soldiers been moved without my orders?" Sheets asked McReynolds.

"The Kiowa killed Fielding and were only moments from killing the lot of us. Someone had to take charge in the absence of a commander."

Even in that half-frozen body, Sheets's eyes flamed.

"If I'd wanted this column moved, I would have left orders to that effect, Doctor."

"But you left no orders, did you, Lieutenant?"

In the light McReynolds could see the white stubble on Sheets's face, misplaced somehow, like whiskers on a child.

"We've had a hard time of it," he said, "as you can see, but these men were brave to the last. There was no heading out for home under my authority." Stepping to the fire, he held his hands out to warm them, eyes sunken and dark. "This is my command," he said, his voice icy, "and no man takes it from me. I consider your action mutinous, McReynolds, and when we return to the fort, you'll stand for hearing."

"A hearing is just what's needed," McReynolds said. "I wasn't the one who abandoned his command."

Pouring a cup of sage tea, First Sergeant Lansdown held his feet against the fire.

"We were lost," he said, "nearly from the start. Only dumb luck we hit the river and headed the right direction, otherwise we'd be stiff as trapped beavers by now."

"Someone stole my maps," Sheets said, looking into the men's faces. "Stole them right out of my saddlebags. Some cowardly thief nearly cost us our lives. Didn't realize they were stolen until we were already committed, by then it was too late to turn back."

"We didn't know which way back was," Lansdown said.

Kneeling at the fire, McReynolds could see the red warrior's blood there in the sand, the battle a distant and vague nightmare. Was it really he who had fought, defeating the fierce red warrior?

In the distance Twobirds gathered wood for the night in her slow and methodical way, her buffalo robe over her shoulders. No matter what happened, life went on for her. No matter whose blood was in the sand, firewood had to be gathered against the night cold. What was she feeling, he wondered, here once again among these foolish men?

"Where did you go," McReynolds asked, "back for the silver?"

"That silver is government property, McReynolds, and it's my duty to recover it. If you lack the stomach for such a challenge, then so be it, but there are those among us who have the fortitude to do what we must. There are those among us who rise to the occasion no matter how distasteful or difficult."

"You should have seen him fight that red warrior," Corporal Number said as he stepped forward. "Me and the men never seen anything like it. Fought him with a knife too small to pare your nails. Dropped him like he was putting a baby to sleep. Dr. McReynolds saved the day, he did, and Twobirds is takin' us home straightaway before the winter sets in, and there won't be no getting lost with her along, I'll bet."

Not a word was said as Sheets stared into the fire, his eyes an inferno of anger and jealousy.

"Lost five miles out of camp, we were," Lansdown said to

himself. "Didn't know up from down or Sunday church. Hell, I ain't never been so lost, and I've been lost plenty."

"Why don't you just shut up, Sergeant. We made it back and without the help of a squaw," Sheets said.

Stepping between them, McReynolds intervened.

"Dohasan says its a hard winter coming and that even the geese are headed south early this year. There's barely enough horses and mules for necessities and damn little time left to get out of here before winter sets in."

"Dohasan is an old woman," Sheets said, hooking the toe of his boot under his knee and pulling it off. "There's ample time. The weather's not that critical, not once we get through the Cross Timbers, and besides, there's every sign of an open winter."

"If we get snowed in," Numbers said, circling the fire, "we're all dead men—snow cover, no grass for the horses, firewood more scarce stock."

"Who the hell are you?" Sheets snapped.

"Corporal Number, sir."

Rising, Sheets walked around him, inspecting him from each angle.

"Number," he said, "Number. Well, Corporal Number, it's none of your business, by God, if I decide to spend the winter on top of this hill or to march you back to Fort Gibson stark naked. Do you understand?"

"Yes sir," Number said, his voice tense.

The north wind whipped among them, like razors on their flesh.

"What's this?" Sheets said, examining Number's new chevrons. "Crooked, halfway down your arm. Sewed on like a green recruit."

"Sewed on in the dark, Lieutenant," Number said.

"In the dark?"

"Yes sir."

"Say, aren't you the one spit up my horse's tail?"

"Shined it clean, just like you asked, sir."

"And didn't you lose your stripes for it?"

"I gave them back," McReynolds said, stepping forward. "The corporal here was the first to help when things were pretty uncertain. It was my judgment that he should have his rank back in order to get things organized."

"And so you countermanded my order?"

"Maybe you don't agree with my order, but it was my order and you should deal with me, not Corporal Number. He had nothing to do with the decision."

Stripes were the soldiers' domain, their livelihood, their status, and even the most exacting officer busted men of rank with reluctance.

"I'd advise you to keep your opinions to yourself, Corporal," Sheets backed off, "or you'll soon find those stripes back in your saddlebags."

Grinning, Number moved away, his crooked gait like that of an old man, but his eyes were young and full of mischief. Pivoting, he squared his shoulders and saluted McReynolds as he had Renfro that terrible day.

Saluting back, McReynolds smiled. So much had changed since that day, so much had happened, and how wrong he'd been about them all. These were not renegades and illiterates but the finest and bravest men he'd known.

"We'll camp here tonight," Sheets said, stiffening. "Me and my men are exhausted and I take it we're no longer under attack. One moment, Corporal Number. Pitch my tent and be sure the flap's southward."

"Yes sir," he said, shuffling on in his arthritic way.

"And make damn sure there are no rocks, Corporal, and level. I want it on level ground."

"Right, no rocks," Number stopped.

"And when you're finished with that, I want you to search every man's gear, Corporal."

"Sir?"

"Every man's."

"For what?" Number said, sticking his hands in his pockets.

"The maps, of course."

Reluctance spread across Number's face.

"Do as he says," McReynolds said.

"Yes sir," he said, "if you say so, sir."

Dragging the tent to a level spot a few feet from the wagon, he began clearing the ground of rocks.

"Search Lieutenant McReynolds's gear first," Sheets said.

A rock dropped from Corporal Number's hand, rolling, stopping on the edge of the buffalo path that twisted down the ravine.

"Lieutenant McReynolds's gear?"

"Start with him. Do it now. That's an order."

In his slow, ambling way he walked toward Sheets. Watching his every move, Sheets dropped his hand to his side arm, but Number walked straight past, to where Sheets's horse stood half asleep, tied to a tree. Lifting its tail, he spat definitively and resolutely into its eye.

The horse looked at Number in amazement before bolting, clawing the air with both front feet, pulling at the reins with its powerful neck, farting in short, violent bursts against the intruder and the reins that now were strained to their limit.

When they broke, they broke suddenly, and Sheets's horse fell backward into the midst of the camp before recovering and galloping away, the saddle stirrups flapping up and down against its sides like an invisible rider, spurring it on, a cloud of dust in its wake as it disappeared over the hill.

Speechless, Sheets watched on as his horse topped the distant rise in full gallop toward Dohasan's camp.

"If I got to do your dirty work," Number said, "I'd just as soon it be cleaning your horse's ass as going against men I respect."

"Stand tall," Sheets howled. "You've defied my orders, driven away my mount, insulted me as your commander." Fuming, he walked around Number, his fingers woven behind his back. "But these things are of little consequence, of little importance. What is of importance, what cannot be excused, is the fact that your treacherous and cowardly behavior may well have endangered these men, foiled the whole expedition." Ripping the chevrons from Number's shoulders, he threw them at his feet. "You'll be a slick sleeve until you die of old age, Number. You'll sleep with the horses, eat with the horses, talk with the horses until you look, think, and smell like the horses." Kicking dirt on the chevrons with his boot, he stared Number in the eye. "If I so much as see your face the remainder of this expedition, I'll have you walking drag with twenty pounds of shot, do you hear? There'll be nothing left of you but a hat by the time we reach Fort Gibson. You're not to speak to me or anyone else in this command. You're not to eat with the men or sleep with them or associate with them in any way. It's horses you want, it's horses you've got. Now get out of my sight before I have you shot for endangering the lives of these brave men here."

Doing an about-face, Number held his head high, looking at no one as he made his way to where the horses were staked, but it was there in his back, in his walk, in the way he carried himself, the pride and honor that was his.

"Richards, get over here, now!" Sheets screamed.

"Yes sir," Richards said.

"You check the gear of every last soul in this camp for those maps and by God you begin with Lieutenant McReynolds or I'll have you horsewhipped on the spot."

"Yes sir."

"And one other thing," Sheets said, "finish with that tent and make sure there are no bloody rocks."

All afternoon Richards searched, even as the sun began to drop on the western horizon, but the maps were nowhere to be found.

Finished with the wood, Twobirds prepared her own bed in a wash where the wind could not reach and where there was protection on three sides. First, she lay cedar branches on the ground and then a small roof of the same across the narrow bank overhead. With a flat stone she dug a trench from around the bed to lead away any rainwater that might come down the wash. Under the head of her bed she placed her satchel and the few belongings she owned.

At the first opportunity, she brought McReynolds to her place and with a motion of her hand, he understood, his spirits soaring because tonight he would be with her once again.

At dusk a lone figure appeared on the horizon, a single horseman, the sticks of his travois protruding over his horse's head like horns. It was a Kiowa warrior sent by Dohasan, a side of buffalo meat strapped to the travois and wrapped in its own skin, a gift to the warrior, Little Knife, and his squaw, Twobirds.

Cutting away the hind quarter, Twobirds placed it on a spit over the fire and by nightfall the smell of roasting meat drifted through the camp and the men's bellies growled in anticipation.

With her knife she cut thick juicy slabs of the roast, handing them to each man, watching them eat, and in her eyes was contentment. Disappearing into the darkness, she took food to poor Number. It would be a hard and cold night among the horses, and Number, being a sociable fellow, would suffer from his banishment. There was no pain so bitter as loneliness and in this place no loneliness so absolute.

Soon the men went to their beds, exhausted and full, satisfied that at least for now their lives were not in danger.

Joining her under her robe, McReynolds put his arms around her warmed body, the pungent aroma of cedar, the earthy scent of her skin.

Beyond the camp, horses stomped their feet and nipped at each other's rumps. Above Twobirds's shelter, the moon rode high, sprinkling ivory light through the cedar branches.

Moving to him, she slipped a cool leg between his, her heart beat against him, her breath in his ear like the tongue of a panther. Tracing the boundaries of her face in the darkness, he touched the delicate wisp of her eyelids, the black sweep of her brow, the line of her opulent mouth.

"Little Knife," she said, and a tingle shot through him.

This woman was his, he'd fought for her, killed for her, won her with his bravery and the blood in the sand. This no man could deny.

Pushing against him, she forbade his hunger, held him back for one more moment, to savor, to know his passion, the texture of his love, endowing him with power, absolving his deeds.

Engulfed, she took him, seized by his thrust, his measure and eagerness, her soul filled with him, this man who faced death for her.

This was the way, the way of honor, and now there was no ignorance nor cruelty nor death so black as to diminish their love. They were as one and the gods and the dead must now accept them.

Arching upward, she forsook her will to the moment and to the ecstasy that consumed her.

Sleeping, they clung to each other for warmth, the cold nipping at the edges of their cocoon, the earth's heat falling away into the thin, clear sky. And in that place the past did not enter nor whisper to them. The world did not exist nor matter, not the difference in kind, not the madman who led them, not the sorrowful braying of the mule beyond, where Number shivered alone.

Sometime in the early-morning hours, when the smoke from the camp twisted like a small black rope from the dying embers, Twobirds slipped from their bed, listening to his breathing, the slow rhythm of deep sleep, and took her satchel from under the pallet.

Naked and trembling, she made her way to the river, walking the shallows like a deer at dawn, water lapping her ankles with its cold tongue, but by morning light her tracks would be washed away, filled with rippling sand and no one would ever know.

Trembling with its weight, she lifted the river-worn sandstone that lay half submerged in the water. Just as the stone broke from her grip she tossed the satchel beneath it and let it splash unchecked into its resting place.

In those mute hours the sound was loud, standing, listening, hands over her breasts, nipples aching still, hard like berries beneath her palms.

Clenching her chattering teeth, she waited. Moments passed with only the ringing of silence in her ears. Persuaded that the soldiers slept undisturbed, she rested a moment before retracing her steps.

With stealth and patience she made her way back, slipping in next to him, snuggling against his warm and musty body, her head in the cradle of his arm.

Without the maps Sheets was lost and her safety assured, and no one would ever find them hidden beneath the rock.

Laying her hand on his hard stomach, her groin stirred. Now his life depended on her and she would do what she must to protect him.

She would not lose another, not without a fight.

Thirty-eight

By the time they broke camp, stowed the remainder of the buffalo meat, and rounded up three of the mules that had broken loose during the night, the sun had risen high in the east. Although still cold, the wind had dropped and the day promised to be fair.

As they mounted up, Richards spotted the band of Kiowa moving south along the river. Lance held high, Dohasan gave them a foreboding salute as they rounded the curve of the river.

"About-face," Sheets ordered.

The men looked at each other in confusion as McReynolds rode forward.

"Lieutenant," he said, "we're headed north, and believe me I know which way that is."

"That's right," Sheets said. "You didn't think for a moment that I would leave here with my job unfinished, did you?"

"What job?"

"To retrieve that government silver."

"Your orders were to return the Kiowa girl and prepare the way for the transfer of tribes from the southeast. As far as I can tell you've accomplished neither of those duties."

"Dohasan will accept the tribes," he shrugged, "never worry about that. With enough soldiers in here, he'll accept the transfer and be damn happy about it. And as for the Kiowa girl, well, we need her to get back to Fort Gibson, don't we, especially without the maps. It's necessary to take her back, that's all, for the good of all concerned."

"It's only the silver you want and you'll kill us all to get it."

"Look, Doctor, that silver is more valuable to the government than all the Indians ever born. If you don't like it, then go with your band of renegades and leave the men's work to the men."

"And what makes you think Twobirds will take you back to the cave, Lieutenant?"

"I'll show you," he said, motioning Twobirds forward.

"He's going back to the cave," McReynolds said as Twobirds rode up, her horse prancing under the rein.

A strand of hair fell across her eyes like a black slash.

"You do not know the way."

"No, but you do," Sheets said.

"It's too late. The winter is upon us. You'll not make it in time." Leaning forward, she spoke, her voice deliberate. "I'll not guide you."

"Then we make camp here and wait for spring, because I'm not leaving without that silver. With ropes and a few men it can be retrieved. It's my duty and I intend to carry it out. Now maybe some of us won't make it through the winter, like the good doctor here, for example. But one thing is for sure, I'm not leaving without that silver, so the sooner we get started, the sooner we get back."

"We cannot stay here," she said. "There's not enough grass for the winter and the buffalo have already moved south. The winds are bitter. Only God's dog survives its sting."

"Well that leaves you one alternative, doesn't it," he said, checking the rounds in the cylinder of his side arm. "We get to that cave as fast as possible and just maybe we'll beat the winter out of here. Otherwise we sit tight. I suggest you make a quick decision, and I wouldn't worry about disturbing your mule skinner at the bottom of that pool. I doubt that he would mind."

"You tempt the gods," she said, studying the distant horizon, "and endanger even your own kind for the metal in the cave.

The snow is in the wind and will soon cover the trail and the tracks of what little game there is. You'll trade all the metal you have for a buffalo robe if you're caught by the winter." Turning in her saddle, she looked down the column of men and then back at Sheets. "I'll take you back," she said.

"Good," he said. "Now that that's settled we can get on about the government's business."

In stunned silence the column moved forward while Twobirds and McReynolds fell back, taking their place behind the supply wagon, the squeak of the wagon wheels conjuring images of Renfro and the many times he'd repaired them to stall for time.

Eyes trained ahead, Twobirds ignored the stone at the river's edge where Sheets's maps lay. She'd underestimated Sheets's willingness to exploit his own men. It was a mistake she would not make again.

For two days they rode, a singular and mad push northward, often starting before sunrise, pressing everyone to their limit.

Two nights they made camp in the dark without even a fire to keep them warm. At drag, Number rode with the horses and mules, sometimes several miles behind the weary column of men.

On a bitter and bleak day they topped the hill and saw Chimney Rock on the eastern horizon, rising upward into the sky, gray rings of gypsum encircling its mass, signifying its eminence on the bleak landscape. But to all who looked on that day, Chimney Rock was not a citadel of inspiration nor a thing of beauty but a grim reminder of their descent into hell.

Once again they camped at its base, the wind whipping red dust into their eyes and scrubbing the skin from their faces. As darkness fell Twobirds appeared, her arms stacked with fuel, and soon a fire of mesquite and buffalo dung flickered in the darkness, steam rising from the pot of boiling water. There was precious little meat left but it was cooked and divided among the hungry men.

The wind dropped with the night and they moved closer to

the fire, holding their hands to the flames, embracing its heat, its protection.

In the darkness beyond, Number stood among the horses, their breaths rising above him as he pressed against them for warmth. Waiting, he watched the campfire, knowing that when all were asleep, Twobirds would bring him a share of the meat.

Unlike most nights, the men did not talk among themselves, the anguish of retreat heavy on their minds, the relinquished miles so hard earned, the uncertainty of their future.

Huddled about the fire like lost children, too tired and discouraged to make beds or to build shelters, they slept at last.

Once in the night McReynolds thought he heard a cry, sitting up, listening, his heart pounding in his ears, but it did not come again.

The cruel night passed and morning rode in on icy winds, Sheets stomping about, cursing the indolence of the men.

"I want a detachment of five," he yelled, "and ropes from the supply wagon. You, Twobirds, and you, Doctor, come along." As he examined the men's faces they cast their eyes to the ground, hoping not to be chosen. "And Number," he said, "for a little visit with his fellow mule skinner."

"Send out a hunting party and gather wood while we're gone," he said to the first sergeant. "Stake the horses out to graze and pack the gear so that we can move out the minute we're back. We're going to beat that snow out of here and we'll do it with a wagon load of silver."

"I know it ain't my place," he said, tucking his coat collar about his ears, "but I consider it my duty to at least bring it up."

"Bring what up, First Sergeant?"

"Well, sir," he pointed his head in the direction from which they had come, "with a little luck we just might beat that snow, although I doubt it. Already it's in the wind, a smell of iron and cold as death. It ain't likely I'm wrong, but let's say I am, and let's say there ain't going to be no snow, least not until we can find our way out of here. Let's say by the grace of God and pure blind luck we just ride on to the Cross Timbers without so much as a hitch. What do we do then, sir, with a wagon load of silver? There ain't no way a man can get a wagon load of silver through the Timbers. They say that bramble's so thick in places that a man afoot has to turn sideways to pass. What we going to do with a wagon load of silver, I wonder?"

Walking to the edge of camp, Sheets looked off in the direction of the Cross Timbers, his hands on his hips.

"We'll go through them, by God," he said. "It takes more than a few trees to stop this expedition. I suppose you'd have me leave that silver to the savages, Lansdown? Well, that's not going to happen, see. That silver's going out of here with me."

"Yes sir," Lansdown said in resignation.

Within the hour Number unloaded the wagon, harnessed and hitched a team of mules, and drove it forward for the soldiers to load into. Under Sheets's orders all supplies were to be left behind to save room in the wagon for the silver.

With reluctance, the soldiers climbed in, hunching behind the side boards to avoid the penetrating wind, muttering among themselves about leaving their mounts behind. All too soon the pathetic caravan crawled across the prairie toward the cavern.

Progress was slow, the wagon bumping and rattling across the rough terrain. By noon the temperature dropped and the wind blew in a relentless, disheartening gale. Under their blankets the men shivered and rubbed at their stiffening fingers.

Chimney Rock faded behind them, the last signature of hope, and soon there was nothing but the wind and the creak of the wheels and the despair of lost ground.

It was dusk when they reached the yawning canyon and stood at its rim, small and insignificant, tiny figures on the edge of eternity.

"We're here. We've made it. We're going in," Sheets said, his voice husky and full of greed.

"But Lieutenant," McReynolds said, "it's nearly dark. Shouldn't we find shelter, make camp, and then go down in the morning?"

"Tonight," he said. "We're going down tonight. Number, you make camp and stake out the horses. Gather wood and build a fire so we can find you in the dark. Fire it high, Number, so we can see. Do you understand?"

Nodding his head, Number began unhitching the team while the others drug ropes from the wagon bed and looped them over their shoulders.

Shadows followed them down the trail, elongated by the setting sun, mute specters swimming beside them on the rock walls of the canyon. Alone as always with the animals, Number watched them descend.

At the bog spring they stopped to prepare torches. All was different now, covered by a thin sheet of ice. In the wind the dry and frozen cattails whispered of lonely places, of sacrilege and desecration.

Soon the torches were lit, soot lifting into the men's faces, clinging to their hair and beards.

None spoke as the brush was parted covering the cave's entrance, tumorous clumps of red berries clinging to bare limbs. None spoke as they descended into the damp blackness. None spoke nor breathed as they entered the hallowed earth where their friend now lay dead. But each man, save Sheets, knew the transgression of the act and whispered a prayer for his own soul.

From the ceiling above them came the hushed whisper of bats grooming for the night's hunt, imperceptible voices from yawning red mouths, noses twisting at the smoke from the torches. Guano crunched beneath the men's feet as they followed Twobirds downward into the earth.

"How much farther," Sheets asked, his voice rebounding against the walls of the cave.

"Just beyond lies the opening, as before," she said, her eyes flickering under the torchlight.

"I have a side arm," he said.

"Yes," she said.

As they approached the narrow passageway, McReynolds's old fears washed over him, the sweating hands, the crushing weight, the suffocating enclosure that lay ahead.

But it was Sheets who cried out, his face contorted at what their torches revealed, the passageway blocked by tons of fallen debris, a jumbled and impassable rubble of rock.

"Noooo," he moaned, "noooo," falling to his knees, eyes fixated on the mountain of rocks that forever sealed away his silver. "Bloody savages," he wailed, "bloody Kiowa."

"No," Twobirds said. "This is sacred ground."

Pulling his side arm, Sheets fired over his head, the deafening volley, the stinging ricochet as the bullet's loathsome whine shifted direction and velocity about them.

"I'll kill them all," he screamed." They've taken my silver."

Determined not to endure one more shot, McReynolds leaped from behind just as Sheets cocked the hammer again. With all his weight he bowled him head over heels, his revolver skidding across the damp floor of the cave and against the wall, firing again from the impact.

Clutching her ankle, Twobirds dropped to her knee, blood dripping from between her fingers.

Rushing to her side, McReynolds examined the wound.

"Thank God, it's missed the bone. We're very lucky." Taking off his bandanna, he wrapped the wound before turning to Sheets. "You could have killed her."

But Sheets only stared at the rubble, as if by sheer determination he could move the tons of rock that stood between him and his silver.

In the shadows beyond the yellow light of the torches McReynolds saw the mesquite post, shaped into a crude wedge for bringing down the passageway. Considerable work and a powerful arm had frayed the end of the post in the process of loosening the layers of rock.

Leaning forward into the darkness, Twobirds pointed to the boot tracks at the edge of the light.

"Not Kiowa, Joseph," she said.

"We'll dig it out," Sheets said.

"You fool," McReynolds exploded, "you lunatic, not in a million years, not if we had all the light and all the time in the world. Not in a million years could we dig this out." Walking to where the side arm lay, he checked the chamber for live rounds. "We're leaving and we're leaving now."

Hobbling behind the others, Twobirds and McReynolds made their way as best they could. The going was slow, her arm slung over his shoulder, her ankle unable to bear much weight.

In sight of the exit, Twobirds gripped his arm.

"Wait," she said.

"What is it?"

"There."

"What? What is it?"

"There," she said, pointing to a small alcove washed in the canyon wall by the ancient waters of the cave, "there in the hollow."

"What is it?" he asked again, kneeling.

"A hackberry fork," she said, "and it grows."

In the dirt was a lone stick, two green leaves sprouting from the dead branches.

"I'll be damned," he said, "I wonder what it means?"

"It means life from death, "she said, shuddering. "We must leave this place now."

The ascent to the rim was slow, hobbling along the path, resting, adjusting to the frigid air. In it was the smell of rusted iron, as Lansdown said, caustic and bitter iron, and up the trail somewhere Sheets cursed the eyes and hearts of the red men who had ruined his life.

By the time Twobirds and McReynolds reached the rim of

the canyon, Number's fire flickered under a serene cascade of snow.

Before entering the camp, they waited, holding each other, to delay Sheets's wrath, to deny the reality of winter's arrival for one more moment.

Thirty-nine

The winds died with the night as the snow fell, flakes the size of dollar pieces, big soft puffs that filled the black sky and plopped on the men's shoulders.

Dragging back an enormous cedar, Number placed the trunk end in the fire to burn off, sitting on the other end to listen to Sheets rant about his lost silver.

Crackling and popping, the fire spewed as it burned its way into the cedar resin, its pungent smell hanging in the still, cold air and somewhere down the canyon coyotes ran a rabbit.

Huge flakes careened from the sky like falling leaves in autumn as the men sipped at their sage tea, steam curling from their cups.

The bandage on Twobirds's leg was pink with blood but in her face was the same mettle that McReynolds had seen in the throwaway wife that night along the river, the resolve to accept what came, whatever it was, to live or die, to endure with courage.

The night passed, interrupted only by an occasional moan from Twobirds as her wound tightened in the bitter cold. At dawn, McReynolds rose to check her bandage, finding the world buried in a thick blanket of snow.

The moon was still suspended on the horizon like an imposing silver eye, its light reflecting across the expanse of snow. First he rubbed the tension from her leg, and then changed the dressing. Stirring, she touched his face before falling asleep again beneath her robe.

Buried beneath the snow like hibernating bears, the men lay scattered around the fire. The prairie was as quiet as he could remember, peaceful but disturbing in its silence. Huddled next to the fire, McReynolds waited for the sun and what little warmth it might bring.

The morning came, not with sun but with bitter winds, the men trembling under its fury as the snow whipped about their feet in white eddies.

The mules hung their heads, ice crystals growing in their nostrils, pink with blood from their cracked and bleeding noses. The leather harness straps were hard as iron from the cold and Number cursed as he tried with stiff and frozen fingers to soften the leather against the fire.

Refusing to mount his horse, Sheets climbed instead into the wagon and buried himself beneath a blanket.

"Chimney Rock is this way," Twobirds said, pointing toward the sea of snow, "but the trail is hidden and the going will be difficult."

The imposing drifts spread before them like waves on an ocean.

"What choice do we have?" McReynolds asked, blowing into his hands to warm them.

"No choice," she said, "your lieutenant has seen to that. We stay or we go. There is no difference now."

Curled under his blanket, Sheets was silent, a pathetic and reprehensible creature in the minds of all. At that moment an idea dropped into McReynolds's head, not an idea so much as a plan, the veracity and finality of which could not be dismissed. Perhaps he'd thought about it before, entertained it in a subliminal way, but this was different, a plot as real as the cold that burned their faces and shriveled their spirits. This was to be.

Justice and all that was decent cried out for Sheets's demise and he was going to do it. How, he was not yet sure, that would come later, but this much he knew, killing was easier than healing; he'd proven that with the red warrior.

"Then let's go," McReynolds said, nodding to Number, who shivered on the wagon seat.

With a snap of the reins against their snow-covered backs, the mules pulled and the wagon creaked forward into the snow.

Excruciating hours passed as they rode in silence, too cold and miserable to speak, each man battling in his own way the desolation, the cold, the hunger. At times the wagon dropped into bottomless drifts, taking all the men to free it, their hands freezing to the iron rims of the wheels as they pushed.

But each hour brought them closer until at last they pulled to a stop at the crest of a hill.

"There," Twobirds pointed into the white horizon, "Chimney Rock."

The mules snorted and stomped their feet as the men stared into the shifting whiteness. Plastered with wind-driven snow, Chimney Rock was nearly invisible. But at last they were home, at least until death or spring set them free, and it would be a cold welcome that awaited.

"Okay," McReynolds said to the half-frozen caravan, "let's go see what's for supper."

Gathered together against the base of Chimney Rock, the men were too dejected even to rise as the wagon pulled into camp.

No game had been found, a fruitless hunt with all tracks leading southward. Only fate and dumb luck led them to a thicket of mesquite within a mile of the camp, a long walk in the drifts, but at least there was wood for fire. Without it they would surely have succumbed to the frigid night.

With precious little food in their bellies or hope in their hearts, they bedded down on the leeward side of Chimney Rock. Like buffalo with their rumps to the blizzard they awaited daybreak.

* * *

As the icy dawn broke, Sheets moved from the wagon into his tent, refusing to take command or even to talk.

Exasperated, McReynolds dispatched a hunting party on his own, but without heart. Even he knew the futility of hunting nonexistent game.

In spite of the pain from her ankle, Twobirds was uncomplaining, standing next to McReynolds as the hunting party trudged over the hill.

"The buffalo and the deer are gone," she said, "because there is no grass and the snow is too deep for them to dig it away. Nothing lives here now but the small animals beneath the snow. If we are to survive, we must learn from them." Looping her arm through his in encouragement, she pointed to areas protected from the winds. "Tell your men to dig holes, to burrow beneath the ground, and there they will find the warmth of the earth. It is dark and damp and offends the pride, but it is what must be done if they are to live."

"And what about food? Are we to prey on each other as well?"

"Tomorrow I will show you how to build traps from hollow logs, for rabbits and for the pack rat, who is as foolish for silver as your lieutenant. Kiowa children learn how to make these traps for amusement before they are able to hunt the buffalo.

"For the Kiowa warrior to take such game brings dishonor," she smiled, "but to die of starvation is no less dishonorable. Send the men for logs, big enough for a rabbit to turn around in, and tomorrow I will show how it is done."

That night McReynolds dreamed of killing Sheets, of choking him with his hands, Sheets's neck beneath his fingers, and then he awakened, his heart thumping from exhilaration.

Rising, he stoked the fire and listened to Sheets's snoring in his tent. Perhaps it should be now, while the others slept, but then they might awaken. If he was to do this thing, it must be covert or at least seen as an accident.

The next day, as promised, Twobirds showed them how to make the traps, simple but ingenious devices. In order for the animal to obtain the bait at the back of the hollow log, it had to squeeze by a notched stick that passed through a small hole in the top of the log. Attached outside to this notched stick was a bowed twig, hinged and levered to lift the door into the open position. The slightest movement dislodged the stick, causing the raised door to drop into place.

It was sound in theory. Whether it could catch a rabbit remained to be seen.

Half the men were given pinole flour for rabbit bait, the other half silver uniform buttons to attract pack rats. Each man was instructed by Twobirds on where and how to bait the traps and how to recognize animal tracks.

"If the track is shiny," she said, "it is old, refrozen from the cold, and is of little value. The track must be fresh, like this." She pushed the edge of her fist into the snow, drawing toes on the imprint. "See," she said, "this is the fresh track of a raccoon. He's very tasty and his hide will warm your bed, and his penis is of bone and can be sharpened into a needle." The prospect of a bone penis made the men smile, but Twobirds went on. "Even the opossum is worth taking, although he smells of death and there is much fat on him, but his flesh will keep your belly from shriveling in the cold.

"Do not throw anything away that's caught in your traps. Learn from the ways of the creatures you hunt or we will surely die. By spring there will be only our bones left in the melting snow."

Once the traps were built, the men were dispatched to set them. Upon their return, they began to dig, burrowing into the frozen red earth, two men to a hole and not too large, since only their bodies would warm them.

So they dug in pairs, like mated birds building a nest. All pretense aside, McReynolds dug for himself and Twobirds.

Only Sheets didn't dig, lying under his blanket, despondent still at the loss of his silver.

Lining his nest with bunchgrass that protruded through the drifts of snow, McReynolds then tested it for size. Like Twobirds said, it was warm, but each time he moved, dirt rained into his hair and ears. Still, it was better than the bitter winds and snow above. One thing for certain, there would be little lovemaking in such a dwelling.

For a week it snowed. Every night and every day the men searched the fresh drifts for their traps. But there was no game, and three of the traps were lost entirely beneath the snow.

"Build new ones," Twobirds said, "and stake them near a tree, five paces, toe to heel, from the base of the tree, and facing the morning sun. Next time you'll be able to dig and find them." With hunger in their faces they looked at her. "Do not worry," she said, "the traps will work. I promise you."

At night the men wormed into their holes, first one and then the other, with little room to turn or to breathe. For McReynolds, each time he entered, the old, suffocating fear returned. It was only her presence that made it bearable.

In the blackness of their lair they clung to each other, taking nourishment and courage from the touch of their bodies. By morning their arms would be dead beneath them and a spider-web of earth built in their hair.

Emancipation from the hole was a difficult task at best, Two-birds laughing at the dirt clinging to his brow and to his chestnut beard now quite long and raggedy.

On the fourth morning, as they exited their lair, their hearts jumped with joy because there before them were the tracks from the night before. At last no fresh snow, and the men flew to check their traps.

From the distance a yell of jubilation and then another and another as the men ran through the snow, their game held above their heads for all to see.

The catch was counted one by one as they returned, five rabbits, three pack rats, and a raccoon weighing nearly twenty pounds, whose foot had become entangled in a trap door. All were dispatched with clubs to save ammunition. Tonight they would eat, and they rubbed their hands together in anticipation.

"Clean them well," Twobirds said as she inspected each of the trophies, and do not throw anything away. What we do not eat, we'll use for bait."

One by one they were butchered and hung to chill, the men rubbing tallow into their cracked hands.

Grinning, First Sergeant Lansdown held up the raccoon's penis.

"Twobirds is right," he said, turning the ivory bone between his fingers. "Arms ready even when he's dead. Course, ain't no more than a darning needle now, is it?"

Slapping each other on the back, the men laughed, the sound strange in their ears.

"Build the fire until the coals are red," Twobirds said, "and cut mesquite sticks for roasting the game. Cut close to the ground where the moisture still lingers in the wood. That way it will not burn away too soon."

Handing Twobirds the penis bone, First Sergeant Lansdown clapped his hands.

"Let's go, boys, because tonight we eat like kings."

Night fell cold, but nothing could dampen their spirits as the smell of roasting meat winged about and set their mouths to watering.

When the meat was ready, according to Twobirds's determination, they fell to, devouring the morsels, sucking the marrow from the bones, wiping the grease from their beards with their sleeves. Even the pack rat was good, with a pungent nutty flavor.

Exiting his tent, Sheets waited for Twobirds to fill his plate. The only noticeable effect of his exile and lack of food was his decidedly baggy pants. Walking about the camp, he looked at the holes dug by the men and then reentered his tent without a word.

With the wind abated, the men stayed longer about the fire, reluctant to burrow beneath the ground where nothing but sleep and silence was possible. Besides, with a belly full of meat, the cold was less brutal and the fire more cheerful.

Working the raccoon penis against a rock, Twobirds ground it to a keen point.

"Must you do that?" McReynolds asked.

"Yes," she said, "the bone is very hard, very sharp. We may need it for sewing skins before the winter is over."

The darkness deepened about them and the day's warmth bled away into the cold, clear air, the stars filling the sky from horizon to horizon. One by one the men went to their beds, until only he and Twobirds remained.

"It's getting late," McReynolds said. "Maybe you should get some rest. You did much work today."

"Yes," she said, laying down the bone, "to my burrow like the rabbit." She paused. "We are going to be okay, Joseph. The winter was early but so will be the spring. It is hard to live this way but it can be done." Tucking her skirt about her legs, she rose. "The most danger is your lieutenant, because there is madness in his eyes."

"Yes," he said, "I know."

"Good night, Joseph. Do not wait too long in the cold."

Throwing a couple more logs on the fire, he moved in closer. It was good to be alone like this. The fire warmed his face and he dozed, basking in his solitude. And they rose from the past to greet him, from so far away now, transitory and fleeting, Renfro, Fielding, the others lost at Sheets's hand. So many had died and so hard, their souls crying out, speaking to him, a turn of the hand once over, they said, and then they could rest.

Awakening, he tossed another stick onto the fire and listened to the snow sizzle away. Why should Sheets be allowed to go on, because he was the commander, because some fool endowed him with that power? From the night, God's dog lifted its voice. Death is nothing, it said, and McReynolds knew that Sheets must die and that he must kill him.

Rising to join Twobirds, he slipped the bone into his pocket.

His medical knowledge had served death better than life so far. Perhaps this was his true purpose.

The next two days brought more snow and empty traps. Loss of hope came easily on an empty stomach and the men once again despaired. To make matters worse, Sheets's funk turned to malice and he ordered muster at daybreak, followed by two hours of marching, a pathetic and sad sight as the men waded the deep snow.

But then on the third day, no snow, and the traps were bountiful once again. As night fell they built the fire high and let the coals glow red and the smell of supper filled the air. Twobirds cut the meat, equal portions for all, and lay aside Sheets's portion on a tin plate.

"He'll want more," she said to McReynolds.

"Let me take it to him," he said.

Snow squeaking under his feet, he walked to Sheets's tent, his decision made. All that was left was to execute the act, sliding the sharpened bone into the meat, handing it to Sheets without hesitation.

Pulling the tent flap closed, McReynolds walked back to the fire. And then it came, a rushing sound as if he'd been punched in the stomach.

The men stood, watching from the fire, instinct alerting them to the unnatural sound that emanated from the tent, mules answering back from the corral at the labored honking.

"The lieutenant's shoving his food again," Number said, "or else calling out one of my mules."

Then Sheets stumbled into the light behind them, eyes bulging, face the color of red war paint as he pointed frantically into his mouth with one hand while holding his throat with the other.

"Seems he's trying to tell us something, sir," Number said, "like he's got a sore throat, or maybe his meat wasn't done to his liking."

Falling to his knees, Sheets's face darkened, snow clinging to his woolen trousers as he seized McReynolds's leg.

From the darkness Twobirds watched, her arms folded.

"You bastard," McReynolds yelled, kicking him away, "what do you want from me?" Vileness and loathing welled up in him even as he ran his fingers into Sheets's throat to dislodge the bone, cursing the day he'd met him. "You can't even die like a man," he shouted as he threw the bone into the fire, the blood and saliva of his enemy covering his hand.

A great rush of air filled Sheets's lungs as he kicked back to life in the snow.

No one spoke or looked at McReynolds but all knew that the moment had passed, that the good doctor's moral code was still intact, that their own chances of survival were now substantially less.

Forty

Avoiding accusation, choosing ignorance over confirmation, Sheets never said a word. Death was as real and certain to him now as the snow at his tent door.

There were times though, that he would sit at the opening of his tent, his pistol in his lap, and watch the men as they went about their work. The fear of reprisal gnawed at his resolve, stole his sleep, forced him ever further into isolation.

Without fail he took his meals alone, probing, examining his food with his fork. Never was he far from fear, looking over his shoulder even as he relieved himself in the bushes. Perhaps McReynolds had failed to rid the world of this monster, but for now at least the marching had stopped, and they were left alone to battle the elements as best they could.

Nearly two weeks passed without snow, and food was once again available, though sporadic and undependable, and in some ways more anguishing because the thought of food was never far from their minds. Would they eat tonight or crawl once again into their holes with empty stomachs? Perhaps tomorrow too, and the day after, the traps would be empty. Perhaps never again would they eat and so each day they waited anxiously for the men's return, waited to see if their arms were high or low, if there was to be joy or black disappointment. But with each day, whether there was food or not, there was always uncertainty, unbearable uncertainty.

Survival was boring work and bickering among the men was

a major problem for McReynolds. There was little to do between checking the traps but to wait, to bear the cold, to think of home.

The men quarreled over the slightest injustice and were intent on placing blame in as many places as possible. So McReynolds organized and dispatched daily hunting parties to search for the nonexistent game and each day there was a head count and each day wood to be gathered, sized, and stacked for the night fire.

The horses and mules were unable to forage for themselves so the men cut by hand the dry grass that protruded through the snow and fed it to them like mothers feeding their children.

Even in the face of the dire circumstances, Twobirds flourished, her ankle healing, her conviction doubling. The situation was better for Number as well, Sheets having forgotten his banishment. Rubbing his empty stomach with one hand while holding the other to the fire, Number would say with great bravado, "Figured my pay's nearly a hundred dollars. Why, with a hundred dollars, I could buy anything I could imagine."

And the men would nod and think of their own paychecks, of what they'd accrued, of what they were going to do with all that money when at last they got home.

But it was Twobirds who kept them going, her head high, her heart strong, her mind always at work. Each day there was a new plan, a new idea, paddle cactus scraped and boiled for pudding, as green and slick as buffalo manure, devil's claws collected by the armload and robbed of their tiny but delicious black seeds, dried hackberries no bigger than spider eggs picked and soaked in water to plump them up and fill the holes in their stomachs.

Sometimes a rare treat would be found, a hatful of scrub oak acorns, promptly boiled until all bitterness and flavor floated away in the steam. The men would dip their hands into the paste and suck the tasteless goo from the ends of their fingers like kids at the cake bowl.

The harder the gale, the more Twobirds bent, and each time she emerged stronger than before. Respect for her among the men was obvious, and they turned to her often, for information, for advice, for solace when their own constitutions began to crumble.

Nearly every day she walked alone, disappearing over the horizon for hours at a time, sparking McReynolds's curiosity until he followed her. At first he tried to keep her in sight as she made her way through the drifts of snow, but with her steady, strong pace, the distance between them increased until at last she disappeared.

Unthwarted, he followed her tracks across the frozen prairie and along the west rim of the basin that overshadowed the valley. Soon even her tracks faded under the sifting snow, leaving only the skittering of ice crystals and the cold whisper of the north wind. Looking over his shoulder, he checked the position of Chimney Rock. As long as he could keep that in sight he could find his way back to camp.

Just ahead the rim broke into a natural path that dropped along the west wall of the valley. Protected from the prevailing north winds, it was clear of snow and McReynolds decided to take a last look before returning to camp. And there in the damp earth her tracks reappeared and he congratulated himself on his resourcefulness.

"Joseph," she said.

Tingles sped down his arms and out the ends of his fingers as he whirled about. Not until she moved did he see her there against the rocks.

"My God," he said, "you scared the life out of me."

"Why have you been following me?" she asked, her hair in a black fall about her shoulders.

"I was worried about you," he lied, the sun-heated rocks warming his face.

"I think you were not worried about me, Joseph."

"I was curious, I guess."

"Yes," she said.

"What are you doing?" he asked, lowering himself against the wall of rock.

For awhile she didn't answer, looking across the expanse of

the valley. When she turned to him, there was a peacefulness in her eyes, a contentment with the world that belied their desperate situation.

"I think you call it praying," she said.

"Praying?"

"Yes," she said, her black eyes lingering on his. "Do you not think there is something larger than your medicine?"

Rubbing the cold from his fingers, he thought. Never had the question been asked so directly. It demanded an honest answer.

"I don't know," he said. "I think maybe not."

"The woman who rode with you did," she said, avoiding Nurse Cromley's name. "Her spirit was strong."

Pulling himself up, he walked to the edge of the path, the canyon sheering away, falling away to terrifying depths, his head whirling as he stepped back.

"Yes," he said, "and we can see where it got her."

Clouds raced through the blue sky as Twobirds walked to the edge of the path. His stomach tightened and he fought the urge to grab her, to pull her away from the brink.

"Be careful," he said, "you might fall."

"Yes, like that, and then no longer of this world. So, these things must be important. They must be thought about, Joseph."

"I see that all is random," he said, averting his eyes, unable to watch, "that whether you fall or not is but fate or individual choice. I see nothing but randomness and infinite possibility." Unable to resist longer, he took her hand, pulling her away from the edge. "What is it that you believe, Twobirds? What makes you so certain?"

The sunlight cast blue swirls in the blackness of her hair, like oil on water.

"I believe in three worlds," she said, "one under the surface of a lake on which the earth floats, another above the sky, and a third the spirits of the four winds which change the seasons. I believe in the wisdom of animals and in the truth of their spirits and in a power above all these things."

"It's good," he said, "to have hope. I guess man needs hope."

A white cloud boiled up from nowhere, startling white columns boiling and churning from the deep blue sky. "But you are an intelligent woman, Twobirds. Surely you don't believe such things."

"You make a joke of me," she said, turning her eyes away.

"No, no," he protested, "but spirits under a lake? It's more than my logic can accept. My science will not allow it."

"Your science then knows all the answers?" she asked, leaning forward, her full breasts against her blouse.

"No, not all, of course, but enough not to believe in spirits under a lake."

"Your science knows nothing," she said, pulling her hair back over one shoulder. "Your science knows so little."

"I've upset you. I'm sorry," he said, cupping her chin in his hand to soften her anger. "I didn't mean to make light of your religion, but there is so much you don't understand." Her skin was alive and supple under his fingers, and his groin warmed. "I'm sorry, Twobirds."

Shaking her head, she forgave him, which was her way.

Ignited by her body, he pulled her down, kissed her hungrily.

"No," she said, struggling against him. But he held her, the smell of her, the taste of her, her exquisite hands against his chest. "No," she gasped, her voice but a distant thing.

"But Twobirds, I thought . . ."

"No," she said again, and this time there was no doubting her resolve.

Heart hammering, he leaned against the rock and fought to reclaim control of his body.

"But we're alone," he said, "and in this place. I want you and I thought you wanted me."

"We cannot," she said, straightening her skirt, her profile silhouetted against the white clouds behind her, "not now."

"But why? I've made you angry, haven't I?"

"It's not that," she said, moving dangerously close to the edge of the rim again.

"Then what?"

"I don't know," she said, tears in her eyes.

"It's the ghosts, isn't it" he said, "the ones who are gone, the ones with no names?" The cold wind blew against his face. "But it was you who said to put them behind us, to not speak their names. It was you who said the dead wanted no more from the living. We have done our grieving and it's over."

"It's wrong, Joseph, to be together. This I know."

"But why?" he asked. "Why now?"

"I am certain," she said.

Stalking away, he fumed with anger, frustration, confusion.

"To hell with you," he shouted over his shoulder. "To hell with you and your ghosts."

"To hell with you," the spirits answered from the canyon walls, "with you and your ghosts."

Forty-one

Not returning to her bed nor asking favors of her again, McReynolds huddled near the fire for warmth, listening to the snoring of Sheets in his tent and to the distant baying of coyotes.

Twice he checked Twobirds's wound, owing her that much, his voice conciliatory, his touch clinical as he examined the scar where the bullet had entered.

And so it was understood, agreed, that things were done between them, and his heart wept for her as he watched her prepare food or gather wood for the fire. At night he dreamed of the small of her back, the pocket of her throat, awakening with his heart tripping.

At first the men too were puzzled by the estrangement between Twobirds and him, but they had learned, like he had learned, that adaptability was the key to survival out here and soon no one questioned it.

In the absence of Twobirds, Number took to McReynolds's side, a constant companion. At first he found the attention annoying, but came to prefer it to the painful loneliness.

"A mule's gone," Number said, pointing to the makeshift corral that lay beyond camp, "as sure as I'm standing here, and there ain't no way that mule could've got down on its knees and crawled under that gate. But he's gone for sure and the lieutenant's going to have my hide tacked and cured if I don't find him soon."

"Maybe you shut him out instead of in," McReynolds said,

sharpening the end of a trap stake, tossing it into a growing pile at his side.

"Ain't likely, is it?" he said. "Even a dumb slick sleeve like myself knows a gate's to shut mules in and not out. Lordy, when Lieutenant Sheets finds out, he's likely to gut me and have me for Sunday dinner."

"Well, he's not likely to know, is he, not unless you tell him."

"Ain't likely I'll stir rattlers," said Number, bending down to stack the stakes into an orderly pile, "not on purpose at least."

"Still, it's peculiar, isn't it? Not like a mule to jump corral. Takes too much energy and planning," he added, with a Renfro flare that pleased him.

"Peculiar, sure," Number said, "and only one answer comes to me."

"What's that, Corporal?"

"Kiowa, sir. Maybe they've come back to steal our mounts and lift our hair."

"Maybe, but it doesn't add up entirely, does it?" he said, tossing another stick onto the pile. "Why would they come back here to eat fried pack rat and opossum and live in a hole in the ground like a prairie dog? Why would they leave good hunting and fresh meat for that?"

"Maybe . . . maybe food ain't what it's all about," Number said, jabbing sticks into the ground to keep the pile from spilling.

"What are you getting at, Corporal?"

"Maybe it's Twobirds, sir. They could've come back for her, you know, and for whatever else they can take in the process."

Maybe so. Maybe that's why Twobirds turned him out. Maybe she knew all along they would return.

"Twobirds would've said, wouldn't she?"

"You'd think so, sir. Still, she's been acting peculiar of late and, well sir, if you'll forgive me for saying it, things ain't the same with you two no more either."

"She's saved our lives here on many occasions, Corporal. We wouldn't be more than tufts of hair and hide by now if she hadn't brought us through. We owe her some loyalty, you and me."

"Yes sir, I know it's so, and I wouldn't for a minute suggest otherwise. All I'm saying is those Kiowa look out for their own and she's still theirs, far as they're concerned. It ain't never done with them, sir, not until it's over."

Sticking his knife into his pocket, McReynolds turned to leave when he smelled something in the air, a feel maybe, a warmth and balm long driven from his memory by the brutal cold.

"Maybe it's nothing but a lost mule, Number, no way of knowing, so don't go spooking up the men. Keep it to yourself until we know for certain what's going on. You understand what I'm saying, don't you?"

"Yes sir, I do, and mules been known to come up missing without Kiowa leading them off, and I guess they could again, sir.

"I didn't mean nothing against Twobirds," he said, loading the stakes into his arms. "Far as I'm concerned, she's the finest ever lived, and I wouldn't ever suggest otherwise."

"I know, Number. Now get out of here before I tell Sheets you lost one of his mules."

"There is just one thing," he grinned, stakes poking in every direction from between his arms. "Don't know if it means much, but there was a boot track not too far from the corral, just yonder where that ole cedar's broke over, where that mule's tracks lead off to the west."

"Boot track?"

"Yes sir, big it was, too."

"Doesn't sound like Kiowa, does it, Number?"

"No sir," he said, rearranging his bundle, "not like Kiowa, 'less they stole boots off some poor soldier, which they could have, I suppose." He paused. "That track's likely to belong to anybody, I reckon, but it's fresh like that mule track and not far behind. Still, why would one of our own be stealing a mule too poor to eat and too mean to ride, assuming of course he didn't have somewhere to go, like a dance or a social meeting."

"It's only a mule missing, Number, and not likely an Indian uprising or an act of treason. Go on, get those traps restaked while there's still sunlight."

"Yes sir," he said, "and thanks for not telling the lieutenant."

The next morning McReynolds was standing at the fire's edge waiting for the rest of the camp to awaken when it occurred to him that he was no longer shivering.

By noon that same day a south wind swept in like a sweet kiss, teeming with life and warmth and the smell of spring on its breath. The men shed their filthy coats and danced about like fools under the thin hot sun. For the first time in many days they believed their lives spared from the savage cold.

Green grass was not far away to fatten their mounts for the trip home, and all knew that game too would soon return and that they could move from their burrows and live like men ought to. Even at that they were a sight to be seen, unshorn, stinking, primeval in every way, and they danced about the camp in celebration like cavemen.

By week's end the sun rose hot and the men rubbed at their burned necks above tattered collars. Warm winds blew from the southwest, melting the snow, and soon even the soggy earth gave up its moisture and baked dry under the persistent winds.

A red powder formed and swirled on its surface as the winds rushed in from their desert stay. Day and night they blew, gusts from all directions, impetuous, violent, lifting blankets, clothes, anything untied, into the air.

One morning early, just as the sun broke, a sudden and ferocious gale sent Sheets's tent soaring to the top of Chimney Rock like a giant kite as he slept half naked on his cot. In spite of his glare, the men laughed uproariously.

Sunsets turned orange and then red like blood as the sky grew dark and ponderous. The sun flushed crimson and hid its face beyond the clouds of March dust.

Day after day the wind blew and even at night it did not subside. The moon blinked and drooped like a fevered red eye and no one slept under its curse, each man huddling under his blanket, listening to the swirl of dirt, wondering how much more he could endure.

When the food was gone, hunger and boredom drove them from their shelters and to their traps. Wrapped in scarves and blankets like old women, they walked the trap line. It was familiar territory to them now and even in the blinding dust they found their way.

As was his custom, Number walked behind McReynolds, the tail of his scarf flapping in the turbulence, but he bore on, head down, voice muffled beneath the folds of cloth.

The first trap was empty and Number held it up for McReynolds to see. The second trap had a half-grown opossum, its prehensile tail looped about its neck, its eyes glazed in feigned death, its tongue lolling from its mouth.

"Playing dead," Number said. "Looks deader than death itself, doesn't he?"

"Hope to never see one again, live or dead," McReynolds said.

With the trap stick, Number whacked the opossum between its ears. Death neither changed its expression nor altered its position.

"Well, he's not playing dead no more," Number said.

The sky darkened above them, not from clouds but from dust riding the winds into the sky.

"What I wouldn't give for a slab of buffalo hump," McReynolds said.

"Well, it won't be long, will it?" Number shifted the opossum to the other shoulder, looking at the distant bank of dust. "Can just hear them buffalo moving north by the hundreds, and pretty soon we'll be knee-deep in red meat."

Optimism was an ingrained part of Number's character, like his boundless and enduring energy.

Within the hour they climbed onto the plateau that lay eastward of Chimney Rock. Prairie grass, waist-deep and dry as tinder, murmured in the wind like whispering girls.

The plateau proved to be their best trap line, small stuff for the most part, rodents, rabbits, an occasional prairie dog. By watching the hawks circle overhead, Number had discovered its bounty. "Bound to be good," he'd said, and it was, especially now that the snow had dissipated, leaving the myriad runways exposed to full view.

The tall grass pulled about their ankles, heavy as water.

"I'll check 'Rat Hollow,' " Number said, pointing to the small valley lying between two swells of earth, "and circle back to 'coon tree.' " Over the winter they'd named their traps by what game was most often found in them. "Maybe you could check 'disappointment creek,' sir, if you don't mind, that is, and meet me at the tree. We could save a little time that way, sir."

Working northward to the small creek, McReynolds cut through the northeast edge of the grass. In the distance he heard what sounded like a clap of thunder. Stopping, he held his hand over his eyes to determine its origin. A flash cut through the bank of dust, close this time, a dry crackle dancing about him. Soon thunder pealed across the plateau and pooled in the pit of his stomach. On the horizon Number stopped and looked back at him as a gust of cold wind surged from the black bank.

When the full force of the wind hit, McReynolds's hat spun into the air.

"Damn," he muttered, spiking the crumpled hat back on his head.

In the distance he could see Number, a tiny figure now against the imposing dust cloud.

Satisfied, McReynolds pressed on to the creek. It barely qualified as a creek, dry most of the time, but now running full of melted snow water.

The trap was empty of course, as it nearly always was, but

he checked the bait and reset the catch anyway, looking for tracks as Twobirds had instructed.

The smell of the campfire reached him on the wind and he wished he were back in his bed. At first it was only a vague uneasiness as he calculated the distance from camp, too far away to smell campfire smoke under the best of conditions.

Clambering to the top of the embankment, his worst fears were confirmed. As far as could he see there were but flames, a boiling, seething inferno. Like a hungry monster it devoured the dry grass, licking and fuming and belching black smoke into the sky.

"Number!" he yelled, his voice consumed by the roaring flames.

Even as he called, he saw Number running before the crown of fire, running before the fury, before the cruelty of flame, wind, fuel.

Already the heat singed McReynolds's beard and burned the moisture from his eyes. Rodents scrambled over his shoes as they tried to flee the terrible heat.

This time his own name rose from his throat. There was no escape, no harbor, no safety, but with one last bid he plunged into the melt stream, burrowed into the fetid muck like a worm under a rock.

The roar came first, a sound not heard until gone, the sky closing above him, a scarlet curtain of fire separating him from life and hope, and the dragon's hot mouth sucked the air from his lungs and the hair on his head curled under the scorching heat, silent screams turned into the belly of the earth. Where was his god now? Where was hers?

Coughing, he spewed slime and water from his mouth as he rose from the mud like an aboriginal man. All about him was death and destruction, a naked and charred place, curls of steam rising from hapless turtles caught in the salvo. It had all happened so quickly, so much destruction, and then it was gone.

Black ash swirled about with each gust of wind and gathered

on his mud-caked face. There was but one thing to do, find Number and take him home. Poor Number, dying like that.

Shivering at the prospect of what he would find, he headed out. Duty called and he would do what he must. With determination he headed for the last place he'd seen Number alive, racing before the crown of fire, his arms waving as the flames reached out for him.

What he found was not Number, but the cremated carcass of the opossum, its blackened body still poised in feigned death. Perhaps there was nothing left of his luckless friend, devoured by the intense and hungry wildfire. In some ways he hoped so. To look upon the twisted and burned body of his companion would be difficult.

With his toe he poked at the charred remains of the opossum and watched it disintegrate into a pile of ash. What an outrageous world, what a cruel and unforgiving world.

At first he didn't recognize them for what they were, parallel lines eastward across the sand and covered with a thin coat of ash. Whisking away the ash with the brim of his hat, he saw that they were tracks, but not wagon tracks as he'd first thought, too uneven, wobbly, like a drunk stumbling home from a bar.

With great concentration and care be blew the ash away and the imprints came into view. Maybe he wasn't much of a tracker, but there was no mistaking mule shoes, not even by him, and those lines in the sand were somebody's heels being dragged along.

A groan came from the thicket at edge of the burn line and there was little doubt who it was.

"Number?" he called.

"Yes sir," he said, his voice weak.

Rushing to his side, McReynolds turned him over, his shirt collar still smoldering, pinching out the coals between his fingers. Number was burned, badly burned, but he was still alive.

"My God, Corporal," McReynolds shook his head, "how did you do it?"

"It's a miracle, sir, a sure enough miracle. I was running hard as I could but that fire was closing in fast. Could feel my blood beginning to boil, but I just couldn't run no more. The gates of hell were right there, a fuming monster fixin' to swallow me down. I never been so scared and so tired all at once."

A gust of wind swept ash into Number's face and he squeezed his eyes shut. Across his shoulders, his shirt was nearly burned away. Out here nothing could be more serious than an open burn wound.

"Take it easy, Corporal. You're alive and little else matters."

"I guess I passed out," he said, "and when I woke, there I was, ropes around my wrists, being hauled out of hell itself by some sort of spirit."

"Who was it?" McReynolds asked.

"Never saw, sir. Never saw nothing but that mule's ass over my head."

"Are you certain, Number?"

"Oh, yes sir, when I see a mule's ass, I'm pretty certain. Funny thing though, it was my mule, you know, the one I shut out instead of in." Groaning, he tried to smile. "No matter to me who it was, sir. Kiowa or not, he's welcome to that mule and I don't care what Lieutenant Sheets says."

Forty-two

The burn was serious, three hands' length across one shoulder and halfway down one arm, third degree, maybe worse.

Like ivory buttons Number's backbone peeked through the burned flesh. Bone infection could be the end of him and it wouldn't be pretty or fast.

"Burned the traps up too, I suppose?" Sheets asked.

"The traps can be replaced," McReynolds said, "but this man can't be."

"Humph," Sheets snorted, "without those traps we'll all go hungry."

"Hadn't been for that spirit ghost, guess I'd be burned up dead, too," Number said, his arm stretched over his head.

"What spirit ghost? What's he talking about now?" Sheets asked.

All soap had long since disappeared so McReynolds poured hot water from the coffeepot over his hands, letting them air dry.

"Someone saved the corporal here," he said. "Pulled him from the fire just in time. There were tracks, mule I think, just under the ash, but no sign of anyone."

Squatting at the fire, her arms full of paddle cactus stacked on a blanket, Twobirds began singeing away the thorns.

"Mule tracks?" she asked, looking up at McReynolds.

"Could have been a horse. I'm not much of a tracker. The

corporal here says it was a mule. Could have been Kiowa or even Osage for all I know.

"Much pain, Corporal?" he asked as he examined the cooked flesh.

"Funny, ain't it, but I can't feel a thing."

"Burned the nerve endings away. No pain is usually good, but not in this case, I'm afraid."

"That spirit ghost have on a uniform?" Sheets asked Number. "Was he little or big? What did he look like?"

"I don't know, sir. Being on fire at the time, I didn't pay attention as I ought."

"Christ," Sheets snorted, his eyes blazing, "if someone pulled me out of a grass fire, think I'd look to see who it was."

"We don't know who it was, Lieutenant," McReynolds said, "but he saved our man here and for that we're grateful."

Laying the cleaned cactus paddles on a smooth rock, Twobirds worked them into a paste, dipping the end of a stick into the paste and handing it to McReynolds.

"Put this on him," she said, "to soften the wound."

"Why not," he said, "there's precious little else to use."

Eyes dark and charged with fear, Sheets addressed the first sergeant.

"Double the guard and prepare to break camp, first light."

"We can't go anywhere yet," McReynolds said, "no supplies, half-starved horses, and this man can't ride with these burns."

"I've made the decision to move out," he said.

"And the corporal?"

"Put him in the wagon," he said, stomping off without looking back.

Reaching for his scalpel, McReynolds watched Sheets's back as he walked away.

"It is not for you to kill again," Twobirds said, clasping his wrist. "You must be the one to heal."

He started to protest, to tell her of his weakness, how it had destroyed him and the ones he loved, to tell her how nothing was left in him but death, no strength, no courage, no will, to tell her how barren and empty was his soul. But she was gone, walking into the distance, her dark hair blowing in the wind.

The sound of camp breaking awoke McReynolds, the smell of horse sweat and leather, the clinking of buckles and snap reins. Like starved phantoms the men worked in the morning dawn, each absorbed in his own thoughts of what lay ahead.

Over night, gulf moisture rode in on shifting winds and a gray haze filtered the sun as it slipped into the morning sky. Beads of moisture clung to the grass that yesterday had burned with blistering heat. Now the men's cuffs were wet to their knees and droplets of water gathered on their beards.

A flurry of confusion erupted each place Sheets stopped, as contradicting orders were issued one after another.

Near the fire Twobirds rolled her bedding, tying it with lengths of rawhide. Kneeling next to her, Sheets whispered something in her ear. Insult lingered on her face as she pushed him away. Like a coyote after a sickly calf, Sheets sensed vulnerability, moving in for an easy kill.

Curled beneath his blanket, Number had not moved from where they'd left him the night before.

"How are you doing this morning, Corporal?" McReynolds asked with all the cheer he could muster.

Quivering under the indignity of his wounds, Number's legs were drawn up in the fetal position. Red streaks burst star-like from the edges of the burns.

"It ain't a hurt, sir, not like you'd think. More like I've been bound by rawhide and left to dry. Can't lift my arm now and my head's pulling back like it was going off somewhere on its own."

Examining his backbone, McReynolds found the spots still clear, no sign of bone infection, but they were beginning to dry. That was not good, not good at all.

Smearing the cactus paste into the open wounds was against

everything he knew and understood about sterile treatment, but what the hell was he supposed to do in this wretched place?

"You're going to do all right, Number," he lied, the smell of cactus on his hands. "You have a guardian angel and you're going to do just fine."

"Yes sir," Number tried to smile. "Got me a considerable sum of money saved up too and no place to spend it. It's been a real economical winter, you might say. The rent's been dirt cheap and the food downright reasonable."

"We're going to load you in the wagon," McReynolds said, wrapping the wounds with makeshift bandages. "It's the best we can do."

"That'll be just fine, sir. I got one free hand to hang on with and more'n my share of pluck."

"That you do, Corporal, that you do."

"I ain't dying out here, see," he said, reaching for McReynolds's hand. "I ain't lettin' Sheets or no man kill me out here. I got me a guardian angel, like you say, and it's you, sir. With a doctor like you right here to get me through, there ain't no way I can't make it."

"Well, I'll do my best, Corporal, and you do the same."

"There is just one thing, sir."

"What's that?" McReynolds said as be folded the bandages to keep out the trail dust.

"It's the Cross Timbers, sir."

"I don't understand."

"They say those thickets are so close a man has to turn sideways to walk through 'em. No wagon's ever going through those Cross Timbers, sir. No wagon, no Number, as I see it, and Sheets wouldn't mind leaving me to the buzzards, not for a minute if it served his purpose, sir."

"Look, Corporal, by the time we make Cross Timbers you'll be well on your way to recovering. It's a bridge we won't have to cross."

"Yes sir," he smiled. "Then I'll just sit back and enjoy the ride."

* * *

With only one wagon carrying Number and the few supplies that were left, they rode into the prairie once again. As the column moved out, as they began their trek southward at last, as they passed their winter burrows dug in the hillside like small graves, all wondered what lay ahead.

Between First Sergeant Lansdown and Lieutenant Sheets, Twobirds rode on one of the pack mules, her black hair twisted in a single braid down her back, as beautiful and regal as the first time McReynolds had seen her.

Bouncing in the bed of the wagon, Number clung to the seat brace with a tenacious grip, his jaw set in determination.

The column ascended the path leading out of the valley and onto a plateau. Stirred by horses' hooves, the burned grass smelled of smoke and death, and neither McReynolds nor Number spoke. But soon they crossed the Cimarron and headed due south through open country, leaving their terrible winter behind.

The column creaked southward like a starved snake, twisting, turning, rattling southward with protruding ribs. The morning haze gave way to midday heat and the humidity pressed upon them and stole what little energy they had.

At noon they stopped to rest but there was precious little to eat or drink. The horses were tied under the shade of a single large elm, their ears drooping from exhaustion, too tired even to pick at the tiny leaf buds on the trees.

The burns Number had suffered would require enormous amounts of calories to heal, so McReynolds gave him water and an extra portion of food.

"How you making it, Corporal?"

"Just fine," he said, raising his eyes. "It's a little tougher than I thought, but I'm making it."

But his contorted face told a different story, a story of misery, of torment, of pain from the endless jostling of the wagon.

"You drink," McReynolds said, "and rest, best you can. You need plenty of both."

"I like having a guardian angel," he smiled, "even if he does wear brass on his shoulders. I've been wondering something, sir, as I was passing the time here in this wagon."

"And what's that?" McReynolds asked, screwing the cap back on his canteen.

Rubbing the tension from his neck, Number squinted his eyes against the sun.

"Why was Lieutenant Sheets in such an all-fired hurry to move out? Would've made more sense to sit it out a few weeks, what with grub, water, and a hole to hide in. Spring grass's just around the corner. Could've fattened the mules up and trotted back home without a hitch."

"There's not much way of explaining Sheets's actions, Corporal."

Under the shade of the elm, Twobirds took down her hair, lowering her head, combing it forward with her fingers and exposing the delicate cut of her neck. "Guess he's got his own ghosts to worry about," he said, looking away.

"Yes sir, guess there's plenty ghosts to go around. I just hadn't planned on being one myself quite so soon."

Two days more they rode, from dawn to dusk, two days southward as the heat began to climb. At a distance, the meadows looked green, winding up through the valleys like delicate ribbons. The horses would quicken their pace at the prospect of food, but once there, the tiny shoots of grass were too small to eat but too big to ignore.

Burying their faces in the dirt, they'd pick at the grass, their abraded noses bleeding from the desperate grubbing in the hardened ground, their big, hungry eyes breaking the heart of every man there.

Watching the horizon, Sheets's arms hung over the limb of a mesquite, a red streak of dirt across his forehead where his hat had rested throughout the day's ride.

"Could I talk to you, Lieutenant?" McReynolds asked.

"You never know what's out here," Sheets said without turning around. "You never know what's waiting to take you down, take you down just like that."

"Lieutenant, I think we need to stop for awhile, wait for grass, send out hunting parties. There are fresh deer tracks here and there, and if we took the time to hunt, I think we could bring a few down, feed the men, wait for grass for the horses. They're not going to make it without pasture. Another couple weeks and they'd be belly-deep in grass.

"Number's getting worse too, serious symptoms, maybe bone infection, and he's dead weary from that wagon. What could it hurt to stop awhile, get things together?"

"There are things you do not understand," he said, training his eyes on McReynolds. "I don't suppose you're aware we're being followed? You didn't know that, did you? Ever since we broke camp, a half day behind, no more."

"Followed?"

"Half day and gaining fast."

Kneeling, McReynolds studied the northern skyline as if, were he to look long enough, he could see what Sheets saw. But there was nothing but blue sky and a single flock of blackbirds disappearing into the sun.

"You've seen someone following us?" he asked again.

"Seen him? I don't have to see him to know he's out there, and he's out there all right."

The blackbirds reappeared, darting through the sky, first to the right and then to the left, then down in a black free fall, as if guided by some unknown force.

"But who?" he asked. "Who could possibly be following us and why?"

"Who pulled Number from the fire? Who buried the silver beneath a thousand tons of rock? I don't know who, do I? But it's my duty to protect my men and that's what I aim to do. We can't be more than a week from the Cross Timbers, a week at most," he said, rubbing the handle of his pistol with the palm of his hand. "No one would follow us in there."

Unsheathing the pistol, he turned the chamber, its oiled click like that of a jeweled timepiece, and then he slid it back into its holster. "It's best to leave these things to me. What I ask of my men, they'll do. This is a man's army and they'll do what's required of them. If they can't stand a hard ride for a few days, then by God, they can just face what's coming over that horizon."

"But Corporal Number can't keep this up, Lieutenant. He needs rest from that wagon."

"This is my last word to you," Sheets said. "Number's wounds are a result of his own stupidity. You leave him or bring him, but don't ask me to jeopardize the safety of my men."

What Sheets described as a hard ride turned out to be three consecutive and torturous days of hell-bent, nonstop riding. By sundown of the third day men and horses were exhausted, trail hardened soldiers collapsing where they dismounted, unable even to unsaddle their spent horses. Neither blistered thighs nor chapped legs nor hungry bellies could detract from their over-powering fatigue.

Twelve hours a day, three days in a row, they had ridden. Twelve hours of Sheets ranting and forcing them on like cattle in a drive. There wasn't a man among them who would not have celebrated his extended and painful demise. But all knew, though none would admit it, that Sheets was capable of getting the most out of his men, and if only through hate, they drove ahead.

But it was Number who suffered, the perpetual bouncing of the wagon, his burns drawing and thickening like leather, his muscles twisting like mountain juniper under the shaking of the wagon. Eyes sunk dark in his skull, his mouth gulped for oxygen. The food was nearly gone, not that it mattered, because he showed little interest in food in any case.

The cactus pulp had softened his wounds, so McReynolds smeared on more. Still, infection was evident now and his head burned hot as a wagon seat at high noon. Perhaps worse was the ominous color of the exposed bone on his back. Covering him from the night chill, McReynolds collapsed in the bed of the wagon.

Dawn rose too soon and found Sheets walking from man to man.

"Get up! Get up!" he shouted. "He's nearly upon us and here you're sleeping like rabbits In the grass. Get up, get up, I say, before it's too late."

"Begging your pardon, sir," Number said, peeking over the side boards of the wagon, "but exactly who is it that's coming?"

"I don't know *who's* coming, Corporal. How do you expect me to know who it is? I haven't exactly had the opportunity to introduce myself and ask who he might be."

"Begging your pardon again, sir, but if you don't know who it is and you ain't seen no one, then how do you know he's about here?"

The insolence of Number's question pushed Sheets's brows into dark peaks, his voice dropping to a sinister tone.

"He pulled you from the burning fire, didn't he? And he's been with us ever since."

"One man could hardly be a threat even to this bedraggled bunch," Number said.

"It's obvious to those who have the brains to think that we're being trailed," Sheet said, fingering his pistol. "I heard him coming last night, riding hard like a man bent to kill, riding hard with evil in his eyes. Daylight caught him, that's all, or he'd have butchered us all in our sleep. Now, mount up, all of you, while there's light to ride."

By noon the sun burned hot on their backs and sweat soaked their shirts. Skin reddened, then blistered under the thin spring day. Shaking his head, Sheets refused to stop at the single murky watering hole they passed at noon.

"You must water the horses," Twobirds told Sheets. "Even Kiowa children know you must water the horses."

But Sheets refused. "We ride," he said. "He is close. Could you not hear him? We must not stop now. The Cross Timbers are close and he'll not follow there."

The column turned southwest into the sun, and the horses labored against the trail as it began an ascent onto a plateau.

Within minutes the lead horse faltered, his back legs spiked for balance, but it was no use, as he fell on his side, his nostrils flaring as he tried to get back on his feet.

"He's done for," Number said from the wagon bed.

But still the shot from Sheets's pistol ripped through the noon heat and through the soul of every man there. The bay horse rose up on his front feet for a single, terrifying moment before dropping into the dust, his life pouring from the small hole between his eyes.

"Damn you!" McReynolds screamed, spittle drooling from his lip, his frustration, his contempt, his despair boiling to the surface, revulsion so complete as to strangle the only humanity left within him.

Leveling the revolver at McReynolds's chest, Sheets cocked the hammer and the cylinder dropped into place.

But for the second time Twobirds intervened, stepping between them, her eyes unswerving, dark as the blackbirds against the sun, pointing to the east, where there on the skyline rose a forbidding black wall.

All else stopped at that moment, unimportant and suspended, as each man struggled to comprehend the magnitude and fearsome impenetrability of the Cross Timbers.

Forty-three

So thick was the undergrowth in the Cross Timbers that sunlight could not penetrate, and cool air bled from its darkness and onto their feet as they stood at its edge and stared into its profusion.

Each man's gear was gone through personally by Sheets and all essentials were ordered left behind, which turned out to be precious little, a few ragged blankets, cooking utensils, keepsakes of no importance except to their owners. The wagon was burned while Number watched on, to keep it from enemy hands, Sheets said.

"It's all right," McReynolds said. "We'll get you through on horseback."

"Just fold me up and use me for a saddle blanket, sir, and shake me out when we get to Fort Gibson."

Every man there knew, just as Number knew, that his chances of survival had dropped considerably with the burning of the wagon.

But it was Twobirds who was the most disturbed, pacing the perimeter of the Cross Timbers like a caged animal, walking its border, staring into its darkness. For the first time since McReynolds had known her, he detected fear in her eyes.

Blackjacks twisted and turned. Bramble wound in tight knurls about their trunks, runners with razor-sharp barbs hanging from every limb. This was not just a forest, but the boundary of hell, and they were about to enter it.

"Twobirds," he said, approaching her as she stood at the edge of camp.

"Joseph" she said, the sun's rays casting shadows upon her proud face, "the Cross Timbers."

Kneeling, he searched the ground for a stick, drawing interlocking circles in the sand as he thought.

"I've watched you," he said, "and this place frightens you. There's no need for you to go farther, you know. You'ye done enough, and there is nothing you owe anyone."

"I've been wanting to talk with you," she said, kneeling next to him. "I know that you're angry, that you believe I no longer care, but you must understand that this is wrong. I'll always care for you."

"Then what is it?" he asked, scratching out the circles, "Why have you driven me away?"

Winds swept through the Timbers, a rush of leaves rolling into its midst like an ocean wave.

"I don't know," she said, "but something is not right. We must wait."

"I don't understand, but then there's been a great deal out here that I have not understood. Perhaps some day?"

"Yes," she said, "perhaps, but for now you must not question it. For now we must get through the Cross Timbers. It is enough."

"You should leave, Twobirds, go back to your people while you can. Sheets is quite mad, you know. No one is safe."

"I will finish this," she said.

And so they entered the Cross Timbers, one by one into the mottled light. Briar abounded and gathered about their ankles, slicing and gouging, blood reddening their britches.

A few hundred yards farther and the forest thickened, forcing them all to dismount and lead their horses. In a silent brood they picked their way through the trees, each man lost in his thoughts, each man irretrievably committed now to whatever lay ahead.

Hardwoods of all varieties thrived in the sand, blackjack, post oak, walnut, dogwood, locust, most of it twisted and knurled, as hard and unforgiving as the land itself.

Here and there would be an opening, never more than a few yards wide, running from the prairie behind like spokes from a wheel. An occasional charred stump was the only evidence of the prairie fires that had penetrated the Cross Timbers. But even such fires were defeated by the undergrowth.

Fine sand sucked at their feet like swamp mud, but it was water-bearing sand, so close to the surface that springs were frequent, sweet and cold and one of the few solaces in the Cross Timbers.

At times the going was so slow, the undergrowth so thick, that they could only wait, unable to move forward or backward until a passage was cleared.

Comforting Number during such waits, McReynolds would tell stories of home, but Number's misery was great, his strength fading, his wounds black with insects that worked at his bandages.

But Number would smile, his head pulled down, his neck corded with pain, as if all were right with the world.

By nightfall the undergrowth thickened again and the column ground to a halt. Cursing at the delay, Sheets's voice cut through the minds and hearts of each man there. Their heads against their knees, their clothing torn and soaked with blood, their minds long since numbed, the men only sat and listened.

First, McReynolds attended Number's wounds as best he could while Twobirds disappeared into the trees, returning shortly, hands dripping with an enormous honeycomb.

Bees still dived about her, the welts on her arms evidence of the battle that had transpired. Long starved for sweets, the men cheered at the sight of the honey, and with great ceremony the comb was divided on pieces of bark.

Not a hundred yards from where they camped, a spring was found, its clear, cold water pooling among the tree roots. Firewood too abounded, seasoned logs of pecan, ash, hackberry, all capable of a steady hot flame, and by dark a luxurious fire roared into the sky.

As always, Sheets sat at a distance, avoiding the company of the men, doing so almost completely now, retiring to the periphery of the camp, insisting that Twobirds alone prepare his food. Even then he examined it with care, turning it over again and again before putting it into his mouth.

Sometimes at night he could be heard muttering of silver and of dark rivers. In the darkest hours, in the quiet morning hours as the stars dimmed and the night plunged into its blackest moments, the cry of "Swinkoe!" could be heard, but no one knew what it meant. No one any longer cared.

Each man was served in turn, Twobirds's dark eyes glowing with satisfaction as the men savored their delicacy. How like a woman she was, caring, nurturing, sacrificing, and yet that endurance within her that no man could equal.

When finished, she sat next to Number, feeding him his share of the comb, squeezing the honey from the wax into his upturned mouth.

"I saw the tracks of the black bear today," she said, "as he too enjoys the gift of bees." Rolling the wax into a ball, she dropped it into her pocket. "There will be many such bears in these timbers. They are very dangerous this time of year. Do not think you can run faster or climb higher," she said, turning to the men. "The bear will be waiting at the top of the tree when you get there."

"Hope he likes his meat rare," Number grinned, "in which case I'd be safe."

"There's too little left for a good meal, Corporal, so I would not worry," she smiled.

Night fell like a black curtain. Overhead the leaves whispered in the prairie breeze, but where they were, deep in the bowels of the Cross Timbers, no breeze blew, no light penetrated, no life spoke. It was a still and dark place, a place unlike any they had ever seen.

They slept little that first night, and sometime in the wee

morning hours, when the leaves murmured high above like the quiet voices of the dead, Sheets could be heard, muttering in the darkness.

Morning came suddenly, the sun already high, tornadic columns of gnats humming above, gathering in their eyes and ears, men swatting at their own faces, pawing at the maddening gnats.

"First Sergeant Lansdown?" Sheets called.

"Yes sir," Lansdown said.

"Take five of the biggest and strongest and blaze a trail through this tangle. The rest will follow, widening the path enough for the horses to pass."

"Sir?" Lansdown asked.

"You heard me, Sergeant. Take axes, knives, whatever you got, and blaze a trail. We're cutting our way out of here."

"But sir . . ."

"And take him," he said, pointing at McReynolds.

"But sir, he's an officer, a doctor. Surely you don't mean to put him to working with the men."

"Do it," Sheets said.

"Don't worry about it, Sergeant," McReynolds said. "I don't mind giving a hand. Twobirds, maybe you could keep a eye on Number here for me."

"We'll be coming behind," she said, to reassure him.

Progress was measured in feet, slow, hard-won feet as they chopped their way through the packed underbrush. It was arduous, brutal work and soon their arms ached from the task.

For awhile they could hear the others working behind, widening the narrow path, but by noon there was nothing but the wind overhead and the constant movement of the leaves.

Taking his turn with the others, McReynolds chopped at the tangle of vines that went on forever, working until his arms refused to lift and then falling back to rest as someone else took his place.

It looked as if they were going to have to chop their way to

Fort Gibson, and no one believed, not for a moment, that there was either the strength or will to pull that off.

A week passed, each new day filled with dread at the wall of underbrush. Each day, they chopped and forged and cursed their way through the Cross Timbers, with no end in sight.

At night as they returned to camp, they fell to their blankets, exhausted from their labor, hands swollen from the work, bodies sore and bitten from the insects that tormented their every waking hour.

Twice McReynolds spotted the tracks of bear in the underbrush, tufts of black, wiry hair clinging on bramble thorns. Twice he warned Sheets to post guard, to at least protect the men from surprise attack. Twice Sheets scoffed, calling him a worrisome old woman.

Eight days in the Cross Timbers without relief, each man nearly to his breaking point, when they came upon a clearing, an oasis burned deep in the Timbers, the random strike of lightning, a haven of buffalo grass, sunlight, and gentle prairie winds, a moment's escape from the choking trees and bramble.

Camp was prepared early, even before the sun began to set, and a small stream provided sufficient water for them to bathe away the week's labor.

Barely able to lift his head, Number lay on his pallet while McReynolds cleaned his burns with water, boiling the bandages and hanging them to dry on a stick driven into the sand.

To reuse bandages was a travesty, but leaving the wounds exposed to the insects was even worse. Maggot infestation was a constant and imminent threat. Three times they'd dug the hideous things from Number's wounds. Had it not been for that, McReynolds would have chosen to let the wounds dry of their own accord.

Already Number's eyes had taken on a pallor. A lesser man would have been dead days earlier under such conditions.

As was her habit, Twobirds disappeared in search of food before camp was settled. The breeze, cooled from its journey across the Timbers, was soothing, and McReynolds took a rare moment to rest. Propping his hands behind his head, he dozed, waking momentarily at the sounds of camp, the men cracking limbs to feed the fire, the stomping of horses' hooves against heel flies, the ever-present cooing of mourning doves in the treetops.

Slumbering, waking, slumbering again, and the luxury of it all, and somewhere in that time before dusk, Sheets moved into the Timbers, his pistol slung low on his leg.

Awakening, McReynolds shook the sleep from his head, his heart pounding in his ears. Something was wrong. How long had he slept? How long since Sheets had gone into the Cross Timbers?

Touching Number's shoulder, he whispered, "Something's awry. I think I'm going to check. Will you be all right?"

"Yes sir, I'll be just fine. Course, I'd planned on dolling up and going dancing, but I'd be happy putting it off."

"Put it off, will you, Corporal? I'll make it up to you later."

"Yes sir," he smiled. "You be careful, hear? Sheets has gone around the bend. Everybody knows, sir." McReynolds smiled.

Uncertain as to the exact direction, he followed the clearing along the stream. Night was falling, shadows moving, dancing, light winking through the upper branches. Wind brushed the treetops like an invisible hand and chills raced down his back. Only then did he remember his rifle back at camp, but it was too late to return now.

Voices came, low, muffled, and he dropped behind a thicket. Candied plum blossoms, white explosions against the green of the Timbers were all about, but not until Twobirds moved her hand did he see their reflection in the water that pooled at the edge of the trees.

Leaning toward her, Sheets's voice was low, menacing.

"He's alive, isn't he?" he asked.

A breeze picked up from the south, the smell of plum blossom strong on the wind.

"I don't know," she said.

The slap was piercing, an insult breaching the evening quiet, Twobirds gasping under its sting.

"Liar!" Sheets screamed. "Tell me. It's him, isn't it? He's come back."

"Yes," she said. "He's taken your silver and soon he will take your life."

Drawing his revolver, he came down across her face with a sweeping and ruthless blow, dropping her to her knees, too stunned even to cry out.

Heedless to Sheets's advantage, McReynolds charged, but the distance was too great. Swinging about, Sheets leveled the revolver at his head, stopping him short, the smell of plum blossoms like funeral flowers hanging in the air. How often McReynolds had wondered about this moment, this moment of death.

"Ah," Sheets said, "Dr. McReynolds."

Like a distant memory, Corporal Adam Renfro stepped from the trees, his arm coming down on Sheets's back in a shattering blow, the revolver spinning from his hand. There was a whooshing sound as air exited Sheets's lungs and he plunged forward into the pool of water.

But even as McReynolds rejoiced for his deliverance, a black bear stepped from the tangle of bushes to his right, plum juice dribbling from its great slobbering mouth.

It turned, much as a man would turn, focusing on Sheets, all others diminishing in significance.

Rising from the water, Sheets's eyes were immense with fear, mud streaking down his face, hand pawing at the empty holster.

But it was Renfro who held the revolver now, turning it first on the bear and then on Sheets.

"Shoot him," Sheets said with trembling voice, his eyes frozen on the bear. "Shoot him, goddamn you, or you'll have the lash."

Motioning for McReynolds to back away, Renfro checked the bruise across Twobirds's cheek, the revolver held before him.

Spinning the chamber, he looked up at Sheets.

"Ain't loaded," he said.

The bear charged, its talons unsheathed, its arms open in deadly embrace, its powerful legs closing the distance in a terrifying charge.

"Stop!" Sheets commanded.

And for a single moment, it did stop, orange light flickering through the branches of the trees.

Then all creation was suspended in a petrifying roar as the bear hoisted him from the water, Sheets's impotent blows raining against its mighty chest, his legs dangling like a doll's in a child's arms.

With a rendering haul, the bear peeled the flesh from Sheets's skull, dropping him back into the water, blood drooling from its flaccid mouth.

"Shoot," Sheets begged, blood coursing down his face.

But his plea rose unheard into the prairie winds, for there was no one left to hear nor care.

Whirling, the bear scooped him from the pool by his back, shaking him like a dog killing a rabbit, flesh and bone defenseless against its crushing jaws.

As suddenly as it came, the bear dropped Sheets's body, a lifeless and bloody rag, and lumbered away into the Timbers. Suspended momentarily in the pink water, the body sank from sight.

So much had happened so quickly that McReynolds couldn't be sure of the passage of time, but when he looked up, Renfro and Twobirds were standing in front of him.

"Sorry 'bout taking that mule, sir, but figured Sheets owed me one."

"But how?" McReynolds asked.

"Sheets caught me with a grazer in that cave," he said, pointing to a scar above his ear, "knocked me out, I guess, until I hit that cold water. I climbed out, black as night it was, and found myself a rock to hide behind. Guess it was providence and fair luck I didn't get hold of Sheets himself in that darkness. So I just followed that torch out of the cave, keeping back as far as I could without losing my way altogether. Went back later," he said, "and brought the ceiling down and planted that hackberry stick. Figured it wouldn't be long 'fore Sheets returned for that silver."

"But how did you survive the winter?"

"Almost didn't. Hadn't been for that Osage hunting party, guess I would've froze stiff as a beaver up there on that rim."

"Where Nurse Cromley was?"

"Yes sir, the same. Guess I'd be just a scalp lock, hadn't been for Nurse Cromley's quick thinking. Cost her that cross she wore and a heap of talk to save my hair. Said I was her man, that she'd saved many from the pox, that she'd see the plague returned tenfold if anything happened to me. It was like God almighty come down from the mountain and spoke hisself. She made believers of them all, including me," he added. "Course, that Osage didn't last the week 'fore some Kiowa lifted his head."

"And Nurse Cromley?"

"Left her early spring, sir, delivering papooses and saving souls."

The smell of plum thickened in the evening cool.

"What now?" McReynolds said.

Handing Sheets's revolver to McReynolds, Renfro turned and pointed to the mule tied beyond in the bush.

"Well, sir, far as the Army goes I'm a dead man, and a dead man's got no rights nor wrongs, as you know. They've no more use of my services as I figure it. All the same to you, me and Twobirds will be on our way. You just keep that raggedy bunch headed east and two, three days you'll be eating slumgullion stew again."

"Are you sure this is how you want it?"

"There ain't a wall in sight nowhere, sir."

Before following Renfro into the Timbers, Twobirds put her arms around McReynolds's neck, holding him for a moment. Then she was gone.

With his thumb, McReynolds released the cylinder of

Sheets's revolver, held it to his eye, and spun the chamber against the fading light. It was empty.

Sunrise broke in a spray of color on the eastern horizon as McReynolds held the reins of his horse, letting his arm rest over his friend's neck.

Leaning forward on the saddlehorn, his recovery well under way, Number looked on. There against the morning sun stood Fort Gibson, as fine a sight as had ever been seen.

A young coyote watched them, motionless, from the grove of locust trees that grew at the edge of the tributary feeding into the Grand River.

In the distance, McReynolds could see Twobirds's cabin, and beyond that the fort garden.

"Ain't it a sight," Number said, shaking his head in disbelief, "and me with enough pay to buy the world."

So much had happened since they'd ridden out that gate to deliver a Kiowa girl to her people. Back there beyond the Cross Timbers were people he'd loved—Twobirds, Nurse Cromley, Adam Renfro. Back there were those who'd died, Bledso, Brandywine, a mule named Molly. Back there his courage had been tested, To,wan,ga,ha, On-da, and even Lieutenant Reginald Sheets.

But none would ever know of Renfro's resurrection, not from him, not then, not ever.

The coyote, God's dog, threw its head to the side, barked sharply, and sprinted toward the Cross Timbers.

THE ONLY ALTERNATIVE IS ANNIHILATION . . .
RICHARD P. HENRICK

SILENT WARRIORS   (8217-3026-6, $4.50/$5.50)
The Red Star, Russia's newest, most technologically advanced submarine, outclasses anything in the U.S. fleet. But when the captain opens his sealed orders 24 hours early, he's staggered to read that he's to spearhead a massive nuclear first strike against the Americans!

THE PHOENIX ODYSSEY   (0-8217-5016-X, $4.99/$5.99)
All communications to the *USS Phoenix* suddenly and mysteriously vanish. Even the urgent message from the president canceling the War Alert is not received, and in six short hours the *Phoenix* will unleash its nuclear arsenal against the Russian mainland. . . .

COUNTERFORCE   (0-8217-5116-6, $5.99/$6.99)
In the silent deep, the chase is on to save a world from destruction. A single Russian submarine moves on a silent and sinister course for the American shores. The men aboard the U.S.S. *Triton* must search for and destroy the Soviet killer submarine as an unsuspecting world race for the apocalypse.

CRY OF THE DEEP   (0-8217-5200-6, $5.99/$6.99)
With the Supreme leader of the Soviet Union dead the Kremlin is pointing a collective accusing finger towards the United States. The motherland wants revenge and unless the USS *Swordfish* can stop the Russian *Caspian,* the salvoes of World War Three are a mere heartbeat away!

BENEATH THE SILENT SEA   (0-8217-3167X, $4.50/$5.50)
The Red Dragon, Communist China's advanced ballistic missile-carrying submarine embarks on the most sinister mission in human history: to attack the U.S. and Soviet Union simultaneously. Soon, the Russian *Barkal,* with its planned attack on a single U.S. submarine, is about unwittingly to aid in the destruction of all mankind!

Available wherever paperbacks are sold, or order direct from the Publisher. Send cover price plus 50¢ per copy for mailing and handling to Kensington Publishing Corp., Consumer Orders, or call (toll free) 888-345-BOOK, to place your order using Mastercard or Visa. Residents of New York and Tennessee must include sales tax. DO NOT SEND CASH.

POLITICAL ESPIONAGE AND HEART-STOPPING HORROR. . . . NOVELS BY NOEL HYND